PRAISE

"*Where Dark Things Rise,* Clark's second novel, is a horrific but tender 1980s trailer-park bildungsroman that drips with authenticity and real magic. Clark's a true-blue Appalachian, and he proves it again in this tale of monstrous entities, dark designs, and wildly imaginative mountain nightmares…"

- POLLY SCHATTEL, AUTHOR OF *SHADOWDAYS* AND *THE OCCULTISTS*

"Appalachian horror has a worthy contributor to the genre. *Where Dark Things Rise,* the master work of author Andrew K. Clark, delivers a thoughtful commentary on rural poverty, belonging, and the demons that haunt all of us…"

- P.M. RAYMOND, ELEANOR TAYLOR BLAND AWARD-WINNING AUTHOR; KILLER SHORTS AND CLAYMORE AWARD FINALIST

"Andrew K. Clark's *Where Dark Things Rise* further cements him as a master of Southern Appalachian folk horror. Breathtaking allegory and pulse-pounding action keep you riveted to the end, and the eclectic, engaging cast of characters will have me thinking about this story for a long time."

- JENDIA GAMMON, NEBULA AND BSFA FINALIST AUTHOR OF *ATACAMA* AND *TO WONDER AND STARSHINE*

"Reading Andrew K. Clark's sequel *Where Dark Things Rise* feels like returning to a familiar mountain cottage and settling into the comfortable sheets of a warm bed while the cold, stormy night whispers promises of visits from both new and familiar horrors—wulvers, gargoyle-faced shadows, and of course, humans so vile you can't wait for them to die."

— DAVID ALLEN VOYLES, AUTHOR OF THE THIRTEENTH DAY OF CHRISTMAS AND TALES FROM THE HEARSE

"*Where Dark Things Rise* is a captivating Southern Supernatural Gothic that affirms Andrew Clark's place as one of the most exciting writers of the thrilling and macabre…"

— CHARLES DODD WHITE, AUTHOR OF HOW FIRE RUNS

"A terror-spiked thrill ride of a novel that leaves room for tender moments of raw beauty and bittersweet nostalgia… Religious trauma, generational curses, folk horror, and themes of found family create a compelling Appalachian Gothic narrative shot through with magic and touches of surrealism. Clark's characters bear their bruises and broken hearts with ennobling pride and a fierce, poetic grace. *Where Dark Things Rise* mesmerizes completely."

— PAULETTE KENNEDY, BESTSELLING AUTHOR OF THE DEVIL AND MRS. DAVENPORT

"*Where Dark Things Rise* is a dazzling, blood-soaked love story, a parable of predators and vengeance, and a smoke-dark thrill ride, and standing at its center is a sixteen-year-old girl who is every bit as terrifying as the evil she faces. I loved Mina, and I loved this book. You will too."

— JAMIESON RIDENHOUR, WRITER AND PRODUCER, PALIMPSEST

"*Where Dark Things Rise* expertly portrays the archetypal 80s high school bully, good guy, rich girl, poor girl, poor girl's younger bitchy sister, racist redneck, et al. In the hands of a less experienced writer these characters are walking cliché time bombs. Clark makes each real, relatable, identifiable, likable or not. Strap in. This book scared the shit out of me."

- LEE STOCKDALE, WINNER OF THE UNITED KINGDOM NATIONAL POETRY PRIZE

WHERE DARK THINGS RISE

WHERE DARK THINGS RISE

ANDREW K. CLARK

Quill & Crow

WHERE DARK THINGS RISE
BY ANDREW K. CLARK
PUBLISHED BY QUILL & CROW PUBLISHING HOUSE

This book is a work of fiction. All incidents, dialogue, and characters, except for some well-known historical and public figures, are either products of the author's imagination or used in a fictitious manner. Any resemblance to actual persons, living or dead, or actual events is purely coincidental.

Copyright © 2025 by Andrew K. Clark

All rights reserved. Published in the United States by Quill & Crow Publishing House, Ohio. No portion of this book may be reproduced in any form without permission from the publisher, except as permitted by U.S. copyright law.

Printed in the United States of America

Library of Congress Control Number: 2025907178

Cover Design by Fay Lane

Interior by Cassandra L. Thompson

Author Photo by Parker J. Pfister

ISBN: 978-1-958228-98-2

ISBN: 978-1-958228-97-5 (ebook)

Publisher's Website: www.quillandcrowpublishinghouse.com

For Casey, in whose light I lean –

PUBLISHER'S NOTE

This book touches on several traumatic themes including bigotry, religious abuse, and violence toward women and children. Please be sure to consult the Trigger Index at the back of the book for more information.

PART 1

"The beginning is always today."

— MARY WOLLSTONECRAFT SHELLEY

1 / GABE & THE WAY BACK

JULY, 1985

Gabe hated sitting in the *way back*—the rear seat of the station wagon, the one that faced the wrong direction. The sun blinded him, wedged low between the mountains. Long shadows swayed across the highway, and a few cars pulled on their headlights. He fiddled with his Walkman, reaching into his backpack for a cassette. He popped out a gospel tape and put in Prince, setting the orange foam headphones over his ears.

"What're you listening to back there?" Mama asked from the front seat, a frown in her voice.

Gabe said, "Reverend Ezra's sermon from a couple weeks ago is all. One where he talks about how Jesus is the Lion of Judah."

"Good boy," Mama said. "Remember, we're *in* the world but not *of* the world."

"Yes, ma'am," Gabe answered. He recalled the bitterness in Mama's face when she'd discovered his rock music tapes, carefully hidden in a shoebox at the back of his closet. She'd made him squirt lighter fluid on them in the backyard and watch them burn. Not only KISS and Led Zeppelin, but every cassette that wasn't gospel. Even Michael Jackson and the Talking Heads. Any music that wasn't glorifying God, she'd said, was glorifying Satan by default. It's one or the other.

He'd been mortified the neighbors might have seen the fire, heard Mama praying loudly for her wayward fourteen-year-old. She'd raised her arms toward the heavens and called on God to purge the evil from her son's mind, mascara tears marking her face. Gabe had cried too, not for being evil, but because he did not have enough money to replace what she was burning. He hid his music better the next time.

In the backseat, he looked at the colorful cover of the Prince tape. The background of the artwork looked like mountains, but a kid at school had pointed out that the landscape was actually the outline of a woman's body. Gabe traced the form with his finger, lingering over the point of her breast. He loved the smell of the cassette, which smelled like the future, like possibility, like sex. In his ears, Prince sang about sadness and forgiveness.

He never understood how Prince could talk so much like a preacher, like every preacher Gabe had ever heard, but also about so many sinful things. How could he sing about sexy things and then talk about God and Heaven? Gabe knew sex was of the world, which really meant the devil. God was something separate. A good person wouldn't allow himself to be so carnal, to dwell on such things. But Gabe loved the beat and Prince's guitar, and while the lyrics sometimes made him feel guilty, the naughty words and their meanings intrigued him. Sometimes, he wrote down the lyrics in a notebook he stuffed in an old coffee can in the barn below the house.

But sitting in the way back was proof you were a kid, and Gabe was sure someone he knew would ride up behind the car to bear witness to this humiliation before they could get out of Buncombe County. He stared into the cars that came up on the station wagon's bumper, ready to duck if he saw someone he knew. What if it was the cute girl from eighth grade pre-Algebra—Mina, the one who wore braids in her long red hair?

It was bad enough his family had an old station wagon with fake wood cladding, much worse that he got stuck in the back with the twins taking up the middle seat. Daddy always put the twins in the middle in case he or Mama needed to get to them. The twins bickered constantly over the same things. Car rides brought out their worst.

"He's looking at me!" Sarah said.

"Uh-uh. She keeps staring at me mean, Mama!" Carl's voice rose in pitch.

The two of them never shut up, never got along, no matter who was around. When they were at home and their bickering wore Daddy down, he'd make them sit in the middle of the living room floor and hold hands, face to face. They'd sit there crying, trying to move as far apart as possible, as if they found each other so repulsive it was painful to touch.

"Stop looking at each other," Mama said. "They's lots of trees along this road, lots of places I can get me a switch if need be."

"You two keep fighting," Daddy said, "and I'll make you sit in the hotel room and hold hands while the rest of us check out the pool."

One night, Gabe had heard Mama and Daddy fighting. Daddy said he didn't like to spank the twins because he felt like it didn't do any good.

"My mama and daddy would just cut their eyes at me, and I knew to get in line," Daddy had said.

Mama said, "You could've used more spankings when you were little." She said her daddy beat her every day, and sometimes her mama too, and they were all the better for it.

Even when she was in a different room, Gabe could picture the rigid lines of Mama's face when she spoke. The only time her face was soft was at church. There, her smile would come easy, her face relaxed and warm. Often, the hardness would return in the car before they left the church parking lot, usually because she had to scold one or more of the children for not paying close enough attention to Reverend Ezra.

Ever since school let out for the summer, Daddy kept talking about taking the family on vacation over to Pigeon Forge, with a stop in Cherokee along the way. Gabe would've rather gone to the beach. He couldn't understand what was so great about leaving one set of mountains in North Carolina to visit another set in Tennessee. Daddy loved spending time with his kids, going on vacation, or just in the backyard when he grilled hamburgers and hot dogs. He was a hugger; he hugged his children close to his chest, holding them there a little too long, like he was always trying to make up for something. Maybe Mama's meanness.

Gabe's eyelids got heavy when the Walkman clicked over to the other side. Now Prince sang about making love in a barn, about making each stroke count. A bright light shone in the car, as if the sun had decided to rise again from its perch behind the trees. When his eyes focused, he saw the headlights of a pickup truck, almost on the bumper of the station wagon. Gabe clicked stop on the tape.

"Why's he riding so close?" Daddy asked.

Mama turned around, looking over her shoulder.

The truck pulled into the left lane, as if to pass them, and when it did, Gabe saw something moving in the truck bed. It was some kind of large animal, almost bear-like. It circled the truck bed, a dark shadow stretching and growing. When the truck pulled alongside them, he saw a pair of eyes emerge, burning like red coals. Soon, the head of the beast became clear; it was more dog-like. It looked like an enormous wolf, but Gabe's brain couldn't process it that way. He'd seen gray wolves before, at the Nature Center in Asheville, but wolves didn't exactly ride in the back of pickups. This one was much larger.

The wolf leapt onto the cab of the truck, the roof buckling under its weight. As the truck pulled farther ahead, Gabe saw a distinct red tint to the beast's fur. Its ears were pinned back to its head, and it bounded back into the bed, the force making the truck bob and weave. There was only darkness inside the cab, no faces visible. His world tilted when he realized it was staring right at him, lips curled back over its teeth. Gabe felt a vibration in his chest—the wolf's growl. He turned around on his knees. Mama and Daddy whispered about the truck, and the twins slept with their mouths open in the middle seat.

The truck pulled ahead of them once more, and the wolf crouched. The world slowed, and Gabe watched the beast leap, the truck bed raising as it departed. It lurched through the air, and Gabe felt the ugly vibration in his stomach again, the deep, otherworldly growl of the beast. It stretched out its body along the front of the car, its full length now the only thing visible through the windshield.

Its paws struck the middle of the station wagon's hood, the beige metal crumpling beneath its weight. The wolf's body rolled toward the windshield as the car swerved madly.

"Christ Jesus, help us!" Mama yelled as the wolf smashed through the windshield, and the crash of glass rang through the car. The tires thumped as the car swerved onto the shoulder of the highway, flying down an embankment before slamming into the earth in a gulley. Gabe's body floated up and over the heads of the twins and into the floorboard in front of them. For a moment, the world rang with shocked silence. One of the twins screamed, but there was no sound. When the quiet broke, Gabe heard the tick of the car's turn signal, the sizzle of the radiator. Gabe scrambled to his knees, fighting back vomit. Carl sobbed quietly, frowning with wild eyes. Sarah screamed.

Gabe pushed open the car door and crawled out onto the ground. Several minutes passed before he could stand. He felt a sharp pain in his right side at the base of his ribs. His arms and legs worked. He stared at the palms of his hands. The car's tail lights lit the world around him. The headlights, smothered in the dirt, gave off an orange glow. Cars passed on the road above, their drivers unaware of the station wagon's plight.

Daddy was wrapped unnaturally around the steering wheel, the lights of the dashboard strobing on his gray face. His eyes were closed, and a ribbon of blood trickled down his head. He wasn't breathing.

Mama's head was back against the headrest, mouth agape. Her eyes stood open, unblinking. In the backseat, Carl called to her. Sarah had stopped screaming and was kicking her legs. Unlike Gabe, they'd been wearing their seatbelts. The pain came again in his side, and he put his hand on it carefully. He did not feel a wound. Maybe he had bruised it when he struck the floorboard. He realized how lucky he was to have hit the back of the front seats instead of flying further up through the car.

"Mama," Carl cried.

Gabe heard something. A deep throbbing grumble that seemed to echo in the pit of his stomach. He was being watched. He turned to find the red wolf facing him about fifty feet away.

For a brief moment, the wolf was visible in the headlights of a passing car, the tips of its fur bristling red, almost the same color as the embers of its eyes, a mix of fur and shadow. The wolf stirred the ground with an enormous paw, flinging dirt and leaves into the air as it slunk toward Gabe, dropping its head.

He considered running, but thought of the twins, still strapped in the middle seat. He faced the wolf with nothing but his Walkman. The wolf took a few steps forward, then came another growl. This one was different; it came from the very earth itself, rumbling up with ancient vibration. It ran through the ground, through Gabe's feet, into his bones. But this sound didn't come from the wolf, but the wolf heard it too. It froze in place, looking past Gabe to the woods beyond. Gabe looked over the roof of the station wagon. There, perhaps twenty feet into the trees, he saw a pair of glowing green eyes. The rumbling continued, more quake than growl.

When Gabe turned back to the wolf, its ears were pinned back, teeth bared. A different look, something akin to fear, smoldered in its eyes. It snarled at the trees.

The red wolf sprinted up the ridge. It looked back when it reached the tree line and held Gabe's gaze briefly before racing through the woods, a ruby glow settling in the trees as it disappeared.

Gabe looked back to where he'd seen the green eyes. Nothing but murk in the trees. He felt dizzy. Realizing he'd been holding his breath, he let go finally and pulled the night air deep into his lungs.

"I'm gonna go get help," he told the twins and started up the bank toward the road, without taking another look at his parents. He didn't want to look at them again, wanting to erase the image of them from his mind. Then he thought about the state of the car, the hissing of the radiator. What if it caught fire? He hurried back down the bank to unbuckle the twins and set them a safe distance from the car at the edge of the trees. He told himself his parents were too heavy to move.

"What was that thing that growled?" Sarah asked.

"There's nothing out here," he said, heading back up to the road.

Gabe flagged down a brown pickup occupied by an old man wearing a John Deere ball cap. The man agreed to go to the next exit and call for help from a pay phone.

While he waited, Gabe sat with the twins at the edge of the woods. They held hands now, sobbing quietly, though no one compelled them to do so. Gabe thought of his cassettes and went to the station wagon, opening the tailgate to retrieve his backpack. There were a couple of preacher cassettes in the backpack. He took them out and left them on the seat.

He walked to the front of the car and forced himself to look in on Mama. He wanted to close her eyes, but dared not touch her. Aside from seeing his papaw, Mama's daddy, at his funeral a few years ago, Gabe had never seen a dead person. He smelled Mama's skin when he looked at her, thinking of the smell of her sweat when she worked outside in the yard and the White Rain hairspray she used to full effect on Sunday mornings. He wanted to feel something soft for her, to touch her cheek, do something a good son would do, but he only stared, thinking about how hard her face looked, even in death. He felt like crying, felt like puking. His hands shook, and he nervously pulled his brown hair behind his ears. He fought back his fear, wanting to look strong before the twins. He stared around wildly, looking for the wolf, afraid it would return. Why had it leapt at their car?

He looked at Daddy. Gabe wanted Daddy to get out of the car and take control of things, help him comfort the twins, and hold him a little too long. He wanted Daddy to take them on to Cherokee, to put on his black socks and flip-flops and walk around the pool, like he always did, oblivious to the snickers of his children and strange children besides. Blood smeared over Daddy's nose and cheekbones, the way the bright white sunscreen would have at the pool if they'd made it to their destination.

When the ambulance came, paramedics covered his parents with white sheets and carted them away. They fussed over the twins and shone a bright light in Gabe's eyes and mouth. Soon, they were in the backseat of a police car. He felt all the energy drain from his body, and he fell back into the seat, clutching his Walkman. He didn't want to hear any music, even Prince. He didn't have the strength to comfort the twins, who huddled close, their heads touching. He scanned the trees for signs of the red wolf. Or of the green eyes that had scared it away.

2 / THE BUS STOP
MINA

OCTOBER, 1987

Mina drew a pair of eyeballs in her notebook. The eyes were large and exaggerated, and she penciled in dramatic eyebrows and thick eyelashes. She quickly sketched a body beneath the eyes and drew a Members Only Jacket on the frame. She looked down at her own brown jacket over her blue summer dress. Where it should say "Members Only," it said "Elemental" in a gaudy font that screamed to the world that it was a knockoff. She examined the jacket straps on each shoulder, pushed up slightly by misplaced shoulder padding under the fabric. She tried to mash it down, making it lie flat like it did on the name-brand jackets. She wondered if she could get one of the girls in Home Ec. class, where they kept the sewing machines for girls to learn on, to replace the label. She hoped Erin, her friend from school who lived down the mountain in the country club, would come through with hand-me-down clothes from her older sister, like she promised.

Mina examined her makeup. She wanted it to look like she didn't have any on. She pictured Krissy Lange from school. Her pool cue blue eyeshadow was a strange mix of trashy and cute, somehow working for her. With her long blond hair and hip-hugging blue jeans, she drew the boys to her the way a red cape draws the bull. Of course, Mina had seen Emerson Schmidt, a guy at school who liked Mina, take long looks at Krissy the way the other boys did, and always a pang dipped in her belly, even though she wasn't entirely sure how she felt about Emerson herself. At least he was good for a ride to and from school, saving her from the annoyance of the sticky bus seats. Mina was tall and lanky at five foot eight, not curvy like Krissy Lang. She had long arms and legs that, coupled with her skinny frame, from a distance made her appear twelve instead of sixteen. She turned sideways to examine herself in the mirror, pulling her ponytail across her chest. If she stood just right, it was long enough to cover the label.

There was a bang on the door, making the mirror slip from its brackets and hit the floor. A crack feathered up the middle.

"You got my hairbrush in there?" Chelsea, her younger sister, pounded the wall with her fists. Mina slipped the mirror back in the flimsy brackets and closed her eyes, as if she could will Chelsea to fall through some invisible trap door under the shag carpet in the hall.

She jerked open the door, holding out the brush. "It's not yours anyway," she said.

"Is too," Chelsea said, snatching the brush and spinning down the hall, never making eye contact.

Mina followed Chelsea down the narrow hall toward the kitchen. Her bedroom was on the opposite end of the trailer from the other bedrooms, meaning she had to cross through the kitchen and living room to get to the family's one working bathroom or to access the front door.

In the kitchen, Mama plopped a spoonful of Country Crock into a hot skillet and laid a slice of bologna in the sizzling pan. Through the half window between the kitchen and the living room, Mina saw Daddy in his recliner. His hair was a tangle of unkempt curls, and he still wore the same clothes he'd had on the night before.

"Ain't Daddy getting ready for work?" she asked.

"Got a catch in his back," Mama said. "I got your breakfast."

Mina eyed the plate of steaming eggs with suspicion. Powdered, she thought, curling her nose. Mama followed her eyes.

"You gotta eat something," Mama said. "They's a couple of heels in that bag over there. They ain't molded. You want me to make you some toast?"

"No, that's okay," Mina said.

"We got some peanut butter?"

The AM radio on the windowsill crackled with a preacher's voice. The Old Time Gospel Hour. *By the time we get to Leviticus, we're getting a handle on the law God has laid out for all mankind,* the voice said with an exaggerated drawl. Mama listened to preachers or gospel music exclusively on her little radio and watched preachers on TV Sunday mornings before taking the kids to the big Church of Hosanna at the edge of town.

A thud made both of them jump. This time it wasn't Chelsea. Daddy had slapped the paneled wall beside his recliner. Mama scrambled to fetch a coffee cup from the cabinet. Her hands shook as she dumped powdered creamer into the cup and poured coffee from the percolator. She stirred to get it the color Daddy liked. He slapped the wall again.

"She's coming, Daddy," Mina said. "Hold your horses!"

"Hold your tongue," Daddy said. When Mina looked through the half window, he was staring up at the ceiling, a hand squeezing his forehead. *Catch in his back, my ass,* she thought.

At night, when Daddy took his beer in the living room, he slapped the wall when it was time for Mama to bring the next one and carry off his empties. If he was in the mood for liquor, he poured it himself at the half window as if he didn't trust a woman to do it right. In the mornings, Daddy's slaps meant he wanted strong coffee and fast.

"He can get his own coffee," Mina said, but Mama didn't answer. She rushed out of the room with a mug that said Champion Paper, carefully watching the coffee lap at the rim.

In the pan, the bologna hissed. Mama had a funny habit of cutting four little slots into the meat when she fried it. She didn't like the way it drew up into a little bowl otherwise. All the food looked disgusting, but Mina's stomach curled with hunger. She grabbed a paper towel and carefully picked up a piece of hot bologna with her fingertips. She laid it on the paper towel and headed for the door.

Daddy was slumped over in his chair, looking at his feet, the hot coffee steaming in one hand, the other still squeezing his forehead.

Mama rushed over and put her arm around Mina. "Don't you want no eggs, no toast?"

"I ain't that hungry, Mama. I grabbed a piece of bologna."

"You wait outside for your sister," Daddy said, not looking up. "You keep her away from that damned Manning boy. Any of them Manning boys. Hell, keep her away from any of the boys in this damned park, and you best stay away from them too."

Mina bit her lip.

"And you better not be catching rides with that country club brat again."

Now he raised his head.

Mina stared at the wall. Daddy's glare warmed her cheeks.

"You been spoken to," he said, his weight shifting in the chair. In old pictures, her daddy was built like her, a lanky mass of limbs. Now every part of him was round and puffy.

"Yes, sir," Mina said.

"These boys ain't got no sense," he said. "Just big man babies. Best you keep your distance."

Outside, Mina stood on the porch waiting for Chelsea. She threw her hip to one side, making the wood porch teeter. It had never been level, and even as a kid, she had loved to make it rock back and forth. She took a bite of the salty bologna. The air smelled fresh, the sky bright and blue. She reached into her backpack to grab her tape player and headphones. She pulled out a cassette and looked at the cover. Two men in suits shook hands, one of them on fire. Ms. Varny, her English teacher, would hold up an image like this and pose a question to the class: *What is the metaphor here?* The human condition? Mina might have answered. She put the blue plastic headphones over her ears and clicked play, then hopped off the porch and banged on the side of the trailer near Chelsea's window.

"All right!" Chelsea yelled from inside.

Three gravel roads snaked through the Whispering Pines Trailer Park. The trailers were laid out on a slant, diagonal to the roads that ran from the back of the park to the entrance, where they merged. Mina's family's trailer was in the very back corner, angled so her bedroom faced the woods. She kept Chelsea in her peripheral vision as they walked toward the bus stop. Leaves almost covered the road, a breeze pushing them along ahead of their feet. Chelsea was walking with "that damned Manning boy."

She's thirteen, Mina thought, *I'm not gonna play mama on the way to the school bus.* She studied the rise of Elk Mountain above the trees. Most of the mountain was covered in woods, with a couple of trailer parks and a junkyard on its southern face, and a few houses sprinkled in here and there. Most of the trailers in Whispering Pines sat on cinder blocks. On a windy day, they rocked gently, a sound

Mina loved. Under a nearby trailer, a dog lay in the shade, tongue lolling in the dirt.

It was a cool morning. Still, she wasn't surprised to see the man everyone called Twist sitting shirtless on his porch. She had never seen the man with a shirt on. She wasn't sure he owned one. In the wintertime, he just wore jackets over bare skin. It was as if shirts were against his religion. He looked comical, his feet on the step below him, his legs so long his knees almost met his ears. His black hair was slicked over, his skin shiny like he was sweating. There wasn't a lick of fat on his bones, his wrinkled head too big for his frame. His pregnant girlfriend, Dana, peeked sheepishly out of the trailer's crank-out windows as they passed. She started to wave but thought better of it. Twist didn't like anyone talking to Dana and gave her hell if she ever talked back. Dana was way too pretty and way too young for Twist. Them being together never made sense to Mina. And now she was stuck with the old geezer, on account of the coming baby. Same story, different day. Girls in these hills always get stuck with a man, never getting a chance to get out of this backwards place. Whispering Pines was full of women like that, including Mina's own mama. One thing Mina knew—that would not be her. As soon as she got the chance, she was gone.

Mina made eye contact with Twist, and as usual, he looked her up and down like a preacher with a secret. Then his eyes drifted back to light on Chelsea. Lately, he'd begun looking at her more, with the same sick hunger he always had for Mina. Mina slowed until Chelsea caught up, blocking the old bastard's view. Twist grimaced.

At the bus stop, kids clumped together in groups. A few from the park wore purple letter jackets, giving them at least one wardrobe item that didn't betray their status as trailer park kids. Chelsea walked with the Manning boy to a group who wore mostly black from head to toe, even though Chelsea was always outfitted in bright pinks and yellows. A few kids sat on the brick base of the sign that marked the entrance to the park, throwing rocks into the trees, betting who could throw the furthest.

Mina was thinking how cold she was in her summer dress when he emerged across the road. It was that Gabe boy from school, the one who lived in the big house through the woods. He was in her Geometry class and Ms. Varny's English class. He'd moved there a couple of years ago—his grandparents' house—after his parents died in a car crash. When he'd first moved to Elk Mountain, he'd come out to the bus stop and stand with his head down, delicately perched like an injured bird, spooked by the slightest sound. He hadn't spoken to anyone at the bus stop for the longest time. Instead, he'd stood off by himself, often with his back to the other kids. Of course, this motivated the trailer park kids to mess with him, teasing him or knocking books from his hands. He never reacted, just bent down and picked up the books or shrugged off the bullying. He didn't seem afraid of them, just annoyed. The new kid always gets picked on, and even though Gabe had already been at their high school, at the bus stop, he was fresh meat. To Mina, he seemed distracted by something else. Always watching the woods, craning his neck around like he'd just seen something strange in the trees. Losing his parents had maybe fucked with his head. Might do that to anybody. Kids at school said he held his mama's hand when she died, that he'd been covered in blood when the ambulance came. Some said he'd been drenched like the girl from *Carrie*.

When they came back to school this year, everyone was astonished to see Gabe had shot up at least a foot over the summer, maybe a few inches taller than Mina. Now he walked with a straight back, nothing like the squirrely little boy he'd been. He had dark brown eyes with sandy hair that lay on his head in waves. Not the tight curls of the preppy boys, just something like a cowlick, though he still tried to part it. None of the kids teased him now. Although he still tended to stand off by himself, he sometimes floated among the different groups of kids at the bus stop, laughing and joking with them. It was the first time she'd seen him smile in forever.

Something else had changed. Before, when he kept to himself, he would sometimes steal a glance at Mina, but always looked away if she saw him. But this year, he hadn't looked away when Mina caught him looking. Instead, he met her eyes and held them, the gold flecks of his irises bearing a kind of defiance. *I see you. I want to see you.* He would even smile at her, and when he did so, she was reminded of the skinny kid he'd been in eighth grade pre-Algebra class, when they'd first met, back when he lived with his parents across town. The kid with a quick smile who didn't hold back a laugh. The kid he'd been before his parents died in front of him.

He looked at her like that now, not looking away when she saw him. Mina turned up the volume on her player. He fished in his backpack, still walking toward the bus stop, and pulled out a Walkman. He put the headphones around his neck and looked right at her. He was wearing a gray suede jacket way too expensive for the trailer park set. When he got to the bus stop, instead of floating to the other groups of kids or standing off by himself, he came toward her. Mina looked away to the trees and back. He was still coming, his face determined, as though he'd just made his mind up about something important. *No fucking way,* she thought.

When he was beside her, he opened his Walkman and studied the cassette as if mesmerized by some new information he'd just discovered. He closed the Walkman and dipped his head at her. She smiled.

"What're you listening to?" he asked.

"What?" She turned the volume down on her player.

"I asked what you were listening to?"

"It's just—" she said. "It's just Pink Floyd."

He didn't make her nervous exactly, but this felt weird. He'd never spoken to her before, and it threw her off. *What was he doing?* Maybe gaining a foot over the summer had given him balls.

"Cool," he said. He was about to say more, like there were a million things he wanted to tell her, when tires squealed down the street and thumping bass echoed around them.

The kids at the stop all looked down the street to see a black IROC racing up the hill.

"Oh Lord," someone muttered.

It was Emerson Schmidt. When the car approached, it slowed, but the music grew louder. Mina cringed when she recognized the song. *Fucking Whitesnake.*

The car pulled up alongside Mina and Gabe. The power window whirred down slowly. Emerson grinned. He looked Gabe up and down before turning to Mina.

"Hey, Cinnamon Girl," he said. "You need a ride?"

Mina hated it when he called her that.

Mina looked at Gabe. He pursed his lips. She looked at the rest of the kids at the bus stop, then back toward her trailer to make sure the old man wasn't watching.

She ran around to the other side of the car.

The kids at the stop *oohed* and *ahhed.* The trailer park girl was getting into Emerson's IROC. Again. Mina knew they were just jealous. He annoyed the hell out of her, but she hated the bus more.

Emerson winked at Gabe. Gabe stuck his hands in his pockets and walked toward the other kids.

"Hey," Mina called after him.

Gabe turned back. "Yeah?"

"See ya in Ms. Varny's class?"

"Yeah," Gabe said.

When Mina got in the car, Emerson revved the engine and popped the clutch. He turned up the music, and as he passed the trailer park kids, he threw a spit bottle out of the car's window. When it hit the pavement, the top popped off and the bottle spun, spraying tobacco spit over several of the kids standing near Chelsea.

"That's, that's like, so gross," Mina said.

Emerson laughed and put his hand on her thigh. She slid away, letting his hand drop onto the leather. "Did you see that shit?" he said, shifting as they hit a curve, Whispering Pines in the rear view.

3 / REVEREND EZRA & THE PILLAR OF SMOKE

Fall is the best time for a good old-fashioned camp meeting, Reverend Ezra thought. Something to stir the souls of the faithful, a force to draw in the lost, seeking redemption, their pockets full of coin. He tapped his toe to the clean gospel music and heard it echo through the valley. The PA system was loud to let the world know—revival was here.

The singers, four men in suits and ties, three women in dresses that broke well below the knee, held onto microphones with fat foam heads of different colors. The bass singer had a yellow head on his, and sang in staggered time, his thick tie catching the breeze. The other men had red, white, and blue microphone heads, their voices swirling together in perfect harmony. A woman with a top-heavy build sang into a purple-headed mic, a silver crucifix wedged tightly in her cleavage. The crucifix was really more of a Catholic symbol, Reverend Ezra thought. Those Catholics wanted to keep Christ on the cross as if he hadn't risen from the grave on the third day. He would need to counsel the good sister to wear a cross, not a crucifix. Help her understand the significance of the resurrection. Her build was just right for the stage. A lot could be forgiven of a body like that. The kind that kept men in the pews, their wallets primed to open.

In the front row, a tiny woman caught the spirit, twisting around with quick, exaggerated jerking. Reverend Ezra watched her, a smile spreading over his face. He stood and held both palms toward her, as if to shower her with even more of the Holy Spirit. He mouthed the words *Go on, sister!* The singers grew louder, like they felt the need to stay just above her voice, which rose with exultant cries. She kicked off her heels and ran the center aisle of the camp tent floor, sawdust swirling in her wake. The woody scent of the sawdust caught in the air, the smell of purity, of brightness, of sins washed away.

The woman moved to the steady *thump thump thump* of the bass. A man in a powder blue suit and hair that fell over his ears, pointed his bass guitar at the congregation like a weapon, bombarding the worshipers with Heaven's holy electricity, spreading it over the fields and into the trees, piercing the entire world with the one true cadence: the very heartbeat of God.

When the singers moved into a moment of a cappella, the faithful swayed, calling out to the woman to let God do his work in her, declaring that he held her in his hands. The singers harmonized:

I shall not be,
I shall not be moved.
Though the tempest rages,
I shall not be moved.
Just like a tree,
that's planted by the water,
I shall not be moved!

When the song ended, the excited woman was so full of the Spirit she fell to the floor and spoke in tongues. A young man in his early twenties, wearing a gray suit and wide blue tie, began to translate.

"In these last days, we must hold tight to the power of Jesus," he said. "We must turn our backs on the evil of the world, the evil things they'd have us do. We must not do these things they tell us to do out of wickedness and in the name of pleasure."

The woman spun on the floor, sawdust in her hair.

Reverend Ezra stood at the podium and leaned into the microphone. "Praise Jesus, the one they call the Christ. Amen, sister. Go on."

"And I saw a rider on a horse, coming down from Heaven," the young man said.

"Go on," said Reverend Ezra.

"And he held scales in his hand," the man interpreted as the woman grew louder, her voice wobbly and fevered.

"And the horseman had green eyes."

Reverend Ezra felt a lump in his throat, the world out of focus for a moment. He pushed it away. "Praise Jesus," he said, his voice echoing through the valley.

"For he has come to judge the quick and the dead," the man interpreted.

"Amen," said Ezra.

"Now comes another," the young man said.

The woman fell still, and the entire tent full of worshipers leapt to their feet, hands skyward, voices lifted to praise what they had witnessed, the clear expression of God's very presence alive and within everything.

When the yelling stopped, Reverend Ezra opened his Bible. He was a thin man, hair naturally raven black, despite being in his seventies. His build was wiry, and though he was shorter than most men, people always said he looked taller in the pulpit, especially when he took the good word and stood before a congregation. He wore black pants, a crisp white Oxford shirt, and a red tie.

He laid his Bible carefully on the lectern and unclipped the microphone, dragging the cable with him as he paced the stage.

"In the year of our Lord, nineteen hundred and eighty-seven," Ezra said.

Someone said *Praise Jesus* and *Go on!*

"In this time and in this place, on October 16th, comes now upon us the words of our Lord Jesus, whom the apostles called the Christ. Let it be known that at this time and in this place, the faithful took a stand."

Amen.

"Let it be known that when the world fell victim to the filthy plague of homosexuality, the evils of drugs and premarital sex, and the pursuits of pleasure and grotesque gluttony, that we, in this place and in this time, the faithful believers in Christ Jesus, took a stand!"

Hallelujah.

"That in order to get closer to God, to get closer to his word and his mighty power, we climbed the highest mountains!"

Amen, Reverend!

"We climbed the highest mountains and began the sacred work of rebuilding. Rebuilding the very faith we share in the power of Christ, in the strength of the Lord Jesus," Ezra said, his slicked-back dark hair glistening under the yellow light bulbs that swung gently above him.

Amen.

"Not just that we should rebuild our faith in a quiet way in our own hearts, but that we should declare it to the world at the top of our lungs, that we should shout it to the whole world with one voice! His voice!"

Amen, brother!

"What greater way for us to show the world what we mean but that we should construct a Temple—indeed, we shall rebuild the very Temple of Jerusalem, a new Jerusalem, right here in these mountains!"

Hallelujah!

"Solomon's temple, brick by brick, block by block, right here, on a peak that is so high the very lips of God shall kiss the chosen."

Amen! Hallelujah!

"Some have mocked the values we instill in our children."

Bull!

"Some have made fun of the Purity Sojourns we require of selected youth."

Boo! Boo!

"Some have said that we put their welfare at risk—but I say to you, it is more of a risk to let them walk the streets of this heathen world, Amen?"

Amen!

"For the lost one who did not come back from last year's Sojourn, we grieve for her parents."

Ezra dipped his head and looked at a family in the third row. A man comforted his crying wife as she leaned onto his shoulder. Ezra pictured the young girl, who'd had the face of a child but the full soft shape of a woman. What had her name been? *Ahh, yes, Heidi.* He remembered the hint of mischief about the girl's eyes, the deviousness he detected that most could not. It was far better that Heidi had disappeared than become an agent of sin in the world. As he thought of the girl, he could conjure the sweet smell of her skin. At the rear of the tent, he saw Sheriff Barnaby, the nosy man who had been sniffing around since the girl had disappeared. *Maybe,* Ezra thought, *we should stick to the whore daughters down on Lexington and Eagle Street going forward. Many would be needed.*

"But mark my words," he said. "Her disappearance is of Satan and not our Lord!"

Amen! Hallelujah!
"And I believe she will be found very soon," he lied.
Amen.
Reverend Ezra looked over the congregation, past the thick wooden tent poles, out over the rolling hills beyond the dirt parking lot. For a moment, he felt something cold in his hands. It worked its way up his forearms and into his chest. He shuddered. A dark mound of shadow, first appearing as a bear, then a huge black panther, skulked between the cars and pick-up trucks out in the field. It shifted back and forth, taking many forms before returning to a pillar of smoke, floating along the ground toward the camp meeting tent.

He tried to find his place again in the text, the words blurring. Was it the one that guarded the boy come back again? The green eyes?

"Praise the Lord?" he said. His voice bent.
Praise God.
"If you are raising your children in his ways, if you are giving them strong roots in the power of God," he said, "you have nothing to fear. And when the select come back from our Fall Sojourn, you'll know that they have been tested and they have been found worthy."
Amen! Praise God.
The pillar of smoke floated closer, reaching the edge of the tent. Faces of bears, jackals, alligators, and other nameless beasts pushed through the smoke, threatening the faithful. And yet, none of the congregants saw what Ezra saw.

"You have no power here!" Reverend Ezra picked up the silver microphone and pulled the cord along the floor behind him, leaping off the elevated stage into the sawdust in front of the pulpit. "If I but summon the words, you must get behind me!"

The congregation fell silent, unfamiliar with the words and current mood of the preacher, whose hands trembled though his expression was solid, his jaw fixed. The faithful looked to Reverend Ezra, then around at each other, with some craning their necks to look outside as if to understand what it was that he saw coming.

Reverend Ezra pointed a bony finger toward the pillar, now so close it ruffled the canvas. "If I call on you and beseech you in His name, if I tell you to get behind me, you must do so."

Reverend Ezra heard a groaning billow from the pillar of smoke before words rang through his head: *Your time has come to an end.*

The Reverend shrank back, the pillar's words stinging his skin. He looked around at the congregation, now eerily silent and perfectly still. Had they heard the voice? Did they see the smoke?

"My time is *now*, do you hear me? We, the faithful, will rebuild the Temple, and you know this to be true," he said. He raced toward the back of the tent, the cord of his microphone now reaching its full length, pulling him back as if he were a dog on a run.

The voice came again, all gravel and rage: *And now comes another.*

"No!" Reverend Ezra said.

When he shook his fist at the pillar, it rushed through the tent and down the aisle; he braced himself against it. When it passed through his body, it dispersed, a million strands of inky black cascading over the congregation and into the night air. He doubled over as a chill dug into his pores, finding its way into every part of him. He unbuttoned his shirt sleeve and rolled it up. He cleared the fabric in time to see the darkness spider vein its way through his forearm. He fell to the floor, lying on his side in the sawdust, and pulled his knees to his chest, curling into a ball.

Reverend Ezra's body expanded, floating, and suddenly he raced through the cool fall air above the mountains into the night clouds. He flew along, the stars and moon so close he could have caressed them with his fingertips. He corkscrewed through the night, feeling the chill overtake every part of him the way frost stretches itself along a pane of glass in winter. He was certain he would never find warmth again, as if his humanity were a thing of the past, the warm blood in his veins a memory, overtaken by the inky stain of some evil constellation.

When he came to, he heard the shouts of the faithful. They stood in the aisle, their hands skyward, the women wailing and the men crying out to the heavens on his behalf. Brother Lemuel helped Ezra to his feet, his pale eyes full of warmth and love. Sister Gail smiled at him from the pews, her helmet hair still as stone. Ezra stood, his knees stiff and locked. He scanned the congregation for the boy. The boy must be the one. The one the pillar talked about. *And now comes another.* The boy with the dead parents. He'd waited this long, hadn't taken him as a baby, unlike King Herod and the Massacre of the Innocents. He'd stayed his hand out of pity and out of respect for the old man, the boy's grandfather, Leonard. Maybe he should have killed Gabriel as a baby, or eliminated his father before he'd been able to spread his seed. They'd always been out there, lingering. Waiting in the darkness to threaten the kingdom.

The pillar gone, Ezra felt a sense of triumph take hold in his bones. He raised his hands toward the heavens and held his chin high. He'd never felt so powerful, so in touch with God, so alive. The sight of him praising the Almighty brought out a kind of wildness in the faithful, some shouting to God, some quoting Bible verses from the sacred King James 1611 edition, some speaking in tongues, some humming the old gospel hymns of their ancestors.

He made his way to the pulpit, scooping up the silver microphone, dragging it along, whipping it over the stage to clear the kinks. He stood taller now, his voice bolder. He knew what had to be done.

"There is no spirit but the one holy spirit of God," he said.

Amen, Brother Ezra.

"Brothers and sisters, you have felt the Holy Spirit alive in this place. It is among us." He held his fist out in front of him, considering the black veins in his forearm before squeezing his eyes shut as tightly as he could. When he opened them, the veins cleared, as though he had willed the darkness away.

Ezra's voice grew soft and deep as he leaned into the microphone. "In a few moments, the choir is going to come up and sing *Just As I Am Without One Plea,* and you will have your chance to not only make things right with God in your hearts and minds, but to open your pocketbooks and pull out the first bricks of the foundation for our new Temple on the Mountain. New Jerusalem."

Amen! Praise Jesus.

"Will you pull the bricks from your pocketbooks?"

Yes! Amen! Hallelujah!

"Will you pull out the cement and the mortar and the foundation of all God has wrought? Or will you lie to God, will you steal from him, will you take all that he has given you and betray him?"

"No!" shouted Brother Lemuel, wisps of blond hair falling over his eyes.

"And so, as they come to play, search your souls. Make sure you are not stealing from the Almighty, focused on a world that is indifferent to his might, indifferent to his message, indifferent to his bloody, agonizing, brutal death on the cross."

Ezra took his seat on the stage to the right of the musicians. He looked out over the large congregation, knowing the foundation of the Temple would soon be built. He knew the effect his gaze had on members during the offering. Like children, they sometimes needed to know someone was watching. And so, he watched them, one by one, as the plate was passed, knowing they felt the weight of his stare. More than once, he saw someone about to pass the plate without making a tithe only to pull it back once they realized Reverend Ezra bore witness to all—he was aware of their indifference, their faithlessness. More than once, he saw them pull out a small bill, then think better of it and pull out more or reach for their checkbooks. Like sheep, he thought, sometimes they must be led.

Reverend Ezra closed the heavy wooden double doors and walked out behind the Church of Hosanna to the graveyard beyond. His shirt stuck to his back, sweat laden, and the cool air gave him chill. The church grounds were immaculately manicured, the grass cut low and the paths raked clean of leaves. Two rows of majestic maples ran the length of the graveyard, standing like sentries watching over the dead. There were no stars, no moonlight, the sky black. He rejoiced at the number of souls saved, the score of congregants who had come down to the altar to pray with one of the elders. Tonight's revival had went well. The contributions for the Temple had been robust, and more would follow. He ran the back of his hand over his head, slicking back the wayward strands threatening to fall in his eyes. He took off his suit jacket and let it drop to the ground, loosening his red tie and pulling the small end through the knot before hurling it away.

The wind rustled the leaves above, and he smiled, feeling a kind of warmth the fall air did not provide. A warmth within the earth, within him. Something only he knew.

He walked the field beyond the graveyard and into the trees, the leaves crunching under his shiny black wingtips. He stood still, basking in the quiet whispers of the forest. He unbuttoned his shirt and let it drop, then pulled off his t-shirt. He stretched out his arms and leaned his head back, staring up into the canopy. He focused on his breathing, controlling each measured breath. Each inhale stretched longer and deeper, until his chest barely moved. He closed his eyes.

He smiled when he felt them around him. On the ground amongst the leaves, red bulbs rose from the earth, growing, floating into the air like flames. The wisps, he knew, were born of the earth, but not of the earth. Like him. They were of something deeper. They swirled around him now, and he opened his eyes to greet them.

"My friends."

The wisps pulled leaves, wildflowers, and tiny limbs they collected from the forest. They wrapped their creation around him, their heat washing over him and settling inside him. They weaved the organic material together, deep red fabric taking shape around his body. It was the same fervent color as the wisps themselves. They worked quickly, weaving and threading together a flowing robe that lit the night. He pulled the deep, soft hood up over his head. Their work complete, they descended back into the earth.

To the wisps, to the night, he said, "And He saw all that He had made, and behold, it was very good."

He thought then of the black pillar that had assaulted him at the camp meeting.

Your time has come to an end.

And now comes another.

Old man Leonard's grandson. Gabriel. Who should have died in the car crash or in his jaws after as he stood by the car. He remembered the smell of the boy, the throbbing of his blood, the way the vein on his neck had danced in fear. What had the boy wielded behind him in the trees? How had it stayed his hand?

He walked through the woods, slowly at first. Then his pace quickened, face hard, his teeth grinding. Soon, his feet left the earth, the red robes finding new shapes and patterns in the air as he flew through the trees. When he returned to earth, his paws pushed the leaves. The Red Wolf sprinted swiftly up the slope toward the mountain's peak. Below him, a highway snaked through the valley, cars' tiny headlights glowing in front of them. When he reached the rock face of the peak, he looked north. Toward Elk Mountain.

He would have to kill the boy and his siblings, the twins.

There would be no other.

4 / GABE & THE MAGIC CARPET RIDE

Gabe sat on the deck behind his grandparents' house. It was a cool Sunday morning, and he listened to the birdsong in the trees above. Did birds sing only one song, or did they have many? He listened to the notes, trying to picture them on the keys of the upright piano in his room in the basement. He wrote the notes down in his notebook, drawing them on a crooked makeshift staff. He thought he had the whole refrain but kept listening to the bird repeat itself to be sure. He wondered if Mina might be outside, just through the woods, listening to the same birdsong. The bird fell silent mid-phrase when Samson came running around the side of the house, sliding on the boards of the deck before leaping against Gabe's leg. Samson was Papa Leo's little terrier mix, white with black spots. The kind of yapping dog that often got so carried away barking, he would give himself a coughing fit. He did that now, not easing until Gabe petted him.

"Well, good morning to you, too."

LilyMa opened the sliding glass door and stepped outside. Her white hair was up in a bun, two long hair sticks holding it in place.

"Don't mind me," she said. "I got your coffee."

She set the hot coffee on the rail beside him. Fixed black the way he liked it, though she and Papa Leo took cream in theirs. Gabe leaned back, looking up through the orange and yellow leaves. The sunlight filtering through the tree limbs made him want to sneeze, but it wouldn't come.

"Thank you, LilyMa," he said, taking up the cup, eyes watering.

She nodded, walking back in the house before he had a sip. She was like that. She wanted to make you comfortable, but not interrupt. She knew how much Gabe liked to sit outside in the mornings, when he had time and there wasn't school. How much he needed the birds. Truth was, he wouldn't mind if she sat down to talk sometimes. She would have breakfast ready soon. It took him a long time to understand that she liked to cook, wanted to take care of everybody. She wasn't doing it out of obligation. It was who she was. She'd cook a full breakfast, have the iron skillet cleaned, all the dishes back in their place—washed and dried by hand—and the kitchen spotless, before she'd sit down to her own breakfast, getting cold on the counter. She refused to heat it back up in the microwave. She hated those things. It was the same at lunch, same at supper. The only time she sat down to eat at the same time as everybody else was for Sunday dinner. Even then, she'd worry herself to death making sure he and Papa Leo had everything they needed.

"Hellfire, Lilyfax," Papa Leo would say. "Sit down and eat, we're fine. The boy can scoop his own beans."

Samson spun in circles till Gabe pet him again, then disappeared around the house, barking. Gabe heard Papa Leo's footsteps, and soon he appeared, the dog running circles around him as he came. He wore a blue coat vest, a dark flannel shirt, and Dickies pants. His seven-day-a-week uniform. Though it was early, he was clean-shaven, his gray and black hair parted neatly, the sunlight catching the sheen of the Brylcreem he wore every day, rain or shine. To Gabe, it made him look like a character out of a 1950s movie. His face was wrinkled, but not as much as a typical man in his seventies. He walked with a straight back, shoulders square, despite sometimes needing a cane for his bad knee.

"Come walk with me," he said. "Got something to show you."

Gabe followed him off the deck and down the bank around the side of the house. He marveled at how quickly the old man moved down the steep hill, with a cane and wearing heavy work boots. When they got to the back, Samson barked excitedly as Papa Leo pulled out an enormous key ring and fiddled with a Master lock on one of the basement doors. There were two such doors on the back of the house, and these rooms didn't connect to the part of the basement that was Gabe's bedroom. He had been in the other one to retrieve lawn mowers and weed eaters. His daddy had once told him Papa Leo built most of the house by hand, so there were weird halls and rooms like these that didn't connect to the main house. Samson did a figure eight between the man's feet.

"Damnit, Samson," Papa Leo said. "Will you get out from under me before I snap one of your little chicken legs?"

Samson stopped briefly, then resumed the figure eight.

Papa Leo clicked the lock open and froze.

"Shhhh," he told the dog. There were gunshots in the distance.

"I am gonna have to shoot that son of a bitch," the old man said.

"Who?" Gabe asked.

"Keeps hunting on my land. I got signs ever where. Reckon he's illiterate. Figures I won't come after him like I did last time."

LilyMa had told Gabe the story of Papa Leo recently running men off the land who were hunting without permission. She'd told him that Papa Leo confronted the two men with a shotgun and offered to introduce them to their maker unless they wanted to get the hell off his land. Now they were back. Papa Leo shook his head.

He opened the doors and walked inside. Gabe could barely see until Papa Leo pulled an overhead light cord hanging from a single bulb in the center of the room. The light illuminated a big blue car. It had flared fenders and a single large door on each side, despite being almost as long as his parents' old station wagon. It was ancient. The kind of car someone's grandma would drive.

Papa Leo beamed. "I know you turn sixteen next month. If you'll take care of it, I know you'll want to be getting around. Take girls out for ice cream."

Samson ran around the car twice before stopping to piss on the back tire.

"Damnit, Samson," Papa Leo said. "Just had her washed. Do you have to piss on ever damn thing you see?"

The dog wagged his tail at hearing his name.

Gabe was mortified. He pictured himself pulling into the school parking lot with this land yacht. Would a girl like Mina ever consider climbing into this beast?

Papa Leo seemed to read his face. "Or you can keep riding your bicycle everywhere. Girls like boys with bicycles too, I reckon. You can get a little cart and tow them around behind you. Just make sure she ain't too big," he laughed. "Backside nothing over half an ax handle. Hard to get her up the hills."

"Yes, no," Gabe said.

It was immense. Enormous. Would it fit in a regular-sized parking space?

"Wow, Papa Leo, I don't know what to say."

Gabe's best friend Lucas had turned sixteen over the summer. He'd gotten a gold 240z. Lucas could park that son of a bitch on the hood of this car.

Papa Leo stuck out his chest. "I been saving her for you. You know she only has about thirty-five thousand miles on her."

"That all?" Gabe said. He looked at the obnoxious curves of the beast, the word OLDSMOBILE spread in grotesque cursive across the enormous grill.

"She rides like you're floating on air. She'll probably last you till you get out of college and get your first job, you take care of her."

Gabe couldn't swallow.

"You're going to college after you graduate, we've talked about this."

"Yes, sir."

"Get you a teacher's certificate, maybe."

"Maybe."

"Maybe this afternoon we can take her for a Sunday drive. Get LilyMa off her chores."

"Yes, sir," Gabe said.

Outside, Samson barked, and Gabe heard a horn honk—three quick beeps in succession. Aunt Clary, he realized, looking at his watch.

On Sundays, Aunt Clary brought the twins to visit with Gabe and their grandparents. Sometimes she came in, carrying a covered dish or two for Sunday dinner. Sometimes she just dropped the kids off, coming back to get them in the late afternoon or just after dark.

The decision to separate the kids had been a difficult one for the family to make when they lost their parents in the car crash. Three kids were just too hard for anyone to take on. Gabe had been sent to live with his daddy's parents, and Carl and Sarah had been sent to live with his mama's sister. Aunt Clary said she wanted to take all the children, but with two of her own, she felt like it would have been too much on her. As for Papa Leo and LilyMa, while most said they were in great health for their ages, the kinfolk agreed the twins were too energetic. At fifteen, his uncle Louis had said Gabe was "practically grow'd" and could take care of himself. Therefore, everyone reasoned, he would be the smallest burden to his grandparents. He could also help LilyMa with Papa Leo, who had started to become forgetful. Uncle Louis used the term *senile*.

Much of the time, Gabe was glad to be shed of Carl and Sarah, who could be quite a nuisance. Some nights, however, when the house on Elk Mountain was still, he longed to be near them, wishing for the days when they would sneak into his bed after their parents had gone to sleep. They would snuggle in, one on each side of him in what Sarah would call a "Gabe sandwich."

That afternoon, after playing outside in the woods for several hours, getting sweaty despite the coolness of the day, Gabe laid with the twins on the couch. LilyMa had fussed over Sarah and Carl, fixing them chocolate chip cookies from scratch after a dinner of pork chops, greens, and cornbread baked in an iron skillet. The house still smelled of pork as the kids wallowed over Gabe the way puppies loll their mothers. He loved these moments, but could sense it was nearing its end when Papa Leo came in and looked at the three of them.

Laying around, even on a Sunday afternoon, annoyed Papa Leo. Finally, he'd had enough, saying, "My God, will y'all go outside and play! Never seen kids that didn't want to be outside."

"They just got here," LilyMa said.

Papa Leo said nothing but went to the opposite side of the house. Gabe heard him pull on the TV.

When Aunt Clary arrived to pick up the twins, she did what she always did, telling Gabe how he was the spitting image of his daddy and how his mama would have been so proud of the good Christian man he was becoming.

Gabe didn't feel like a good Christian. On this Sunday, like most Sundays, he'd woken up early enough to go to church, but he hadn't gone. Papa Leo and LilyMa didn't go to church regular. While he missed his mama and daddy, he did not miss Mama harping about the evils of being in the world, and how she'd dragged the family to church every Sunday morning, Sunday night, going to Wednesday night service, to revivals, and any other service she could find. Gabe knew Reverend Ezra's fall camp meeting was going on, and he was relieved he didn't have to go. But this made him feel guilty, sinful. Sometimes he heard his mama's voice in his head, telling him how low he was to sit and listen to rock and roll music, talking about girls the way he did with Lucas, or reading so many books that weren't the Bible. Everything but the Bible.

"I'll never forget the funeral," Aunt Clary said, "the way you stood by their caskets and shook hands with people just like a grown-up. Your mama would have been so proud."

Aunt Clary could not stop talking about the funeral, even though it had been over two years. She talked incessantly about how handsome Gabe's father had looked, how radiant and God-like his mama had been, her shock of chestnut-colored hair styled up in a way she could never fix herself. Both parents had been shown in an open casket, their mouths stretched hideously with makeup caking their faces to make them look less pale. Gabe had touched his daddy, reaching in to put his hand over the cold shape of his father's. He'd had no such urge to touch his mama and felt mean about it. Part of him regretted not touching her, especially with everyone watching.

"At least they didn't suffer," Aunt Clary said. Turning to Papa Leo and LilyMa, she said, "Y'all heard about Mrs. Redding, up Barnardsville way?"

"No," LilyMa said, smoothing back wisps that had fallen out of her bun. "I haven't seen her in years, why? What's wrong?"

"She's eat up with cancer," Aunt Clary said, a tinge of what sounded like joy in her voice. "Eat up with it. They say it's only a matter of time." Turning to Gabe, she said, "I know it was sudden-like for your folks, but at least they didn't suffer for years like people with cancer do."

Gabe looked at the twins. They had been playing on the floor until Aunt Clary brought up their dead parents and ravenous cancer. Now they watched her, mouths open.

"What's cancer?" Carl asked.

"Course, Mrs. Redding ain't been living right, not for years," Aunt Clary said.

"It's a disease that eats people," Sarah said to Carl.

Aunt Clary said, "The Lord works in mysterious ways. You don't follow his ways, he says, *'vengeance is mine.'*"

"That's horseshit," Papa Leo said.

"Leo!" LilyMa said, eyebrows raised. She wasn't scolding him for disagreeing with Aunt Clary, Gabe knew, but for cursing in front of the twins.

For Aunt Clary, for Mama, for a lot of Christian folk Gabe knew, Jesus was a boogeyman hiding in the bushes, ready to pounce on a sinner or wayward Christian. Yes, he'd died for everyone's sins, and yes, he did great things, like miracles for the downtrodden. But he also gave people cancer or heart attacks, or had them die in other horrible ways, because they had not lived right or because they had mocked him in some blasphemous fashion. Even though Gabe tried not to think this way, he sometimes wondered what secret sins his parents had committed that resulted in them dying in a car crash, leaving their kids orphaned.

Once when Aunt Clary was alone with Gabe, she'd queried him incessantly about the car crash and the way the Red Wolf had leapt into the windshield of the family's car. "I believe you seen the Devil himself," Aunt Clary had said. "He come after your parents because they were such good people. That's what he always does to the faithful." A chill worked up Gabe's spine when he thought about it. Over time, he'd almost convinced himself the wolf hadn't been real. But he could still hear its growl, see its teeth. It came to him in his nightmares.

When Aunt Clary loaded the twins up in her shiny new Dodge Caravan, she headed up the driveway with the same three honks she used to herald her arrival. Samson went to barking, as did every dog on Elk Mountain, including those from the junkyard to the south and all the dogs from the trailer park through the woods. Somehow, every trailer in Whispering Pines had at least one dog, several with three or more. They all barked as Aunt Clary and the twins disappeared over the hill.

Gabe thought about the twins, about Mama and Daddy, the way they had lain in their coffins with plastic faces. He looked at his watch and thought about going to read before bed. He imagined rushing through the morning to get to the bus stop, where the best part of his day would begin. That's when Gabe thought of her, of Mina—of her green eyes, her summer dresses, her spare smile, and how he was sure one day soon, she'd talk to him. Really talk to him. And maybe that son of a bitch Emerson Schmidt—whom everyone called Emerson Shit—would get a flat tire and wouldn't be able to squeal his tires up the road to give her a ride. Or maybe, just maybe, Mina would prefer to ride in Gabe's giant blue granny car. After all, it would be like riding on air—a real Magic Carpet Ride. He vowed to go to bed early, to rush the night along to bring morning, the bus stop, and a glimpse of Mina and her long red hair.

5 / EMERSON & ALL THAT WITCH SHIT
MINA

Emerson treated his car like he was mad at it. He sped up in the curves, never touching his brakes, the tires complaining, the car leaning. Not that Mina could hear the tires over the stereo blasting Ratt. It was the kind of stereo where you felt the bass in your chest, the kind that cost more than most teenagers' cars. Most of her friends didn't even have cars. Certainly not the kids living in Whispering Pines. When they hit a new curve, she slid across the seat, her thigh touching the back of Emerson's hand on the gear shift. He grinned at her, dropping his big head suggestively. She pulled on the door handle to center herself in the seat, the back of her knees sticking to the leather while the rest of her glided back and forth, the seat slick with Armor All.

When they hit a straightaway, Emerson's hand left the gearshift and found her leg just above the knee. He slid it up, pushing the hem of her dress. She began to regret accepting his offer for a ride home after school.

She rolled her eyes, picked up his hand, and positioned it back on the gearshift.

He glanced at her, jaw set, and turned the music up louder. She watched his large arms work the steering wheel, considering his blue Izod shirt with its collar turned up. The Swatch that perfectly matched. Emerson always matched. Shirt, jacket, socks. Always. It was like he just stepped off a mall billboard. He was probably dressed by his mother. She pictured the woman, whom she'd met only once, with her Farrah Fawcett bangs and white pantsuit. Mina imagined her slicking Emerson's hair down like he was five. Laying out his clothes each morning.

When they approached the entrance to the trailer park, she turned to fetch her backpack from the backseat but was surprised when they sped past the entrance. She turned her head as it went by.

"Where are you going?" she asked.

"Would you just relax?" Emerson returned his hand to her leg. Once again, she used both of hers to position it back on the gearshift. He ground his teeth. She pulled at her ponytail, something she did when she was nervous. She let go of it when she realized what she was doing. *It's not a big deal*, she thought. He probably just wants to go on up the mountain, find some bigger curves that he can drive too fast into. Maybe shoot us off the road to a fiery death. No big deal.

Emerson turned onto a dirt road, slowing briefly to make the turn before flooring the gas.

Mina bounced on the seat, her head bumping the headliner.

"I have to get home," she said. He just grinned and kept his eyes on the road.

Emerson drove them deep in the woods. Mina knew the road. At the end of it, there was an old junkyard. She and Chelsea had walked its perimeter many times, peering through at the rusty cars that lined the kudzu-covered fence. Dogs growled at them from the other side, warning them to keep their distance. One time, somebody had thrown poisoned meat in, killing a few of the dogs. Somebody said they'd ripped off the old man who ran the place, taking parts and throwing them over the fence to load in a pickup. They got the cash box, too. After that, the man had his new dogs trained never to take food from anyone but him. The next boys that tried the meat trick, one of them had a chunk taken from the back of his leg before he got back over the fence.

Emerson slammed on the brakes and the car slid sideways, gravel striking the wheel well. He turned down the music.

"I have to get home," Mina said. "Daddy will be expecting me."

"Relax," he said again.

"Fine. I can walk from here," she said, reaching for the door. He pulled her back by her shoulder.

"Emerson—"

His face softened. "It's a pretty day. We can just have a little fun, then I'll take you home."

She watched the leaves falling from the trees onto the hood of the car. Orange and yellow streaks on the black paint.

He reached across her again, pulling the lever on the side of her seat. It reclined, her feet coming off the floor as she tried to keep herself upright.

"Emerson, no," she said.

Then he was kissing her neck, his arms around her, and pulling her toward him. He breathed into her neck, and she could smell his cologne. Polo. Way too much Polo—enough to douse the entire football team. It mixed with the chemical scent of his hair mousse, making her feel sick. She pushed him off. He sat back in his seat, glaring.

"I have to get home," she said.

"Mina, Mina, Mina," he said. "What am I going to do with you?"

"It's not a big deal," she said. "I can walk home from here."

"I ain't done with you yet," he said, his eyes roving.

She pulled at the hem of her dress, straightening the fabric.

"You always this uptight, Cinnamon Girl?" he said.

She tried a different tack. "Want to go look through the fence at the junkyard? It's not far."

"I want," he said, "to see what's under that dress."

Her face flushed, but not with embarrassment. As much as she'd tried to convince herself otherwise, she knew this was coming. Guys like Emerson didn't give girls like her rides to school. It was always about this. Not just guys like Emerson. All guys.

"You'll have to find another girl for that," she said.

He cupped his hands and rubbed them together. They were soft compared to her daddy's, but Emerson was big. A wrestler. His skin might be soft, but he was strong.

She tried the door again. He reached across her and slammed it shut.

"I keep taking you to school, dropping you off. I took you to the pool."

Over the summer, Emerson had picked Mina up and taken her to the Beaver Trail Country Club pool down the mountain. She'd been astonished when they went through the gate, staring at the huge trees lining both sides of the road, the entrance seeming to go on for miles before you saw the first house. The pool was enormous, Olympic-sized, with swimming lanes on one end, big Maple trees around it, and a view of the golf course below. The only pool Mina had been in before was the county pool, which boasted views of an asphalt parking lot and the highway. She had felt instantly out of place. She'd been the only girl, Emerson and his five guy friends sipping beer from red solo cups and sniggering about which of the country club moms they'd like to bang. The women seemed like they were from a different planet. They walked on heels and wore pearls to the pool. Mina remembered hoping Erin, her best friend, would show up, since she lived in the community, but she never did. Since that day, Emerson had constantly brought up the pool, as if it were something she owed him for.

"And you still haven't shown me what's under that dress," he said.

She looked out the window. This was so predictable. She'd pretended like this wasn't who Emerson was. Lied to herself about why he took her to school, a place where he barely acknowledged her. At school, he hung with his friends, flirting with Krissy Lang and her girlfriends. All Mina got was a quick wink when he passed. Sometimes he'd lift his chin. She was good for a ride to school, someone to feel up in the car. A trailer park girl to fuck in the woods. Not the kind of girl he wanted to go with, to date.

"I really like you," he said. "I'm sorry if I came on too strong."

"Oh, is that right?" she asked.

"Yeah," he said. "Some of the other guys at school, they're scared of you."

She met his eyes.

"It's true," he said. "You're always carrying some big book you're reading. They're all intimidated."

"No, they aren't," she said.

He slid toward her. "They are, but I'm not. I think you're kind of pretty."

He was trying to seem kind, but his face wasn't. He seemed annoyed that he had to talk her around, like he was bored with it all.

"I'm just going to take the bus from now on," she said. "You don't have to pick me up anymore."

His lip curled. He leaned in. She turned her head to avoid the kiss.

"Let's just have some fun," he said. "I haven't had a redhead before."

"Emerson," she said, putting her hand on his chest, pushing him back. "It's not gonna happen."

He scowled, balled his fists. For a moment, she was sure he'd try to hit her.

"I think," he said, grinding his teeth, "that maybe you should know your place."

"That right?" she said. Her ears burned. "You think you're gonna show me my place?"

"Maybe," he said.

"Big Emerson Schmidt—Emerson Shit—you're gonna show the trailer park girl what she's good for?"

He squared his shoulders and puffed out his chest. She knew he hated the nickname. Knew she was pushing his buttons. "Damn right," he said. Then he was on top of her in earnest, pushing his hand up her leg.

She banged her knees together, cracking his fingers. "You piece of shit," she said. "I said no."

She tried to bite his lip but missed. He tucked his head into her neck, panting like he'd been running. She pushed at him again, then reached for the door.

She looked over his shoulder at the trees. The light bent there, as if she were looking through old glass. At the tops of the trees, a shadow fell over the branches. It came to life, slithered like a snake. She closed her eyes.

"No," she said, but not to Emerson.

His mouth was open on her neck, and he pinned her to the seat, his body heavy, his shoulders over hers.

Then she was in the trees, the world gray, looking down at the black IROC sitting sideways on the dirt road. She saw herself through the sunroof, her head back, his body swallowing hers as she pushed at him.

"He's just a boy," she said.

Emerson pulled away from her, eyebrows arched. "Who's just a boy?"

She looked past him. "He doesn't know what he's doing."

He looked insulted. "I know exactly what I'm doing, and you're gonna love it. All the girls love it."

The shadows in the trees grew long. They expanded and

stretched, long tentacles of black gripping the limbs. Mina watched them grow, frowning.

"No," she said. "Don't."

"I'll teach you tricks you can use on other guys," Emerson said. "They'll high-five me in the hall," he said.

"Don't hurt him," she said.

He pulled away again. "What?"

That's when it came. Up through the earth, shaking the roots of the trees, racing up the trunks to bend the sky. A growl so deep it rattled Mina's teeth. It shook the car, a thousand times louder than the stereo had been. Emerson looked around wildly. The growl seemed to go on forever, the bass of it curling in waves so loud it hurt her ears. Emerson scrambled back and put his hands over his ears, looking out of the window in time to see an enormous black cloud descend over the car. The entire world went black as a night with no moon. Mina couldn't see him, the car, or the trees. She couldn't see her own hand in front of her face

"What the fuck?" Emerson said. He fumbled through the center console. "Mina?"

"I'm here," she said.

He clicked open his Zippo lighter, striking it. It didn't light at first, the spark strobing as he frantically worked the flint. He dropped the lighter and scrambled to find it on the floor.

He struck it again, and the flame took. When her eyes adjusted, Mina saw Emerson's face. His eyes were wide, his lips stretched in a grimace. The car windows were pitch black.

"Mina," he said, voice trembling, "what's happening?"

In the driver's side window, she saw the shadow faces.

Emerson followed her eyes. A huge, monstrous face lurked in the window. Something between beast and man. It looked like the gargoyle faces Mina had once seen on a field trip to the Biltmore House. Bulging eyes and sharp teeth and lolling tongues. Another appeared beside it, then another. Gargoyle faces lined the car windows, and Emerson held the lighter out in front of him, twisting in his seat. A big one huffed at the window, its breath fogging the glass.

"Don't hurt him," she repeated.

"Oh my God," Emerson said. His hand shook, the flame wobbling in the pitch.

The growl came again, up through the earth, shaking the car windows. The faces showed their teeth, long canines throbbing.

Mina knew it was her fault; she had done this. Brought the darkness that swallowed the car, swallowed the trees, consumed the world. She'd done it, but she hadn't meant to. She never meant to. It was an involuntary reflex, like when the doctor tested your knee with that tiny hammer. She tried to shrug away the darkness, but it only deepened, the faces pushing against the glass, windows creaking as if they might shatter.

"Mina," Emerson said. He looked at her for comfort, then dropped his eyes to his lap, his shoulders slumped.

"It will pass," she said. It always passed, like a wave of anxiety. She just needed to breathe, to slow her heart. She focused on her breathing, the way she'd read to do in books: in through her nose, out through her mouth.

Then the shadow faces spoke.

Know your place, they laughed, mouths moving in unison. A chill tickled Mina's scalp.

"Leave us alone," she said.

Let us eat him, they said. *Oh, Mina, let us eat him.* Their voices were deep, but whiny like demonic children.

"No," she said.

She reached for the door latch.

"Mina, no, please," Emerson begged. His voice rattled like a boy going through puberty. Gone was the swagger, the low punch it held earlier. "Don't leave me here."

"I won't be needing a ride to school anymore," she said.

"I'll give you rides," he said. "I won't touch you again, ever. I swear."

"I know you won't," she said.

"Just don't leave me," he said. "Not like this."

"I'm gonna go," she said. "This will pass. Just sit still and don't talk to them. Don't look at them, okay?"

"Please, Mina," he begged. "They'll attack me."

"They won't," she said. "I won't let them." She tried to smile. But part of her did want them to devour him whole and spit out his bones.

"Please," he said.

When she exited the car, the cloud and the gargoyle faces parted for her. She walked away, her hands held out in front of her. She couldn't see the road or the trees. Then an orange glow lit the way before her. She saw spikes along the path in the woods, a head on each spike. Dozens, then hundreds. There were men's heads, the heads of wolves, of bears. Mountain lions. Cats and dogs. Monster gargoyle heads. She tried not to look at them, tried to follow the advice she'd given Emerson. They showed their teeth, animated, alive. Their jaws snapped as she passed.

It was worse this time. The worst it had ever been.

She remembered the first time she'd summoned the shadow faces. She couldn't have been more than eight. Daddy had hit Mama in the kitchen. Some fight over money or liquor, maybe both. Mina had balled her fists, feeling like she would explode. The curl in her stomach came, and she leaned into her anger. She wanted to hit Daddy, wanted him to fall through the earth, be eaten by worms. The shadows crept in through a window, spreading like tentacles over the ceiling. A face descended, and its long neck wrapped around Daddy's neck. He stood paralyzed, reaching for his throat before falling. He lay on the floor, red-faced, while Mama screamed and pounded on his chest. An ambulance had taken Daddy to the hospital. When he came home, he drank even more. And while he still bowed up and cursed Mama, he never raised his hand to her again.

Mina didn't want this. Any of this. She wanted to be in her room at home. Reading a book or listening to some music. She didn't want Emerson's dumb ass to give her rides. She'd only done that so she wouldn't have to hang out with the trailer park kids any more than she already had to.

She didn't want to live in this fucking town, in Whispering Pines, to be stuck in these mountains that rose up in all directions to block her escape. But she wouldn't get stuck. She wasn't stuck. She didn't want the dark clouds, the black smoke full of shadow faces. She'd never asked for this. Why her? Why had the shadows come to her?

She'd tried so hard to keep them at bay, to push them away in those moments when anger rang her bones. Even in the car, Emerson's lumbering body over hers, she'd just wanted to push him off and run. She didn't want to be saved. Didn't need saving. She wanted the faces to leave her alone. She didn't want the earth to growl beneath her feet.

The spiked heads leaned toward her. They whispered to her in a language she didn't understand. They circled her, and something strange happened—a sense of peace washed over her. Each time the shadow faces came, she'd been seized by fear and anger, but now she felt a strange comfort in their presence. It was as if she were at home here in the dark, in the woods, swallowed by shadow. Maybe it was the one place on earth she could find peace. The faces twisted around her, and she finally let go. She fell back into them, and they were everywhere, as soft and warm as a big mattress in a fancy hotel. She relaxed into them, and the shadows held her, her body never touching the ground. Instead, she rose up through the canopy, above the trees, up above Elk Mountain. The sky, which had been blue before, now waxed winter gray. She looked south and saw Whispering Pines, heard the trailers rocking on their cinder blocks. To the west, she saw a house. She'd seen it before, walking through the woods with Chelsea, but she'd never been inside. She saw a pickup truck in the driveway, a blue and white Ford F-150. She recognized it —Gabe's grandfather's truck, the one he'd used to pick up Gabe from school a few times.

At the edge of the woods near the house, she saw something moving. A glimpse of red. Some kind of animal. When it turned toward her, she could see it was an enormous red wolf, as tall as a horse. It froze in place, stopping its creep around the house. It lifted its head skyward. It growled and bared its teeth. Did it see her? The earth—or maybe Mina herself—roared back at the wolf, shaking the trees, the same supernatural growl that terrorized Emerson before. Then she floated back to the earth, the shadows receding into the trees and dissipating into the leaves on the ground. The shadow faces, the spiked heads—all of it was gone. The thought of the wolf should have terrified her, but instead, she marveled at how there were more dark things than just the shadows she could conjure.

She'd made it to the road and was headed down the mountain when she heard the IROC's tires leave the dirt road and grip the pavement. Emerson drove slowly—something she didn't know he could do—pulling up alongside her. The power window whirred down. She didn't look at him.

"What was that back there?" he asked.

"I just don't know what you mean," she said.

"You pulled some kind of trick on me. Some witch shit."

"Did I?"

"Yeah," he said like he was trying to convince himself. "You pulled something over on me."

She stopped walking and faced the car.

"Emerson," she said. "Just go home."

He looked around nervously, perhaps expecting the shadow faces to return. He shook his head.

"Krissy and all those girls at school," he said. "They only talk to you because of me."

"That right?"

"They wouldn't be your friends if it wasn't for me," he said.

"They're not my friends," she said.

"Anyway," he said. "You're through."

She wanted to laugh. "Am I?"

"I'll tell everybody what a whore you are."

"You do that."

"I'll tell them you had to have it every day after school. Right in my car. That you couldn't get enough."

She leaned toward the car window. "I'll tell them you got spooked in the woods and pissed your pants."

"I did not!" he said, looking down as if to check. "You're just a trailer park whore."

"I should have let them eat you."

Emerson shuddered. The window purred closed and the car lurched down the mountain. But Mina had bigger things to worry about than Emerson Schmidt's big mouth. Things like the shadow faces and the red wolf skulking around outside Gabe's house. Had it really growled at her? Had she really been floating in the sky? Had the strange wolf seen her there? And why had her instinct been to growl back, to engage this thing she didn't understand?

Emerson's tires squealed on the road. She heard the thump of the stereo return as he hit the first curve. He didn't touch the brakes.

6 / CONVERGENCE
GABE

Gabe got home in the early afternoon after LilyMa took him to the dentist. He was rubbing his sore jaw, book in hand, on the couch, when Papa Leo marched through the living room.

"That son of a bitch," Papa Leo muttered.

He wore a flannel shirt, unbuttoned, and the white t-shirt he wore underneath was bright against his tan skin. A pistol stuck out of his pants pocket. He opened the sliding glass door and stepped out onto the deck. LilyMa entered the room, wringing her hands in front of her.

"What is it?" Gabe asked.

"The hunters," she said. "He said they're back, but I didn't hear anything. Did you hear any gunfire?"

Gabe stood in time to see Papa Leo leave the deck to walk downhill toward the woods.

"Go after him," LilyMa said, her voice shaking. "He's not thinking straight. He'll get himself killed."

Gabe laced up his Air Jordans, licking his finger to wipe a scuff from the Carolina blue leather, and headed for the door. He put his hand on LilyMa's arm. "Don't worry," he said. "I'll look after him."

She frowned, nodding.

Gabe found Papa Leo deep in the woods below the house. As always, the man was spry, and Gabe hurried to keep up. It was a brisk fall day, and bright leaves rained down, covering everything. After a few minutes, Papa Leo froze in place. He cocked his head to one side, listening for the hunter's gunfire, or maybe the sound of their feet ahead in the dry leaves. His hand hovered near the pistol. Gabe stood still, behind a tree, not wanting Papa Leo to know he was there, that LilyMa sent him to watch out for him.

"I see you, you bastard," Papa Leo said.

Gabe felt his skin prick at his grandfather's angry tone. He thought of running down and standing in front of Papa Leo. The old man might just shoot somebody.

Papa Leo walked forward slowly, peering through the trees. Gabe craned his neck and looked beyond, trying to catch a glimpse of the hunters. He saw nothing. If they were there, they weren't wearing a hunter's orange protective gear. They blended into the trees. Invisible. Maybe they did this because they were hunting on private land? Maybe they felt sure no other hunters would be around. No one to worry about except the old curmudgeon who'd run them off before. They didn't fear the old man. But they didn't know Papa Leo.

"I see you," Papa Leo repeated. "Come on out of there." His voice was steady. If he felt any threat from the hunters, he didn't show it. He stood straight, his hand resting lightly on the pistol grip.

In the trees, Gabe saw something move. Something red. An unusual color for hunters to wear. He moved from one tree to another to gain a better view. Terror ran through him, through his skin and his bones and into his clenched jaw when he saw it.

The Red Wolf emerged from the trees, moving slowly toward Papa Leo. Gabe couldn't swallow; he felt he might choke. It was the same wolf, the same Red Wolf from the back of the pick-up truck, the one that leapt onto the car. The one that killed his parents. The wolf approached a large oak in the clearing, maybe ten yards from where Papa Leo stood. It circled the tree, its body wrapping unnaturally around the bark, more snake than canine. It dropped its head and approached.

Papa Leo didn't budge. His hand left the butt of his pistol. Gabe wanted to yell for him to run, thought to leap from behind the tree to yell at him. But his feet wouldn't move, trapped as though concrete were poured over them.

Leo, my old friend, the wolf hissed. It spoke, but its mouth didn't move.

The wolf could talk? Had it talked to Gabe the night of the car wreck? Had he heard this voice before, perhaps in his dreams?

"We ain't friends," Papa Leo said. "Not no more."

The wolf laughed. It walked a wide circle around the man, its footfalls so heavy the dry earth shook beneath it. Papa Leo didn't follow the wolf's path. He stood still, staring straight ahead. Why wasn't he running?

The shadows have returned, the Red Wolf said.

"You are the shadow," Papa Leo said. "You slipped into darkness back then, and now you wallow in it. You could've let go of it. But you didn't."

I am worse than the shadows, the Red Wolf said. *Far worse.* It bared its teeth.

"Have you come to eat an old man?" Papa Leo said. "But then, you're pretty old yourself."

I am an ancient thing. I am older than the Earth itself.

"You're still a scared orphan boy down deep. I can smell it on you. You're eat up with it."

The days of the ancient wulvers are over, the Red Wolf said. *Yet someone conjures the shadows. Wields them against me. A pillar of smoke and fire. But I, too, can bring flames.*

"You made your choice," Papa Leo said. "You gave yourself over to it. Did you think you'd end up in a field of flowers being fanned by angels?"

Your grandson, the Red Wolf said. *He brings the pillar of smoke, threatens all I have built.*

"My grandson? Gabriel?"

I should have killed him when I had the chance.

Gabe's pulse quickened.

"They say you're rebuilding the Temple. Up Mulwin Rock. Would you become like the Blue Man? Something so gnarled and twisted?"

The wolf growled low. Gabe felt it rattle in his stomach.

Wake was a fool. His kingdom built on the sand. I build my house upon the rock.

"The Blue Man burned for his sins. You were there."

The wolf approached Papa Leo. It stood a head taller, though all four paws were on the ground. Fine bright red light flickered over the tips of its fur, as if some strange electricity surged through its body.

"I ain't afraid of you," Papa Leo said. "You and me? We can go to Hell right now." He pulled the pistol out and pointed it at the wolf's head.

The wolf leapt forward, biting down on the barrel. It jerked the gun from Papa Leo's hand and hurled it into the woods. It turned its back on Papa Leo, dismissing him and pacing toward the trees.

I should have wiped out your seed when I had the chance.

Ice ran through Gabe's veins.

"You leave Gabriel out of it. He's got nothing to do with this."

He has everything to do with this. You taught him to wield it, didn't you?

"He knows nothing of the past. Nothing of what we went through. Nothing of your evil."

I do God's work.

"There's nothing of God in you, Preacherman."

Gabe stared at them. What did that mean? Why did Papa Leo call the wolf a preacher?

I will come for the boy again. I will tear his limbs from his body.

"You'll do nothing of the sort."

I'll sever his head and swallow it whole. I'll take him at school, along the road. Wherever I can find him. You can't protect him.

"He's not a part of this. You leave him alone, you hear me? I'll kill you myself. I'll hunt you down like a dog."

He brought the pillar down from the sky. Just to taunt me. I will make him pay, just as I made his mother pay. Her incessant questioning. Her nose too long for her face. Its eyes narrowed. *I'll wipe your seed from the face of the Earth. I'll eat them all.*

Just then, the earth rumbled as if an earthquake moved beneath them. Gabe held onto the tree to stabilize himself. The Earth didn't just quake. It roared, as if some ancient beast had awakened, as if the whole earth were a giant lion, hungry and angry. He looked for the source of the roar. It hadn't come from the wolf. This was something else.

There! The Red Wolf spun around. *Do you hear it?*

Papa Leo looked confused. For the first time, his hands showed the slightest hint of a tremor, a glint of fear in his eyes.

That's your boy. He's doing this. He taunts me even now. Where is he?

"It's not him," Papa Leo said. "I've kept all this from him."

The Red Wolf raced past Papa Leo, its shoulder knocking him to the ground. It ran up through the woods, past the tree where Gabe hid, toward the house.

There you are! The wolf howled in the distance. *Hiding in the sky. The pillar won't protect you. I'm coming for you, boy!*

7 / FAITHFUL REWARDS
EZRA

In the days after confronting Leo at Elk Mountain, the Red Wolf stalked Gabriel as he rode the bus to and from school, to baseball practice, to music lessons, to and from his friend Lucas's house. There were times he could have pounced. Times he could have taken the boy in his teeth, severed his delicious jugular. But Ezra was patient. Deliberate. He would wait for signs of the boy wielding his power, perhaps in a teenage moment of weakness or rage. A moment when, overwhelmed by his boyish frailty, he would call the shadows down from the trees. But it didn't happen. Each time he got close, the boy was oblivious. Either that, or he pretended not to sense Ezra's presence. No matter. Eventually, the boy would give in and show himself. And when he did so, he would die. Then the Red Wolf would finish Papa Leo and the twins, leaving none to oppose him. But other matters needed attention. The boy would have to wait.

The men carried gas lanterns, casting amber light in the trees as they walked in a quiet procession up the winding dirt road along the edge of the mountain. Reverend Ezra had forbidden flashlights with their ugly yellow beams. They walked through an open clearing before finally reaching the trees atop Mulwin Rock.

Reverend Ezra led the way, the flame of his lantern behind a pane of red glass, casting the trees ahead in deep shadow. He wore his long red robe, rather than his normal uniform of black or gray pinstriped suits. Some of the men had raised their eyebrows when they saw his robes, but no matter. The time for façade had passed. Let them see the real Ezra. Let them behold his glory.

When he saw the patch of trees at the peak, he held his lantern high.

"It won't be long now, brothers."

Some of the men were out of breath, perhaps feeling the effects of the elevation. He heard them panting, the blood rushing through their veins. These were the most loyal men, elders of the church—the ones he could trust, or those about whom he had some intimate knowledge, something to hold over their heads. These men were eager to please him; there was power in that. Years of being their pastor had brought him knowledge. Sins confessed in late-night meetings or those made with shaky voices in his office at the church. Some struggled with alcohol or pills, some with affairs they'd conducted with other women of the community or of the congregation itself. A few had, in fits of frustration, struck their wives, and had come to the Reverend for absolution or so that he might testify to the law on their behalf. Those were the most easily manipulated.

He led them through the patch of woods at the peak. The outer rim of trees was mostly bare of bark; deep grooves ran across their trunks like wayward river veins, as if a sleuth of bears had ground their claws on them. Some of the men gasped when they saw it. He smelled their fear, palpable and throbbing. *Good*, he thought, *good*.

When they reached the edge, above the rock face of the peak, the outline of the Temple came into view. The earth smelled musky, as if it were freshly turned. Blocks marked the old footing of the former structure, jagged and gnarled.

"Come, brothers," he said. "Gather together in a circle."

The men did as they were told, standing shoulder to shoulder.

"Good," he said. "Look around you, brothers. This is what I have foretold."

The men looked at the foundation of the ancient structure, at the enormous trees, and the cliff face beyond.

"Here," he said. "You see the glory of what once was. Of what shall be again."

The man nearest him breathed hard, his mouth agape. His bald head caught the red light. It was Brother Charles, one of his most faithful and trusted. The only problem with Charles was his wife, Sister Gail—the kind of woman who was always asking questions. She'd stopped Reverend Ezra after service recently. Questioned him about the rebuilding of the Temple, where it should be located. As if that were her concern, as if she were entitled. She was a woman who didn't know her place, her face always puckered and dull. Reverend Ezra put his hand on Brother Charles's shoulder. The man's breathing slowed.

"Here. Here we will rebuild the Temple. Our new Jerusalem. Right here, right in our time."

The men nodded their heads. There were a few muffled *amens*.

"Now, brothers, as the Apostle Paul, I am called to a higher power. I am not a man who has taken a wife, who feels the burn of desire which I cannot control, as so many of you do."

Some of the men looked at each other.

"For my bride is my faith, the ministry. My bride is the very church itself. But I know that you are weak, that you do not have the power to withstand the temptations of this world, and so most of you have or will take wives, and this is not evil. This is of God.

"But remember, brothers, this is what God *allowed*, not what he thought best. No, in 1st Corinthians he tells us that it is good for a man *not* to marry. But he understood that many of you would have to marry, to take a woman, to satisfy your wicked, filthy needs. God gave you wives because of your weakness, but your wives grow worldly and defiant, my brothers, amen?"

Amen said a man in the back, leaning in closer.

"The women want to bring you away from God, away from the church, away from my teachings, for this is the way of the world and this is the way of women. Remember Eve defiled Adam in the Garden. She was full of wickedness; she bore no self-control. No woman has self-control."

Several of the men nodded their heads now, with more conviction.

"So, God gave you women to help you because of your weakness, and in return, the women exploit your weakness and seek to drive a wedge between you and your faith, between you and your very God! Amen?"

Amen.

Reverend Ezra crossed his long fingers in front of him.

"And so, this Temple. It shall be only for the sacred few."

Amen.

"It shall be only for the chosen."

Yes, amen.

"You shall never bring any man here who has not been chosen."

Amen.

"You shall never bring a woman here—ever, under any circumstance."

The men fell silent. They looked at one another. Brother Charles broke the silence with a firm *Amen, Reverend Ezra*. Brother Charles knew, more than most, the trouble of a busybody woman.

"You will guard this temple as the sacred place it is, and you will give your very lives to protect it."

Yes, Amen.

"My brothers, follow me."

Ezra walked past the foundation of the Temple toward the tall black trees that stood beyond. The men followed. This group of trees was older and larger, more majestic, than those of the greater forest. The ground around them was different, the soil darker and richer, as if enchanted.

Ezra lifted his arms, his back to the men.

"For I have laid before you treasures, heretofore unseen."

Ezra's hands began to throb red in the low light of the woods. The light pulsed from his fingers as if to the beat of some unseen drum, casting his face in grim shadow. Some men grew visibly frightened, glancing from one to the other. The trees around them glowed with amber light, and the men could see. Finally, their eyes were open.

There, suspended in the trees, were women and girls. Their eyes were open, but they did not seem to breathe. Their bodies were perfectly still. There were women with brown faces, girls with fair skin and freckles, ones with blonde hair, some with red and brown and pitch-black hair. Some had short hair, some long hair that swept over their shoulders. Some wore dresses, some pants, some were in their underwear. The men gasped; several stood with their mouths open.

Only Brother Lemuel was unsurprised, having seen these treasures before. *He is my right hand*, Ezra thought. He gave Brother Lemuel a knowing smile, and Lemuel dipped his head in acknowledgement of the power of the moment.

"For I have given to you treasures immeasurable," Reverend Ezra said, turning toward the men, his arms still outstretched, his fingertips extended, illuminated.

Some of the men walked toward the trees and put their hands on them to find them cold to the touch, as if the trees ensconced the girls in frozen glass. As they drew closer, the men saw the wonderful shapes of the women's bodies, the long limbs of the girls. Some men began to smile while others' eyes began to well with tears.

"Can we," one man asked, "touch them?"

"When the Lord's work is done here, there will not be two dozen trees holding such marvelous fruit. No, my brother," said Ezra. He put his hand on the man's shoulder. "No indeed; there shall be hundreds if not thousands of trees that bear such fruit, but only for the faithful, those faithful to me, who submit to me, to the power of the one true Temple."

The man nodded.

Reverend Ezra considered the girls in the trees. In one wide oak, he saw Heidi, the young girl from last year's Sojourn. The one Sheriff Barnaby kept asking about. He'd saved her from a life of sin by putting her here in the trees. He considered her filthy mouth, her shapely body, and his face twisted with disdain.

"And I assure you, only here, in the majesty of this place, are these wretched creatures free."

Ezra's arms dropped slowly to his sides, and the red glow of his fingertips began to fade. So too did the lights in the trees, the girls disappearing into darkness.

A man standing near one tree rubbed his hand over where a woman's body had been. Now the surface was rough bark, the smooth, glassy surface having receded.

Ezra smiled at the man. "Fret not, my brother, for I go to prepare a table for you that is beyond any of this world. You shall feast in this temple before the second frost moon, and these trees shall bear you fruit."

The man looked into Ezra's eyes. He nodded. He was a believer.

"And you shall know a peace you have never known."

Amen.

"And you shall be full for the first time in your life."

He turned to the other men. "And so now, my disciples, you understand. You know your just rewards." His voice rose, echoing in the mountains around them, his voice becoming something else entirely. It was unnaturally deep, grinding like the gears of some terrible machine. That of the Red Wolf. *Build my Temple. Be about my work.*

When the men looked upon him, they were astonished to see his face warped and changing. The shadow of the Red Wolf fell over his countenance. The men were afraid. And it was good.

8 / MINA & THE PDA POLICE

The bus lot was the only place at G.W. Clayton High where public displays of affection were allowed. If kids held hands in the hall or attempted to steal a kiss at their lockers, a previously unseen teacher or administrator would materialize out of thin air to block the action and enforce feigned chastity. The kids called them the PDA Police. But at the buses, kids stood face to face, French kissing or necking in full embrace, their hands roving over each other's bodies, hedonistic and unfettered. Beyond the lack of adult interference, there was something about the lot that made the teenagers lose their inhibitions. At the bus stop, they seemed hellbent on providing lusty displays of their passion despite the chorus of sniggers from younger kids, the mocking sounds of smooching, and jeers of disgust. Here, they *wanted* to be seen, to put on a show. Even nerdy boys found girls to kiss at the buses, coming to homeroom with lip gloss smeared faces.

Clayton's bus lot even boasted a pair of kissing girls from time to time, which drew quite the crowd. The pair of girls changed every few months, by half. The constant half was Bev, a stocky girl with a short boy's haircut. She wore a chain wallet, like the redneck boys, and put on enthusiastic displays with a new girl every few months. *There's somebody for everybody*, Mina thought. Only for Bev, there were a lot of somebodies. To Mina, Bev was one of the coolest girls at Clayton. Except for all her makeout sessions on the buses.

Disgusted, Mina weaved in and out of the lusty lovers and delighted voyeurs on her way to the main building. It was almost Halloween, and the sky was palpably gray, fitting her mood. Riding the bus again after her daily rides in the slick IROC was a bit of a fall from grace, but she was happy to be shed of Emerson's ham-handed groping, his dumb matching shirts, and stupid music. In her headphones, *the Rocky Horror Picture Show* soundtrack blared "Let's do the Time Warp Again!" After all, 'twas the season. Erin had mocked her for playing it the last time they hung out at her house.

"Keep Halloween in your way," Mina had said. "And let me keep it in mine."

Clayton High spread out over the hills in a series of four flat-roofed buildings, dull and gray. In the early 1970s, maybe around the time *Rocky Horror* had been in theaters (Mina had never actually seen the movie), the buildings must have looked sleek and modern. Nearly twenty years later, everything about the campus felt stale and boring.

Mina had been aware of Gabe's gaze when he'd walked down the center aisle of the bus. He'd looked for a seat nearby, but they were occupied, and she'd sat near the center so no one could sit beside her. He'd still smiled at her, passing to the back of the bus. Mina hadn't returned the smile. She'd had enough of dudes. Enough of their dumb donkey grins, games, and expectations. She wasn't in the mood to talk to him or anyone else. She wasn't going to date anyone until she got far from Clayton High, far from Asheville, from these stupid backwood mountains. Of course, college guys would probably be the same or worse. She might just stay celibate; nothing wrong with that. If a boy like Emerson tried to fuck with her again, she'd make him ugly cry like the big wrestler had done in the woods.

Near the doorway to the main building, she saw Erin sucking face with Lucas. Of course, she was. Lucas was tall, with straight brown hair, always parted to the side, wayward strands threatening to fall in his eyes. Now his hair fell over Erin's pixie face, which he seemed to be trying to eat whole. They hadn't ridden the buses to school, but they knew the unwritten code. So they took a detour from the student lot through the football field to walk in by the buses, where they were free to hold hands and make out.

When she saw Mina, Erin pecked Lucas's cheek and skipped over.

Mina clicked stop on her tape player. "I love the smell of hormones in the morning." She smirked.

Erin beamed, bumping her shoulder. "Good morning to you, too." Behind them, Gabe and Lucas punched each other's arms.

"Hope you ladies have a nice day," Lucas said.

"Yeah," Gabe said, pausing.

Mina looked over her shoulder at him and tried not to smile. Turning to Erin, she said, "You get your sister's clothes, those blue jeans?"

"I got them. Why don't you come get them tonight?" Erin said.

"Your place?"

"At his," Erin said, tilting her head toward the boys behind them.

"Lucas's? Where does he live?"

"No," Erin smiled. "At *his*." She gestured toward Gabe.

Mina shook her head slowly.

Erin leaned in and whispered in Mina's ear. "Lucas says he's got it *bad*."

"Got what bad?" Mina asked, feigning ignorance.

"Got it bad for you, girl, that's what," Erin said. "Say seven? Me and Lucas will be over there. I'll bring the clothes."

Mina bit her lip. *Goddamnit*.

Inside, they parted. Erin and Mina headed toward their lockers near the Senior Bench, Gabe and Lucas down the opposite hall. The Senior Bench ran along a huge window overlooking the rest of the campus. It was a row of wooden benches painted in purple and gold, Clayton's school colors. Another unwritten rule at Clayton High was that underclassmen weren't allowed on the bench. The only exception was underclass girls who were dating senior boys. But only girls who dated seniors. One delusional sophomore boy dating a senior girl tried to break the rule once. Some of the jocks had dunked his head in a toilet for the offense. *Know your place*. One of the most important rules at G.W. Clayton.

Mina was closing her locker when she felt something hit her back. Change clanged against the metal locker and onto the floor around her. She looked down to see a handful of nickels and dimes at her feet, then turned to the bench. In the center, with his perpetual flock of preppy jocks, sat Emerson Shit. He offered her a wide grin. Some of the guys were pointing at her, laughing. She shot Emerson the bird and turned back to her locker. More coins. This time, they met their mark, stinging the back of her bare legs under her summer dress, a few coins pelting her back.

"I hope that's enough," he yelled. "You've done it for less."

Before she could think it through, Mina marched across the white tile floor toward him. Some seniors on the bench *oohhed* and *ahhhed* as she came on. A boy said, "You're gonna get it now, Emerson."

"I already had it," Emerson said.

Krissy Lang stepped in front of Mina before she could get to him. Several of Krissy's girlfriends flanked her, blocking her path.

"Move," Mina said. The back of her legs stung but she tried not to let it show on her face.

"Move where?" Krissy said. Her blonde hair was up in a ponytail, the front teased up into a hairsprayed claw. It tilted toward Mina like a weapon. She was chewing bubble gum, the pink wad bulging her jaw.

Mina looked past Krissy to Emerson Shit. The girls around Krissy circled tighter, blocking her view.

"Why are you protecting that idiot?" Mina said.

"It's a free country," Krissy said. She popped a bubble with her front teeth. "And I ain't protecting nobody. I just don't like you. Where did you get that dress? The Salvation Army?" She turned to the girls, giggling. "Your granny called, she wants her dress back."

Mina looked down at her dress.

"You look like trailer trash, but I mean, you are," Krissy said. "So..."

"You got a lot of room to talk." Mina gestured with her eyes at Krissy's tight shirt, unbuttoned to flaunt her generous cleavage.

Krissy stuck out her chest even further. "Why don't you run along, little girl, before you get your ass beat."

Mina took a step toward Krissy with balled fists, her neck hot. "And just who is gonna do that?"

Krissy's high-heeled boots enabled her to almost look Mina in the eye. "Just because he fucked you don't mean he likes you." Mina took another step forward. "Now you're just projecting."

She felt the shadows growing at the edges of the high ceiling above the Senior Bench. They called to her with whispered voices. Gargoyle faces formed in the corners, thirty feet above them. Mina could pull them down in a frenzy—she could picture it. Lifting Krissy up and throwing her through the window to the smoking area below.

She imagined the spaces that would open in Krissy's skull when she struck the concrete, pink like her bubblegum.

Someone pushed in beside her. It was Erin.

"Krissy," Erin said, drawing out the word with dripping sweetness. "It's so good to see you!"

Krissy wrinkled her nose.

Erin put a hand on Krissy's shoulder. "We're always surprised when someone lets you off your leash. Good for you!"

Krissy slapped her hand away just as an alarm went off, a shrill echo through the halls. Krissy and the other girls turned toward the exit through the math hall. The kids on the bench began to file out onto the quad. This was maybe the fifth time someone had set off the school fire alarm in the past two months. It had to be those redneck idiots again.

"At least it called the dogs off," Erin said, smiling.

"And so it goes," Mina said. "For a day or two, maybe."

As they filed out behind the other students, Mina saw Mr. Bachman standing with Danni, a freshman girl she knew from Spanish Club. While all the other teachers tried to keep students calm and orderly as they exited the building, creepy Mr. Bachman leaned in toward Danni. As they passed him, Mr. Bachman traced a finger along the pattern of Danni's letter jacket, along the G in G.W. Clayton, positioned at the girl's breast.

"What the fuck is wrong with this place?" Mina shook her head.

"They've been dating a while," Erin said. "She keeps walking around wearing his blue blazer, follows him like a puppy."

"Dating?" Mina said. "He's old. Like old enough to be her father old."

"Yeah," Erin said. "The girls think he's cute, though. Even with a broken arm."

Bachman was the wrestling coach. Supposedly, he'd broken his arm mountain climbing, something he bragged about when he wasn't yelling at the guys on the wrestling team. Guys like Emerson Shit, who learned a lot from Mr. Bachman. About wrestling and how to grope little girls like Danni, whose black hair curled at the tips where it met her purple letter jacket.

"I can't wait to get out of here," Mina said.

"It ain't that bad," Erin said. "There are worse places. My aunt lives in Tallahassee. You think *we* got rednecks?"

In the math hall, a crowd of kids broke off from the stream to circle one of the pillars near the far wall.

"What's all that?" Erin asked.

"God knows," Mina said.

They followed the students peeling off toward the column, then Mina saw it. A picture was on the column. It was a poster-sized caricature drawing of a black man with exaggerated minstrel lips. Beside them, a black boy named Kevin saw the poster at the same time. He grimaced and turned away.

"Shit," Mina said.

"I know," Erin said, watching Kevin's face.

Kevin was one of the best writers in Miss Varny's class, reading his poems to the class with a deep baritone voice Mina loved. He was maybe the only kid in class who got as much joy from a poem as she did.

At the far wall, Randy Todd and a bunch of his redneck cronies smirked. Those boys wore jeans so tight you could see the rings of the dip cans in their back pockets. Randy was always stirring up shit. At least once a month, he and his boys put up something racist in the math hall near the exit and pulled the fire alarm so most of the student body had to see it on their way out. People said Randy's daddy was in the KKK; he was always going on about how race wars were coming, how they would cleanse America for the white people. He had a gun rack in the back of his jacked-up Toyota pickup and a rebel battle flag plate on the front. In the school parking lot, he was known to blare heavy metal and, of all things, rap music.

Miss Varny cut briskly through the sea of students and tore down the poster. She ripped it to shreds and threw it in a waste basket.

Mina stared at Randy. He held his head high, his chin jutting out. Anger pulsed through her. "What the fuck is wrong with this place?" she repeated.

Erin shrugged.

"Come on, girls, outside," yelled Miss Varny.

Mina marked it all down. Every bit of it. She thought of the shadow faces, of the way they came out in their anger that day with Emerson, even in broad daylight. The way she'd made the whole world black on Elk Mountain. She thought of all the people who needed to see what she could do, who needed to be put in *their* place for once. She thought of Emerson's smug face on the bench, throwing coins at her, telling everyone at school she'd gone all the way with him every day in his car. She thought of Mr. Bachman's stubby finger on Danni's chest, the way he strutted around like a peacock, Danni by his side, in front of other teachers, students, the principal, everybody. She thought of Twist's leering eyes in the trailer park, of Randy's smug hatred, the way he constantly tried to keep the black kids at Clayton on edge. People that didn't deserve his bullshit. What if a shadow crept along outside his window, reached in one night, and threw him off the mountain where his people lived and slept in little houses around him? What if the shadows took up a big stick—no, a club—and used it to break both of Emerson's legs? What kind of wrestler would he be then? Pivoting around with crutches and a double leg cast. He wouldn't even be able to sit on the Senior Bench, much less put freshman girls on his lap the way he liked to do. And Mr. Bachman. What if he had a couple of broken legs to go along with that broken arm? How many high school girls could he seduce in a full body cast?

No more, Mina thought. *No more Ms. Nice Girl.*

9 / THE CATS & THE BIRDS
GABE

That afternoon, Gabe sat on the front porch, watching the sun streak orange behind the trees. This time of year, it got dark early, something Gabe loved, though Papa Leo and LilyMa went on and on about how Daylight Savings Time was damned foolishness. Papa Leo stepped out on the porch, Samson at his feet. A red-throated hummingbird buzzed around one of the small nectar feeders outside the house, hanging from the eaves. Samson hiked his leg and peed on one of LilyMa's clay planters.

"Hellfire, Samson," Papa Leo said. "Do you have to piss on ever damn thing you see?"

The dog walked calmly to another planter and lifted the opposite leg, christening the red pot.

Papa Leo packed his pipe and struck a wood match. The tip clacked in his teeth; it was shiny and black, ringed with dark brown wood accents. The smell of burnt apples filled the air. Papa Leo's blue flannel shirt was untucked.

He said, "Our people have been in these mountains since before the Revolutionary War." He lifted his chin. "Did you know that?"

"I didn't know that, exactly," Gabe said.

"We were here before Washington crossed the Delaware, before Grant marched through and burnt Atlanta to the ground."

"Umm hmm," Gabe said.

"Say," Papa Leo said, "have you seen my shotgun?"

"No?"

"The over under, my big one."
"No, sir, I ain't."
"I think Lilyfax has took to hiding my guns."
"Why would she do that?"
"Hell if I know."

But Gabe knew all about it. She'd asked for his help hiding the guns, mostly in the attic. Papa Leo had been getting worse in the days after Gabe had seen him with the Red Wolf. One day, he'd driven into town looking for a policeman buddy of his who'd been dead for about five years. He'd gotten lost downtown, asking folks how to get back to Patton Avenue, even though he knew Asheville like the back of his hand. Another time, he called Gabe by his father's name and seemed confused when Gabe corrected him. It was coming on quicker now.

Samson came running from around the side of the house, a blue bird in his teeth.

"What in *the* hell?" Papa Leo said.
"I've never known him to kill a bird," Gabe said.
"He didn't kill it. It's them damned cats."

Papa Leo loved animals, big and small. He put up feeders and baths all around the yard, drawing in the birds. Then when he saw some scrawny feral cats on the mountain, he started putting out bowls of dry food for them. He couldn't stand to see anything hungry, but he jumped on the cats when they hunted the birds he'd attracted. He didn't seem to see the contradiction of drawing in birds and cats to the same space. What would happen when the cats did what nature called them to do.

"You still practicing your piano?" Papa Leo asked.
"Yes, sir," Gabe said. "Thank you for setting it up in the basement for me." The piano had been Gabe's father's and had been in storage after the wreck. One day, Gabe came home to find the upright piano in his basement bedroom, across from his bed.

"If I knew how to read music," Papa Leo said, "I'd be the damnedest songwriter that ever lived."

"I can teach you how to read, it ain't hard," Gabe said.

"You can't teach an old dog new tricks." Papa Leo smiled. "I'll just listen to you play."

A car came down the driveway. It already had on its headlights, though it wasn't yet dark. It was Lucas's 24oz, the gold paint shimmering in the remaining sunlight like the surface of a lake through the trees.

"Y'all kids gonna play games in the basement?" Papa Leo asked.

"I think so," Gabe said.

"Don't let your grandmother wait on you hand and foot. She'll worry herself to death with people in the house."

"No, sir, I won't."

Papa Leo stepped off the porch toward the side of the house. He turned back.

"Ain't it your birthday soon, boy?"

"Next week, the 27th," Gabe said.

"That's right," Papa Leo said, "November 27th. That's your birthday."

"No," Gabe said. "It's October. October 27th. Next week."

Papa Leo squinted, then nodded before disappearing around the house. November 27th had been Gabe's father's—Papa Leo's son's—birthday.

When Lucas pulled up, he was laughing at something. Then Gabe saw the back of Erin's head in the shadows of the car, her face in at his neck. He squirmed like it tickled.

When they got out, Gabe said, "Pretty sure that sort of thing is frowned upon while driving."

Erin laughed. Her brown hair was short, the edges feathered slightly in the front. Her face was red like she'd just come in from the cold. She reached behind the front seat and pulled out a big black trash bag. She heaved it up on her shoulder, carrying it like Santa's sack.

"What's all that?" Gabe asked.

"Girls' clothes. You want some?" Erin said.

"Girls' clothes? What for?"

"They ain't for you, silly boy. They're for her." Erin lifted her head, pointing with her chin.

At the tree line, Mina appeared. Her long red hair was up in a ponytail, and she was walking so fast it danced. Holy shit! Mina was *here*? Gabe smoothed his hair and looked at the old N.C. State t-shirt he was wearing. Why was he wearing this ugly shirt? Why hadn't Lucas and Erin warned him she was coming? Was his room clean?

His face warmed, and he shot Lucas a look. His friend arched an eyebrow, grinned. *That bastard.*

"Figured you wouldn't mind," Erin said, jabbing Gabe in the ribs. She put her hand over her eyes. "Everybody knows you got it bad. She's a cool glass of water, ain't she?"

"Shhhh," Gabe begged.

"You brought them!" Mina said.

The girls met in the center of the yard, and Erin dropped the heavy bag.

Mina looked past Erin to Lucas. "Couldn't your boyfriend carry it? He's always flexing his muscles in gym class."

Lucas shrugged and punched Gabe in the arm. Gabe twisted. He raised his hand toward Mina. "Hey," he said.

Mina smiled and dropped to her knees to dig through the clothes. "Oh my God," she said. "There's so much!"

"Got some Jordache in there. Vanderbilt jeans, too. My sister's a bitch, but she's got style."

Mina pulled out a pair of jeans and a tie-dyed t-shirt. It was blue with orange and red mixed in. She ran to a cluster of trees and shed her jacket. She fussed with the buttons of her dress.

"You boys better turn around," Erin said.

Mina kicked off her shoes and tiptoed behind a big oak. Gabe felt his cheeks warm. She was changing in the front yard. In *his* front yard. Mina with no clothes on. Outside. Here. Right now. It was all too much.

"Oh my God, Gabe, don't peek," Erin teased.

"I wasn't peeking!" Gabe said, a little too loud.

"I'll kick your ass," Mina said.

She was smiling when she reappeared. She held her jacket and dress out in front of her before depositing them in the black bag.

"There's shoes at the bottom too," Erin said. "My sister's got big feet like you."

Mina skipped over to hug Erin hard.

"Thank you," she said.

"It's no problem," Erin said. "They look way better on you anyway."

When Mina pulled away from Erin, the t-shirt slipped off her right shoulder. It was a little too big for her. Gabe saw a cluster of freckles at her collarbone. They shone like stars in the low light, and for a moment, something inside him hurt. Physically hurt. He stared at the constellation of freckles, thought of the galaxy of freckles, the universe that must spread down her back and over her body. Beautiful freckle stars made to brighten the world. He thought of touching them, of tracing the freckles down her back, the most interesting paint-by-numbers sketch of all time, in all the world. When she pulled the shirt back in place, his legs almost folded. He stumbled, though he'd been standing still.

Lucas grabbed his shoulder. "You okay there, big guy?"

"What? Yes," Gabe said.

In the basement, the kids sat around a wooden coffee table and played Scrabble. Gabe tried to focus on the game, but Mina was like a new person, a new girl entirely with those blue jeans and the tie-dyed t-shirt. He was losing badly, placing three-letter words like "C-A-T" and "B-O-G" while Mina crushed everyone, dropping first a Q on a triple-word tile, then a Z.

LilyMa fussed over them, just as Papa Leo predicted, bringing them soda and freshly baked cookies. The smell of them filled the house for several agonizing minutes before they were ready. As soon as she brought them down, the teenagers scarfed them down, one after another, as if they'd never eaten cookies before.

LilyMa had her hair up in a tight white bun. She wore a flowing white shirt with colored blocks of fabric along the sleeves. It was one of her "damned hippy shirts" per Papa Leo. He often teased her about how the '60s had changed her, turned her into one of those white women who discovered yoga and Buddhism. On her section of the bookshelf in the living room, there were a lot of books on meditation with titles like *Zen-Dawn in the West* and the *Science of Being and Art of Living*, their authors sporting long beards and brown skin. LilyMa never let on that Papa Leo's taunts bothered her one bit, and one early morning when Gabe couldn't sleep, he'd found her outside on the back deck, legs crossed tightly, humming quietly, hands at her side.

She couldn't have been more different than Gabe's mama. Sure, Mama had worn her hair up in a tight bun sometimes, but it always looked angry on her, harsh. Back in eighth grade, he'd brought home pictures of classmates. It was customary to exchange them when the packets came in after picture day. His favorite, even back then, was one of Mina. He'd kept it in his Bible like a bookmark, so he could look at it when Mama did her nightly devotionals—a time when she read three or four chapters from the Bible and everyone talked about who they wanted to pray for before they each prayed aloud in turn. One night, the picture of Mina had fallen out of Gabe's Bible to the floor where Mama sat on her knees across from him and the twins. She'd snatched up the picture before he could retrieve it. She'd studied it, eyes squinting, lips descending into a frown. In the picture, Mina had worn a blue button-up shirt, kind of like a man's Oxford. The top button was unbuttoned, but the shirt was very modest, barely betraying the fact that she was a girl, unlike her fitted summer dresses.

"Kind of girl you bring home pictures of," Mama had said, "says something about the kind of man you are becoming, the kind of Christian. This little one will regret it one day. That she didn't learn to keep her *buttons buttoned*. Instead of showing the world everything she's got, her sinful body, throwing meat before the wolves."

Gabe had snatched the picture back and found a better hiding place for it. Mama would have hated the tight blue jeans Mina had on now, the slipping t-shirt. Was it sinful to think of her this way? Is that why it hurt so much to look at her? Gabe pushed it all away and tried to get back in the game.

LilyMa brought more cookies and a bag of chips under her arm, when Lucas said, "Did you hear Erin's been called up?"

"Called up?" Mina said. "Are you serious?"

"My parents are making me do it," Erin said, picking some Scrabble tiles out of the box lid.

Being "called up" was a Church of Hosanna thing. Part of what they called Purity Sojourns. A group of teenagers would be dropped deep in the woods, someplace where they would camp, fish, and cook their own food with some youth ministers to make sure they stayed in line. It was all about getting close to God. Gabe had never been on one, but this would have been his year, the year his mama would have made him go. On these excursions, teenagers were taught about their horny sinful natures, the perils of drugs and homosexuality, and how remaining sober and celibate was the only way to salvation. Problem kids—those who had been caught partying or having sex or seemed like they might be gay were at the top of the selection list.

LilyMa set the potato chips and dip on the table.

Mina frowned. "Tell them you won't go."

"They won't listen," Erin said. "My big sister went a few years ago, and my dad is big in the church. Deacon or something?"

"A girl went missing last year on one of those so-called *sojourns*," LilyMa said.

Erin said, "I know. They say they're adding some more youth leaders this year. For safety's sake."

"You don't have to go up on no mountain to get close to God," LilyMa said. "God is everywhere all around us. She's in everything."

"She?" Lucas laughed.

"Might be," LilyMa said. "You don't know. And neither does Reverend Ezra or any of those holy rollers at Hosanna." She looked at Erin. "Tell your folks you won't go. Tell them you're scared, if you have to."

"Her parents know she ain't scared of nothing, that's the problem," Lucas said. He smiled. "They know better."

"I know the woods better than most of the other kids out there. Probably the youth ministers, too. We might live in the country club, but my dad made us camp like settlers when we were kids. Called it survival training. I'll pack some hunting knives, my compass. I'll be fine." She put her hand on LilyMa's. "Don't worry," Erin said. "I can take care of myself. And thank you for the cookies."

Lucas opened the chips, and the kids dug in. LilyMa shook her head and slipped up the stairs.

"Why are your parents making you go?" Mina said.

Erin and Lucas looked at each other.

"I'm on my mom's shitlist," Erin said.

"Why's that?" Gabe asked.

"Well," Erin said, dunking a chip into some French onion dip. "They think I'm sexually active."

"I'm shocked," Mina said. "But why do they think that?"

Erin wiped her mouth with the back of her hand. "Well," she said as she tilted her head toward Lucas. "Genius here left a condom in my nightstand. That's why."

Lucas shook his head. "You can't blame this one on me. You told me to put it in there."

"Yeah," Erin said. "*Under* all my shit. You put it right on top, like an idiot."

"You never said to put it under everything."

"Shouldn't have to," Erin said.

"So they're trying to cure you from it?" Gabe said. "That it?"

"Something like that," Erin said. "Only I'm trying to figure out how to get the location so lover boy here can sneak up the mountain." She traced a finger along Lucas's bicep. "Maybe this little *sojourn* won't be so *pure* after all." She smiled, her teeth white.

Lucas seemed embarrassed. "That'll make it all worse, I get caught corrupting you while they're trying to save your soul from eternal damnation."

"Just so many things to do in the woods, we'll sneak off, just the two of us," Erin said. She seemed to delight in Lucas's discomfort. "Find a new way to pray."

"Ewww," Mina said. "You two are gross." She looked at Gabe, then reached for a cookie.

"Stop," Lucas said. "I don't want you to go. Seems dangerous after Heidi went missing."

"Tell them you won't go," Gabe said. "Just tell them, straight up."

"I might as well tell them I don't want to be baptized or that I don't want to be a Christian anymore. That I'm converting to Buddhism or lesbianism. That's about how well it would go over."

Lucas was about to say something when a loud boom rang outside. It was close, echoing like a cannon through the open basement door. The four of them ran around to the front of the house to find Papa Leo, pointing his shotgun up into the trees. Smoke circled the tip of the barrel.

"Papa Leo," Gabe said.

"Shhhh," he said. "Listen. Do you hear it?"

Gabe and the others stood still. He heard nothing. He looked back at the other three. Mina shrugged her shoulders.

Papa Leo cracked open the over under and fed it two more shells. "That son of a bitch hunting again. That was a warning shot. Next one's liable to scatter in his ass."

Gabe looked up at the night sky. There was only a shard of silver moon nestled in the stars.

"People don't hunt at night, Papaw. You sure you heard something?"

Papa Leo seemed to consider this. He tilted his head, listening. "He's out there. I know he's out there."

Goosebumps prickled over Gabe's skin. He thought of the Red Wolf. "Did—" he started. "Did you see something?"

Mina stepped beside him. She looked up into the trees, her green eyes catching the moonlight.

"Leo," LilyMa said from the porch. "Did you get up in the attic?"

"Why would I get in the attic?" Papa Leo asked. His face was serious, as if he really didn't catch her meaning.

"Come on inside," LilyMa said. "We can worry about those hunters tomorrow."

"Goddamn it, woman." Papa Leo scowled. "This is between me and him. This is for the men to sort out."

"Oh, I know that," LilyMa said, winking at the kids. "You menfolk can sort it out in the morning."

Papa Leo laid the barrel against his shoulder and turned sharply toward the house as if marching in formation. "You kids," he said as he passed, "don't stay up too late, and for God's sake, keep it down."

"Yes, sir," Gabe said.

"We should be getting home anyway," Lucas said.

"Mina," Erin said. "Ride with us. It's dark through the woods."

"I'm fine," Mina said.

"I'll walk her," Gabe said. There was a curling eagerness to his tone; he regretted it as soon as the words passed his lips. "I mean," he stumbled. "I'll walk you home. If you want. I mean, I don't mind."

Mina smiled. She looked him up and down. "Okay, whatever."

Erin and Lucas looked at each other, then back at Mina and Gabe. Lucas gave Gabe a thumbs up, but he pretended not to see it.

"I need to get those clothes," Mina said.

"I'll get them," Gabe said, sprinting toward the basement without waiting for a reply.

"Don't be strangers," LilyMa said to Erin and Lucas. "We like having y'all over. And you too Mina, it's good to finally meet you."

When Gabe returned, he saw Lucas's tail lights disappearing through the trees. He threw the black bag over his shoulder and they headed through the woods.

Mina stared ahead. "I don't need you to carry my bag or to walk me home just because it's dark."

"Oh, I know that," Gabe said.

Though it was a cool night, he was sweating. He wiped his forehead with his free hand.

"The two of them are something," he said.

"Stuck together like glue," she said.

"Like a pair of lovebugs."
"It's kinda sickening," she said.
"Yeah, really gross," he said.

Gabe could hear Mina's breathing. He thought again of her freckles, of her bare shoulder when the shirt slipped.

"You know," he said. "I'll be driving soon."

"Yeah?"

"It's my birthday next week. I'll get my license."

"Cool," she said.

"If you get tired of riding the bus," he said, "you could catch a ride with me. I mean, if you want to."

"Is that right?" she said. He couldn't see her face in the shadows but could hear the smile.

"Keep you off the bus anyway."

"Yeah, maybe," she said. "But I don't much like getting rides with boys."

"I ain't like those other guys you hang around."

"Sounds like something Emerson said when he first came around offering me rides."

"Well, it ain't a Camaro, exactly—"

"Erin said you got a big blue boat car?"

"It's enormous," he said. "But Papa Leo says it rides like you're floating on air."

"Oh, that does sound promising."

"Yup," he said.

They walked in silence for a few minutes, leaves crunching under their feet. Then Mina's toe caught a root, and she slipped, their shoulders bumping. Gabe reached out to steady her and caught her hand in his. Without thinking, he held onto her hand and interlaced his fingers with hers. She gripped his hand back, not pulling away like he expected. Did she know how he felt about her?

When they reached the road, the streetlights at the entrance to Whispering Pines lit up the trees around them.

"Okay," she said. "I've got it from here."

"I don't mind walking you to your door," he said.

"You don't know my old man," she said. "That won't fly."

"Okay," Gabe said. He set the bag on the ground between them. A breeze lifted the ponytail from her back.

He leaned toward her. Would she let him kiss her?

Mina stepped back.

"Look, Gabe," she said. "You seem like a nice guy, but—"

"The infamous *but*," he said. "There always seems to be a *but*."

"It's not like that," she said. "I'm just not wanting to be like Erin and Lucas. I'm not looking for something serious."

"Me neither," he lied.

"Really?"

"Yeah, they're sickening. We've already established that."

She smiled. "See, I'm not staying here," she said.

"You're moving?"

"Yes. No, I mean...not till I graduate. I mean, I'm not staying in Asheville. I'm going as far away as I can, soon as we graduate. You understand?"

"Where will you go?"

"Whatever college is furthest from this place that gives me scholarship money."

"So," he said, "New Zealand? Somewhere like that?"

"Exactly, New Zealand. I've always wanted to go to school in New Zealand."

They both laughed.

"It's probably already tomorrow in New Zealand," she said. "It's already the future there."

He took her hand again. "I understand. I don't want to stay here either. But you've got two more years of high school. We can hang out till then, right? Then you can run off to New Zealand in search of your future. I'll just be sitting back here on Elk Mountain, bored to death."

"Maybe. I mean, sure," she said. "But I don't want anything serious. I'm not getting stuck here."

"I'd never be dumb enough to try to pin you down," he said.

She smiled again. Her freckles sparkled like diamonds in the streetlight.

"Okay, well I gotta go, my dad is going to be pissed enough as it is."

"Okay, so I'll see you on the bus?"

"Sure."

She picked up the bag and took a step toward the street.

"And after I get my license, you'll want to ride to school sometimes?"

"In the big hig blue boat car?"
"Like floating on air," he said. "A real magic carpet ride."
"Well," she said. "That does sound delightful."
"Okay," he said.
And she was gone.

10 / MINA FINDS HER PLACE

Mina followed the path through the trees to the center of the trailer park. She wove in and out of them, a shortcut she could run in her sleep. She dreaded getting home. Daddy was gonna be pissed. Because it was close to ten on a school night, because she'd been at Gabe's house, because she'd been out with a boy. It wouldn't matter that Gabe's grandparents had been home. He wouldn't believe that anyway.

Her 4.0 average wouldn't save her. The college brochures she'd ordered, all the books strewn around her room. None of that mattered in Daddy's mind. It didn't matter that she got that Good Citizenship Award in eighth grade. That she was in the BETA Club. It didn't matter that she steered clear of partying and drugs. Weed, horse, and huffing on back porches in the trailer park; pretty snow-white cocaine spread out on fancy glass tables down the mountain at house parties in the country club. She barely touched any of it, but there was guilt by association. You grew up in the trailer park, that's the kind of girl you were. Who you were expected to be.

For the most part, Mina had steered clear of boys, too, unlike most girls she knew in the park who got reputations for being wild. They acted as if the hot aluminum boxes made them feral beasts somehow, primed to spread their legs for anybody with a car or who bought them beer, any asshole who would take them cruising to the mall or tell them they were pretty. She pictured Karen, the girl who lived in a cute yellow trailer near the entrance. She remembered splashing in a kiddie pool at her house when they were both in kindergarten. Karen had gotten knocked up last year. She'd dropped out of school, gotten a job as a cashier at Ingles, and gone on food stamps. Mina went to see her after she had the baby. The baby had screamed the whole time, its face pinched, filling diaper after diaper. Karen dropped them into a stinky pail by the foot of her bed, still covered in the pink Raggedy Anne sheets it sported in elementary school.

You weren't expected to get out, to rise above it. Mama hadn't. Mina had seen the pictures: the baby bump Mama sported in her fifteenth year. Mina was that bump. Mama talked about it now like it had been God's will all along. Like God couldn't think up anything better for a trailer park girl.

Mama had been forced to drop out of high school, lest the lusty implications of a round belly infect all the kids like a disease in the water. When Mama talked about it, it was never a cautionary tale, something to be avoided. For parents like hers, it was a prophecy. Inevitability. Sure as the sun rises in the east and sets in the west. Get knocked up, drop out. Have babies, stay dumb. Stay down. Know your place. *Fuck that*, Mina thought.

She rounded the corner of one of the trailers and saw a man up on his tiptoes, peering into a window. He was shirtless and shoeless, wearing dirty blue jeans. His skin was gray in the flickering lights of the televisions in the trailers on both sides, his hair standing up like he'd stuck his finger in a light socket. Mina turned to go the other way, but when she did, the trash bag on her shoulder scraped the trailer's siding. For a moment it stuck, the plastic caught on one of the aluminum rivets. It screeched when she pulled free. The man spun to face her—Twist.

Mina ran, weaving between trailers, her heart in her throat. Why was Twist looking into a trailer that wasn't his? She was only a couple of rows from home when she came around a corner to find herself face to face with him.

She moved to go around him, but his long arm shot out and grabbed her wrist.

They were both breathing hard. He was sweaty and greasy, smelling of sardines and saltine crackers, his favorite meal. She looked into his dull eyes, and he grinned. His long salt and pepper gray hair danced as he panted. He looked like the mad scientist from the *Back to the Future* movies, only his face was drawn and wrinkled. He grinned, his mouth full of crooked teeth.

"Mina, merry, quite *contrary*," he said.

"Let go of me, you old bastard."

"Sure," he said. "Soon as you tell me what you're doing out so late, you little scamp."

"None of your goddamned business."

His bony hand clamped around it like a vice. She pulled as hard as she could, but the man's feet were planted like they were buried in concrete.

He said, "You been out with a boy, I'd wager."

"Let go."

"Just tell me what you do with them boys. What they do to you. Then I'll let you go."

Mina gritted her teeth. She longed for a weapon. She wished she had a knife to plunge into his gut. She thought about bringing forth the Shadow Creatures to tear the disgusting man limb from limb.

"That's all you got to do," he said. His lips curled up over his gums. "Just tell me what you let them do to you." He looked at her chest. "What they do to your body? Tell me and I won't tell your daddy you was sneaking around the park all hours of the night."

"You're disgusting," she said. "My daddy will kick your ass."

He leaned in close. "I ain't afraid of your daddy or no one else."

"What were you doing looking in that window?"

His smile disappeared. "Is it that country club boy? The one with the sports car? That the one you been off in the woods with?"

"Let go," she repeated.

He sneered. "Jeans is hard to work with in a car though, ain't they? Always told mine to wear skirts. Easier, much easier."

Mina pictured Dana, Twist's pregnant girlfriend. She was much younger, not pretty exactly, but way more attractive than any woman Twist should have been running with. She was very pregnant and, because the rest of her body was skinny, her belly gave her the appearance of a tick about to pop. She often sat on their front porch, staring at the little gravel road that ran between the trailers. Seemed like at any moment she'd get the nerve to take off running up the hill, away from Twist.

Everybody in the trailer park knew that Twist beat the poor girl.

They didn't have epic fights out on the yard like Mina's parents or some of the other adults in the park, smashing beer bottles on the concrete and cursing at the top of their lungs. No, their fights were one-sided, with Twist yelling at the girl, calling her a dog, and yanking her behind closed doors to give her a whipping. Once Mina had spoken to Dana out near the park mailboxes, and Twist had appeared to drag the girl back to their trailer by her hair. Dana had fallen, her knees scraping the gravel. Mina had yelled at him to stop, but he'd only tightened his grip and yanked harder, as if Mina's words had egged him on, made him even meaner.

He asked, "What's in the bag, missy? What did that country club peacock send you home with?"

"None of your fucking business."

Mina ground her teeth. Twist was like all the rest. He saw her as just another feral mountain girl, a thing to be used and discarded. Someone who would never amount to much. Someone you could grab and harass under the cover of night, do what you want with. Who cared about a little trailer park whore, anyway? Her heart had been racing, but now it slowed. Calmness washed over her; she slowed her breathing and focused on each breath. In through her nose, out through her mouth. In the trees behind Twist, she saw the shadows weaving through the treetops. *Okay*, she thought. *Come.*

He seemed to sense the change in her demeanor. His forehead scrunched as he studied her face. She smiled back at him.

"I warned you, you old bastard," she said.

His voice was softer now. "Just tell me about them boys, I want to hear about the boys. Then you can run along."

More shadows formed in the trees, and the shadow faces sneered down.

He whispered, "Just tell me what you let them do."

"I let them do everything," she purred.

"Yes," he moaned.

A rope of shadow descended from the tree behind Twist. It coiled on the ground. Mina thought of a snake, and it became a snake, a head emerging at the tip, a horrible, twisted gargoyle face. It slithered along the ground toward Twist. *Yes,* she thought, *yes.*

"Tell me," he said.

"I let them do everything. Whatever they want. I want them to do it," she said.

"All the boys?" he said. His face became animated. He watched her lips.

She looked down his skinny frame; his jeans were loose, held up by the twin pegs of his jutting hip bones, no belt. One wrong move and his britches would hit the ground. "All the ones that want some," she cooed, leaning in. "All of them."

The shadow snake rose behind Twist, its misshapen head a foot taller.

"Of course," he said. "All the boys want to."

She grinned. Her mind raced with hate. She hated Twist, every man that looked at her like he did now, every adult that acted like she was nothing, every stupid boy at Clayton High, the jocks and the goths and everything in between.

"I want you to die," she growled.

Twist's eyebrows rose.

"What?"

"I should break all your bones, throw you around like you do that pregnant girl of yours."

His brow dropped, and he tightened his grip.

She pulled the shadow snake closer with her mind. She was calm. Free. *No more Ms. Nice Girl.*

The snake struck Twist between his shoulder blades, its fangs ripping into his flesh, and he immediately released her hand. It coiled around his body, pinning his arms to his sides. Twist looked around wildly, down at the shadows that tightened against him, choking off his breathing, then desperately up at Mina, staring into her eyes. She snarled, and the earth growled below them. The snake tightened around Twist's stomach, lifting him from the ground. The shadows stretched around his neck, and his face went white. He fought to breathe, and Mina balled her fists. The tighter she squeezed them, the tighter the snake gripped.

"I'm gonna choke you till you kick out," she said.

He shook his head. His lips tried to form words, but couldn't. Finally, his eyes rolled up in his head.

"But that would be letting you off too easy. I want you to remember this moment. I want it to haunt your dreams. All your days."

The shadow snake pushed through his skin into his body, and he fell to the ground. The remaining shadows raced along the earth, dissipating between the trailers like chimney smoke. Twist lay on the round, veins of black spidering through his bare chest and arms, as if the darkness pushed its way into every pore, filling his very bloodstream.

Mina picked up the garbage bag and threw it over her shoulder. She stood over Twist, bending at the waist to look him in the eyes. "Fuck with me again," she said. "I dare you."

Twist looked at her. He panted, frantic and wild.

Mina left him there on the ground. She did not run, didn't worry about what Daddy might say when she got home. She walked slowly along, as if it were a beautiful spring morning and she bore not a care in the world. There was so much to do. So many things that needed fixing. She thought of Emerson's ugly grin on the Senior Bench. Of Krissy Lang. Of the racist boys down the math hall. Of the perverted wrestling coach. Of all the adults who'd judged her for where she lived, who looked down their long noses at her. All her life, they'd wanted to keep her down. *Know your place.* Mina knew her place in the world. It was time to show everyone where she belonged.

11 / SISTER GAIL INTERVENES

All day long, dark thick clouds hung in the sky. There was never the smell of rain, nor hint of lightning or thunder. The sky was more winter gray than mid-fall, and the sun itself made no appearance, the late afternoon like dusk, a premature darkening taking hold.

Sister Gail crept along the trail that cut through the woods up Mulwin Rock. A few days earlier, she'd followed her husband Chuck up the mountain along this same trail, hidden. She'd had to head back before she reached the top so she could get a covered dish ready for Sister Rice, who'd recently lost her mother. But she followed Charles up far enough that there would be no way to get lost or not find her way to where he and the elders were led each night by Reverend Ezra. She turned up the small canteen she'd brought and took a drink.

Why had all this been a secret? Were secrets of the Lord? Reverend Ezra had a secretive streak about him, everybody knew, but Sister Gail didn't know why. God wasn't one for secrets. He always laid everything out in the light, exposed everything and everyone, and she thought there might be a need for some daylight in the congregation at Hosanna, a church she'd been a member of since she was a child. Things had grown so fast, so swiftly had the number of savings and baptisms multiplied, and now with Reverend Ezra on AM radio and on television, the man seemed to have forgotten why God had recruited him to the ministry in the first place—to save souls.

Sister Gail stumbled over an exposed root as she climbed the mountain. The day grew darker. It wasn't just that the men kept going off for long periods of time, taking her Chuck with them, it was the Purity Sojourns that the pastor kept promoting that gave her pause. There was something about them that didn't sit right with her. Sure, it was a great idea in the beginning, to get the young people fired up for God, get them to thinking about their purity, sending them off into the woods to pray and find God. She remembered her Papaw used to talk about how a man could get closer to God, quite literally, by scaling the mountains. Up on the highest peaks, he said, you were in the heavens, and God was so close you could feel him on your skin. So it was with the Purity Sojourns, Sister Gail thought when Reverend Ezra had introduced the idea; there couldn't be anything better than to give teenagers something to do besides go off and drink around bonfires or fornicate in the lofts of old barns or in the back of their cars. Get out into the natural world that God had created, take nothing but food, water, and your Bible...so many young men had come back on fire for God. Young women, too. But then something happened.

Just last year, a young girl went missing. They'd never found a body, but Sister Gail was sure she was dead. And in the *Citizen* newspaper, there were stories of other girls missing. Some were prostitutes from Asheville, most of the others from poor parts of the county—kids that had been raised in old shacks covered by tar paper or in Asheville's ghettos.

These things were odd, and they bothered Sister Gail, but then she'd get into church on Sunday morning and Reverend Ezra would speak so beautifully, the love of God lighting on his every word, every powerful gesture of his hands, every *Amen* and *Hallelujah*. She would sit in the pew, her hand over Chuck's, her eyes full of tears. The Reverend Ezra really was a good man, she thought, even now. Just maybe misguided.

But when they took Chuck from her on so many weeknights, not just on Wednesdays or Sundays or during camp meetings, and when Chuck said she could not be a part of the work he was doing...that's when Sister Gail became flooded with doubt. Why couldn't she come along, she'd asked Chuck, and he'd lectured her about how wives were to be subservient to their husbands and not to question the ways of the Lord.

At church one Sunday, the Reverend talked about rebuilding

Solomon's Temple, right here in the mountains, and she was so excited she'd rushed over to the Reverend after service.

"When are we breaking ground on the new church?" she'd asked, picturing a vast sanctuary, twice as big as the current one, with the existing building converted to a school or social hall for prayer meetings and Rotary clubs and what not. "Are we going to build the new sanctuary over in that field on the west side of the grounds?" she'd asked, unable to contain her excitement.

The Reverend had stopped shaking the hands of church members at the back door and stood silently for a moment, looking her up and down. Finally, with a hint of disdain just below the surface of his voice, he'd said, "I go to prepare a place for you. If it were not so, I would have told you."

His hand on her shoulder was more dismissive than his eyes.

"You, Sister Gail, are stuck in thinking that what matters is the *physical* world around us, but remember," he said, smiling, "we are *in* the world but not *of* the world, we are of something higher, and so I speak of things that are not of this world, but of something beyond."

Sister Gail blushed, and the people around her looked at her knowingly, all seeing her ignorance, the mistake she'd made in not understanding the spiritual nature of the good Reverend's metaphor about Solomon's temple. She'd walked to the car as fast as she could that day, hid her face in her hands, wiping away the tears as Chuck got in to drive them to the Calabash Buffet for fried shrimp with some of the other church folk.

Even after this, she'd stood solidly behind the Reverend, believing in everything he strived to do for the community, for the church, both the believers and the lost. But over time, she realized he was trying to take her Chuck away, and that was a bridge too far.

Once Chuck had been taken in as an elder, and meetings started happening on weeknights and sometimes all day on Saturdays, he'd become a stranger in their home. He barely spoke to her, and when he did, it was in a dismissive, agitated tone, as if nothing she had to say held any value whatsoever. When he got dressed in the mornings, he did so in the bathroom and turned his back to her when they spoke. And so, last Saturday, in the bright morning sunshine, she followed him as he drove his truck deep into the woods, off the main road, following a series of dirt roads until finally he'd gotten out and continued on foot.

Today, in the thick gray light, she'd retraced her route along those old country roads, passing ragged tobacco barns and rusty grain silos covered by kudzu vine. She parked the station wagon off the road so it wouldn't be visible. She'd taken Chuck's little canteen, filled it with water—her only cargo—and headed up the mountain.

Deeper in the woods, the world grew dim, daylight dampened by the remaining leaves of the trees that murmured on a shallow breeze. High in the woods, the air seemed too thin, and Sister Gail had some difficulty breathing. She wasn't sure if the air had changed or if she was just tired from all the walking. It felt like the trees were closing in on her, choking off her air. It was a steep climb, and in some places, she worried she'd lost the trail. Looking around her, though, she knew that there was only one way to go to find out what the Elders and Reverend Ezra were so secretive about—up.

When she reached the peak of the mountain, the land began to level off, and in the distance, she saw a cluster of dark woods ahead. At the edge of a drop–off, accentuated by the bare rock of the mountain's face, there was a building.

As she got closer, she saw the building was really just the start of one. There were cinder blocks laid out in the footprint of what would be a huge structure when completed. Nearby, inside the walls of the new structure, there were ruins; the footing of some old building covered with black mold and sprouting mushrooms.

Sister Gail smiled. So they really were doing it! They were building Solomon's Temple right here. A warm joy rushed over her she could only attribute to the Holy Spirit. Was the good Reverend keeping this from the congregation to surprise them and to unleash a great revival among the believers? That had to be the reason for the secrecy, she decided, and she cupped her hands together, overwhelmed by the Spirit.

She looked at the men's handiwork, studying the block they'd laid, when her eyes were drawn to the footing of the old structure, to the mushrooms that sprouted from the black blocks. These mushrooms were different from the ones back down the mountain, the white ones that grew in the yard, or those that sprouted from the cow patties in the fields. These mushrooms were ugly, with large red flat heads. Sister Gail walked closer, and as she looked at the heads, she could see they were covered with dark spots. They reminded her of the spider eyes she'd seen in books, rows of dark eyes that seemed to pull her in somehow. The world had grown gloomy, and when she looked up into the trees, she saw only shadows. Though there was no sun to draw them out, the shadows were there, just the same.

Dare you come to this place?

For a moment, it didn't register. She'd heard something, but was it really words? Was someone there, out in the trees, talking to her?

Oh ye of little faith, Sister Gail.

"Reverend Ezra?" the woman asked, her voice trembling. The voice sounded like the Reverend, but there was something unnatural about it. It was deeper than the Reverend's, more hostile.

So unworthy, so impure.

Now, Sister Gail knew the voice was not the Reverend. It grew resonant and metallic, rolling around her head like a bad dream.

She looked down at the mushrooms with spider eyes, half expecting the voice to come again from the outgrowths, drawing her in to stare at them. Then an amber glow began to form in the trees.

In dozens of trees, maybe a hundred, she saw them. Silhouetted in the trees, the bodies of women and girls. One girl was naked, others wore thin robes that clung to their bodies, highlighting their breasts, arms, and legs.

Sister Gail began to recite the Lord's Prayer. There was nothing else to do in the presence of such evil. What was this place? What does this have to do with the church, with Solomon's Temple, with her Chuck?

One of the largest trees of the forest glowed brightest, and Sister Gail felt her eyes drawn to it as she had been to the spider-eyed mushrooms. As she looked at it, she saw something emerge. It was tall, like a horse. One of the horsemen from the end times?

Its head angled around the tree, and the body came into view. It was no horse. It was a huge wolf, much larger than the ones Sister Gail had seen on the television, much larger than the ones she'd seen on that field trip with the kids to the Columbia Zoo.

The Red Wolf tracked forward with slow, measured steps. It did not seem unnerved by her presence, and there was only the hint of a low growl she felt at the base of her stomach.

She looked up to the heavens, wondering if God was listening, if he was close to her now at this high elevation where the air was thinner, the way her Papaw had said he would be. She looked at the girls in the trees, frozen in time. She wondered how God could let these things go on here, just under his bright heavens.

The wolf stood ten feet from her. It had stopped moving and now silently showed its long teeth. There was a red tinge to the tips of its hair, and there were moments she could see right through it, as if it were translucent. The leaves crunched under its weight, letting her know it was not a shadow.

Sister Gail thought about yelling for Chuck. She thought about yelling for the elders, or Reverend Ezra, Jesus, anyone at all who could hear her call out.

"Jesus God Almighty," she said.

He can't hear you here.

The voice was deep and low, rustling at the base of her spine like an itch she couldn't reach to scratch.

"Will you put me in the trees with the other girls?" Sister Gail asked.

The wolf lowered its head and pulled back its lips even further. A deep cackle found its way up through the ground, through her legs, and into her stomach. The Red Wolf was laughing.

You?

The wolf circled her, its nose nudging her cheek.

You? But look at you—you're so old and ugly. What need have I of you?

Sister Gail tried to still her shaking hands.

You? You're good for eating, the wolf said. *I hunger.*

She recited the Lord's Prayer louder now.

"Hallowed be thy name, thy kingdom come, on earth as it is in Heaven."

The wolf opened its mouth and lowered its head above her own. There came the crunching sound of bone, and she saw the wolf had dislocated its jaw to open wider, the way snakes do. Its jaws slipped over her head, the long teeth scraping the top of her skull, digging into her skin. For a moment, Sister Gail thought to run, picturing the path back down the mountain, her place on the green couch at home. But her body would not move, as if held in place by some unseen force. Then she saw her Chuck, standing nearby in a brown robe, watching. She tried to call out to him, but her mouth, her throat... nothing worked, and the emptiness of Chuck's eyes told her he was not coming for her, he would not intervene. The wolf did not bite down, but began to swallow her, working her head and shoulders down his long throat, her face and neck thick with saliva. Soon she was inside the wolf, marveling at how quickly it had all happened.

Now Sister Gail began to descend, as if into the folds of the earth. She was rushed along a sea of inky black, heavy waves washing over her and carrying her along, caught in some current not drawn by the moon. Looking down into the depths, she could see clouds below the surface, and below them, the dark woods where the Red Wolf stood, affixing his jaw back into place with a crunch. She recited the Lord's Prayer until she could no longer catch her breath. The light went out.

PART 2

"The night wind began to come down from the hills, but it felt like a breath from another world."

– FRANCIS MARION CRAWFORD

12 / MINA SPLASHES DOWN

The next morning, everything was new. Mina took her time at the dusty makeup mirror perched on her dresser, admiring the way the new-to-her blue jeans fit her body. She chose a different tie-dyed shirt to wear today, the fabric streaked purple and blue. It was a little big, like the others, and she had to tie it taut to keep it from slipping off her shoulders. She loved all the jeans, but some of the tops were just too preppy for her—little polo shirts with bright colors and white collars just weren't her thing. She put the clothes she liked in her dresser, the preppy tops in a pile at the foot of her bed for Chelsea.

She took a couple bites of lumpy instant oatmeal in the kitchen. Mama was listening to the Old Time Gospel Hour again. When she went to the bathroom, Mina switched it off. Daddy was in the living room, nursing a hangover. They didn't speak as she passed through the room. She waited for Chelsea outside the trailer, striking the siding when she didn't come fast enough. Tired of waiting, Mina thought, *fuck it*. Chelsea was big enough to walk without an escort. She stepped onto the gravel road between the trailers and headed to the bus stop.

Everything felt different. The world fresh. Partly it was the clothes, but it was also her new sense of purpose, the wrongs she had the power to right. Not even Twist's leering on his front porch, knees up to his ears, could dampen her mood. She met his eyes and stared back hard. Twist looked away first, something he never did. She thought of the shadow snake that had wrapped around his gray body and smiled. He'd not soon forget that night, and he'd not put his hands on Mina or any other girl in the park again. Not even Dana. All that was over. She would see to it.

As she neared the bus stop, Gabe emerged from the tree line opposite the park. It had been a mistake to let him hold her hand. To give him false hope. There would be no guys—not now, not ever. She thought of the way Gabe's puppy dog eyes had peered at her in the streetlight. Earnest. Too earnest. In the end, wouldn't he be just like the other guys anyway? They'd come to you nice, saying all the right things, then they'd show their true colors. And even if he wasn't like Emerson Shit, he couldn't be that different when it got right down to it. She thought of her dad's stupid saying: *a boy has got him a pecker.* Even if he was the best guy in the world, she didn't have time for that shit. There were things to do. Wrongs to right. She had to knock some people off their high horses in her last couple of years in Asheville, then she'd be long gone. She'd get the fuck out of here and never look back.

At the bus stop, Gabe's puppy dog eyes found her again. He looked at her as if they were still standing in the woods the night before. Mina gave him a half smile and turned her back, cranking her music. She felt a little guilty turning from him, and he did look cute today, but this had to be done. Rip off the Band-Aid. In her ears, Meatloaf sang, "Whatever happened to Saturday night?" Halloween was almost here. Today felt like Halloween. The sky was clear, and the air smelled clean from late-night rain.

At the bus stop, a few kids were throwing rocks into a crater-sized pothole near the entrance to Whispering Pines. One of the rock throwers was the Manning boy, and sure enough, Chelsea was soon by his side, laughing like rocks hitting muddy water was the most fascinating thing she'd ever seen. *Pathetic.* Mina turned her back again, fussing with a strand of hair that fell in her eyes. She was lost in her thoughts, thinking about how ridiculous it all was: high school, the way kids acted at the bus stop, the stupid ritual of it all, when someone grabbed her.

Gabe.

He spun her around by the shoulders, putting his back between her and the road. *What the fuck?* She jerked off her headphones, ready to tear into him when cold water splashed the side of her face, a wall of water cascading over Gabe's back. She heard tires slipping on the road. She moved around Gabe to catch Emerson's IROC speeding up the hill. Gabe ran out into the road and shot Emerson the bird. Hanging out of the passenger window was Krissy Lang, her head cocked back, laughing. Neither of them lived on Elk Mountain. They'd made a special trip just to pull this.

Mina squeezed her fists together, feeling the rustle of the shadows in the trees overhead. Gabe looked up, hearing the leaves rattling in the trees. When the IROC was gone, disappearing over the ridge, Mina let it go. The shadows died away.

The trailer park kids who hadn't been splashed were all laughing. One of them shouted, "Holy shit! Did you guys see that?"

"That sorry son of a bitch," Gabe said. He shook the water off his hands, then ran his fingers through the mud in the back of his hair. He'd jumped in front of the coming water to keep it from hitting her. What's more, if Emerson had misjudged by a few feet, the car could have hit him. Mina wiped a streak of mud from his face and touched the sleeve of his gray jacket. His suede jacket. Real leather. She could smell it.

"Oh my God," she said, pulling the sleeve. "I'm sorry. They ruined it."

Behind them, the bus rolled up, its brakes hissing.

"It's no big deal," Gabe said. He took off the jacket and balled it up, throwing it into the woods. "We better go or they're gonna leave us." Streaks of brown feathered over the collar of his white shirt. The mud was everywhere, especially on his jeans and in his hair.

Gabe walked onto the bus, his head high, ignoring the sniggers as he walked down the aisle. He sat near the back of the bus and scooted to the window, leaving enough room for Mina. She eyed the empty seats behind him and almost walked past. He looked out the window, as if not wanting to pressure her to join him. At the last minute, she sighed and slipped into the seat beside him, their legs touching.

She put her headphones over her ears. *This changes nothing*, she told herself. She wasn't becoming Erin, the way she wrapped herself around Lucas every day. Or worse, she wasn't going to be like Karen or her mom. There was no way she would get stuck here.

"Thank you," she said, looking straight ahead. "You didn't have to do that."

"I know," he said.

She looked at his hair. The back of it was curling, wet with caked mud. She ran her fingers through it, pulling out the clumps. "I'm just getting the mud out so you won't look like an idiot at school."

"Okay," he said.

When her neck got hot, she stopped.

"Yeah. It's pretty much hopeless," she said.

"I figured. Any bets on which teacher gives me crap about it first?"

"Hmm." She furrowed her brow. "I'm betting the Driver's Ed guy, Mr. Portman."

"Why him?"

"Because his clothes are always super clean and ironed with creases. He's gonna take one look at you and just know you're trouble."

"I am, though."

"You're what?" she asked.

"Trouble," he said.

"That right?"

She couldn't stop the smile that raced up when she met his eyes. *Goddamnit.* She looked away and clicked play on her cassette. He put his hand over hers. She wanted to get up and move across the aisle to the empty seat. But she didn't. This was bad. But it didn't change anything, she reminded herself again. Okay, so she was holding his hand. But no way would she ever suck face in the bus lot at school. Never. Still, there was something nice about it, his skin warm against hers. Gabe shifted his hand, and she opened her palm. Their fingers intertwined, their hands fitting together perfectly. There was something familiar about it all, something that made it seem like this wasn't new. The stupid smile came back again. She couldn't stop it. She looked away so he wouldn't see.

Fuck.

13 / SWEET SIXTEEN
GABE

A few days later, Gabe finally turned sixteen. Papa Leo and LilyMa had a small birthday dinner for him at the house. Mina, Lucas, and Erin came over. Papa Leo had pulled the Magic Carpet Ride around front and waxed it shirtless under a cool fall sun. LilyMa made fried chicken with all the fixings and baked Gabe's favorite: yellow cake with caramel icing. They'd all sung "Happy Birthday" to him, Papa Leo dropping his voice an octave below his natural singing voice and making all the kids laugh. When his parents had been alive, Papa Leo never failed to call first thing on Gabe's birthday, always at the butt crack of dawn. His daddy would wake him and hand him the corded phone. He would say hello, and Papa Leo would immediately launch into that year's exaggerated version of "Happy Birthday." Sometimes he crooned like Frank Sinatra, hitting each note with a kind of pomp. Other times, he drew every syllable out like Hank Williams, his favorite country singer.

Gabe hadn't wanted a party; once it started, he just wanted it to be over. He wanted to get his license and take Mina for a drive. He wanted to drive her to the movies, maybe to the moon. The next day, Papa Leo and LilyMa took Gabe to get his driver's license. Once he passed the exam, they'd made him pose for pictures in front of the sign at the DMV, holding up the little rectangular piece of plastic. They took Polaroid after Polaroid, LilyMa shaking the film to make sure she got the shots she wanted. Gabe was mortified, worried that someone he knew from school would see him posing for pictures with his grandparents outside the DMV.

"Can we just go?" he asked.

"Soon as she gets enough pictures to fill a book," Papa Leo replied, laughing. "Now smile like you mean it, damnit."

It took an extra day to get him on the car insurance, so it was Friday before Gabe pulled up to the bus stop and offered Mina a ride to school. Some of the kids sniggered at the big tank of a car. Gabe paid it no mind. Mina said yes and got in. Halfway there, a serious look crossed her face.

"My God," she said.

"What?"

"This *is* just like riding on air!"

"Shut up," Gabe said.

"Just like a magic carpet! I kinda dig the Magic Carpet Ride."

"Told ya," he said.

After school, Mina asked him to meet her parents, but she made him drop her at the bus stop.

"You can't just drive right up to my place," she said. "Daddy will blow a gasket sure as the world."

"What do I do then?"

"Just take your car home and walk over. You'll seem like a fine teenage boy instead of a menacing threat to his daughter's chastity," Mina said.

"Okay."

"If they meet you and realize you're not a jerk, it won't be a big deal for you to give me rides to school. And so we can go out some time, like to the big Halloween bonfire on Saturday?"

His face lit up. "You got it. I'll walk over and try to be all presentable."

Gabe parked the car at Papa Leo's and jogged the shortcut through the woods toward Mina's. The trailer park sloped downhill. Standing at the entrance, it was possible to see the tops of all the trailers, most of them dull white with oxidized crystals, some with painted roofs and hints of rust at the edges. They sat on cinder blocks and Gabe imagined them tumping over onto their sides in a hard wind. The trailers sat diagonal to the gravel paths running through the park, each about twenty feet apart with a small grass yard between them and a gravel parking pad that could accommodate one car. If folks had more than one car, they had one parked on the pad and one pulled up into their small front yards.

When Gabe passed, he heard a motorized groaning from the top of the trailer. The antenna moved slowly, changing directions. He remembered the antenna box that had sat on his family's TV when his parents were alive. Daddy would tell him to go to turn the big knob on the box when he wanted the signal to come in clearer or when he changed channels. The box would grind, a little orange indicator moving between the directional labels—North, South, East, and West. The groaning antenna motor reminded him of Daddy, of how they would find college football games to watch in the fall, sometimes switching between the TV's three channels to check the scores of other games during commercials.

The last trailer in the park—Mina's—came into view. It was a white trailer with a blue stripe down the middle and gold accents at the top and bottom. There was a crowd in the front yard. Mina's dad was there, along with a tall, skinny man everyone called Twist. A man close to him had his shirt pulled over his expansive belly and rubbed it slowly, donkey grinning. Another, shorter man rubbed his chin, staring at the belly, deep in thought. Listening to them talk, Gabe figured out the man with his belly out was called Stump, and the short man looking at it was named Dick.

"Pure muscle, I tell you," said Stump. "I don't give a damn, go ahead. Hit it."

Dick considered this, raising his hand and balling it into a fist before relaxing it, letting his hand fall to his side.

"Goddamn it, Dick," a tall man named Twist said. "He said you could do it. He's asking you to do it. Just do it. Hit the son of a bitch. Right in the belly."

"Go ahead," said Stump. "Hit it as hard as you can. There ain't a bit of fat on my body, that is all wadded up muscle."

"You're crazy," Dick said. "Under all that blubber, maybe." The man named Dick bit his lip.

Twist held a dark glass bottle in one hand and two paper cups in the other. The bottle had no label. He poured the brown liquid into the paper cups and handed one to Dick.

"Liquid courage," he said.

Dick took the cup and tossed the drink back.

"Go on ahead now," said Stump. "Pure muscle. I won't feel a thing."

Dick crushed the paper cup and let it fall to the ground before raring his body back like he was about to throw the first pitch at a baseball game, his eyes narrowing. He swung his fist hard into the center of Stump's stomach, catching him just at the belly button. Dick's fist went deep in the other man's stomach. It jiggled like a bowl of jelly. Stump bent over, gasping, the breath knocked out of him.

Everyone laughed, and Mina's dad took the other paper cup from Twist and turned it up.

"Pure muscle," Mina's dad said, laughing, training his eyes on Gabe as he walked into the yard. Gabe had hoped not to be spotted, at least not until Mina came out.

Mina's dad looked at Twist and said, "Looks like a gentleman caller for one of my daughters."

Twist smiled and hooked his thumbs in his belt loops, leering at Gabe.

"Dogs always come sniffing around where the cats keep," Twist said. The man had too much skin on his face, bunched up to form deep wrinkles on his cheeks and forehead. The deep creases reminded Gabe of the paper lanterns they had made in craft class in middle school. His face seemed decades older than his body.

Mina's dad took a few steps toward Gabe. He wasn't tall, but he was broad-shouldered, his hair a mass of brown curls spiraling on his head.

"Suppose you're here to see my Mina."

"Yes, sir," said Gabe.

"You two boyfriend and girlfriend now?" her dad asked.

"We're just friends that visit is all," Gabe said. *Friends that visit?* Gabe thought. *What the hell does that even mean?*

"Friends that visit," he repeated. He looked over his shoulder at Twist. "They're friends that visit, Twist, you hear that?"

"I heard," Twist said, pouring more brown liquid into a paper cup and handing it to Stump.

Mina's dad stuck a thick finger in Gabe's chest. He spoke under his breath. "I may not know a lot of things, but one thing I do know is that a boy has got him a pecker."

Gabe felt his face flush. He couldn't decide what to say, so he said, "Yes, sir."

"You put your hands on my daughter, and you'll regret it."

Gabe shook his head.

"You get her knocked up, you ain't living here. No, sir."

Gabe looked at his feet.

"You'll have to raise your puppies in Old Man Leonard's basement. Yeah, I know your grandpappy. Everybody on Elk Mountain knows him."

"Arrested half of us back in the day," Stump said, laughing.

Gabe looked Mina's dad in the eyes. He wanted to say that he wouldn't do Mina like that, that she wasn't like that, but nothing came out.

"Best thing for you to do is keep it in your pants, son."

"Yes, sir," Gabe said.

"I see you two have met." Mina walked across the yard.

"Yes," her daddy said. "I was just welcoming, umm. Say, what is your name, boy?"

"Gabe."

"Yeah, Gabe. I was just welcoming him to our humble abode."

"I see that," Mina said. "Have you done your Bad Dad song and dance? Do you wanna get your guns out and clean them in front of him? Sharpen your machete?"

Mina's dad frowned. Gabe smiled nervously. Twist glared at Mina, then looked away, a shadow over his face. Mina stared back at him, the edge of a smile at her lips. Gabe studied them both, sure something had passed between them he'd been too slow to catch. Twist turned and walked briskly away, not saying goodbye as he turned up the bottle to take a swig.

"We had our talk," Mina's dad said finally, watching Twist go.

"Okay then. Glad we got that out of the way." To Gabe, she said, "Come meet my mom."

"Okay," Gabe said.

"Remember what I told you," Mina's dad said. He pointed two fingers at his own eyes, then one at Gabe.

"Yes, sir," Gabe said.

After spending a few awkward minutes with Mina's mom and sister, Chelsea, they walked out of the park and into the woods between the trailers and the junkyard to the north. Mina's mom had been almost warm, but she'd seemed very nervous to Gabe, wary of his presence.

"Thanks for doing that," Mina said.

"Happy to," Gabe said.

"I know it's a pain in the ass," she said.

"It was fine."

Mina kept a fast pace, staying a stride or two ahead.

"They're having a big bonfire out in Sand Grove tomorrow for Halloween," she said, bouncing on the balls of her feet. "It's Halloween! How cool is it that Halloween falls on a Saturday this year? We should go."

"Do we really want to drive all the way out there to hang out with all those rednecks?" Gabe asked. He immediately regretted complaining about the drive. More time in the car meant more time with Mina.

"There'll be all kinds of kids there. A lot of different people from school are going."

"That's what I'm afraid of," Gabe said.

"It's Halloween. We have to do *something* for Halloween. You got a better idea?"

"Not really," he said.

Mina spun as they walked, her arms extended. "It's the most wonderful time of the year."

"Isn't that Christmas?"

Mina lowered her head and closed her eyes like she was dealing with a small child.

"Okay," Gabe said, "but do we have to dress up?"

"Only if you want to be one of the cool kids."

"I have no idea what to wear," he admitted. "Where will I get a costume by tomorrow?"

"Hmm," Mina said. "We can figure something out."

"What are you gonna be?"

"Me? That's easy. I'm going as a witch."

"Of course you are," Gabe said, smiling. He felt a little pang of anxiety when he thought about it all. Mama had never let them dress up for Halloween. She'd called it a Satanic holiday, the Devil's Christmas. Instead of dressing up for Halloween, she'd always look for a revival or tent meeting for them to go to instead. Of course, all that was ridiculous, but still...the thought of it made him nervous. Lucas had taken him to one of the bonfires out at Sand Grove in the past, and while Lucas had fit right in, cruising around the hayfield talking to everyone, Gabe had felt out of place, not knowing what to say or what to do with his hands. He wound up just stuffing them in his pockets and offering a head nod to everyone as if he were above it all, too cool.

But this would be picking Mina up and taking her somewhere. Kind of like a date. He knew he'd take her anyplace she wanted to go, anytime. If he had to get dressed up like a little kid for Halloween, he'd figure it out. Anything to hang out with her.

"What should I be?" he asked.

Mina stopped walking and stood in front of him. She was tall for a girl, the top of her head level with his eyes. She scrunched up her forehead, deep in thought, and tugged at one of his earlobes as if it held the answer to the costume quandary.

"Okay," she smiled. "I've got it!"

"You do?"

"Yeah," she said. "I'll be the red-headed witch, and you'll be a vampire."

"A vampire? I don't have time to find a vampire costume before tomorrow."

"That's just it. You don't need a costume."

"Don't I need like a cape or something?"

"Vampires don't have to wear capes. Haven't you seen *Lost Boys*? You just wear like a cool jacket—maybe that black leather bomber—and I'll paint your face white."

"I have to wear makeup?"

"Don't be dense. It's Halloween. Lots of people will be wearing makeup."

"Boys too?"

"The cool ones will. You're definitely one of the cool ones. At least this year." She grinned.

Gabe looked up at the fall sky. "So, you're saying I wasn't one of the cool ones until I met the red witch?"

"Basically," she said.

He dropped his eyes to meet hers. "I'm good with that."

"Good," she said. "Pick me up at seven."

"Anything for you, my witch."

Mina stopped for a moment. She looked into his eyes, then dropped her gaze to his lips. She leaned toward him as if to kiss him. At the last second, she turned and her lips landed on his cheek. It wasn't a peck. Instead, she let her lips linger there; he could feel her breathing against him. When she pulled away, she stayed close, and he leaned toward her, thinking that's what she wanted. She backed away, half smiling.

"Can you skip?" she said.

"What?"

"Can you skip?" she repeated. She turned and began to skip down the trail back toward home.

He tried to skip, but his feet tangled and he almost fell.

"Apparently not," he said, laughing.

"It's okay," she said. "Vampires have an eternity to learn how to dance. I'll teach you. How is it," she asked, "you can play the piano, but you can't skip through the woods?" She looked him up and down and shook her head. She pursed her lips.

"I have no idea. It's like dancing. I can keep time on the piano, but I can't make my feet move right for dancing."

"When are you gonna play your piano for me?"

"Whenever you want. Anything for the red witch."

"What about running?" she said.

"What about it?"

"Can you run, at least?"

She didn't wait for his answer. She sprinted down the trail, leaves spinning around her feet. He chased after her. She was fast, but he soon caught up to her. When they reached the road, they stood panting. She stared at his lips again.

"So," she said, looking away.

"Yeah?"

"See you tomorrow. Seven sharp." She didn't wait for a response. She took off running across the road, her ponytail swirling. Gabe watched her for a long time, the leaves prancing along the ground behind her.

14 / JEEPERS PEEPERS
MINA

Mina dried herself off, stepping out of the shower as Chelsea banged on the bathroom door.

"Hold your horses!" Mina said.

"If you used all the hot water, I'm gonna kill you!" Chelsea yelled.

She was one to talk, Mina thought. She took up the bathroom for more than an hour, or until Daddy threatened to come and do his business with her right there in the shower. Their trailer had two bathrooms, but only one worked. Chelsea had long brown hair and thought it was her right to take her time drying it in the bathroom, while Mina dried hers cross-legged on her bedroom floor.

She tucked a towel around her body, then took a second towel and wrapped it around her head. It got caught on the light fixture, making it cock back and bang into the ceiling as if propelled by a spring. Chelsea poked her pink tongue out as Mina pushed past her down the narrow hall and headed toward her room. Daddy sat in his recliner, feet up, a NASCAR race blaring on the television. In the kitchen, Mama stirred a boiling pot of noodles for mac and cheese.

Back in her room, Mina eyed the black witch gown draped over the bed, tracing her fingers along the lace hem, and smiled. She checked the clock—5:30. Almost time. Gabe would be by to pick her up at seven. It was Halloween at last! No other holiday seemed as exciting. Did that make her weird? If so, she was good with it. Normal was so fucking boring. In a few hours, they'd be at the bonfire, away from the blaring football game, away from Mama's preacher radio, away from Chelsea's whining.

Mina took the towel off her head and dried her hair. It fell over her face as she worked, and when she pulled it back, a bright flash of light blinded her. The curtain rod in front of her window had fallen again—the curtain rod that Daddy kept promising to fix—and the window to her bedroom was completely exposed. An orb of bright white shone through the window. It was so dazzling she had to squint.

"What the fuck?" Mina yelled.

"Language! What's wrong in there?" Mama called from down the hall.

"My curtain fell, Daddy still ain't fixed it!" Mina said.

Mina felt her skin ripple with goosebumps. The orb of light floated with staccato motion, the world around it dark.

Mina backed against the wall beside the window to be out of view, and the light moved to the far angle, as if it sought out her hiding spot. When her eyes focused, she realized this wasn't something magical; it was just a man-made light, something like a spotlight. Was it a person holding a light? It looked like a camera flash, but it didn't flash. Then she understood. It was someone outside her window with a camcorder.

Fucking pervert, she thought.

Then the light disappeared. Mina slipped a t-shirt over her head and stretched the curtain over her window, securing it with thumbtacks. She pulled the edge back. It was already dark outside, a strain of street light filtering through the trees at the edge of the park. There was no sign of anyone. Her mind clicked through possible offenders. Someone from the park? Twist? Maybe. She remembered him looking into one of the trailer's windows. But camcorders were expensive. She'd never seen anyone in Whispering Pines with one. Camcorders were for rich kids' parents to film their little brats playing baseball or performing at piano recitals. Parents like Emerson Shit's. And it was Halloween—kids would be out pranking. Maybe that's all it was.

After she calmed, Mina put on the witch dress, then sat and began applying white makeup. She'd deal with the camcorder jackass later. No way was it going to ruin her night. No way. She picked up the copy of *Atlas Shrugged* sitting on her desk and let it drop to the floor with a thud. She was sure the stupid book had been chosen for her college-prep English class solely for its size and daunting number of pages. She recalled the way some of her classmates toted the big volume through the halls like it was a badge of honor, as if the size of the book said something about their intelligence. The book itself had brief moments of interest buried in long, dry patches of laborious text that had all the grip of a bald tire.

Mina looked across the floor, at the once-golden shag carpet coming up at the edges near the wall, then to her small wooden bookshelf. She'd gotten it at the park-wide yard sale last year. It was a bit rickety at first, but she put some nails in it to make it sturdier. Daddy had suggested she paint it pink, stuck on the idea that she was still five, when everything in a girl's room was pink, like little girls couldn't fathom other colors. But Mina liked the light wood grain, something like pine but not as soft.

On the shelf beside some cassette tapes, she saw her copy of *The Two Towers* and looked longingly at its red cover, the spine barely bent or marked. The book had been a rare find: used like most of the books she had on her bookshelf, but so lightly used it felt new. Her copy of *The Hobbit* had writing in the margins and a dedication to a kid who either disliked the book so much he sold it, or he cared so little he'd lost it somewhere, or worse, tossed it in the trash. Soon she'd finish the stupid school reading assignment and be back in the land of hobbits, elves, and dwarves. A world better than Whispering Pines. A world better than Asheville.

Mina was weaving her hair into a side ponytail to wear under the pointed witch's hat she'd borrowed from a theater kid at school, when she heard a scream on the other side of the trailer. Chelsea. She didn't think much of it at first; Chelsea was always loud, always a bit melodramatic. She'd probably seen a mouse. The family had a problem with mice lately, working their way through the cupboards or along the floor of the kitchen and living room, feasting on the vast wealth of crumbs around Daddy's recliner.

The scream came again, and Mina ran out the door and down the hall.

Someone flipped the light on, and Daddy lumbered along, half-drunk maybe, while Mama tried the door to Chelsea's room.

"Chelsea," Mama said. "Open the door!"

She screamed again.

"There's somebody outside!"

Daddy tried the door, realized it was locked, and leaned into it, pushing the door open as the latch snapped, the lock giving way under the pressure of his weight.

Chelsea was on her bed, holding her softball bat, staring out the window. She wore a yellow Panama Jack t-shirt and white underwear.

Mina followed her gaze out the window. Between the open curtains, a bright orb, the same light Mina had seen in her window earlier. Why hadn't she said something about it when it happened to her?

Daddy whipped across the room. The light went out, and he cranked open the window.

"I seen you, you piece of shit! I seen you," Daddy yelled, running out of the room and down the hall toward the front door. Mina followed on his heels, and soon they were outside, standing in the tiny front yard.

Daddy ran out into the road and paced.

"You son of a bitch, come back out here and let me get a look at your peeping Tom ass!"

A few of the neighbors came outside and stood on their porches.

"Be a man and come face me."

Mina had never seen her daddy like this. There was no uncertainty in his movements, no sign of the tentativeness he often showed with decisions. He stood with his gorilla arms held out from his body. After a few minutes, he walked over and kissed Mina on the forehead. His face was warm, and his stubble scraped her as he pulled away. She couldn't remember the last time he'd kissed her. He used to kiss her and Chelsea on their foreheads every night before bed when they were small.

Chelsea came onto the porch, still in her underwear.

"Did you catch him?" she asked.

"Get in the house," Daddy said. "You ain't got any clothes on! He don't need to peek in no windows, you out here showing your buttcheeks off to the world."

"Oh my God," Chelsea huffed, slamming the door.

Mina's heart raced, and her blood smoldered. She walked out into the road, hugging herself. She looked in the woods, past the dumpster at the back of the park, where they caught her eye. There, up in the trees, just barely visible by the street light near the dumpster at the back of the park, the shadows formed. She closed her eyes and felt the shadows stretching across the tops of the tree limbs, black forms folding in on themselves like a kaleidoscope. Then she was one with the shadow faces, seeing through their eyes, racing over the roofs of the trailers. She saw everything all at once, somehow, every trailer, every person in the park. A man grilled in his backyard at the front of the park. Some kids smoked on a porch. She saw everything but the Peeping Tom. There was no one with a camcorder, no one loitering suspiciously. She scanned toward Twist's trailer. She could see into his window, where he sipped whiskey at a rickety fold-up card table. Dana sat opposite on an old couch with wooden arms, hugging her swollen belly, a strawberry bruise blooming on her cheek. Mina marked it down.

Then she rode the waves of the shadows south through the woods. There was nothing. No one was there. Whoever had been peeping in on them had vanished.

15 / THIS IS HALLOWEEN
GABE

There was no way Gabe was going to be late. Mina had said seven sharp, so Gabe pulled into the Whispering Pines Park at 6:58, the headlights of the Magic Carpet Ride striking her trailer right at seven.

Erin and Lucas had met at Gabe's house to ride along to the bonfire.

"Oh my God," Erin said to Lucas, "we need to borrow Gabe's car when we wanna go parking. Check out this back seat! It's as long as my bed."

"We could do a lot of damage to each other back here," Lucas laughed.

"All right—this car may never be this clean again, keep it PG back there," Gabe said, peering in the rearview.

"Only people I know who drive an Oldsmobile are like a hundred," Erin said.

"That's it," Gabe grinned. "You definitely can't borrow my car now."

"What's so funny?" Mina asked, sliding into the car and slamming the door.

"Girl, you look good," Erin said. "Best. Witch. Ever."

"Thanks," Mina said, peering over the headrest. "What in the world are you two supposed to be?"

Gabe had the same reaction when he'd seen them hop out of Lucas's 240Z. Erin had on tall heels, a short black leather skirt paired with a pink top, and huge hoop earrings. Her cheeks were painted bright red. Lucas sported bell-bottom jeans, a yellow velvet shirt, and a wide-brimmed hat with a feather.

"I'm a lady of the night," Erin said, leaning into Lucas, "and this here is my pimp."

"You guys are idiots," Mina said. "Really, truly."

"Don't be jealous," Lucas said.

"Your boy didn't even dress up!" Erin said.

"Did too," Gabe said. "She's just gotta paint my face."

"You're wearing jeans and a leather jacket. You know, like every other day of the week," Erin said.

Mina put a hand on Gabe's shoulder. "He's a vampire. I just have to paint him up to look dead."

Gabe pulled out of the trailer park and headed down the mountain.

"You should pull over," Mina said. "Let Lucas drive so I can fix your face."

Gabe felt nauseous. He still wasn't entirely on board with wearing makeup. Especially out in public.

"No can do," he said. "Insurance."

"No big deal," Mina said. "It won't take a minute. We can do it at the bonfire before we get out of the car."

"I really don't have to wear it," Gabe said.

"You really should pull over," Lucas said. "This backseat is enormous. You and Mina can get more acquainted back here. Swear me and Erin won't look."

"Christ," Mina said.

"Watch this!" Erin said. She laid out completely across the seat, her head in Lucas's lap. "Look! My feet don't even touch the other side. It's a car with a built-in bed!"

"Magic Carpet Ride indeed," Lucas said.

Gabe shook his head. He looked over at Mina, who rolled her eyes.

"Only one problem," Lucas said.

"What's that?" Gabe asked.

"This thing has only got an AM radio!"

"Yeah, I'm going to have to talk Papa Leo into letting me put a tape deck in this beast. And cut some holes back there for speakers."

"Never fear, I brought my boom box," Lucas said.

Soon Rush's "Limelight" blared from the backseat.

On the drive, Gabe rested his hand on the seat between them. One downside of the big car was that Mina was pretty far away. She'd have to slide closer if they were to hold hands. She didn't take the bait, and eventually, he put both hands back on the wheel. Mina checked her makeup in the visor mirror.

When they got to the bonfire, Gabe pulled off the dirt road onto a cluster of freshly cut hayfields. Cars and trucks were parked haphazardly in the nearest rolling field. Gabe tried to park near the top of one of the crests, afraid the Oldsmobile might get stuck. The field was dry, and dust swirled in the rearview.

Erin and Lucas were out of the car before Gabe could get it in park, Rush still blaring in the backseat. Mina pulled out her makeup kit, and he rolled his eyes.

"You think this witch is going to hang out with some mortal high school kid?"

"Do we really have to? They're definitely going to make fun of me."

"Sir, you are a vampire. We didn't come this far for you to phone it in now."

"Okay."

Mina bent over the seat back to turn down the boombox, her long legs stretching out below the hem of the witch dress. She turned around, catching Gabe looking.

"Don't be a pervert."

"Who? Me?"

"Yeah, you."

She smiled, and even through her white makeup, he thought he saw a hint of red to her cheeks.

She slid across the seat toward him and lifted his hair, moving a makeup brush swiftly over his forehead. She was so close he felt her breath on his neck. He didn't know where to look, so he rolled his eyes up to stare at the headliner, then down to look at her neck.

"Be still!" she said.

"I am," he said.

After a couple of minutes, she moved back to survey her work. She scrunched up her nose. "Yeah, we'll need a second coat of that white powder. You don't look dead yet. You just look like you need a tan."

"Oh no," he said. "I must look utterly dead. Keep going."

He felt a lift in his stomach when she slid in close. After she applied another coat of powder, she pulled out a tube of lipstick.

"Umm, what's that for?"

"Umm, for your lips, you big dummy."

"Vampires don't wear lipstick."

"Real vampires don't need lipstick," she said, grinning. "Their lips are always coated with blood."

"True," Gabe said.

"I don't have any blood handy, so..."

She took her time, angling the lipstick head against his lips before sliding back across the seat to examine her work. She narrowed her eyes. "My God, you're kind of *pretty*."

"Shut up," he said, looking at himself in the rearview.

"I'm sorry, but it's true."

Gabe lifted his palm to his lips, thinking of wiping away the lipstick.

"Don't you dare," she said. "I'm just fooling."

"Yeah, right."

"No, I mean it," she said. "You look like a badass vampire. I wouldn't dare mess with you."

"Why in the world did I agree to this?" He winced.

"Total badass, for real," she said. "Let's go."

When they climbed out of the car, they met at the front, and Mina took his hand as they walked toward the bonfire. After a minute, she stopped and stared at his face.

"What is it? Do I look bad? Seriously?"

"You're really *pretty*," she said.

"Oh my God. Stop it."

"Like Doctor Frankenfurter."

"Who?" Gabe asked.

"Never mind." She rolled her eyes.

When they got to the bonfire, forty or fifty kids were milling about. The hayfield sloped downhill from the fire, several large hay bale rolls casting deep shadows along the ground. Above, a cluster of clouds obscured the moon, a scattered few rays of brilliant light finding their way through. To the west, there was a small pond, maybe fifty feet across, the outlines of a few kids huddled around it in the distance. Someone was blaring Bon Jovi from a pick-up truck backed up near the fire. The music was so loud the panels of the truck vibrated. Several boys sat in the bed of the truck drinking beer. Between songs, someone whistled, perhaps at Mina. If she heard it, she didn't react. Gabe stretched his shoulders and put his arm around her.

A lot of the kids were wearing costumes. There were a couple Jasons from the Friday the 13th movies, a few Michael Myers masks, even a Pinhead. Some dude wore a little kid's Casper the Friendly Ghost costume, and some kids covered themselves in white sheets with eyes cut out. There were werewolves and a few witches, though none as fetching as Mina. There was even a white kid dressed as Michael Jackson, with dark makeup on his face. He kept trying to moonwalk on the dried hay stalks. Out of all the costumes, there was only one pimp and prostitute. Soon, a dozen kids were gathered around Lucas and Erin, sniggering and pointing. Erin held her chin up. Nothing in all the world seemed to embarrass her. On the contrary, she twirled and held her hands out, clearly enjoying the attention. Lucas beamed by her side, flipping the purple feather on his hat and adjusting the wide collar of his shirt. Beside them, a few kids shot-gunned beers.

Gabe felt the same as the last time he'd been to one of the bonfire parties with Lucas, not sure what to do or say. Mina was unusually cheerful. Occasionally, she let go of his hand to go talk to different groups of kids. When she did, he stuffed his hands in his pockets and just looked around or tapped his toe to the beat of the song blaring from the pickup. After one such excursion, Mina returned with two bottles of Bud Light. She handed one to him and turned the other up to take a swig.

Gabe took a small sip and brought the bottle back down.

Mina looked at the beer in his hand. "Oh, come on, take a big sip, Mr. Vampire," she said.

"I don't know. I have to drive later."

"Yeah, *much* later," she said. "You'll have plenty of time to sober up."

The truth was, Gabe had only had beer a few times, and each

time he'd panicked when he felt the buzz come on. He always heard his mama's voice when he drank, sermonizing over the evils of alcohol and how, when folks let themselves try it, even once, they got addicted right away and became drunks, immediately losing their jobs and families. Or worse, wrapping their cars around trees when they tried to drive. Gabe pictured the Magic Carpet Ride wrapped around a tree, remembering the smell of antifreeze and smoke when the family's station wagon had crashed off the highway.

Mina put a hand on his shoulder. "It's okay. Just chill out."

Gabe pushed thoughts of Mama away, the image of her face after the wreck, mouth agape. *Just chill*, he told himself. *It's a party, for God's sake.* He turned up the bottle and took a few deep swallows. The beer tasted good. Cold and crisp. He was glad she'd come back with beer instead of wine coolers, which girls always seemed to prefer. They were so sweet they turned his stomach.

Mina smiled. "See, it isn't hard to have a good time on Halloween."

Behind them, some kids were yelling near the fire.

Someone said, "They're doing keg stands, let's go!"

Erin said, "I want to do it! Lucas, let's go!"

"You're wearing a skirt," Lucas said. "Like a really short skirt. How the hell are you gonna do keg stands in a skirt?"

Erin didn't wait for an answer. She jogged around to the other side of the fire, her tall heels poking into the dirt. Lucas shook his head at Gabe and Mina.

"Come on," Mina said.

"Keg stands?" Gabe said. "Really?"

"Not us," she said. "But let's go watch."

When they got around the bonfire, there were several kids crowded around a beer keg. Some big dude was doing a stand, two of his buddies holding each leg. Gabe drew up when they got close and made out who it was. Mina squeezed his hand. It was Emerson Shit.

Emerson's aqua polo shirt was riding up his chest, his pale midsection a shock in the light of the bonfire. Beer ran up his cheeks and into his hair. After a few moments, he stood up and pumped his fists at the sky. His cronies encouraged him, yelling his name and slapping him on the back. After the celebration, he took his shirttail and wiped his face, slicking back his beer-soaked hair. Then he saw Mina.

For a moment, he seemed frozen in place, like he didn't know what to do. Then he set his jaw. He grinned and took a step toward Gabe and Mina.

"Finally dressing the part, I see," he said, looking at her dress and hat.

"Guess so," she said.

Emerson looked at Gabe. "You supposed to be a boy witch?"

"Vampire, you nimrod," Mina answered.

"Yeah, okay," Emerson said. He let his eyes roam over her. He licked his lips suggestively.

Gabe stepped between them, blocking his view.

"Careful, boy witch, you might get more than you bargained for," Emerson said.

"Careful," Mina said, stepping around Gabe, "I might make you piss your pants again."

Emerson's face soured. He and Mina stared at each other until Emerson finally looked away. He turned back to his friends.

"Where'd that cute little freshman girl go?" he asked.

"Which one?" one of his friends laughed.

"The little red head one, my new *cinnamon girl*?" he said, winking at Mina.

"Oh, Val? She's around here somewhere."

"Yeah, let's find her. She needs a trip to the loft."

Mina glared at them as they walked away.

Since they'd arrived, Gabe had seen several couples make their way to the barn at the far end of the field. It had been that way the last time he came to a bonfire party, too. The barn was a bit infamous as a place kids went to make out or to lose their virginities.

They watched a few more kids do keg stands, laughing when they fell over and when one boy got up and started puking so close to the fire his hair singed. Then Erin stepped to the keg.

"My turn," she declared.

"You can't stand on your head in a miniskirt," Lucas said.

She leaned toward him and whispered, "But I have on underwear."

He threw up his hands. "You can't be serious."

"I mean, they're tiny, but I have them on." Erin slurred her words as if she was already buzzed.

"Shhh," Lucas said, looking around nervously.

"Listen here, cowboy," she said. "I'm doing a keg stand one way or the other, so maybe you should come hold my skirt?"

"Okay," he said. "Just give me a minute." Lucas ran out into the darkness. He came back panting, putting his wallet back in his pocket. In his other hand, he held a sheet he'd bought from one of the many sheet ghosts at the party. "Okay, put this on," he said.

"Lucas," Mina said. "Don't let her have too much. She's already talking funny."

"I know," Lucas said. "But once she gets her mind set on something, there ain't no stopping her."

It was true. In the last month or so, ever since Erin had been chosen for the Hosanna Church's upcoming Purity Sojourn, she'd grown wilder and wilder, as if she were on a quest to prove she was anything but pure.

Lucas slipped the sheet over Erin, and soon she was on her head, chugging beer. Lucas was holding her feet, trying to cinch the white sheet.

Kids yelled, "Chug, chug, chug!"

"Gabe! Give me a hand," Lucas said.

Gabe took one leg, cinching the white sheet around it. People hollered her name, cheering her on. Suddenly, she kicked her legs out, and the sheet fell, exposing her legs. Her skirt rode up her hips, and Gabe—and everyone—saw her black underwear. They were sprinkled with little orange pumpkins. The crowd chanted even louder at this, but the show was over quick, as Lucas pulled her skirt in place and helped her up. She stood and thrust her hand up like Emerson had done, but with fingers horns up.

"Woooooooo," she yelled as everyone cheered.

Gabe saw Mina at the edge of the crowd, staring toward the barn. Her jaw worked.

"What is it?"

"Emerson."

"What about him?"

"He just took that freshman girl, Val, into the barn." She crossed her arms and glared at the barn.

"Shit."

"Yeah."

Then Gabe felt a dip in his stomach. Why did Mina care so much? Was she jealous? "What's the big deal?"

"She's just a little kid," Mina said.

"She's like a year younger than us. She's not a kid."

"Yeah, but she's innocent."

"How do you know?"

Mina stared at him. "Emerson is a creep, Gabe. She doesn't know what she's asking for."

He thought about this. "I mean, she's going into the barn with him at a bonfire party. I'm pretty sure she knows what's up."

"He'll chew her up and spit her out," she said, crossing her arms. "Somebody needs to put him in his place. *I* need to put him in his place."

"Well, did he drag her in there or did she walk in there willingly?" he asked.

Mina glared at him. "I didn't say he knocked her over the head and dragged her in there. Jesus! But she's probably drunk and doesn't know what kind of guy he is."

Gabe put his arm around her, but she shrugged away.

"You don't get it," she said.

"You don't want him to treat her bad. I get it. But do you think she'd have stopped if you'd told her what kind of guy Emerson is?"

Mina was quiet for a moment. She shook her head no and balled her fists; the wind kicked up on the field, blowing dust in the air. Shadows above cleared, and moonlight flooded the barn in white light.

"Do you want to go home?" Gabe asked. "I can tell Lucas and Erin it's time to go."

Mina looked at her watch. "It's only ten, I don't want to go home." She turned back to Gabe, and her face softened. She uncurled her fingers. "It's too early. I am not going to let that dirtbag ruin our night."

Gabe smiled. She had called it *their* night. "Well, okay then." He held out his hand. "What's next, my dark witch?"

Mina stepped past his hand and put her arms around him. "You're the coolest vampire at this party."

"You think?"

"Definitely. Maybe the coolest vampire in Asheville."

"That's high praise."

Mina stepped back and put a finger to her mouth, deep in thought.

"I've got an idea," she said.
"What is it?" he said. "Anything you want."
"Anything?" she said.
"Yup."
"Okay," she said. "Remember you said that." She looked around, standing on her tiptoes to peer through the crowd. "Stay here, I'll be right back."

"Want me to come with?" Gabe asked, but she was already gone. He looked for Lucas and Erin, finally spotting Erin dancing in the bed of the pickup truck, now blaring Def Leppard's "Pour Some Sugar on Me." Erin spun around, her hands high. Lucas leaned on the edge of the truck bed with his arms crossed. He didn't look jealous or uncomfortable; he stared up at Erin and simply took her in. The same way he always looked at her. Dumbstruck, like she was the most amazing thing he'd ever seen. He wasn't trying to get her down out of that truck bed, wasn't warning her not to make a scene, like other guys might do, afraid of other guys watching their girl dance. Maybe this was why their relationship worked. Lucas had the sense to just let Erin *be*. If she was happy, he was happy. She was spinning around with one of the dudes in the truck, their arms stretched out. Lucas just laughed and sipped a beer.

"Hi there," Mina said.

Gabe turned and smiled. She looked past him at Erin dancing in the truck and shook her head.

"She has fun," he said.

"*We* need to go have some fun," Mina said.

He raised an eyebrow. "Yeah?"

"Yeah."

She held out a joint.

"Whoa," Gabe said, pulling at the collar of his shirt. It suddenly felt too tight.

"Yeah, I went and found Ramey."

Ramey was the go-to kid for pot at Clayton. Nice kid, always well-dressed, with a penchant for skinny leather ties and a swooping Flock of Seagulls haircut. A bit on the nerdy side, but quick with a joke. He didn't fit the Nancy Reagan ad "stoner kid" stereotype. Not by a longshot.

"I want to smoke with you," Mina said.

"I have to drive."

"Will you quit with that? It's early," she said. "You'll have plenty of time to come down. Don't worry."

Mina grabbed his hand and pulled him away from the bonfire, past the pick-up trucks and parked cars, past several big hay bales, to the upper hayfield beyond.

16 / GABE & THE MAGIC KISS

From their vantage point in the upper hayfield, Gabe and Mina watched the bonfire, the parked cars and trucks, the barn, and the pond. Some kids started shooting off fireworks at the pond, lighting the sky with bursts of orange and blue and gold. After a few minutes, they began shooting bottle rockets at each other across the pond.

"Shoot low, not at my face, asshole!" one of the kids yelled.

"Fuck," said one kid when he was struck by one of the rockets, catching his shirt on fire. He leapt into the pond, and smoke sizzled around his shadowed frame.

"Jesus Christ, the water's cold," he said.

"Idiots," Mina said.

The fire didn't stop them. They continued to whoop and holler as they played, shooting rocket after rocket, sparks sizzling in the water.

The night was cool but comfortable. For the first time since they'd arrived, Gabe felt calm. He always felt better away from the crowd. Mina took off the witch hat and pulled out a book of matches. Thick strands of her red hair were woven together and pulled to the side in a ponytail resting on her shoulder. He tried not to stare, but, despite the witch makeup, she'd never looked more beautiful. He looked away each time she caught him looking. Part of him still couldn't believe he was here with her. It didn't matter that she still held part of herself back, bristling at the notion of ever being anyone's girlfriend. None of that mattered. They were here. They were together.

Mina lit the joint. She pursed her lips as she held in the smoke for what felt like forever. Finally, she released it and smiled. Gabe tried not to think of the drive home. He wanted to just *be*. He was excited to smoke with Mina—to smoke weed for the very first time—but nervous energy pinged through him.

When she handed him the joint, his fingers shook. He took a small drag and tried not to cough. He held it back, but Mina held up her hand.

"Uh-uh," she said, shaking her head. "You barely hit it. You have to hold it in longer." She smiled, her bright teeth showing, a narrow beam of moonlight spotlighting them in the field. Her freckles were barely visible beneath the witch makeup. Gabe imagined wiping it away to kiss each freckle in turn. To kiss each freckle a thousand times.

Gabe hit the joint again, forcing himself to hold in the smoke, though his lungs smoldered. Mina watched him with a kind of mischievous amusement.

"You're enjoying this," he said.

"Maybe. You ever smoked before?"

"Just cigarettes," he said.

They took turns hitting the joint until it was gone. After a few minutes, Gabe lay back on the ground, the first waves of the high washing over his skin like a thousand gentle pinpricks. Mina lay back with him, their shoulders touching. Clouds again obscured the moon, the world dark, but it didn't dampen Gabe's mood. The air was clean and bright in his lungs as the world slowed. His skin felt sensitive, too sensitive for the leather bomber, so he took it off.

"Are you cold?" he asked, prepared to cover her with it.

"No," she said, so he balled the jacket as a pillow and placed it under her head.

He pushed himself close against her so their arms and legs touched. She took his hand, and he felt her warmth move through him, in through his fingers, up his arm, and over his chest. An involuntary smile formed on his face, and he laughed. They both laughed. Above them, the clouds came alive, dancing in front of the moon. They raced across the sky, the moon peering in and out upon them, a gentle strobe effect gliding over their faces. The movement felt radiant, and the sky seemed to press down on Gabe's body, anchoring his limbs to the earth with a kind of snug heaviness.

"Why are they moving so fast?" he said.

"Isn't it beautiful?" she asked.

Then Mina unlaced his boots, old black work boots Gabe polished with Papa Leo's shoeshine; they seemed more appropriate for vampire attire than his Jordans. She took off his boots and socks. When his feet touched the cool straw, they felt alive, and everything seemed to tickle. First, his feet itched, then his shins and legs. It wasn't the kind of itch that required a scratch; instead, the sensation was invigorating, this simple act of touching the earth with his bare skin. Mina touched the tops of Gabe's feet with her palms.

"What're you doing?" he asked.

Mina didn't answer. Instead, she lowered her body over him, lying on him, her weight coupling with that of the pressing sky. She looked in his eyes, and he looked at her lips. They were swollen and red, like she'd just applied fresh lipstick, but he knew she hadn't. Then she kissed him, slow and deliberate, their tongues touching. Gabe felt heat surge through him from every place their bodies touched. This kiss was different. She kissed him like she meant it, something she'd never done before, always seeming to hold most of herself back. He felt feverish, but in a good way. In the best way.

Gabe felt something in his mouth as they kissed. At first, he thought it was her tongue, then he thought it was his own. But it was neither; something foreign, not part of her mouth or his. It tasted earthy, the way rich soil smells when a field has been turned by plow. When she pulled away, the foreign thing was still in his mouth. He raised up and spit it out into his palm.

"What in the hell is this?" he asked.

"It's just a mushroom," she said. "It's no big deal."

Gabe studied the mushroom in his palm.

"You don't have to," she said.

He tried to speak but couldn't form words.

She smiled. "It's okay."

Gabe looked into her dark green eyes. He put the mushroom on his tongue, and it slid down his throat like a raw egg yolk. Mina touched his Adam's apple with her fingertips, coaxing it down.

"That feels nice," she said.

At last, he could speak. "It tastes like dirt."

"It will open you up," she said, "to new worlds."

He sat up, his stomach tightening. Mina pushed his shoulders gently back down.

"It's just a 'shroom," she said. "Ramey gave it to me, kind of a bonus. He said they were really good."

"Mina," he said. "I have to drive later."

"It's all natural. It'll make you feel good." She kissed each of his cheeks, and her lips grazed his forehead before sliding down to kiss each eyelid. Her lips felt hot on his skin, making him forget about the mushroom.

"The famous poets and artists of old," she said, "would eat these mushrooms to open their minds to new things. This or opium or absinthe. Maybe you'll find a new kind of magic now; maybe you'll write me a beautiful poem."

"I can't write poems. I don't understand poetry," he said. "If I had a piano, I could write you some music."

"Then write me a song," she said.

"There aren't many pianos in hayfields," he said.

"Then close your eyes," she said, "and just feel the keys."

Gabe closed his eyes and felt them roll up in their sockets. He saw the keys of a piano floating in the fall air above them. He touched them, stroking the keys. His fingers moved over them, and notes rang around them. They were far away at first, but he felt them all, pulled them closer. He moved his hands along the keyboard.

"I hear it," he said.

"What does it sound like?" she said, moving over him.

"They're your notes," he said. "They belong to you. They're what I feel when I look at you."

"Keep playing," she said, her lips to his forehead. "I can hear them too."

Gabe kept playing, a song taking shape.

"It's in B minor," he said. "Your song. It's in B minor."

"Yes," she said, "that sounds right."

Mina lowered herself upon him again, their bodies touching. He felt the place where her toes met his shins. She kissed his neck, her teeth grazing his skin. She consumed him, and yet somehow, he continued to play her song, though she wrapped her arms and legs around him. She pulled him closer with her strong legs, their bodies together, on fire.

"My Mina," he said. "Can you hear it?"

"Play my song," she said.

He could feel his fingers moving over the keyboard, hear the click of the hammer hitting the stretched piano strings. He knew the song, though he'd never played it before. It was both new and familiar somehow, with chords that stretched and augmented beyond his ability to reach, yet he was doing it. Each hand stretched to notes and octaves that were impossibly far apart, but Gabe played them easily.

"There's a door," she whispered in his ear. "Do you see it?" She bit his earlobe. "Do you see the door?"

"Yes," he said.

"What color is it?"

"It's red," he said.

"Why is it red?" she said.

His hands left the piano keys, and he embraced her, wrapping his arms around her. The music did not stop. Instead, he saw the piano keys stretch along her back, and he continued to play them, note upon note in rising crescendo. She was a magical new instrument that made the music of the heavens.

"The door, Gabriel," she said.

"Yes?"

"Why is it red?"

"It's the color of blood," he said. "Of all the blood in the world. The blood of Christ."

"Yes," she said. "The blood."

He saw blood come down from the woods to wash over their bodies. He watched it wash from the upper hayfield to the one below. It pooled in the pond where the kids shot brilliantly colored bottle rockets. Somehow, the river of blood didn't seem scary. Instead, it felt peaceful.

"What else?" she said.

"The door. It's red like your hair," he said. "It glows, Mina, and I can hear the music. I am playing it. A song I never knew how to play before. I've tried so long to find it. I can play it now! The keys are on your back. They're in your skin. They're all inside you."

"Yes," Mina said. "Play me, Gabriel. Find my melody."

Gabe continued to play the song, feeling her body against his own. Her fingers and hands, legs and toes, her chest against his. All of her against all of him.

Then the world went dark. The red door darkened too, and the door grew dusky vines that sprouted from black soil. Gabe heard something on the other side of the door. His skin rippled with gooseflesh when he heard it again. A growl. The Red Wolf on the other side of the door.

"He's here," Gabe said, his jaw clenched. "He's here, and I will kill him now."

Mina nuzzled his neck in the afterglow. "Who's here, my Gabriel?"

"God is at the door."

"Yes," she said. "He's behind the door and in the trees and in the clouds."

"Yes," Gabe said.

The world went dark again, and Gabe heard the growl once more beyond the door.

"No," he said. "It's not God."

"What?"

"He's here."

"Who's here?"

"The Red Wolf. And I will kill him."

Mina froze. She stopped kissing his neck. Her hands stopped moving over his body. "What?"

"The Red Wolf is at the door."

"The Red Wolf?"

"The one that killed my parents."

"The Red Wolf killed your parents?"

"Yes. And he wants to kill me; he thinks I have come to take his power."

Mina kissed his neck again, but more tentatively. "And how would *you* take his power?"

"He spoke of shadows, of the pillar of smoke."

Mina went rigid.

"No," she said. "We're just high. That's all. You're just high. It's okay. Just relax."

Gabe shook his head. He put his ear to the door and listened. It was freshly painted, and some of the paint came off onto his skin when he touched it. He rubbed the paint between his fingers. It wasn't paint. It was blood.

The growl came again, up through the earth, rattling the red door.

"He's here," Gabe whispered again. "Now."

"No," Mina said. "It's just the two of us here." She stood up and paced around Gabe in a circle, fixing her dress. "Just the two of us."

The door creaked, the wood frame shaking. The wolf pushed against the door from the other side.

"He's coming in," Gabe whispered, and the world fell away.

17 / MINA RISING

When Gabe mentioned the Red Wolf and the pillar of smoke, ice edged into Mina's veins. She pulled away from him, frozen, their lips inches apart. Then she heard the door creak, and heard a growl that hit her deep in her stomach. She looked around wildly—where was it?

"It hurts!" Gabe said, his eyes shut tightly, eyeballs working their sockets.

"What hurts?" she said, her voice rising.

Gabe's hands balled up, and he curled onto his side.

"The teeth," he said.

"What is it?"

Gabe's jaws were grinding, his face distorted. For a moment, he looked like someone else, his face like one of the shadow gargoyles.

"My side," he moaned.

Mina pulled up Gabe's shirt and saw the wounds forming from his waistline to under his armpit. Dark red wounds opened in his flesh spontaneously, like some type of stigmata. She looked around, seeing nothing. Down in the field, someone screamed. She looked back at Gabe, at the patterns forming in his skin, bright red, as if cut into him with a knife. Circles and patterns.

Mina stood. Clouds multiplied overhead, masking the moon. The fields were almost completely dark now, save the lucent embers of the weakening fire. The headlights of the truck went out. At the edge of the field, near the barn, Randy Todd and some other kids lit a cross on fire. She heard someone speaking in a language she didn't recognize. An unnatural voice, octaves below that of a man. She heard Gabe cry out behind her, looking to find him twisting on the ground. Her fear grew, rushing up into her throat and to her temples; she heard her own heart beating. She tried to push it down and thought about what Gabe had said about the Red Wolf, the way it killed his parents. She remembered the way it gazed up into the sky at her that day above Elk Mountain. Then her fear transformed. She balled her fists, her face tight.

"It's okay, Gabe," she whispered. She pressed his wounds with her palms, kissed them, getting blood on her lips. He tasted like salt and iron. The Red Wolf was here for her Gabriel. The Wolf would take him from her, just as she'd come to realize what he meant to her? Now that something—someone—in this goddamn world finally meant something to her? It happened, in spite of how hard she'd fought to close herself off from everyone. He had found a way in. And now the wolf would take him right where he lay, not even showing himself, through some kind of dark magic? The night was cooling, but sweat formed at her collarbone, trickling down her chest.

She stood and faced the fields below.

"Where are you?" she yelled.

Some kids milled near the bonfire, but there was no other movement.

She closed her eyes, tensing her body. She felt the shadow faces swell in the trees behind her, working through the limbs. She called to the darkness, summoned it, basked in it. She saw their ugly gargoyle faces, the way their heads snapped at her upon the spikes that day outside Emerson's car. Now they crept through the woods in the mountains above the fields.

"That's a good trick," she whispered to the wolf. "Come out and show yourself." She ground her teeth, jaw working, tears streaming down her cheeks.

"Come!" she yelled, and the earth groaned like an earthquake took form beneath her.

The kids at the party began to run now, fleeing in all directions. Someone tried to start a car, but it wouldn't turn over.

Mina walked down slowly from the upper field, and the world grew quiet, save for the shadows that pushed against the trees behind her, the forest aching as though the tree limbs groaned under the weight of an ice storm. The wind kicked up, sparks swirling the bonfire.

"Come out," Mina said. She lowered her voice. *Come see what I can do.*

Just then, one of the kids near the pond shot a bank of fireworks into the air. The darkness was split, just for a moment, and the outline of the wolf appeared out in the open near the tree line, down near the barn and burning cross. Some kids screamed.

She crept down the field, toward the place where she'd seen its outline before the darkness returned, the flash of the fireworks gone. On the lower field, the kids parted for her with somber faces. Then they ran when they saw the shadow creatures racing down from the woods. Some of the kids ran toward the parked cars, others for shelter in the woods. They shrieked as they ran, the only kids remaining too drunk to understand, some falling to their knees as though Mina were some new dark goddess, one they suddenly knew they should fear completely.

I knew you'd show your true self, boy, the wolf growled.

"I'm no boy," she said.

They were close together now. Mina held her hands out to her sides, pulling the shadows closer. She formed them in her mind: grotesque shadow bears, monstrous gargoyles, sleek black monsters. They were ugly and beautiful, all powerful, and they would crush the wolf for hurting Gabe. They would break his bones, tear him limb from limb. She smiled, picturing it.

When she got to where the wolf's shape had been, she saw nothing. Then his growls echoed around her.

Who are you? It said. *I know you not.*

"I'm the one who has come to break you," she said.

I see your little playthings. I saw you in the sky before. In the pillar of smoke?

"It was me," she said, spinning, looking for the wolf. "Show yourself so I can crack your ribs wide open and feed you to the fire." Gabe's moaning on the ground returned to her. Somehow, the wolf bit down into his body still. Salty tears licked her cheeks, and she wiped them away.

"You're wasting time," she said. "Show yourself."

There's no mention of you in the prophecies. No images of you in the lore. There was something like doubt in its voice.

"And yet here the fuck I am," she said.
This is a trick. You're an impostor. The boy tricks me, does he not?
"Come and see for yourself," she said.

The Red Wolf growled. Its long snout emerged from the shadows, hair bristling crimson and glowing, not as a reflection from the bonfire or burning cross, but as if some powerful light emanated from within its enormous body.

The shadow creatures Mina conjured stampeded across the field, their heavy paws and clawed feet stirring the dust. There were dozens of them, then hundreds. They rushed past her, the hem of her dress swirling in their wake. They bore down on the wolf, their horrible faces twisted with anger, their jaws snapping in anticipation, the crunch of their teeth echoing ridge to ridge.

The wolf did not run. It snarled, stirring the dirt with its paw. The shadows growled back so loudly they shook the earth.

There was a twist of shadow and dust and smoke as they leapt at the wolf. Through them, Mina saw the wolf on its back, the shadow beasts holding it down, sinking their teeth into its flesh. Trying to find their mark. A swirl of anger and violence, the crunching of paws striking the earth, the horrible cry of the gargoyles, the dreadful grinding of their teeth. The wolf pushed back briefly before it was consumed. She saw the shadow faces attacking, grabbing, and biting over and over. With horror, she realized that as they bit into the wolf, their jaws snapped closed, as if the wolf was as intangible as them. It was the same when the wolf crunched down on the shadows; while it was able to push them around the field with its enormous body, it could never find a weak spot, no flesh in which to sink.

Mina felt the hair rise on her neck. She tried to push it away, but her fear was stubborn. Finally, the Red Wolf emerged from the shadows, skulking toward her, its head low. The shadows pooled along the ground around it, having lost all form. The wolf stretched its neck high. It stood taller than a horse, its body long, muscles rippling beneath its fur.

Who gave you these dark gifts? It asked.

Mina said nothing.

No matter. I'll see for myself.

Then the wolf was inside her head, shuffling through her memories.

"No," Mina whispered.

The Red Wolf needled in her head, like an itch she couldn't scratch, and saw Daddy on the floor after hitting Mama. It saw Mina at school, at home, at church. Being talked down to by Mrs. Smith in the second grade, listened to the old bat telling her she'd never amount to anything, that she better learn to knit or sew to make herself useful, not to worry that she was slow at math, slow at reading. She had been slow at everything, unable to read for nearly a year after her peers. The way she'd sweated and cried over math worksheets in the fifth grade; it took her twice as long to finish a problem. But then she learned to work harder than everyone else. How she had been able, finally, to read at the 12th grade level by the 7th grade. How she'd passed everyone in math, sitting in 10th grade biology class in the 8th grade, the older kids marveling at how she got back quiz after quiz with an A+ written on the page. The wolf worked through everything, though Mina tried to push him back, tried to conjure the shadows again, which now seemed melted, just wisps of smoke whispering along the ground around the wolf's feet as it padded around her.

Remarkable, it said. *I can see your thoughts, but never could see those of the boy, as if a dark cloud kept me out each time I tried.*

The wolf saw, too, her fear of being trapped. Her determination not to get stuck in Asheville, a baby on her hip, a man thumping the wall, demanding to be served.

How marvelous! How beautiful! Your fears laid out for me as if on a table.

"Get out of my head."

Then the wolf nuzzled her neck with the top of its head. *The light taker came to you. To a boy it once came.*

The wolf showed Mina a boy on his knees in the woods, a dark shadow behind him in the snow.

"Papa Leo," she whispered.

He was so angry. He wanted to burn it down—everything in the world. Wanted to kill everyone on earth, to punish them for looking down on him. Just like you.

"Stop," she said. The tears came again. They burned her cheeks as they ran down, smearing her white makeup.

The only thing I can't see. Your name. What is your name, girl? What do they call you?

"No," Mina said. Then she felt the word slip up her throat and out of her mouth in a whisper, coming though she tried to stop it, as if she was possessed. *M i n a*, she whispered.

Mina, Mina, Mina! the wolf hissed. *And the boy. How you must care for him to throw yourself at me this way. I can destroy you by destroying him.*

Mina closed her lips tight and shook her head, but the wolf was inside her mind again. He saw her on top of Gabe in the field. The way she'd kissed Gabe's eyelids, wrapped her arms and legs around him, tried to pull all the heat in the world inside her body.

Oh my, the wolf said. *So much passion passing between you. But this is but a crush, something passing like in the trees.*

"Love is real," she said, but her voice shook. She felt as if she might lose her balance. "There are beautiful things."

No, it said. *All is ugliness. All is hate.*

Mina tried not to feel it. Tried not to think of Mrs. Smith, of Twist, the bus stop kids, the folks all trying to pin her to the mountains, to the park, to a fate befitting her birth.

Yes, the wolf said. *That's right, let it unfurl. Slip under its curtain.*

Mina shook her head. Closed her eyes.

You and me, the Red Wolf cooed. *Let's burn down this city, this whole world. Together. You can have the boy. Anything you want. If you will bow down and serve me.*

Mina set her jaw. She pulled at the shadows that pooled along the ground. They began to rise slowly from the earth, finding form once more.

The wolf looked around and saw them forming around where they stood.

You're making a grave mistake.

"I will break you," Mina said, her voice losing the shakiness it held before.

It's a false choice, the wolf said. The wolf ran a paw over its snout, as if cleaning itself.

The horrible gargoyle faces pushed forward from the shadows and circled the place where they stood.

The wolf showed its teeth. *Remember you did this. You forced my hand.*

The shadows rose, first rising a few feet off the ground, then ten, then a hundred. They swirled around Mina and the wolf, a wall of storm and shadow. Mina felt her breath slow, her hands balled into fists, her biceps twitching.

The wolf pounced, coming so quick Mina barely had time to duck. The wolf's head descended over her own, its jaws almost snapping closed so quickly she felt the force of the wind they stirred over her face. But one of the gargoyles leaped forward, its terrible face twisted and hideous. It held the wolf's jaws in its hands, keeping them from crushing Mina's skull. She tried to pull back, but something held her in place, the same force that pulled her name from her lips. A single canine caught on her forehead, pushing into her flesh. It burned, and the wolf twisted its head so the tooth slid down, opening a gash that stretched from her hairline down the left side of her face. Blood ran into her eye, and it burned.

Mina dropped her chin to her chest. She looked down and saw the wolf's leg pushed against her, its enormous paw dwarfing the size of her foot. It felt tangible and real against her foot, somehow less transparent than the rest of its body. She concentrated on it and twisted her body free of the wolf's grasp. She dropped her face to the paw and bit into it as hard as she could, a shadow gargoyle joining her.

The wolf howled in pain and stepped back.

When Mina rose, she saw it stumbling away on three legs, holding up its injured paw.

He shall bruise thy head, the wolf growled, *and thou shalt bruise his heel.*

Then the shadows consumed the wolf, reaching for his other paws, for anything they could bite. But once again, there was nothing for them to latch onto.

The wolf laughed. It ran through the shadows and up the hill toward the tree line. There it stopped and looked back over its shoulder at Mina.

Think about what I said. It bared its teeth. *You'll bend the knee, or I'll kill your Gabriel. The twins, the old man. I'll wipe their seed from the face of the earth.*

Mina scowled.

And then I'm coming for you.

Then it was gone.

18 / MINA'S REVENGE

When the wolf disappeared, Mina heard the pickup truck start up again, music blaring from its speakers once more. Some kids stoked the bonfire, throwing logs upon it until it swelled up twenty feet or more. They acted like nothing had happened. Had they seen anything?

Lucas approached her, his face white. She didn't know if it meant he'd seen what happened with the wolf or if something else troubled him. He reached out to touch her, but she backed away.

"Gabe is in the upper field," she said. "He's hurt. Carry him to the car."

"What happened?"

"Get him and put him in the car," she said. "Get Erin. Get them both in the car. We're leaving."

"What happened to your face?" he asked. "Mina, what's happening? I seen a monster."

Mina wiped her cheek and looked at the dark blood on her palm. She tasted something metallic on her tongue. Was it the wolf's blood? Had she really wounded him?

Mina seethed. She looked around, eyes wide, for any sign of the Red Wolf. Her skin felt alive. As if she could feel everything in all the world, every wisp of the wind, every bit of dust and ash falling on her skin. Her anger pushed her heartbeat faster and faster. Her breathing quickened; soon she was panting. She wanted to chase the Red Wolf into the woods, to make it pay for what it had done to Gabe. *Her Gabe.* But she needed to get him home, to tend to his wounds and make sure he was okay. She turned away from the car when she heard some kids whooping behind her, near the barn.

Emerson Shit came out of the barn. He grinned like a Cheshire cat.

"You get her?" some boy asked.

"Damn right, I did," he said.

The boys cheered and began to chant his name.

"Emerson! Emerson! Emerson!"

Then Emerson pulled something from his pocket and held it over his head. It was a pair of pink cotton panties. He pumped the underwear up and down as if it were an enemy flag seized in battle. This made the boys around him get louder and louder.

In a doorway on the second story of the barn, Mina saw a figure in the shadows. It was the freshman girl, Val. The one Emerson called his new *Cinnamon Girl*. Her shoulders trembled.

Mina felt everything well within her. All the anger she'd ever felt. The anger of every kid in the field, every kid in the whole world. She exhaled.

She focused on Emerson's gloating face, his cheeks pink from the cold. Or exertion. Or both. She felt the shadows rising around the barn. She pushed them together, twisted her hands into claws. She imagined a cat. An enormous cat. Bigger than the Red Wolf.

A grim panther scream echoed over the hayfield. Every kid at the party froze. Someone clicked off the tape in the truck's stereo. The world fell silent again; the only sound was the soft crackle of the bonfire.

Then came the sound of heavy footfalls. The Shadow Panther stalked through the middle of the hayfield, the partying kids parting for it, some sprinting for their cars or the pond. When it passed Mina, she saw the faces of gargoyles, snakes, and wild dogs in its body, as if they balled up all together to form this monstrous beast. It was ugly and beautiful. It screamed again, a short staccato burst. The earth shook as it sprinted toward the barn.

Mina looked at Emerson. He met her eyes and she smiled at him. He had the same look of fear he'd had in the IROC the day the shadow faces had darkened the world. He stuffed the freshman's underwear in his pocket, but then, as if he thought better of it, he fished them out and let them fall to the ground.

He turned to run as the panther pounced, its long fangs ripping into his calf. He fell to the ground, screaming.

The panther circled, its breath visible in the cool night air. Emerson stood, and when he did, the panther's paw whistled through the air, slapping him face down into the earth.

He rose to his knees, and it slapped him down again, its claws digging into his back.

He screamed.

Then the panther padded toward the boys who had been cheering his conquest. They scattered like rats; it chased one behind the barn. His scream was snuffed out as quickly as it came. It caught another boy and hurled him into the creek.

In front of the barn, Emerson stood. He shook all over, his legs weak, stumbling around as if drunk.

"Mina," he said, his voice hoarse.

She frowned.

"Mina," he said again. "Make it stop. I'm sorry. I'll make it right."

She laughed. She was aware of the eyes of all the kids on her. Her laugh grew higher pitched. This dumb boy. This waste of space.

Then the huge sliding door of the barn behind Emerson began to creak like something had pushed against it.

"Mina, please," Emerson said, taking a few steps forward.

The barn door shattered as the panther pushed through. It screamed again, leaping at Emerson and catching him in its enormous teeth. It flipped him up in the air, perhaps twenty or thirty feet; when Emerson came down, he landed feet first. The revolting crunch of bone echoed as he met the hard earth flat-footed. The bones in his legs snapped, and he cried out briefly before losing consciousness.

The panther receded into the shadows cast by the barn, disappearing into the cracks in the wood siding.

Mina walked over to Emerson, squatting down and rolling him over on his back. She put two fingers against his neck and felt his pulse. It was slow, but it was there.

She walked from the barn toward the bonfire. The kids parted for her as she came. One girl stepped forward. Val held Mina's witch hat in her hands. Mina smiled and cleared some fallen red hair from the girl's eyes, carefully tucking a strand behind her ear. Val blotted Mina's face with a blue bandana. The wound stung when she touched it, and Mina was reminded again of the wolf's fang, the way it had dug into her, creating a small trench in her skin. Her shoulders twitched, but she pushed back the pain. She put the hat on Val's head and walked past the bonfire up the field toward the car.

From the crowd, another girl stepped forward. It was Krissy Lang, dressed as a sexy genie from the TV show.

"What did you do, you bitch?" Krissy said.

Mina walked toward her, aware of the other kids' eyes on her.

"Little old me? This little trailer park girl?"

"I hate you," Krissy said.

Mina balled her fist and punched the other girl hard in the cheek. She fell on her back. Mina waited for her to get up, but she stayed on the ground, holding her face.

In the backseat, Gabe lay on his side. Mina raised his shirt and checked the wounds from the wolf's teeth. They spread out from his beltline to his neck, each wound the size of a jagged quarter. In the back, on the floorboard, Erin was laid out, snoring. Lucas sat in the passenger's seat.

"Put Erin on her side in case she pukes," Mina said.

Lucas did as he was told, returning to the passenger's seat when it was done.

"You're driving," she said.

He slid behind the wheel without speaking.

Mina took her place in the passenger seat. She flipped down the visor and examined her face, tracing the long wound with her finger. It began at her hairline and dipped to the edge of her eye crease. It was beautiful.

Lucas started the car. At the edge of the field, police lights emerged.

19 / PAPA LEO TRIES TO REMEMBER

Sometimes things set before Leo's eyes plainly, out in the open. Things like ideas, memories, and people. He could walk over and pick them up off the shelf like a trinket or a book. He could hold them in his hands, and they were real, tangible. But sometimes the things on the shelf appeared behind wavy glass, like that of an old building, or the stained glass of a church window. Sometimes they fell to the bottom of a deep pond. He could see their shape, make out their color, even their texture, the way they would feel if he could touch them, but they were beyond his reach. There might be an idea of a thing, of a memory, but the tangible aspects of it, the complete thought...These were unreachable, resting in the clay at the bottom.

When Gabe was laid out on his bed in the basement with Lilyfax bent over him, cleaning each wound with alcohol, the world had been crystal clear. Papa Leo knew who he was, where he was, what he must do. Anger rose within him as quick as water rises in a flash flood. He studied the jagged wounds on the boy, not unlike the wound he carried for years, and still bore the scar of. Later, in the bathroom, he'd pulled up his shirt and looked at it. Where the row of teeth and the tusk had punctured his skin when he was just a boy. And just as the memories of who he was and what he must do were lucid for him, so too was the memory of the girl, his girl—Lilyfax—pulling him out of the jaws of the beast that day, midway up Mulwin Rock, out behind the old church that no longer stood. He could see Lilyfax's face as she did it, seeing her face in every memory and moment since that day. Each nightly kiss at the icebox before they turned off the light. Each morning hug. And how every time, out of the thousands, he'd bent slightly to kiss her forehead. Her face was never obscured like the objects below the water in the pond. He always knew her face, even when words jumbled nonsensically in his head and he was unsure of everything, making him angry and nervous. It was as if time ran together where she was concerned. The mature woman before him, the defiant girl she'd been, with the devilish widow's peak and her ever-present mischievous streak—he saw all the versions of her. She became ever more beautiful to him as time passed, as if she were a thing polished by wind and sand, forces that destroyed other, less permanent things. They only made her stronger, more refined. The girl and the woman were the same, and he never had to reach into the pond for her. She was always there, just as she'd said in the beginning, that day she'd held his hand and whispered, "I've always known you."

But everything else, everything else but Lilyfax, was and could be washed away. And when he sat on the bed beside Gabe—Gabe, his precious grandson—he knew what he had to do. It was obvious and tangible, as if he held it in his hand. Coming for his grandson was a step too far for the Red Wolf. He would have to go after him now. He knew where Lilyfax hid his guns. He might not remember his damned name tomorrow, or where he left the Phillips head screwdriver—the one he kept in the house that kept disappearing, almost daily—but he could almost smell the steel of the guns, his handgun and the over under, no matter what. He always found them, no matter how elaborately she hid them, and maybe his remembering was for this purpose. His purpose. Like God himself knew that Leo needed to find them, needed to slay Ezra, the wolf, perhaps the last thing he would do before he forgot everything and the world went black.

It wasn't about the hunter that kept trespassing, although that son of a bitch deserved a slug too, but to protect his own against the darkness that lurked in the trees, the way the ancient wulvers had done so long ago. Ezra was too far gone now. He was unsavable. He had to die. What was it they'd called him so many years ago? *The Little Priest.* Yes, that was it. That was the nickname they'd teased Ezra with when he was young, his black hair slicked back like crow feathers. It was one thing for Ezra to be on the other side of town, wallowing in his own darkness. It would have been one thing if he'd come after Leo. But to come after Gabriel? Leo knew he'd have to stand against the beast. No one else would or could. And in that form, when Ezra became the wolf...in that form, he was too strong to kill. Leo would have to find the man. A man has flesh, fragile flesh that can be torn.

Leo would have to find Ezra when he walked about town as a human, as the preacher man. He'd have to shoot him down like a dog before he had the chance to change. He would likely get caught. Someone would see him, or the police would in some way trace it all back to him. He calculated all the ways they'd do this, drawing upon his own time on the Asheville Police Department, first as a beat cop, then later as a detective. Yes, they'd find him. Eventually. He'd go to jail. Die there. Nobody would believe the story of how this preacher, this wolf in sheep's clothing, was also a monster. Leo would go to jail, and he was fine with that. He'd lived his life. Well, he was fine with it all except for losing Lilyfax. He pictured her visiting him at the penitentiary. How they'd long to touch each other, how there would be glass between them. How those last kisses, each night in the kitchen before bed, would end. It was horrible to contemplate, and yet it must be done. He'd finally be locked up just like his old man had been. There was no other way.

He was thinking about it, forming a plan for how to deal with the Red Wolf, when Gabe's eyes popped open, and he sat up in bed, shaking. Papa Leo put his hand on Gabe's shoulder.

"What is it, boy?"

Gabe looked at him sideways, as if his neck couldn't turn his head. "Nightmares. Nightmares upon nightmares."

"They're all over now. Once you have them, they're gone. They can't return unless you keep figuring on them, rolling them over, inviting them back. You understand?"

"Yes, Papa Leo." Gabe relaxed and eased his head back onto the pillow.

Papa Leo brushed the hair from Gabe's eyes. Suddenly, the water deepened, and he looked down into the depths of the pond where the boy slept, all the other objects and ideas Leo had been contemplating beside him in the silt. They looked old and covered in moss, as if time had passed them by. He would have to do whatever it was that he had been thinking of doing soon. But that was just it. He couldn't remember what he had been thinking about.

What was it? The plans he had been making? They were important, but they were slipping from him down into the depths, beyond his reach.

He looked at the boy, and something bubbled up. He laughed out loud—a big hearty laugh like his daddy used to have when he thought of a joke. The boy on the bed opened his eyes and smiled.

"What's so funny?" the boy asked. Leo suddenly did not know the boy, but he did seem familiar, maybe because he looked like someone else, perhaps someone he'd seen in a movie.

"I just thought of something funny," Papa Leo said.

"What's that?" the boy asked. He had earnest eyes, the kind that told you he cared about what you had to say, and Leo studied their deep brown color, the flecks of gold that caught in the light from the high basement window to the east.

"You know, people can put on airs," Papa Leo said.

"Yes," the boy said.

"They put on airs and get all gussied up in their fancy clothes and walk with their chests poked out and want you to think how they're really somebody," he said.

"Yes, Papa," the boy said.

Leo didn't know why the boy called him Papa. That didn't make sense, but his face was kind enough, so he let it pass. Maybe the boy—the knowledge of the boy—was in one of those wavy boxes at the bottom of the pond.

"Then you might see a man in his fancy clothes, chin so high he can't hardly see out his eyes. You might see that son of a bitch in the bathroom. He might step away from the urinal, nod his head at you, and just walk out of the bathroom without washing his goddamned hands."

The boy laughed, a little uncomfortably.

"I once saw the mayor in the toilet. Short, smug bastard. Always dressed just so, you know what I mean? Always had his hair just perfect. A ring on his pinkie finger. That kind of bastard. He come out of the stall and walked right past the wash station."

The boy smiled again. There was something kind about the smile. A smile that put people at ease.

"So I seen the mayor, in all his finery, completely decked out, shoes shined up perfect, pretty silk tie, white shirt. Suit. He goes in the bathroom, walks out without washing his hands and then he's shaking every damn body's hand in the whole room. Right there, after just handling his damned old pecker."

"Gross," the boy said.

"It's one thing if you're out in the woods and there ain't no bathroom, no sink. And out there you won't be shaking nobody's hand no way."

The boy winced, as if in pain.

"What's wrong with you, boy?" Papa Leo asked.

The boy seemed confused. "Just my side again."

"What happened to your side?"

The boy furrowed his brow. He didn't say anything, just looked away. Papa Leo reached down and pulled up the boy's shirt. There were a number of wounds spread out on his belly and across his chest, each covered with a piece of gauze and held in place by medical tape.

"Looks like something got ahold of you good," Papa Leo said.

"Yeah, something did," said the boy.

Papa Leo looked around the room. He wasn't sure where he was. It looked like someone's basement, turned into a bedroom.

"Is this your room?" he asked the boy.

"Yes, Papa Leo," the boy said. "You set it up for me. Built this bed. Don't you remember?"

There was something like pity in the boy's eyes, and it flipped a switch inside Leo. He didn't like that look of pity, the way the boy looked at him like he was some fragile thing. The boy didn't know a goddamned thing about him. The things he'd seen. He was the kind of man who had done things in his life. Struggled, fought, scraped by. He'd been in fights with people. He couldn't picture them at the moment, see the faces of people he'd beaten, defended himself against, but they were there, he was sure of it. He pictured the face of a man; it was a mugshot, black and white. The face was clean in the picture, but Leo saw it bloodied, the man's nose mashed out flat. Leo knew he'd done it, beat the man to a pulp. But he couldn't think of why. There must have been a reason. A damned good reason.

But this boy, looking at him with pity in his eyes. *Damn him to hell.* Leo wasn't one to abide fools, so he turned his back to the boy. He wasn't going to hit him like the man in the picture, but he wanted to.

Then a woman came into the room. She had white hair up in a

bun, held up with two sticks at cross angles. She was beautiful, and Leo knew somehow that she belonged to him, and he belonged to her, but he didn't know her name right away. She was carrying a bowl of something warm, steam rising toward her chin.

"Good," she said. "You're awake." She was talking to the pitying boy on the bed.

"Sit up," she said. And the boy did, wincing. The beautiful woman set the bowl in the boy's lap. Grits. There was a pat of butter on top, rapidly melting into a swirl of yellow.

"I used to eat grits when I was in the Marine Corps," Leo said.

"It wasn't as good as mine," the woman said.

"I don't doubt that," Leo said. "You look like a woman who knows how to make them good. The good old-fashioned kind on the stove, stirred slow. In the military, they made it watery, and it had no flavor. No salt, no pepper, nothing."

"Oh, mine is better than that," said the woman. She looked at the boy, and when she did, her face lit up bright as the stars. She had a dimple at the edge of her cheek, and when Papa Leo saw it, he felt his stomach dip. He wanted to put his lips into the dimple.

"I joined up soon as they let me," Papa Leo said. He felt around in his pocket. There was a pack of cigarettes in there, and he took it out. They were Camels. He felt in the other pocket for the box of wooden matches he somehow knew was there. Somehow, the matches and cigarettes were familiar things that were present when everything else faded. The dimple on this beautiful woman—it was the same way. Leo smiled at her and hoped she'd smile back. She did.

He lit the cigarette and spit out a flake of tobacco that stuck to his tongue.

"Would you mind going outside with that cigarette?" she asked. She nodded at the boy when she said it, like the boy was too precious for cigarette smoke. Papa Leo looked at him. He ate his grits slowly, like he didn't much care for them, after this woman had gone to all that trouble. At that moment, he hated the boy and his damned pity, a brat that didn't appreciate good food put right in front of him. Leo wanted to leave the room, but he didn't want to leave her presence. He couldn't bear the thought of being outside when she was inside. He looked her up and down. She had long legs, below a hippy skirt with bright streaks of color. She was long and lean, and carried herself with magical elegance. She held her chin up, but not in a haughty way; the tilt of her chin said she knew who she was, thank you very much. Leo wanted to follow her wherever she went. Just to look at her would be enough.

"Yes, ma'am," he said anyway, remembering her request to take the cigarette outside on account of the fragile boy on the bed. He felt a sharp pain in his side when he stood; it felt like someone had stuck him with a screwdriver.

"They almost didn't let me in the Marines," he said. "On account of me being wounded." He pulled up his shirt and felt the scars there. He remembered the way the military nurse had examined the wounds, tracing them with her fingers. The way she'd shaken her head slowly as if he were too damaged to fight those Korean bastards. This boy had similar jagged wounds.

"You poor thing," the beautiful woman said. She bent down and looked at the scars like it was the first time she'd ever seen them. "But scars on a man can be attractive. I'm sure the nurse had to let you in on account of how the scars just made you more handsome, even more handsome than you already are."

Leo smiled, meeting her eyes, and had to look away. How did this beautiful woman, in this strange basement, know about the nurse? Did she really find him handsome?

"They almost didn't let me in on account of it," he repeated. "I was trying to get in the Marines so I could go kill those sons of bitches over there, you know, during the war."

"You were very brave," the beautiful woman said.

"I don't know if I was brave or just full of piss and vinegar," Leo said. He laughed, wincing when the pain returned.

"How'd you get that scar?" the boy asked. He had straightened up now, holding the bowl of grits in his lap.

Leo's eyes dropped to the floor. "I don't know, but it was very painful."

"You were gored by a boar," the beautiful woman said. "Remember?"

He tried to remember, reaching into the pond for one of the boxes on the bottom. It had the answer. It had to be there somewhere.

"Seems like it burned when it happened, and all the time after," he said, after a while.

The beautiful woman turned to the boy and said, "He was gored by a wild boar. I was afraid he'd bleed out before we could get him help."

Leo studied the woman's face. How did she know things about him that he didn't know about himself? He saw her face, a younger version of her with dark hair. He saw her pulling him along the ground after he'd been wounded. She was strong for a woman; stronger than many men. Images flipped by. A beast growling at him, a boar, but with a long snout and rows of teeth like a jackal.

"You were there," he said to her.

"I was there," she said. "I've always been there."

"You've always been there," Leo repeated. And somehow, he knew she had been.

Then the waves washed over him, and he felt his skin prick. He rubbed his free hand over his chest. He almost knew the boy on the bed again, knew the boy was bound to him in some way. He studied his face. He knew he knew the boy, but he wasn't sure how.

"Thom?" he said to the boy, thinking the boy was his son, the one he'd sometimes called Junior.

The boy looked to Leo, then to the beautiful woman.

"I'm his son, Thom's son," he said.

"Thom has a son?" Leo said.

Thom. Papa Leo could see him—the son that bore his first name. But Thom couldn't have a son of his own. He was just a boy himself. None of this made sense. Pictures of his son flooded him. He saw the boy, the way he'd taken his little red wagon to the top of the crest on the gravel road out in front of the house. Before there were any other houses or that junkyard on Elk Mountain. Thom had raced down the steep hill and hit a tree. He'd laid in this very room, and Papa Leo had seen to him on a morning just like this. Doctored his wounds in this very room, sitting on the edge of the bed with a cigarette, talking to the boy about how he needed to be more careful, that he was going to kill his damn self if he didn't watch it. Thom had nodded, tears on his cheeks. Then the beautiful woman—Papa Leo looked up at her now, his Lilyfax—she had poured peroxide on the scuffs on his knees and elbows. No, it wasn't peroxide, it was mercurochrome. He could see the red streaks on the boy's limbs before Lilyfax applied the Band-Aids.

"Your boy—our boy—was the one you called Thom," Lilyfax said. "This is his son, you remember, *Gabriel*."

Papa Leo looked at the boy on the bed. He did not remember any of it. Thom growing up, marrying, having a son of his own. This boy, Gabriel. He could not remember any of it. Time had rushed past him like a fast-moving river that washes away its banks, robbing him of everything.

"Of course, I do," he said, faking a smile. He reached for the boy's knee, gripping it over the blanket. "Of course I remember Thom and this here boy."

The boy smiled at him, pity returning. Papa Leo looked away as Lilyfax put her hand on his shoulder.

"You've always been brave about things," she said.

"Brave or full of piss and vinegar," Papa Leo said.

"Maybe some of both," she said, smiling.

When the smile came, he calmed for a moment. Until other images trickled into his mind. His eyes darkened. *The Little Priest*," he whispered.

"What?" said Lilyfax.

"Oh, nothing," Leo said, taking his hand off the boy's knee and standing.

He thought about his guns. The pistol, a revolver he'd been given when he retired from the police force as a retirement present. The shotgun he'd bought for himself many years ago. He remembered the day he bought it. A man behind the counter set it down on a cloth for him to examine. The way the shells had clacked in the box when the clerk pulled them out. What store had it been? Maybe Western Auto? Or was it Sears & Roebuck? He remembered bringing it home, shining the barrel with a handkerchief. The words *Made in Italy* engraved elegantly in the steel.

Then his cigarette burned his fingers. It had burned down to the quick. The burn snapped him out of his recollections, and thoughts swamped his mind, one after another, too quick for him to process. He thought of how Lilyfax hid the shotgun in the attic last time. His brain ticked off all the places it could be now and settled on the other basement room—the one adjoining this one—where the furnace was. He saw the groove in the ductwork rising from the old furnace, where it flattened out on top. That's where the guns would be. He was sure of it.

He looked at Lilyfax and smiled. He took the cigarette butt and flipped it into the toilet in the bathroom across the hall, focusing on the furnace where the guns were hidden. He had to remember all this. He couldn't let it slip away, or he would fail. He walked back into the room and kissed Lilyfax on the cheek, right at the place her dimple formed when she smiled. He couldn't let on about the guns. About what he had to do.

Papa Leo walked over to the bed and kissed Gabe on the forehead. It all came back to him. The Red Wolf. The way it had attacked the boy, though he lied about it to try to keep it from his grandfather. When Lilyfax lifted his shirt to doctor his wounds, Leo was able to see the outline of his teeth, perfectly spaced apart. He didn't know how the boy's shirt hadn't been torn, but it didn't matter. He knew what he had to do. Now he just had to keep a few things straight in his head: the place where the guns were hidden, Ezra, and where he needed to go to find the man. He wasn't sure where Ezra kept house these days, but he knew where to start. The Church of Hosanna. Ezra would show up there eventually. And when he did, Leo would put an end to him, once and for all.

20 / GABE & THE LIFTING FOG

It was mid-November before Gabe's wounds eased. He'd been in a deep fog in the days after the bonfire and the Red Wolf's bite. For nearly a week, he'd felt ever hungover, but not from the mushrooms or pot. It was like something new and dark wound its way through his veins. He couldn't stop thinking about the Red Wolf, feeling strangely connected to it now, as though their fates were so intertwined there was no altering the trajectory upon which they both traveled. Gabe felt it in his bones—he'd see the wolf again. It would come for him and the twins.

In those dim early days, he slept all day and all night, rising above the surface only to slip quickly beneath it again. The only moments of brightness came when Mina appeared at his bedside, her smile a bright jewel that hung in the air, pushing back the darkness at the edges of the room that threatened to rush in again.

Though the world was a fog for Gabe, Papa Leo had fallen under an even deeper shroud of dementia since Halloween. Often, he would hear Papa Leo's feet on the stairs, and the old man would appear at the landing, surprised to find him there. Or perhaps he was surprised it was Gabe and not his father. He had come to call Gabe by his father's name, Thom. The looks Papa Leo had for him were almost scary, as if he thought he'd come across a stranger in his basement each time. Some foul intruder to be expelled. Once, Papa Leo came down the stairs and stared at Gabe for a solid minute before taking out his pipe and lighting it, something he normally wouldn't do indoors, as LilyMa forbade it. The old man stood there and smoked the pipe, the tip clicking against his teeth, his eyes on Gabe like he was figuring out how to deal with the stranger in the basement.

"And just who in the hell are you?" he asked.

"I'm Gabe," Gabe had answered.

Papa Leo had looked around the basement as if lost and said, "I've no memory of this room."

Sometimes, Gabe heard Papa Leo yelling at LilyMa upstairs, her occasionally yelling back at him. He could never quite make out the words, but Papa Leo seemed to grow angrier each day, and more than once he'd apparently hurled something across the room. It wasn't clear if Papa Leo was throwing things at LilyMa or if he was just throwing breakable things against the walls to vent his frustrations.

As scary as Papa Leo could sometimes be, LilyMa worried Gabe most. He remembered her silently crying the day after the bonfire as she dressed his wounds and traced their outlines with her finger. When she became aware of Gabe watching her, she quickly wiped away her tears and forced a smile, her voice rising with fake happiness, perhaps to ease his worry. She seemed lost in thought, figuring on something deep in the recesses of her mind. Gabe injured and Papa Leo losing it...perhaps it was all becoming too much for her.

"These aren't so deep," she said, putting a square of gauze over each wound, affixed with medical tape. "I don't think you'll scar."

Gabe tried to smile back at her. He put his hand on hers, but she moved away. He wondered if she knew about the Red Wolf, that it was coming for Gabe and the twins.

"Lay back and rest," she ordered. "Let me be about my work."

Mina had been different since the bonfire. When Gabe was well enough to go back to school, they rode together in the Magic Carpet Ride, mostly in silence with Mina sitting so far against the door there was no chance of holding hands. Sometimes he tried to find a classic rock station on the old AM radio in the car, but whenever he found a station, it was inevitably drowned out in a mile or two by a gospel station with a stronger signal. It was like preachers on the radio were all the people of Asheville had a taste for. It was strange to have a preacher barge in over the Rolling Stones. Eventually, Gabe stopped trying. He thought about the arguments he could use with Papa Leo to get him to agree to installing a tape deck with an FM receiver in the car. Of course, with the way Papa Leo was going, it might be

LilyMa he'd need to convince. Papa Leo wouldn't recognize Gabe or the Magic Carpet Ride soon.

Erin and Lucas visited them once in Gabe's basement bedroom, the door open and cool fall air whooshing in as they laughed and drank soda. He left the door open each night after dinner in hopes Mina would come by, as she sometimes did. Of course, he would have happily rushed through the woods to visit her, but there was no place to hang out. Mina's dad was not a fan of boys coming to visit his daughters, let alone sitting in their bedrooms.

Most nights, Mina didn't come, and Gabe would pass the time reading or plucking at the upright piano. He didn't remember much about Halloween, just snippets of images: the moments Mina's body hovered over his, the electric power of her lips on his, the excruciating pain when the Red Wolf bit into his body, somehow remaining invisible. What haunted him most was the music he played that night, Mina's song that stretched out in floating piano keys on the clouds and along her bare back.

It was the only song Gabe played these days, constantly forming the chords with his left hand, the trance-like melody with his right. While he could remember some of it, most of the notes escaped him. He was left with maybe a third of what should be there, and he wasn't sure if he'd forgotten part of the song or if he'd never finished composing it to begin with. He also had the sense that, in the lamplight of his basement bedroom, he simply could not reach all the notes that needed to be played. Somehow, under the low sky in the field, when the keys stretched out along Mina's back, his hands seemed much larger, allowing him to reach notes across multiple octaves at once. Still, he made progress on the song each week, remembering more of the notes and writing them down in his staff bar notebook, terrified he would forget them.

As fall wore on, the days grew shorter and the nights came on quick and cold, and even though Gabe had to dress in layers and even though Papa Leo complained about how his hard-earned money wasn't intended to heat the whole goddamned outdoors, he kept the door open each night as he read or played Mina's Song.

One night as he waited for her, gooseflesh spread over his arms and legs. He stared down the hall from his bedroom in the direction of the open door. He was suddenly afraid. He'd left the door open on the off chance Mina would come visit, but an open door could bring other, uninvited visitors. Like the Red Wolf. Gabe stood and walked toward the hallway, hearing a growl beneath his feet. He thought of running, but he knew there was no escaping the wolf's reach. Without even showing itself on Halloween, the wolf had reached through the night air to tear into his flesh. What hope of outrunning the Red Wolf did he have if it could do such things?

Outside, he heard Samson yapping.

"Come in here, Samson!" Gabe said.

The dog appeared, running around his feet. He reached down to pet him, but he was too excited to stand still. Samson ran out of the bedroom toward the open door.

"Come back!" Gabe said.

There were footsteps in the hall. He froze. They were lighter than Papa Leo's and didn't bear the thump of his work boots. LilyMa never entered this way.

From the shadows, Mina emerged. Her hair was down, cascading bright red over her shoulders. She wore Gabe's brown leather bomber jacket and a black turtleneck sweater with a pair of Erin's sister's old blue jeans. There were holes in the knees.

"Did you leave this door open for me?"

"I was hot," Gabe said, smiling.

"It's forty degrees," she said.

Samson ran back in the room, sprinting between them, as if he couldn't make up his mind about who to seek affection from.

"Some kind of guard dog you got there." Mina laughed.

"Nothing gets past Samson," Gabe said. He reached down and rubbed the dog's belly. Samson stopped sprinting and rolled over on his back. His leg kicked as if Gabe had found his funny bone.

"Hopefully, whoever breaks in won't know how to give great belly rubs," Mina said.

"I believe he'd step over my dead body for a belly rub," Gabe said.

Mina sat down on the piano bench. She laid her hands on the keys, sliding her fingertips between the black keys.

"You know, I heard you playing."

"You did? When?" Gabe gave Samson one last pat on the head and joined her on the bench.

"In the woods on the way over. It sounded nice."

He furrowed his brow. "I don't quite have it yet."

"Have what?"

"Just something I've been working on."
"Will you play it for me?"
"It's not ready."
"Just play what you know."
Gabe put his hands on the keys. "Soon," he said.
"Is it the song you played in the field? My song?"
Gabe looked down at the keys. "Yes."
"My song in B minor?" She said, thrumming her fingers over the black keys.
"You remembered?"
"Of course, I remember."
"I know this is going to sound crazy, but I learned the whole thing in the field. Played it all out over and over. Only now I can't get it quite right, like maybe I'm not good enough to play it."
"Want to hear something crazier?" she said.
"What's that?"
"I heard it too. That night in the field, I heard you playing it."
Gabe looked at her.
Mina said, "Play it for me now. Please?"
He played the opening bars of *Fur Elise*.
"I'm pretty sure that's not it."
"What?" He grinned. "I made this little tune up, just for you."
Mina rolled her eyes. "Okay, Ludwig."
He let the tune morph into a ragtime song he learned when he first started lessons.
"Oh yeah," Mina said. "This is more me, to be honest."
"I thought you'd like it."
Gabe stopped playing when Samson began growling at the door. He bared his teeth.
"What is it, little guy?" Mina said.
Samson ran down the hall and outside, barking.
"Samson, come back!" Gabe called after him.
"Probably chasing a cat," Mina said. "There's like a million cats in your yard, you know that right?"
He stared down the hall to the dark doorway. After a moment, he sat down on the bed.
"Thank you for playing for me," Mina said.
"You're welcome."
"Thank you for playing everything *but* my song."

"Soon, I promise."

"You've been saying that since Halloween."

"I want to have it just right for you."

Mina looked him in the eyes, then quickly away. Maybe it had been the wrong thing to say.

"Gabe," she said, her eyes falling to the floor. "I'm not who you think I am."

He didn't answer right away, wondering if he'd been too direct in talking about Mina's song, letting his feelings for her be so transparent.

"I'm not who you think I am," she repeated. She walked over and sat beside him on the bed.

"You mean you're not the cool, brilliant girl I think you are? Are you trying to tell me you're not that cool?" Gabe said.

"Your wounds. The night at the bonfire. It's my fault, all of it."

He shook his head. "No, Mina, you don't understand."

She stood and walked to the corner of the room. "No, Gabe, *you* don't understand."

"The wolf, Mina. I saw it before Halloween night. It killed my parents. It's like something out of a horror movie. It is after me. It's stalking me. I put you in danger that night."

Mina turned to face him with tears in her eyes and shook her head.

"My papaw, Mina," Gabe said. "He has something to do with it all, too. I don't really know what, but the Red Wolf came here, to the woods right behind the house. Papa Leo talked to it like he knew it. Like he'd known it for years. Like they were old friends."

Mina said, "I'm not talking about the Red Wolf, Gabe. I'm talking about me."

He approached her, but she turned away.

"There's something inside me," she said. "Something dark."

"What do you mean?"

"I can...do things," she said. "See things."

Gabe nodded. His blood ran cold thinking about what she might mean.

"Erin is going on that Purity Sojourn this weekend," she said. "I have a bad feeling about it."

Gabe shook his head. "I know. I wish she wouldn't go. Her parents suck for making her."

"I keep imagining her getting hurt somehow. It's like I can see it," Mina said. "Who thinks like that?"

"Erin hurt?"

"It's just," Mina started, "I thought I could control all this, but I can't."

"Control what, Mina? Do you mean you and me?"

"You and me?" she faced him. "What about you and me?"

"I don't know, isn't that what this is about? Is that why you're saying all this?"

"Everything isn't about us, Gabe, don't you know that?" Her voice cracked.

He looked at his feet. He held up his hand, then let it drop again.

"You're just really important to me," he said. "I don't mean to always make it about that. About us, I mean. You're just something special."

Mina approached him and put her hand on his chest. "You're important to me, too. But there's so much more going on. I don't understand why this is all happening. Why us, you know?"

"I'm getting better," Gabe said. "My sores are almost healed. I'll barely have any scars."

"Gabe," she said. "I have wounds, too, only no one can see them."

He put his hand over hers on his chest and looked at the scar on her face.

"Show me," he said. "I can handle it."

She looked up into his eyes. "What if you can't?"

"I can," he said. "I'm going to figure this whole thing out. The Red Wolf, my grandfather, all of it. I am going to figure it out and I'm going to take care of it somehow. Then we can get back to normal. We can just *be*. You know?"

"Just be," she said. She looked at his lips, then back to his eyes.

"Yeah," he said. "We can just be, I don't know, normal."

Finally, she smiled. She put a hand to his cheek. "I think..." She trailed off. "I think we're way past that now."

"Probably," he said, matching her smile. He looked at the turtleneck, taking in the way the black fabric contrasted with her perfect porcelain skin.

She leaned toward him, their lips close. Gabe closed his eyes and moved closer. Their lips had only just touched when they heard Samson yelping outside. No longer barking—crying out in pain.

They ran out into the night air.

Samson's cries continued for another moment before stopping abruptly.

"Over there, it came from over there!" Mina said, pointing to the first cluster of trees near the driveway. They ran into the woods and looked around, but nothing was there. They stopped running, facing each other, panting. They listened for Samson but heard nothing.

"Gabe, there," Mina said. She pointed at something on the ground.

He bent down and scooped it up. It was Samson's orange collar with its small, bone-shaped tag with his name and his county rabies vaccination tag.

"Samson!" he called out.

At the house, the front porch lights clicked on. Papa Leo and LilyMa walked out onto the porch.

"What was that?" LilyMa said.

"Samson!" Gabe called out again.

Mina said, "Let me see the collar."

Gabe handed it to her, and she turned it around and around in her hands.

"What happened?" LilyMa asked. "Was that Samson?"

"He's just slipped out of his collar," Gabe said. "Don't worry, we'll find him. We're going into the woods after him."

"Let me get you some flashlights," LilyMa said, stepping into the house.

"Oh my God," Mina whispered. "There's blood on the collar." She held up her fingers to show Gabe that they were streaked with blood.

Gabe ran to the front porch to retrieve the flashlights from LilyMa.

"Who are y'all looking for?" Papa Leo said.

"Oh, it's nothing. We'll be right back, Papa Leo," Gabe said.

The old man lit his pipe. "Well, don't stay in the woods too long this time of night. I'm sure whoever you're looking for will come back soon. It's a pretty night. Maybe they just wanted to take a walk, get outside for a while." He turned and walked into the house with his lit pipe.

Gabe and Mina raced through the woods, their flashlight beams bouncing in front of them. Every so often, they would stop and call out to the dog. In the distance, an owl cried. Mina trained her flashlight up into the trees where the owl's yellow eyes glowed like torched coals.

"Do you think an owl attacked him?" Mina asked.

"Maybe," Gabe said.

They walked on for a few more minutes. They were climbing a small ridge when he spotted something ahead of them. He sprinted toward the small body nestled in a pile of leaves.

"Samson," he said, approaching slowly. "You're okay, boy."

When he reached the body, he shook it gently. It did not move. He scooped it up and turned back, Mina's flashlight in his face.

"I got him, but he's not moving," Gabe said. Then he looked down.

Samson's head was missing. Where it should be, part of the spine protruded. Blood ran through Gabe's fingers and down his hands. He dropped the body.

"No owl did this," he said. He sank to his knees, an ache spreading through his stomach and up into his chest. "No. No. No," he said. He rubbed his small rear leg, the one Papa Leo always called Samson's chicken leg.

Mina was beside him; her body shook, her shoulders rising as she caught her breath. She began to cry. They sat on the ground together, shoulder to shoulder, heads touching as they sobbed.

"I don't understand," Gabe said.

"He did it." Mina sobbed. "He'll never leave us alone."

Gabe looked around for the head. He felt sick run all through him.

"We have to bury him out here. We can't let LilyMa or Papa Leo know. They won't be able to handle this."

"Yes," Mina said. "Okay."

They cried as they pulled back the blanket of leaves covering the ground, and their fingers hit the cold earth. A few more weeks, and the ground might have been too hard to turn by hand, but they were able to move the dirt. Darkness had fully fallen before they had a hole deep enough for Samson's little body.

"We have to find the head," Gabe said. He picked up Samson's little body and placed it carefully in the shallow grave. When his fingers touched the open wound at the neck, grazing the little spine, his stomach gave way. He dropped the body and sprinted to a nearby tree to vomit. When he returned, Mina was raking dirt over the body.

"But the head," he said.

"It's not here," she said. "He took it."

Gabe fell to his knees and watched her work. His eyes burned, and tears glazed his cheeks.

"Why?" Gabe asked. "Why did the Red Wolf do this?"

"To hurt you. To hurt us." Mina said. She stood and ran the back of her hand over her forehead. "We have to kill him. I have to kill him. He left us alone for a season, but he's back. He's telling us he's returned for us."

"Mina, no," Gabe said. "I don't want you wrapped up in all this."

She glared at him. "I'm in the thick of it."

Gabe took her by her shoulders and gently turned her to face him. "Mina, the Red Wolf has taken my mama and my daddy. It wants me and the twins. If I come out of this alive, I can't lose you, too."

"You won't," Mina said, her face hardened. Her eyes changed; she looked like someone else.

Gabe tried to recognize her features, to reckon with the girl in front of him. She wasn't Mina somehow. She looked around, up into the trees, and around the mountains, illuminated by a quarter moon.

"Maybe," she said. "Maybe he's still here."

Her face continued to change. Gabe let go of her shoulders and took a step back.

"If he's still here," she said, "I'll find him."

There came a rustling in the tops of the trees. Something formed there in the gloom. There were dozens of them, creatures of some sort, slithering around the limbs like snakes at first, then racing from limb to limb, jumping from tree to tree like monkeys. He couldn't make out what they were, but where there had been dozens, there were now hundreds. They raced south down the mountain, leaping through the tops of the trees.

"Mina," he said. "What are they?"

Then he looked at her. Her eyes were glazed and white, the irises and pupils gone.

Gabe's heart kicked in his chest.

"Mina?" he said. "What are they?"

"They are me and I am them," she said. "We are many."

21 / REVEREND EZRA & THE CIRCLING VULTURES

The Predicant stood at Ezra's desk early on a Monday morning, and in his hands, he held a red box.

"I've brought you a gift," he said.

When he saw the Predicant's hideous smile, Ezra realized why the man rarely smiled. It was so shocking that he recoiled a bit before quickly recovering to proffer a smile in return. Pale pink lips stretched out to reveal milky white teeth and gums that were almost as white. The Predicant had long white-blond hair with eyebrows and eyelashes that matched and pallid skin that burned easily in the sun. He was much taller than Reverend Ezra, six foot three, with large hands and long, thin fingers. He paired a light pink tie with a tan suit that made his blond hair and anemic flesh appear even more pasty.

It wasn't just the dreadful sight of the thing; smiling was for the unburdened, and like Ezra. The Predicant carried the weight of God's work on his shoulders, the heavy yoke of service. Like Ezra, he was bound to all that should be done—all that must be done—in the name of the Lord. It was like an affliction; gone was the frivolity of human pursuits, the banality of the secular man.

Ezra eyed the red box. "Our gifts are not of this world, Brother Lemuel, but of the one true God."

Lemuel was the Predicant's earthly name. Ezra had bestowed upon him the title of Predicant to reward his faithfulness, rising from deacon to elder to become something more important in the ministry at Hosanna, more important to Reverend Ezra himself.

The Predicant said, "True gifts are bestowed only by God, but I give with all humility." The Predicant's accent was slow and southern, his voice an octave higher than the register of a man.

Ezra took the red box. It was covered with a fine material that felt like silk. He looked up at the Predicant; his grotesque smile widened. Ezra had to look away.

"You must open it," said the Predicant.

Inside was a pair of sunglasses. The lenses were not dark or mirrored. Instead, they were bright red, the frames silver and round.

Ezra beamed, trying to avoid looking at the Predicant's face.

"I do approve the color."

"Try them on," said the Predicant.

"Later, Brother Lemuel. But thank you for your kindness." He closed the box and ran his fingers over the silky texture.

He gestured for the Predicant to sit. He did so, his distorted smile dissipating. Lemuel crossed his legs, so long they bumped the wood panel at the front of Ezra's desk. He clasped his long hands together on his lap.

"I trust," said Ezra, "that the preparations have been made for the Sojourn." For a second, his ankle stung, making him wince.

The Predicant relaxed into the chair. "It will be our most ambitious Sojourn yet."

"Praise the Lord," Ezra said. "How Many?"

"Twenty-seven lost will participate," said the Predicant. "I have seen to the selection of each one personally."

"And you will, of course, see to the sin-purge yourself?"

"Of course."

"Tell me about the selected."

The Predicant pursed his lips. "They are the most troubled, most afflicted we could find. Many use illicit drugs. All have given themselves over to a reprobate lust to one degree or another. Some bask in the plague of homosexuality. One is a wild child, a deacon's daughter."

"Excellent. They must turn from their sinful ways and move into God's light," Ezra said.

"They will turn or suffer," said the Predicant.

"If any cannot be turned," said Ezra, "bring them immediately to me at the Temple."

The Predicant's eyes narrowed. He shifted uneasily in the wooden chair.

Ezra was amused. "Speak, Brother Lemuel. Do not hold your tongue."

"With all due respect, Reverend Ezra, do you think that wise?"

"Is God unwise? Are his ways the ways of fools?"

"It's the Sheriff, my lord," said the Predicant. "He burrows into our flesh like a tick. He continues the search for the young girl, Heidi, who went missing from last year's Sojourn."

"And? What does this have to do with our work?"

"If more of our youth go missing, more trouble will wash upon our shores."

Ezra didn't respond. He tented his fingers in front of him, looking at Lemuel.

"It's not just the Sheriff, I'm afraid."

"How's that?"

"I've learned that the Sheriff has asked for additional resources from the state. The SBI is going to take on the investigation. Since no body was ever found, the case remains suspicious."

Ezra rose to peer out the window at the woods beyond the sanctuary. In the trees, there gathered a wake of black vultures.

"If more go missing, the investigation will only escalate," said the Predicant. "I think that's why the sheriff asked to see you."

Ezra ran his fingers over the grain of the wooden walls. He'd chosen a deep cherry wood color and specified the crown molding be thick and substantial. The sheriff had called yesterday to arrange a meeting. *Another meeting.* How many times would he do this? The sheriff was sticking his nose where it didn't belong, but having the state bear down on Hosanna was something else entirely. Yet, men always tried to interfere in the work of God, did they not?

"Let them come. Let all of them come. I fear them not," Ezra said.

"They'll cover the mountains like ants, combing through each blade of grass. They'll be in our financial books; they'll swarm Mulwin Rock. They'll find the Temple."

Ezra met the Predicant's eyes and squinted.

"Then they'll meet the Red Wolf."

The Predicant closed his eyes. "Should we not stick to the poor, the whores down in Asheville? Those that won't be missed?"

Ezra sat, never taking his eyes off the Predicant's. "If they can't be turned, they will serve. God gave us all free will. Let them decide for themselves."

"As you wish," said the Predicant. With that, he rose to his feet.

"Brother Lemuel. Thank you again for the gift."

The smile threatened to return; Ezra averted his eyes.

"But forget not, brother, what we are called to do. We answer not to men. In uniform and otherwise."

"Yes, sir," said the Predicant.

Ezra watched him leave.

The Predicant was close. Close to ascending, just as Ezra had once ascended from human form. His training was well underway. It wouldn't be long before the Predicant would find his own aura, his own darkness to wield. What would the shadow girl do then? He was sure the Predicant would one day be his replacement at the Church of Hosanna. If not him, then whom? Though he had no plans of going anywhere soon. Regardless, the Predicant had the kind of unimpeachable character and drive that was needed. He had the resolve. Because Lemuel had not taken a wife, just as Ezra had not taken a wife, he was not susceptible to many of the evils the world could use to take down a man of God.

The Predicant had no earthly vices that Ezra was aware of. He did not drink, nor smoke, nor indulge in narcotics. He did not seem to desire women the way the other Elders did. Ezra had tempted the man with the girls in the trees, and not once had the Predicant shown a penchant for lust. Because he didn't crave women and had not taken a wife, Ezra had even arranged for him to be tempted by a man. The Predicant had shown no interest in sex with the young male prostitute and had, therefore, passed all of Ezra's tests. In fact, the Predicant had invited the prostitute to church.

There were two things, however, that gave Ezra pause. One was the unnatural smile of the man. How could he lead a flock of his own if his very smile could terrify small children? Perhaps he could be taught to smile more gently, with the kind of warm smile Ezra himself used to bend others to his will? Or maybe he should be taught to never smile, and in that way come across as a kind of Puritan, one who didn't smile because he was ever on fire for God. The second factor in Ezra's hesitation was the very thing that had drawn him to the Predicant in the first place: his ambition. He was a seeker, like Ezra, with an insatiable desire for knowledge. He constantly read books on philosophy, the occult, and theology. Being a seeker was good. Yet sometimes, when the Predicant looked at Ezra with a sidelong stare, Ezra imagined the Predicant sizing him up, considering what it would take to seize ultimate power for himself, to wrest control of the kingdom from Ezra before his time, the same way Lucifer rose to challenge God.

Ezra walked to his desk and opened the red box. He took out the glasses, carefully unfolding the arms, and put them on. They fit perfectly, the world awash with scarlet light.

It was midmorning before Sister Margaret ushered the Sheriff into his office. Ezra stood on the wine-colored area rug in the middle of the room to meet him, having donned his suit jacket and put on a purple tie.

"Sheriff Barnaby," he said, gripping the Sheriff's hand hard. "What a pleasure to see you again."

Barnaby was a broad-shouldered man with short brown hair, feathered straight back on his head. Though he was a bit soft in the middle now that he was in his fifties, his frame was still athletic and strong. He had the thick, tan neck of a farmer and wore a khaki-colored uniform with sharply pressed creases. He held his hat in his hand.

"Thank you for seeing me on such short notice," said the Sheriff.

"Of course," Ezra said, gesturing to the pair of chairs near his desk.

"I need your help," the Sheriff said, placing his hat on the edge of the desk.

Ezra eyed the hat with disdain. "I am always at your service, Sheriff, but we've covered this ground before. I am sure I don't have anything new to tell you about our sweet Heidi. Such a shame she's still missing after all this time."

"I'm not here about the girl," said the Sheriff. He pursed his lips.

"No?" Ezra said. "Then please tell me how I can help. Is it time for the yearly department fundraiser?" Ezra opened his desk drawer as if looking for the church checkbook.

"No, sir." The Sheriff ran his fingers through his hair and placed his hands on his knees. "We do that in July. I'm here about one of your congregants."

"Okay," said Ezra. "Who might that be?"

"Are you familiar with a woman named Gail Owenby?" The Sheriff retrieved a small notepad and pen from his pocket.

Ezra felt cold run over his skin. He pushed it away. "Sister Gail. Of course. She's a wonderful woman of God. Married to one of our Elders, in fact. Is she in some kind of trouble?"

"Maybe," said the Sheriff. "We don't know much yet, but it appears she's gone missing."

"Missing?" said Ezra. "My goodness. Are you sure?"

"We're sure," said the Sheriff. "From what we've been able to piece together, no one has seen her for at least three weeks."

"Is that so?" said Ezra. He recalled her unwanted appearance at the Temple. The sweet smell of fear that pricked her skin, the fine sweat that beaded at her neck. Her foul taste.

"Strange part is her husband, Charles—he never reported her missing. We received a tip from one of the couple's neighbors and a missing person report from one of their children, a daughter, who lives down in Shelby."

"Brother Charles is a stalwart of the faith here at Hosanna. A remarkable man. As I said, he's an Elder. A man of impeccable character, I've found."

"Well, he didn't report his wife missing. Didn't mention it to anyone." Barnaby glared into Ezra's eyes.

"That is odd," Reverend Ezra said, holding the man's gaze. "I remember their daughter from services years ago. She was always quick to volunteer in the nursery. Delightful young woman."

"What do you know about Mr. and Mrs. Owenby? Is there anything you can tell me about their relationship?"

Reverend Ezra shook his head. "I counsel many of the Elders, many of the congregants. They sometimes request prayers for relationship problems, marital issues, that kind of thing. We don't condone divorce as anything other than the terrible sin it is. But I can't recall anything but happiness between those two. Brother Charles is one of the kindest and most devoted husbands I've seen. They seemed quite normal."

"Did you notice her missing?"

"There was a time," answered Ezra with a grand sweep of his palms, "when our congregation was young and small. When I was intimately aware of all our members, their comings and goings. When there were so few of us, I knew when someone skipped a service or was ill, or perhaps when they became caught up in the world and began to backslide. These days, however, with the sanctuary being so immense and us being blessed with so many members, the way our ministry has reached the television and radio, I'm afraid I am unable to keep account of my sheep like I once did."

"I see," said the Sheriff. "So, you haven't noticed Mrs. Owenby missing or Mr. Owenby coming to church without her? From what we can tell, he's continued about his normal life, going to work, attending church, as if he ain't bothered in the least by her absence."

"Soon we'll even be on cable television," said Ezra.

"Tell me about Brother Charles."

"Yes, of course. Brother Charles is a devoted husband," said Ezra. "If his wife were really missing, I can't see him being anything other than deeply distraught."

"Not coming to the police, not telling anyone, not mentioning it all? He hasn't carried on like a man that's distraught." The Sheriff thumbed through his notebook as if looking for something particular. "We've questioned Mr. Owenby a few times now. He's been cooperative, but completely devoid of emotion. If, as you say, he's a devoted husband, that seems a bit odd, don't you think?"

"I am not sure it's odd, Sheriff."

"No?"

"As I said, Brother Charles is a very devoted man. To the church, to his family, to the community. But Sister Gail—"

"What about her?" asked the Sheriff.

"How can I put this politely? My Grandmother would have called her *busy*, if you catch my meaning."

"A gossip? She was one for gossiping, is that what you're saying?"

Ezra shook his head slowly. "I hate to speak ill of her. She meant well. But yes. She was a bit of an unhappy woman, at times, often involving herself in the affairs of others unnecessarily. Asking too many questions, that sort of thing."

"Asking too many questions of whom?"

"No one in particular. Just as I say, utterly *involved*. Perhaps in an unwanted way with some of the other congregants."

"I'll need a list of the people you're talking about. Anyone who can give us insight into their relationship."

"Of course," Reverend Ezra said. "Let me think on it, and I'll provide a list to Sister Margaret out front. You can follow up with her."

"Okay," said the Sheriff, taking down notes on the small notepad. After he stopped writing, he seemed deep in thought, holding the tip of the pen to his lips.

"Well, if there's nothing else I can help you with, Sheriff," said Ezra, starting to rise from his chair.

"One other thing," said the Sheriff. "The daughter in Shelby. Apparently, she talked to her mother on the phone from time to time."

"Always a sweet girl, as I said before," said Ezra.

"Apparently, Mrs. Owenby talked to her daughter about how her husband had begun to withdraw from the home. That he was involved in something unusual with the church."

"Unusual?" asked Ezra.

"Yes, something Mrs. Owenby described to her daughter as *secret* activities. Things Charles wouldn't talk to her about, seemed not to want her to know about. Said he was disappearing after supper each evening till way up in the night or early morning. Got any idea what she might have been talking about?"

Reverend Ezra looked down at the desk, then met the Sheriff's eyes. "We are a traditional church, Sheriff, as you may know. We believe that women have important roles to play in the congregation. Working with the children in Sunday School or Vacation Bible School, for example. And it is also important that strong, Godly women be involved in the counseling of the younger women in the church, that kind of thing. But we believe the ministry, the Elders, the deacons; these roles are exclusively for men, as laid out clearly in the Bible."

"I see," said the Sheriff.

"Brother Charles, being an Elder, had meetings to attend, functions to participate in, the purview of the men of our congregation. Now, most of the women of our church understand this, understand their place in the congregation—that they are to be subservient to their husbands in all things, just as we men must be subservient to God. Some women, however, influenced by the secular world, the evils of humanism, and the wickedness of radical feminism. They will sometimes question these principles. I'm sure you understand, having a wife of your own, how this can be a problem."

"I do have a wife," said the Sheriff. "But what you're saying is Mrs. Owenby disagreed with your ideas about the place of women at Hosanna?"

"I don't know that to be the case, per se," said Ezra. "But if she's describing the humble service of a Godly man in such secret and clandestine terms, then I'm afraid she questioned God's Law. Just as you enforce man's law, Sheriff, the spiritual laws laid out for us by God in the Bible are mine to enforce."

"I see," said the Sheriff.

The Sheriff closed his notepad and put it in his pocket. He carefully clipped the pen beside it.

"I'll check with Sister Margaret in a few days on that list. I need to talk to anyone in the congregation who was close to Sister Gail, get a sense for any activities she was involved in here at the church."

Reverend Ezra smiled, cupping his hands. "Of course. We will provide you with any assistance you need. But one question, Sheriff, if you don't mind?"

"Sure," said the Sheriff.

"Do you not think it possible that Sister Gail has, in fact, simply abandoned her husband? Is it possible that in her sinful questioning, she might have taken up with another man, or even, in this day and age, with a woman?"

"You're suggesting that Mrs. Owenby could have left her husband for another man, or that it's possible she's a lesbian?"

"I would have considered both options impossible, at one time, given all I know about the good sister. But with her questioning God the way she'd come to do, we can't be certain. And if she's done this, run off with another man or in some other way abandoned her husband, she may never be heard from again. She could be in California right now, basking in sin, away from the eyes of her church, away from the eye of God."

Sheriff Barnaby rubbed his chin. "We never rule anything out. Ever. Just like the case of the missing girl from your church last year. We have never ruled anything out." He stared into Ezra's eyes. "And, Reverend, I'm sure the eyes of God are on California, not just North Carolina."

"Of course," said Ezra. "But it's quite a sinful place. She could go someplace like that and just disappear."

"We'll find her," Sheriff Barnaby said. "And we've not given up the search for Heidi."

"Praise the Lord," said Ezra. "I love your confidence, Sheriff Barnaby. I trust in God, and pray ever *without ceasing*, that they be returned to us unharmed."

The men shook hands near the doorway. After Barnaby left, Ezra washed his hands in his private bathroom, scrubbing the tops and sides of his hands so long they stung. He thought again of the sheriff's smugness, of his thick jaws, of his obsession with the missing girl. Let him come, Ezra thought, let them all come. There were darker concerns than the ambitions of men.

Ezra looked out the window. More vultures sat tall and black in the treetops. They were waiting for him, he knew, to pick the meat from his bones. Then his eyes were drawn to the parking lot to the east. He saw Old Man Leonard's F150 pickup truck sitting there. The man wasn't in the truck; it was parked diagonal across two parking spaces. Let him come too. Let them all come: Sheriff Barnaby, the SBI, Old Man Leonard, the girl and her shadow beasts, the black vultures, faithless and godless all. *Let them come.*

PART 3

"The fiend in his own shape is less hideous than when he rages in the breast of men."

— NATHANIEL HAWTHORNE

22 / ERIN'S PILGRIMAGE

Erin hopped out of her dad's truck at six a.m. Saturday morning at the Church of Hosanna. Six fucking a.m. Not only was it stupid early, it was cold as hell. Lucas would have said it was cold as a brass witch's titty, and he'd have been right. So not only did Erin have to go camping with a bunch of weirdos and listen to Jesus freaks preach at her all weekend, she was going to freeze her ass off too.

Mom helped her pack the night before. Together, they stuffed four big sweatshirts and three pairs of jeans into the one bag allowed for each kid. Mom had been particular about how Erin needed a hundred pairs of thick socks. She was positively obsessed with what underwear Erin packed, making sure she only brought total granny panties that practically rode up above her belly button.

"No one is going to see my underwear, Mom," Erin had said.

"If you'd kept it that way, you wouldn't even be going," Mom said.

Today, Erin wore a pair of jeans, brown lace-up boots, and a purple Western Carolina University sweatshirt she'd gotten from one of her cousins. She lugged a thick green snow jacket with a fur-trimmed hood, tugging at its hem as she stood in line.

Erin tried one last time to beg her mom not to make her go, but Mom just frowned, saying it was the Lord's will and that she hoped Erin would think about her actions and try to be a better Christian. A better young woman. Dad had hardly spoken to her at all since her mom found the condom in her nightstand and told him about it. He'd become a grunter, knocking on her door and mumbling single words like "Dinner" and "Night."

On the ride to the church, she'd tried to talk to him. "Dad, I'm sorry," she said, her voice shaky.

He never took his eyes off the road. "Let's talk when you get back."

Why had Mom told him in the first place? Was it because her dad always doted on Erin and she resented it? She certainly hadn't ratted out Erin's older sister for every little thing she'd done. Maybe she wanted to drive a wedge between them? *Mission accomplished, Mom.*

Dad had stopped coming up to see her at bedtime on school nights, the way he'd done since she was small, sitting on the edge of the bed, asking about her day before saying a quiet prayer over her, his hand on her foot over the covers. He didn't hug her before school like he used to, and when Erin took it upon herself to hug him, his hands hung lifelessly at his sides, as if she was now tainted. At first this had just pissed her off, but as the days wore on, she felt an ache in her stomach, as if his quiet disapproval had opened a wound deep inside her. All for a stupid condom. Wasn't Erin smart for not being another teenage statistic? Couldn't they give her credit for that? That stupid rubber had convinced them she was so bad she needed to get off in the woods to have all her sins washed away and, maybe, her virginity restored. Jesus could do that, right? What bullshit.

The buses the church chartered were plush and new, with modern high-backed chairs that reclined and headrests that cradled your head. They were a far cry from the buses at school with their low vinyl seats and persistent smell of sweat and piss. The buses were warm, the heat cranked high to fight the cold November morning, and when the kids got to their seats, they found Hardee's bags with sausage biscuits. Erin wondered if they wanted to make the kids too fat to want sex.

A balding youth minister passed out goodie bags full of candy, a new King James 1611 Edition Youth Bible, and a variety of gospel music cassettes, as well as tapes of Reverend Ezra's sermons. No other music would be allowed on the Purity Sojourn. The kids were forbidden to bring anything secular, and a stocky woman with a librarian hair bun and a clipboard told them, when reading out the rules, that any *worldly music* found on the trip would be cast on the campfire.

"Besides," the hair-bunned minister had said. "You'll come back so on fire for Jesus you'll never care for anything that doesn't glorify his holy name."

A tall man with white-blond hair so bright it hurt Erin's eyes stood in the back, taking it all in, his hands behind him. While the rest of the ministers wore khaki camping gear with bright Church of Hosanna golf shirts, he was dressed in a navy suit paired with a red tie and hiking boots. He wore weird red sunglasses even though the sun wasn't even up. Every time Erin looked in his direction, he glared back at her, his eyes dark behind the red. She was relieved when he got on a different bus. He gave her the creeps.

A chubby black kid named Kevin sat down by Erin on the bus. At school, he was teased for being in the Chess Club, and everyone said he was gay because he was shy around girls. Erin looked around at the rest of the kids. They were some strange cross-section of teenagers from Clayton and a couple other nearby high schools. There were some jocks she recognized from the football team, a few stoner kids, a girl named Shannon that half the boys in school claimed to have felt up, some plain vanilla kids that she didn't associate with anything in particular, and several kids who the rednecks at Clayton harassed for being gay. There was Bev, who wore a chain wallet and kissed other girls at the buses, Kevin, and Jack, who had hair with fake-looking yellow highlights, like he sprayed his hair with Sun-In and laid out all day. He had the most beautiful bangs.

Erin felt sick when she thought about all these kids being forced to come on a stupid holy roller camping trip in the woods just because their parents decided they were "bad kids." Kevin and Jack had never hurt anyone in their whole lives. Nor had Bev, for that matter, but they were all being singled out because they were different. And herself. Why was *she* here? Because she liked Lucas—no, she *loved* Lucas. The condom in her drawer must mean she's a bad person, full of lust that can't be quenched? It was all so ridiculous. Erin thought of a quote she'd seen somewhere, maybe in the newspaper. It said something like "telling kids not to have sex is like telling them not to eat; it works until they get hungry." Wasn't it normal to want to be close to another human being? And Bev and the others: did they not have their own hunger? They could ignore it, of course, for a while, but eventually it would gnaw at them like real hunger. And then what would they do? It wasn't something you could get over, like a cold.

Erin wouldn't forgive her parents for this. They were such fucking hypocrites anyway. They got married when Dad was twenty and her mom just seventeen. And they'd supposedly dated for years before that. They expected her to think they didn't have sex before they got married? The thought of them being physical was revolting and made her want to puke. But if Mom could get married at seventeen, who was she to judge Erin anyways? Besides, Erin *loved* Lucas. This wasn't a fling.

She tried that argument with her mom when everything went down. "Look, Mom," she said. "I'm in love with Lucas. It's not like I'm out banging all the guys on the football team."

"You just shut your mouth, young lady," Mom said. "You don't know the first thing about love."

But she was wrong. Lucas was the brightest star in the sky, had been since the day Erin first laid eyes on him in the sixth-grade lunchroom, after all the elementary school kids in the county got dumped into Clayton Middle. They hadn't gone together in middle school, but when they were freshman, Erin had found any excuse to talk to him, joining the stupid Beta club and even showing up at his games, even though watching baseball was totally like watching paint dry.

The first time Lucas really noticed her was at one of his games. She'd worn some white shorts and a red tank top, dragging a couple of her girlfriends to the game and getting them to scream Lucas's name when he took to the pitcher's mound. And when he hit a homerun on his second at-bat, Erin leapt up and down on the bleachers, ecstatic, her hair—she had long hair back then—bouncing around her shoulders like a scarf caught in the wind. Because the ball had gone past the fence, Lucas's run around the bases had been more of a victory lap than a base run. He pumped his fists in the air and did a slow jog, but somewhere around shortstop, his eyes lit on her in the bleachers. He almost tripped when he rounded third, like he'd forgotten how to make his feet work. Couldn't take his eyes off her, looking back over his shoulder after he passed the base. After the game, Erin sent one of her friends over to tell Lucas she wanted him to take her to Tastee Freeze for a banana split. That day, watching her eat ice cream, he fell like a heavy stone dropped into a lake. What Erin hadn't counted on was how hard she'd fall for *him*.

Thinking back on it, Lucas hadn't even flinched when she'd cut off her long hair and gotten the short boy's haircut. He'd said he loved it right away, telling her he liked how he could see her neck before burrowing into it. But Dad? He sulked for a week after she cut it off. Just like now.

After a while, the bus driver began blasting gospel music. Not just playing it loud—blaring it so loud the speakers in the ceiling rattled. It hurt Erin's ears.

"Hey, can you turn that down?" she asked, but the volume was so high there was no way he could hear her. Erin unbuckled her seatbelt and stood up. That got his attention. He glared at her in the mirror.

"Take your seat, young lady," the driver yelled.

"Not till you turn this shit down," she yelled back. The kids on the bus all started clapping, whooping and hollering in agreement.

The driver turned down the music. "What did you say?" he asked.

"The music is too loud," Erin said.

"You teenagers like loud music," he said. "Now take your seat."

He turned the music even louder, the windows shaking with the bass. A deep male voice drawled out the lyrics: *Up from the grave he arose! With a mighty triumph o'er his foes!*

Erin walked to the back of the bus, rolling her eyes at the scowling librarian lady.

The minister shook her head, her black bun twitching on top of her head. "You need to sit down," she said, grabbing Erin's forearm.

Erin shook her off and made her way to the back row. On an empty seat, she perched on her knees and looked out the back window. The bus leaned into the sharp curves they were on now, having left the interstate a few miles back. Erin studied the cars that snaked along behind them. There. Behind an old pickup truck, she saw Lucas's golden 240Z. She'd been unnerved when she got to the church and saw no signs of him. But there he was, following the buses so he'd be able to find the campsite. Erin had persuaded him to sneak up around midnight each night. He didn't want to come and potentially get her in more trouble, but she insisted. Three days was a long time to go without seeing each other, and she wasn't about to be bored all weekend. She'd play her little part, sitting by the campfire and singing "Jesus Loves the Little Children" or whatever, but when everybody went to sleep, she'd sneak off to be with Lucas. Let the camp counselors smoke on that.

23 / GOSPEL DOWN
ERIN

The trek up the mountain was a pain in the ass. After the buses left the paved road for a dirt road thick with gullied veins, the limbs of the trees had scraped the metal roofs of the buses, bearing the timbre of nails on a chalkboard. The driver eventually turned down the gospel music; it appeared he could not praise the Lord and focus on the rutted road at the same time. The road hugged the edge of the mountain on one side and featured views of spectacular drop-offs on the other, making Erin completely nauseous. She wondered if Lucas's car could even make it up the winding road. Eventually, the dirt road ended, and they were told to gather their gear from the rear of the bus to continue on foot. It took another hour to reach the campsite; by the time they got there, Erin was sweating, the collar of her sweatshirt clinging to her neck.

Gospel music was already playing through speakers in the assembly tent when they approached.

My hope is built on nothing less, than Jesus' blood and righteousness

I dare not trust the sweetest frame but wholly lean on Jesus' name.

The campsite was near a mountain peak, situated in a clearing ringed by large trees, mostly oak. Canvas tents were set up around a burning campfire. Two large tents sat at the head of the camp, one for assembly, the other for dining. Small sleeping tents finished the circle, each large enough to fit four or five kids. The counselors instructed them to drop off their belongings and set up their sleeping bags in their assigned tents. Erin was astonished to learn her tentmates were Bev, Kevin, Jack, and an impish boy she didn't know named Cody. On every other church outing, the boys and girls were strictly segregated by sex; as Erin watched the other tent assignments, she noticed boys and girls were separated in every other case. Then it dawned on her: she was being put with all the gay kids.

"Excuse me, ma'am," Erin said to Librarian Bun with the clipboard.

The woman stopped and peered at her over her horn-rimmed glasses. "Yes?" she said.

"I'm wondering about the tent assignments," Erin said. "I think there's been some kind of mistake."

"We know that all things work together for good to them who love God, to them who are called according to his purpose," said Librarian Bun.

"Okay, but there are three boys in my tent. They always separate us by gender."

Librarian Bun looked at her clipboard and flipped through the pages. "No, there's no mistake." She smiled broadly, revealing crooked lower teeth beneath a perfectly straight top row. "Everything according to His purpose."

"It's not just that," Erin said, looking around her as if she'd find the right words hanging in the air. "The kids in my tent. They're, um, different from me."

"Different how?" The woman tilted her head, bun cocking right. It looked like a ball that might roll off her head.

Erin couldn't think of how to say it, but she needed to know why they put her in a tent with all the gay kids. Had someone told the youth leaders she was a lesbian? In the end, she didn't want to give Librarian Bun the satisfaction. "Nothing. It's fine."

The woman straightened, bun recentering. She smiled smugly. "Good. Remember: many are called, but few are chosen."

"I'm sorry?" said Erin.

"That's from Matthew. You don't study your Bible much, do you, Miss Erin?" said the bun.

"Oh, okay. I knew I'd heard it somewhere."

The woman looked her up and down. Her eyes settled on Erin's hair. "That's a short haircut for a girl, don't you think?"

"Yeah, I really like it, though. A lot of girls are getting cuts like this."

"Are they? Church girls?" Bun raised an eyebrow.

"I don't know, yeah, some maybe."

"I don't think so," said Librarian Bun. She pursed her lips and flipped the pages back over on her clipboard. "Now go get your name tag in the main tent."

Erin joined the queue for name tags. Cody was behind her in line, but she didn't speak to him. When she got her name tag, it read "Erin" in large letters. Beneath her name, in smaller font, were the words *God's Girl*.

"Oh my God," she whispered. She looked over Cody's shoulder at the name tag in his hands. It read *God's Son* beneath his name. Erin rolled her eyes.

After everyone had found their tent assignments, rolled out their sleeping bags, and retrieved their name tags, they gathered by the fire.

"Sit down Indian-style," said one of the youth ministers, a red-headed man in his early twenties with an overly earnest face. After everyone sat, he said, "Kids, you're in store for an amazing few days. Lives will be changed, hearts set afire for Christ. You will go home full of the Holy Spirit, each and every one of you." At this, the other camp counselors clapped their hands. The kids looked around at each other, and a couple began to clap, then the rest joined in. Erin kept her hands in her lap. A few yards away, Erin noticed Bev doing the same.

"But before we begin the activities of our Purity Sojourn," he said, "we have something very special for you."

"Amen," someone said.

From the assembly tent on the other side of the fire, Reverend Ezra emerged. He raised his hands in the air like a football player who just scored a touchdown. He wore a charcoal pin-striped suit like it was Sunday morning. He had on a red tie and shiny black wingtips. He walked around the fire toward the seated kids. Erin noticed he walked with a slight limp. She noticed dust on one of them at the same time he did; he frowned. He looked around at the youth ministers. Librarian Bun approached him sheepishly. She nodded at the Reverend and knelt before the soiled wingtip. She let down her hair carefully, eyes downcast. She knelt and used her hair to polish the shoe. She stood and gave a half-bow before returning to her place in the crowd, quickly reassembling her bun. Reverend Ezra did not acknowledge her.

"I praise God for such an amazing assembly of youth," he said with a smile. Erin could not get over how small he looked, with narrow shoulders maybe half the size of Lucas's. He always appeared so much larger at church, up on stage. There was something youthful and vigorous about his face, despite being in his seventies; he had less wrinkles than Erin's daddy who was barely fifty. She wanted to dislike the man but found herself drawn to him somehow. Even when he said something she disagreed with, she felt that pull, and understood why he'd been so successful at building a flock of followers.

"I want to first thank our youth ministers—yes, give them a round of applause." He gestured to the ministers, and the kids clapped dutifully. "They have given up the precious resource of time to be here with you, to counsel you in God's ways, to change lives for the Lord, Amen?"

One of the jocks in the back said, "Amen," and the other kids craned their necks to see who'd spoken.

"Come, Brother Lemuel," said Reverend Ezra, gesturing to the creepy blond man. The other man dipped his head in an aw-shucks kind of way and walked over to stand by the preacher. He towered over Reverend Ezra. Taking off his red sunglasses, he put them in his shirt pocket. Reverend Ezra seemed to stare at the sunglasses before they disappeared.

"I want you all to be aware that the leader for your Sojourn this year is Brother Lemuel. He's been named Predicant by the Church of Hosanna, making him the chief elder for all our ministries. So for him to spend time with you here these next few days tells you how important we view this ministry, how crucial y'all are to the future of our church. The Predicant's role is to supervise the youth ministers as they guide you through your Sojourn, and he may counsel some of you directly, depending on what God calls him to do. Amen?"

A chorus of *Amens* circled through the youth ministers from a couple kids on the ground.

"Your job, youth of Hosanna, is to open your hearts and minds to all God has in store for you. Until Tuesday morning, your every thought belongs to God. You must let go of all worldly thoughts and pressures. You must give yourself over to Him and do exactly as you're told. It was willed by God for you to be here, and you are all among the chosen." Reverend Ezra began to pace in front of the fire, balling his fists in front of him. "You were *chosen*. Do you know what that means? It means you are special. You were chosen by God to be here, just as Jesus once walked on the earth among men and chose his disciples and apostles one by one. They didn't all want to follow him right away, no, sir. Some of them resisted God's call and had to suffer before they understood God's plan for their lives. Over the next few days, the Predicant and youth ministers may ask you to do things you don't fully understand. They may ask you to do things you find uncomfortable, Amen?"

Amen echoed among the youth ministers.

"As it is said in the Holy Scriptures, 'be patient when thou art changed to a low estate. For gold is tried in the fire, and acceptable men in the furnace of adversity.' So fear not the trials you may endure here, and when you return to the secular world. For you will have been tried by fire, just as gold is tried. If you give your heart over to the Lord, you can emerge as gold emerges from the fire. Amen?" Then he added, "At this time, I'd like to ask the Predicant to say a few words."

The Predicant stepped forward, dipping his head when he passed Reverend Ezra. He adjusted his tie before he spoke, fidgeting.

"Thanks to the good Reverend Ezra," he began, "for taking the time out of your busy schedule to visit with our youth, who need the firm hand of God upon them. We are thankful for your guidance and the wisdom of your teachings."

Erin was shocked at the Predicant's voice. It did not fit his appearance in any way, being much higher-pitched than the reverend's. He drew out his words a bit like Erin's aunt from Florida, with a low country southern drawl.

"To the youth, I tell you, you will be part of the greatest Purity Sojourn in the history of the Church of Hosanna. We have wonderful food, fellowship, and activities planned for you, but it is important you open your hearts to the Lord. As Reverend Ezra said, this will not be all fun and games. We will challenge you. Challenge you to let go of your worldly ways, challenge you to let go of the evil, humanistic ideas you learn in our ungodly public school system. To free yourself from the radical, dark ideas of Hollywood and its homosexual agenda. Here, before God, let a woman be a woman and a man be a man."

Reverend Ezra said "Amen" and held his palms up toward the Predicant. "Go on, brother."

"All these foul, wicked things must pass, ashes to ashes, dust to dust. We will make you uncomfortable at times as we share the gospel with you. As we challenge you to read your Bibles aloud to each other. As we form Prayer Circles to focus on your individual needs and worldly challenges. You may not like what God has to say, but that doesn't change the words put down in his infallible scripture." He dropped his head and spoke more slowly. "You *will* listen. And you *will* hear. And you will be changed by God. For it is the only way—the only way you can walk in the light.

"Some of you may have heard the weatherman is calling for snow. Don't let this concern you. It's snowed during our sojourns before, and, if anything, it lit a fire under those in attendance. Each of you has warm sleeping bags, strong and secure accommodations, and a fire to keep you warm. I am confident you'll be so full of the Holy Spirit, you won't feel the cold."

In the afternoon, the kids ate bologna sandwiches on white bread in the dining tent while gospel music played from a generator powered PA system, echoing on the ridges around them. Erin's sandwich was so dry, she only ate a third of it before tossing it in the trash. They were given various chores to perform. Erin and a few others were tasked with erecting tiki torches around the campsite. The cold made it difficult to drive the wooden bases into the ground; some of the torches split at the base as they tried to push them into the frozen dirt. A youth minister eventually produced some small garden shovels for them to use.

As she worked, Erin focused on the campsite and the landmarks around it. She'd told Lucas to come meet her north of the camp at midnight, but they'd snaked around the mountain so many times she wasn't sure which way was north. When night fell, she was sure she could use the North Star to find due north. When she'd told Lucas to meet her north of the camp, he'd asked how he would know which direction was north.

"Ain't you got a compass, you big dummy?" she'd laughed.

But his face had grown serious; he didn't have one. And so, she gave Lucas her compass and prayed the night would be clear enough for her to find the stars. But heavy gray clouds hung so close they seemed to hug the tops of the trees. If the clouds remained, she might not be able to navigate out of the camp. She imagined Lucas sitting in the first cluster of trees to the north of the camp while she wandered around in the woods till she got lost. That would be just her luck.

24 / THE PRAYER CIRCLE
ERIN

When dusk came, it advanced with long tree-drawn shadows, edging along the ground toward the camp tents. The kids were gathered by the fire for another Jesus pep talk, this time given by the bald bus driver. He wore a thick jacket over a bright blue Church of Hosanna sweatshirt. The temperature dropped, and many kids donned toboggan hats and earmuffs. Erin put on the green coat she'd brought and pulled the hood up over her head. The wind was bitter cold. She noticed the other kids shaking around her and had difficulty stilling her own body. After what amounted to a mini church service, complete with hymn singing, preaching, and an altar call to an imaginary altar down in front of the fire to which zero kids responded, they were divided into groups called Prayer Circles. Librarian Bun handed out the Prayer Circle assignments, and each circle was paired with a youth minister who held up a sign with a number to tell the kids where to go.

When Erin got to her Prayer Circle, she was mortified by two facts. First, her Prayer Circle minister was none other than Librarian Bun herself, and second, her circle was comprised of her tent mates. Was she going to have to hang out with the same fucking gay kids all weekend?

Librarian Bun sat at the head of the group. She smiled, saying, "Let us open our group with a word of prayer." She set the clipboard beside her and placed a big black Bible on her lap. She put her hands in front of her and laced her fingers the way children are taught to pray.

"Our Heavenly Father, we pray you'll be with us this night. That you'll cover us with your grace and power, that we'll feel it in our blood and in our very bones, dear Lord. We pray that these troubled children will turn from evil and abandon the lust in their hearts. That they'll turn their eyes on you and away from the wickedness the dark one has put into their minds and bodies."

Erin opened her eyes. The other kids were looking around at each other.

"I pray, dear Christ," Librarian Bun continued, "that you'll call on them to forsake the darkness and give themselves over completely to your service. So they may be saved from eternal damnation and the horrible, terrible pain of your Lake of Fire, final eternal home for the damned."

Erin met Bev's eyes and rolled her own. When she looked back at Librarian Bun, she was mortified to find that the woman's eyes were open as well. She'd seen the gesture.

"Amen," said Librarian Bun, her lips spreading to grimace.

At first the Prayer Circle felt a bit like Sunday School. Librarian Bun would throw out a question to the group like, "Why do you think it's important to remain sexually pure?" and the kids would fight back sniggers before parroting something their parents had said or they'd heard in church at some point. It was all so ridiculous that Erin could hardly sit still. She squirmed, crossing and uncrossing her legs to get comfortable. She hated every minute of it.

Librarian Bun looked at her sideways. "Is the spirit of the Lord dealing with you about something, Erin? Is there anything you'd like to confess to our circle, to God?"

"Um, no," Erin said. "I'm just tired of sitting on the ground."

"Imagine how uncomfortable you'll be if you bypass this opportunity for salvation and wind up in the flames of Hell," Librarian Bun said.

"Excuse me?" said Erin.

"Are you pretending you didn't hear me?" Librarian Bun said.

"I heard you, but I've been in church all my life—"

"Church pews are full of people going straight to Hell," said Librarian Bun. "They sit there, week after week, pretending to be Christians. But God sees their hearts. God sees your heart, Erin."

"Does she?" Erin said. She laughed to herself when she thought about LilyMa calling God "she" in front of Lucas and the others.

Librarian Bun leaned toward her, pointing a fat finger. "You're very close to committing the only sin God said in the Bible could not be forgiven, couldn't be washed away, even by Jesus's blood."

Erin looked at her lap, trying not to smile.

"Blasphemy is the highest of all sins. Don't let me hear you say anything like that ever again."

"You don't know if God is a he or she," Erin said.

Librarian Bun bit her lip and turned to the other kids in the Prayer Circle. She gestured at Erin. "May the rest of you not mock God the way this wayward child does. For the wages of sin is death."

There was a little more discussion, with Librarian Bun changing the subject to premarital sex and the importance of saving one's virginity for marriage. Erin fought the urge to roll her eyes again.

"You will all memorize a specific, unique Bible verse that is applicable to your...situation," Librarian Bun said. She handed a slip of paper to each and asked them to read aloud.

Kevin read his first. "Romans 1:27, 'And likewise also the men, leaving the natural use of the woman...'" Kevin paused and looked around at the others.

"Go on, Kevin. Read your verse. These are the words of God."

Kevin looked at the paper for a moment. "'...and likewise also the men, leaving the natural use of the woman, burned in their lust one toward another; men with men working that which is unseemly, and receiving in themselves that recompense of their error which was meet.'"

"Good, Kevin. You will memorize this verse tonight. You will say it before our little Prayer Circle each time we meet."

"Why does he have to memorize that one?" Bev asked. "There's lots of Bible verses."

"Do you have a problem with the word of God?" Librarian Bun asked.

"No, it's just...I mean... That is ridiculous."

"So, God is ridiculous to you? His word's folly?"

Bev dropped her head. "I didn't say that."

"Since you're so opinionated, why don't you read yours?"

Bev lifted her slip of paper so she had enough light. She shook her head slowly.

"Go on," Librarian Bun said.

Bev met Erin's eyes and seemed to resign herself to the moment.

"Romans 1:26, 'For this God gave them up unto vile affections: for even their women did change the natural use into that which is against nature.'"

"See," Librarian Bun said, her eyes squinting with smugness. "That wasn't so hard." She looked around at the kids in the circle. "These are the words of God. They're not *my* words. I didn't write this. God did. We must obey if we are to live in his light."

"This is bullshit," Erin said.

"Miss Erin, I've had about all I can stand of you tonight. You're certainly starting things out on the wrong foot. Do you want to wash dishes every night after evening meals? Is that what you're telling me with this persistent back talk and ungodly language?"

"You're raking them over the coals."

Librarian Bun smirked. "Them? What about you? Why don't we hear your verse?"

Erin looked down at the piece of paper in her hands. Just get it over with, she told herself. "Okay, Proverbs 7:21-27, 'With her fair speech she caused him to yield, with the flattering of her lips she forced him. He goeth after her straightaway, as an ox goeth to the slaughter. Let not thine heart decline to her ways, go astray in her paths. Her house is the way to Hell.'"

Librarian Bun smiled, pleased with herself.

"It's really long," Erin said. "I'm supposed to memorize this, and this, like—is this supposed to be me? I'm the *she* tempting men to the house of Hell?"

"So many of you wicked children, questioning the word of God. Which part of the verse should we pick out, and which part should we keep, Miss Erin? Which of God's words offend you?"

So that was it, Erin thought. Somehow, what her mom and dad had said about her, Lucas, and the condom had gotten to the youth ministers at Hosanna. This *Purity Sojourn* was about bashing them over the head with what they'd all done. For the gay boys around the fire, their verses would be about how evil it was for a man to lie with a man, for Bev, the same but with women. Erin was just a whore all the way around with a lesbian haircut that called her straightness into question. She couldn't swallow.

"Cat got your tongue?" Librarian Bun said. Her grin grew larger, more toothy. "Devil got your tongue?"

"Fuck this," Erin said finally, throwing her verse onto the fire.

Librarian Bun interlaced her fingers as if she were delighted. "How about the rest of you? Do you want to test God as Miss Erin has done? Or do you accept his words?"

No one moved to throw their papers into the fire.

Erin's eyes burned. She stood. Only then did she realize the Predicant was watching them from the shadows. She sprinted past him toward her tent. When she got inside, she dropped to her knees. She felt like she was on fire. As if everything in the whole world burned inside her. Why were they treating them this way, like they were the most horrible creatures in the whole world? That bitch had called her a *loose woman*. She stretched out on top of her sleeping bag, pulled her pillow to her face, and bit into it as hard as she could.

Later, when it grew quiet outside, the smell of food wafted from the dining tent. Erin heard kids laughing and looked out to see them lining up to eat. She was starving. The sandwich hadn't been enough to hold her over all day, and it smelled like they were grilling hamburgers and hot dogs. She walked quietly to the tent, her arms crossed, keeping an eye out for Librarian Bun and the other youth ministers. She didn't see any of them. She joined the line with a group of kids she didn't know. When she got to the front, a youth minister in a thick hairnet asked her what she wanted out of the items laid out in tin containers above lit Sterno cans. There were hot dogs, macaroni and cheese, hamburgers, baked beans, and potato chips. It all smelled amazing; Erin felt frail and weak from hunger.

"Just a burger, please, and some baked beans."

Hairnet began to scoop beans onto a plate. The Predicant emerged beside her, taking her hand and dumping the beans back into the tin container. Hairnet looked at him, confused. He said nothing but shook his head. The woman looked at Erin with sad eyes.

"Next!" she said. The kid behind Erin stepped in front of her, and Hairnet took his order.

"What?" Erin said. "I don't get to eat?"

The Predicant glared at her, saying nothing. He pursed his sickening pink lips, daring her to say something else. He stuck out his chest and adjusted his tie.

Erin walked around the dining tent for a moment, watching all the kids eat their burgers. She picked up a red solo cup of iced tea from a table at the edge of the tent. She half expected the Predicant to emerge and slap it out of her hand. What the fuck was wrong with these people? If we don't play nice, they don't let us fucking eat? Her stomach grumbled as she left to pace around the fire. When she returned to her tent, she found Cody on the opposite side, sobbing.

"What's wrong?" Erin asked.

"Those verses. They're just so mean. Why are they doing this to us?"

"Did they let you eat?" Erin asked.

"Yeah, why?" said Cody.

"They didn't let me have any food," she said. "I guess you can't curse at your youth minister and throw your Bible verses on the fire, or you lose eating privileges."

"Oh my God," said Cody. "This place is horrible."

For a moment, Erin couldn't breathe. Her rage choked her.

"I'm sorry," Cody said. "I would have saved you some of mine."

Erin thought about meeting Lucas later. Maybe he'd have some beef jerky or a banana? He always packed jerky and water when they went hiking. Erin hoped to God he had something. *Anything.*

At lights out, the kids went to their respective tents. Erin, Bev, and Kevin lay on one side of the tent floor, Cody and Jack on the other.

"These people are crazy," said Kevin. "I can't believe the way they're treating us."

"And why in the hell are we in the only co-ed tent?" Bev asked.

"I think I know," said Erin, sitting up in her sleeping bag.

"Why?" Bev asked.

"Look around at us," she said. "They think we're all gay."

"Duh," said Jack. "All our verses were about that. Well, all of them except yours." He tilted his sun-kissed head toward Erin.

"Mine was about just being a whore in general," she said.

"So why put the gay kids in one tent?" Bev asked. "Aren't they worried we'll be gay together?"

"They put me and you in here," Erin said, sweeping her hand toward the boys, "to be bait for these three."

"Gross," said Cody.

"I know," said Erin. "But that's the only explanation. They think if they mix us together, y'all will all figure out how to be straight. Do what nature calls you to do."

"But you're not gay," Bev said. "Are you?"

"No," Erin said. "My parents sent me here because they found out I'm doing it with my boyfriend."

"I'm not even gay," Cody said. He studied his hands. "At least I don't think I am. I never thought about it. I mean, I've thought about it, but—"

"But they keep going on and on," Kevin said, "about sexual purity. About saving yourself for marriage. Then they put you in here to tempt us?" He began rifling through his duffle bag. He dug under his clothes, and then became so exasperated he dumped the contents out on his lap. "Where is it?" he said.

"What?" Bev asked.

"I had some Oreos in here, and some other stuff. It's all gone."

"They took your food?" Cody asked. "Why?"

"So you couldn't give me anything," Erin said.

"These people aren't Christians, they're psychos," Bev said. She punched her palm.

"All I know to do," Erin said, "is we just need to play their game while we're here. We're going to have to nod and say, 'Yes, sex is bad, and I'm a horrible person who needs the blood of Christ to save me.'"

"And we'll have to say we hate gay people and read our little verses like we believe them," Jack said.

"Yup," said Erin. "Act contrite. Act convicted. Act. If you don't, you won't get to eat, and we'll all be miserable all weekend."

"Maybe we should pair off by sex outside this tent," Bev said.

"Yes!" Erin said. "That's brilliant. You three, don't hang with other boys, hang with Bev or me. Let them think their little scheme is working. That you've seen the hetero light. And you," she said to Bev, "you can't talk to any girls."

"The big bad lesbian has turned," laughed Bev.

"Why do they hate us so much anyway?" Kevin said. "We didn't do anything to anybody."

"It's not about that," Erin said. "They pick and choose what they want out of the Bible. I have this fight with my old man all the time. The Bible has these verses about gay people, right? It also says we can't eat shellfish or pork and that gluttony is a deadly sin. But how many fat preachers do they take to Bible camps in the woods to make them skinny?"

"Like, every preacher is fat," Cody said. "Except Reverend Ezra. He looks like he never eats."

"He's one weird dude," Bev said. "Always made my skin crawl."

"Not as weird as the Predicant." Erin shivered.

"He wears red to copy Reverend Ezra," Cody said. "Don't you think?" His blue eyes caught the lamp light.

Gospel music began blaring outside. Erin looked at her watch—10:30 p.m.

"I thought it was lights out?" Bev said.

The music was really loud, echoing around the ridges above the campsite. Even louder than it had been on the bus.

"Maybe they want to send us to bed with the right thoughts. Mind control, like in *1984*," Kevin said.

"What did you say?" Erin asked. The boy repeated his sentence, but the music was so loud she couldn't hear him. They had to lean close together and yell in order to be heard.

"It's to keep us from talking," Bev said. "So we can't connect the dots like we've been doing."

"If we can't talk," Jack said, "they keep us alone, isolated. More open to the crap they're trying to drill into our heads. There's no escape."

The kids all looked at each other. Erin had never felt so much sadness in one place. She wanted to scream. To get out of the tent, to run down the mountain. To escape. But if she went home, her parents would send her back. And if she went to Lucas's or Mina's, how long before the church notified her parents? They'd have the police out looking for her. They'd already told her that if she didn't do the Purity Sojourn, she was going to be forced to go to some Yankee Christian boarding school. For a year! That was the only thing that made the Purity Sojourn look okay. It only lasted three nights. It would be like ripping off a Band-Aid. Just get it over with, and she could tell her parents she's sorry she had a condom.

The music was too loud. Eventually, they gave up trying to talk and settled into their sleeping bags. Song after song played over the PA system. Every third or fourth song, the same one repeated, a bluegrass hymn Erin had heard before in church. She put her head under her pillow but could still hear every word.

Were you there when they nailed him to the cross?
Were you there when they nailed him to the cross?
Sometimes it causes me to tremble
Were you there when they nailed him to the cross?

Why did they keep repeating this stupid song? There was a mandolin strum she'd liked when she heard it in church. But here in the tent, the sound felt sinister and sickening. Erin balled up on her side. She looked at her watch. It was 11 p.m. Almost time to meet Lucas. She'd hoped to get some rest before she snuck out. Then she remembered she didn't know which way to go.

"Do any of you have a compass?" Erin asked.

"Nope," Kevin said. The rest of her tentmates nodded in agreement.

"Do any of you know which way is north?"

"North is straight back behind the Assembly Tent," Bev assured her.

Lucas would be there waiting for her, in the first cluster of trees. Just a few more minutes, she told herself. Then she'd get to see him. If she could just hold on without going insane.

25 / ROUND MIDNIGHT
ERIN

Outside, it was snowing. Big fluffy flakes that covered the ground where they landed. Gospel music still blared, and the tiki torches sizzled as they caught the snow. Erin didn't notice anyone outside the kids' tents, but when she started through the campsite, she saw a couple of youth ministers, bundled up in their jackets, keeping watch by the fire. Erin backtracked to the edge of the campsite, circling around in the shadows to clear the assembly tent and make her way north. Overhead, not a single star was visible, the clouds blocking out any light they may give alongside the moon. A streak of white burnished the stormy snow clouds in one corner of the sky.

She had to walk maybe a thousand yards to get to the tree line beyond the campsite. The farther she got from camp, the more tolerable the music volume became. Erin stuffed her gloved hands in her coat pockets, feeling her insides tremble. She knew the cold had more bite because she hadn't eaten. She felt hollow inside, like her stomach was pulled against her spine. When she reached the trees, she looked at her watch. It was midnight. Lucas should be here. The trees were old with thick trunks; she petted them as she passed, her gloved fingers finding the grooves of their bark. She looked around. She knew he wouldn't exactly be waving a flashlight; any light could be seen from the camp.

"Lucas!" she whispered. "Lucas!"

She trudged through the brush, staying close to the tree line and the field that spread out toward the campsite. The last thing she needed to do was get lost. She felt weak as she walked, hunger gnawing her insides. She'd give anything for the dry sandwich from lunch. Though there was less snow on the ground in the trees, she saw it begin to lay in the field. She walked along, whispering his name, when suddenly she was lifted in the air, someone bear-hugging her around the waist.

"What the fuck?" she said.

His lips were at her ear, nuzzling her fur-lined hood out of the way. "Well, hello there, beautiful."

"Lucas," she said, turning to face him. "You came!"

He held a blue plastic flashlight in his hand, which he kept trained on the ground. "Of course I came. Did you think I could go days and days without some Erin?"

"Nope," she said.

"Besides," he said, "I knew how mad you'd get if I didn't. Hell hath no fury and all that."

"I'd have killed you cold."

"I know," he said. "I could see the headline. 'Local boy killed by raging girlfriend he wouldn't help break curfew.' No way could I go out like that." He looked through the trees to the campsite. "They're playing music at midnight?"

"They've been playing it for hours."

"It's so loud. I could hear all the words from way down the mountain. What the hell?"

"They're trying to torture us."

"But why?"

"This is a Purity Sojourn, remember? They've got to purge every evil thought. If you play that music, nobody can think a single sinful thought."

"God, that's awful. And it's not even good music."

"It's like the preaching at Hosanna," she said. "All fire and brimstone, all the time."

"I'm sorry, baby," he said, pulling her close. He hooked his fingers in the belt loops of her jeans, lifting her green coat.

"It's cold," she said, pulling the coat down. "I'm freezing my ass off out here."

"If the snow piles up pretty deep, will they call this whole thing off?"

"Are you kidding? They'll keep going unless the Rapture comes." She leaned into him, finally calming. The day had wrecked her, but this was just what she needed. "Tell me you've got some food. Jerky. Something."

"I don't have anything. You're hungry?"

"They didn't let me eat anything for dinner."

"What? Why not?"

"I'm too bad of a sinner," she said. "Sinners don't get food. Just good, compliant Christian girls get to eat."

Lucas shook his head. "These people are bonkers."

"How far away is your car?" she asked. "You got anything in there?"

"No, I didn't think about it. I had a Whopper on the drive."

She punched him in the stomach. "Don't talk about fucking Whoppers, oh my God."

"How about a cigarette?" he said. He took a pack of Camel Lights from his pocket and shook one out.

"Oh my God, yes," she said.

He pulled out his lighter and struck it for her.

"Turn your back," she said. "We don't want them to see the lighter or the cherries."

They smoked with their backs to the campsite. Lucas kept his free arm around her, pulling their sides together tight. The smoke burned Erin's lungs. She inhaled and held it for a moment before blowing it out through her nostrils. It wasn't as good as a Whopper, but it was pretty damned good after the day she'd had.

Lucas took a drag. "My uncle was a POW in Vietnam," he said. "Said those bastards kept them awake for days at a time. Trying to break them down. Said big brawny dudes, who'd been through the toughest training back home, Marines, Special Forces dudes. Said they started to sing like canaries about day three. Spilling their guts. Telling every damn thing they knew. Ratting out their fellow prisoners, telling who was an officer. Anything they were asked."

"That's terrible," Erin said. "Somebody tells you you're bad long enough, you start to believe them. They're trying to break us down. Break us like wild horses. Lucas, they got gay kids in there. Bunch of them are in my tent. They're trying to turn them. Bashing them over the head with every Bible verse about it."

"You're joking."

"Making us memorize verses. Making them memorize ones about how terrible it is for a man to lie with a man and all that."

"They give me the creeps."

"Stop being a dick, Lucas. Are you listening?" She put her hands on her hips.

"Yeah, no. They shouldn't be doing that. That's terrible."

"Guess what my verses are about? The ones I have to memorize?"

Lucas kissed her on the cheek. "Are they about hiding your condoms better?"

Erin pulled away from him. "This ain't funny, Lucas. All mine are about loose women in the Bible. About *whores*, Lucas. How they corrupt and destroy the good prophets and all that shit."

"I mean," Lucas said, grinning, "you did corrupt me."

"Fuck you," Erin said. "I wish you were in those tents getting preached at. I don't deserve this."

Lucas straightened. "I know. I'm sorry. You shouldn't be treated like that. You're not like that."

"Would it matter if I was?"

"What do you mean?"

"Are you saying I'd deserve this if I was like a loose girl? I'd deserve to be preached down to? I'd deserve to be food and sleep-deprived? Someone should teach me a lesson?"

"No, that's not what I—"

"You said it like I shouldn't be treated like that because I'm not a whore. But you're saying some people do deserve to be treated like that?"

"No way," Lucas stammered.

"No, they don't," she said. Her voice was shaky, tears welling in her eyes, and that pissed her off.

"I'm sorry, Erin. I love you. I'm sorry your parents made you come. It's my fault."

"One of them, the ministers," Erin said. "He'd stone me to death if he could get away with it. That's how much hate is in his eyes."

Lucas tried again to hug her, but again she twisted away.

"You'd be right there with them," she said. "If this was Biblical times. They never talk about the men. It's always the women."

"Jesus stopped them from stoning a woman," Lucas said, his face lighting as if he were super proud for paying attention that one day in Sunday School. "He said they couldn't stone her unless they had no sin, remember?"

Erin said, "You know how many times I've seen youth ministers check out girls at Bible camps? Look at them like they could eat them? No different from men on the street somewhere. They do it all the time. Teachers at our school are exactly the same. They'd be the first ones to pick up the stones, you know? All the while wishing they could fuck the whore on the ground getting stoned."

"Erin, I'm sorry. I am so sorry you're being treated this way. You don't deserve it, but yeah, you're right. No one does."

"I'm just so sick. I want to run down this mountain. Get in the car with you. Let you turn on the heat. Get me some fucking food, for Christ's sake. Get away and never come back to this stupid camp. Never set foot in another goddamned church my whole fucking life."

"I know."

Erin frowned. "You don't know. You really don't. My daddy thinks I'm trash now. Just because of that stupid condom. If you were his son, if he had boys instead of girls... If he'd found a condom in your nightstand, he'd be high fiving you right now."

Lucas didn't answer.

"You'd be a stud. He'd like that. If he had sons, that would be a good thing. Then he'd look down his nose at the other kids. He'd think, *at least he's not gay like so-and-so's kid*. But me? I'm tainted now. Unless I come back to from this fucking camp smiling and quoting Bible verses, dressed in virginal white."

Erin sat down on a fallen log. Nothing had gone the way she wanted. Not for a long time. She hadn't thought the Sojourn would be like this. In her mind, she pictured something like summer church camps. Yeah, you'd have to memorize Bible verses and listen to preaching and gospel music and all that. But you'd also play volleyball and go for hikes and play with those giant carpet checker boards. And she'd wanted to be happy to see Lucas. She had been until he opened his stupid mouth. She had been so excited to sneak off from camp to see him, to feel that little thrill from doing something wrong. She hadn't thought about it being this goddamned cold. She'd imagined Lucas meeting her with a blanket they'd spread out and lay on, looking up at the stars or making love. She didn't know she'd be hungry, and cold, and so angry. She was so fucking pissed. And sick, she felt sick, like she might puke. But there was nothing in her stomach to throw up.

Lucas sat beside her and shook out two more cigarettes. They lit them and smoked in silence. He put his hand on her leg. She wanted to move it, but she didn't have the energy and, after a moment, it felt nice. Even through his glove and her jeans, she could feel the warmth from his hand.

"I'd do anything for you, Erin," he said. "I'd do anything. I'd die for you."

"A little dramatic, don't you think?" she said.

"I mean it," he said.

"You being here," she said, putting her gloved hand over his, "you being here helps. Thank you for coming."

"It's not enough," he said. "It just ain't enough."

"If you'd have brought food," she said, smiling. "That might have been enough."

"Promise, I will tomorrow night. But they'll let you eat tomorrow, won't they?"

"I don't know," she said. "I'll try to be a better sport tomorrow. Play the game. Say I'm sorry for being such a lusty wench."

"I love when you say *wench*," he said.

"Of course you do," she said. She leaned and kissed him. They sat like that for a moment, holding their cigarettes out, kissing until Erin heard a crunching sound, like a limb breaking. Someone was coming. Someone was in the woods, not far from where they sat. She pulled away from Lucas and saw in his eyes that he'd heard it too.

"Fuck," she said, and they put their cigarettes out on the downed tree. Lucas clicked off his flashlight.

They sat still for a few moments, listening. Something moved deeper in the woods, coming their way. They climbed behind the downed tree. Erin pulled Lucas further down, afraid the ball of his toboggan hat stuck up too far.

Whatever it was, it came down the path they'd walked. It sniffed the air, perhaps picking up the lingering cigarette smoke. Its snorts sounded like a horse's as it walked past them with heavy footfalls, its nostrils working loudly. Then it was gone. They stayed behind the log for several minutes, just to be sure, their hearts slamming in their chests so loud Erin couldn't tell hers from his.

"What the hell was that?" Erin whispered.

"A bear, maybe," Lucas said. He scanned the trees, then stepped out and lit the ground with his flashlight.

"Aren't the bears hibernating?" she asked.

"Maybe they woke up 'cause of that music," he said. "But these tracks ain't bear tracks."

"What was it then?"

"I've never seen a footprint this big," he said.

Erin joined him. The thin beam of the flashlight lit a wide paw print. It was as wide as Lucas's foot was long.

"Be careful going down to your car," Erin said.

Lucas put his arms around her. "I will," he said. "But I don't want to leave just yet."

"I'm freezing, Lucas, you're freezing. There's no way to keep warm out here."

"We can try," he said with a sly smile.

"I'm worried about you getting home in that car. It's not like the 240z is good in the snow."

"Don't worry," he said. "I seen the forecast. I put chains on my tires."

"You are a wonder," she said, leaning in to kiss his cheek.

"You're the wonder," he said, kissing her.

He tasted like sweet tobacco. Even in the freezing cold, she loved the smell of him.

"I have to get back," she said.

"I know," he said.

Erin checked her watch as she walked along the edge of the field toward the campsite. She could feel Lucas's eyes on her—at least, she hoped it was Lucas. But he would watch her till he saw she was safe, she knew that much. She clicked the light on the side of her watch. It was three a.m. Gospel music still blared, echoing around the field.

26 / ERIN'S TRIBULATION

The gospel music went off around five a.m. Erin knew because she'd never gone to sleep. After she'd gotten back, she watched the others as they rolled around, trapped in a fitful state of half-sleep. When they cut the music, the other kids in the tent were tossing and turning. Promptly at six a.m., someone started playing the trumpet. It sounded like the son of a bitch was right outside their tent, the horn pointed straight at Erin's throbbing head. He played Amazing Grace three times all the way through.

"Fucking Christ," Bev said, rolling onto her back.

"I'd rather be in Hell," said Kevin, pulling his pillow over his head.

Soon, youth ministers were walking by, shaking the outside of the kids' tents.

"Time to rise and shine! It's a beautiful day in the Lord."

"Shoot me," said Jack.

In the dining tent, kids scarfed down scrambled eggs and biscuits, opened and smothered with gravy.

When Erin got in line, she saw the Predicant standing at the food table. She tried to ignore him because food smelled so good. But eventually she met his eyes through his stupid red sunglasses. He had this way of looking at her sideways, turning his head slightly so she could only see one eye glaring back at her, like he could see better that way. He shook his head slightly, telling her she couldn't eat. Erin wanted to scream. She wanted to grab one of the metal spatulas and beat him to death with it. He crossed his arms, daring her to stay in line, daring her to try to get food. She gritted her teeth and avoided his evil eye and stood until she was first in line.

"A little of everything, please," she told the woman scooping food. Erin watched, mouth watering, as the woman heaped gravy on top of scrambled eggs and an open biscuit. She practically ran to the nearest table, forgetting to pick up a fork and napkins. As soon as her paper plate hit the table, she watched as it was snatched up in front of her. She saw the Predicant's back as he walked away. Erin seethed. She marched out of the tent and right into Librarian Bun.

"Miss Erin, such a gorgeous morning, don't you think?" Snow flurries blew through the cold air, and about three inches of snow lay on the ground.

Erin didn't answer. She looked at the snow, already dirty from the foot traffic.

"Are you hungry, Miss Erin?"

Erin met her eyes.

"Maybe," Librarian Bun said. "Maybe today you can get full of the Holy Ghost. What do you think?"

"Maybe," Erin agreed. She imagined biting the woman's fat face, digging her teeth into her beefy jowl, tearing off a piece for a souvenir.

"God is with you," Librarian Bun said. "Don't turn your back on him."

When she got to the campfire, the red-headed youth minister handed her a push broom. A bunch of kids were clearing the snow in front of the fire. Others were carrying metal folding chairs from the assembly tent, forming a semicircle before the fire. Erin tried to push the snow with the broom head, but it had hardened from the cold; the bristles slid over the snow. After struggling for a few minutes, Erin let the broom handle drop to the ground.

"We are all going to do our part here, Miss Erin," said the red-haired youth minister. He picked up the broom handle and put it in her hands.

"The snow is frozen," Erin said.

"You'll have to use some elbow grease," he said.

She pushed with the broom, finally breaking a chunk of snow free.

"I mean, don't you have a shovel or something?" she said.

"Only the slothful complain about the tools they are given. Put your back into it," he said.

Then someone took the broom from her. Bev slammed the broom head down in front of a pile of snow and pushed hard. Several sheets of snow broke free, and she pushed them fifteen feet to the growing pile from the other sweepers.

"Miss Bev," the red-headed minister said. "That chore was assigned to Erin. You're not to do her chores."

"I don't mind none," Bev said, winking at Erin. "The Lord called to me. Spoke to me directly, told me to help."

"But—" started Red Head.

Bev put her hand on her hip. "Are you saying that if the Lord calls you to do something, you shouldn't listen to him? You're telling me not to listen to the Lord?"

"That's not what I am saying," Red Head said.

She slammed the broom head down again, pushing another huge sheet, maybe six feet wide, across the ground to the massing pile.

"Thank you," Erin said. She felt weak. Her head throbbed, and she saw stars when she closed her eyes. Red Head stomped away.

The morning service was similar to yesterday's, with mandatory Gospel singing and two different youth ministers preaching and reading from the Gospel. At the end of the service, the youth ministers encouraged any of the kids, if they were so moved, to stand and give their testimonies.

One of the jocks, the "amen" guy from yesterday, stood first.

"I just want to thank the Lord Ever Almighty for working in my heart. I feel closer to God up here with y'all, out in the elements like this, out in this snow. I couldn't get enough of that Gospel music last night; I was so sad when it was turned off. I missed it. It was so beautiful and gave me such beautiful dreams." He turned and winked to a couple of the other jocks in his group. "I rebuke all the sinful ways of my heart," he said. "And I can't wait to get home. I will make a difference in my school and my community, telling everybody I meet about the Lord, whether I'm in the grocery store with my mama or the locker room."

Amen, said one of the youth ministers.

"In fact," he went on, "I told my roommates in my tent last night. I told them I'm going to start a Prayer Circle for all the athletes in my school. We'll pray every day before school and before every game

God will make us victorious, and we will crush our enemies. On the field, I mean."

"Amen," said one of his jock buddies.

"Okay, anyone else?" said Red Head.

A sheepish girl with a bouncy brown ponytail stood next. "The Lord wants good things for us, I know that now, after coming here to this Purity Sojourn. The Devil wants us to do bad things. And every time I'm told to do bad things, I'll know it's the Devil doing. And you know what?" she said. "I ain't gonna listen! I'll just hum a hymn or praise Jesus if someone tries to hand me a cup of beer or a joint or whatever. I'll just open my little red New Testament my mee-maw give me, and I'll tell them about the Lord, right then and there."

Erin wanted to roll her eyes, but she was too weak.

After a few more kids gave testimonies, they all had to sing another song, "Just as I Am." While they were singing, Erin noticed Librarian Bun putting a few fold-up chairs close to the fire. After the song, Red Head asked if anyone wanted to come down and be saved or rededicate their lives to the Lord. This time, several kids went down. For a moment, she thought maybe she should go. Not because she felt the conviction of the Lord, but so all the ministers would think she did. If she went down, she reasoned, they might let her eat lunch. She should do it, just suck it up and go down, pretend to pray. But something inside her kept her still, as if a heavy stone sat on her lap. She felt Librarian Bun's eyes on her. She seemed to sense the struggle within Erin. She knew what Librarian Bun wanted her to do, and it made her want to do it even less.

After the altar kids had been prayed over and petted on, Librarian Bun stepped up. "One thing we are charged with this week is helping you, the youth of Hosanna, understand what's at stake. Do we seem like fanatics? Maybe so. But you have so much to lose! So much to lose if you don't follow God. We don't want that for you. We want you to understand. This is life and death, Heaven and Hell. We feel burdened for you. Remember, Jesus sweated drops of blood in the Garden of Gethsemane."

She walked over to the chairs beside the fire. "For our next game, we'll need a volunteer. Who wants to step forward and show their love for Christ?"

A few kids raised their hands.

"Thank you, praise Jesus. No one can tell me that our kids don't love the Lord," Librarian Bun said. "Who else? Oh, praise God," she said. "Come on down, Miss Erin."

Erin looked around the crowd. Who was she talking to? Was there another Erin?

"Yes, Miss Erin, don't be shy, I saw you raise your hand. Come on."

"I didn't raise my hand," Erin muttered. Then Red Head lifted her from her chair.

"Move it," he whispered in her ear. Through the flames on the other side, Erin saw the Predicant standing on a picnic table.

"But I didn't raise my hand," Erin repeated.

Red Head was behind her, pushing her to the front of the group. He led her to one of the metal chairs close to the fire. Erin felt woozy, her legs like wet spaghetti noodles. She wanted to let herself fall to the ground. Anything to stop this headache. Once she sat in the chair, the fire felt amazing. For the first time in what felt like days, she felt warm. She took her gloves off and let her hands warm over the fire, gaining feeling back in her fingers.

"The matters we speak of on the Purity Sojourn," Librarian Bun said, pacing in front of the fire. "They are of life and death. They are of Heaven and Hell."

Some of the other youth ministers offered perfunctory *Amens*.

"Now, all of you. We want you to close your eyes. Imagine what it will be like if you turn from your sinful, wicked ways. Imagine being in God's presence."

No one had closed their eyes, and Hair Bun frowned.

"Close your eyes, all of you," she scolded. "Think about that. About having total peace. No struggle. No strife. Just imagine."

Erin closed her eyes. Librarian Bun let the moment linger for so long she almost fell asleep. It was beautiful. There was no gospel music blaring in Erin's Heaven. No Librarian Bun, or Predicant, or Red Head. There was no downcast father, no busybody mother. Her head bobbed as she slipped under.

"Now!" Librarian Bun yelled, jerking Erin awake. "Now you've seen the peace of God. I want you to imagine the opposite of peace. Imagine the chaos and ugliness, the fire you will feel, if you decide not to follow God."

Suddenly, the fire went from comfortable and calming to overwhelmingly hot. Erin tugged at the collar of her sweatshirt. Then the fire grew hotter. She opened her eyes. Instead of being six or eight feet away, she was now within four feet of the orange flame. She looked behind her as Red Head and another youth minister slid her chair closer.

"You think the struggles you feel in life," Librarian Bun said, "are so difficult. Being popular at school, or maybe being not so popular. A teacher giving you a bad mark. Your parents making you go to bed at a certain hour, not letting you stay out late with your friends. You think these things are difficult, and maybe they do feel painful in the moment. Maybe they do. But I call on you now to think about what it will be like if you continue on your current path. If you fail to heed God's call. You might think, I'm young, I've got time, right? You think I'll turn to God one day, when I'm older. I've got plenty of time. Well, what happens if you die in a car crash next week when you get home, back down off this mountain? Can you imagine it? Dying without the Lord? What will your fate be then? It's a far cry from the peace of God, isn't it?"

The ministers pushed Erin's chair closer. She was within three feet now. The heat washed over her face, and sweat ran down her back. Her feet began to burn.

"Stop, okay?" she said.

She slid as far back in her chair as she could, her head leaning back into one of the minister's arms on the back of her seat.

"Stop," she said again.

Librarian Bun walked close to her chair.

"Please," Erin whispered.

"Does Miss Erin look comfortable?" she asked the other kids.

"No," some of them muttered. Some of them looked around uncomfortably. Some of them grinned, as if they were enjoying watching Erin squirm.

The ministers pushed her closer. Erin tried to roll out of the seat, but Red Head held her in place by her shoulders. Through the fire, she saw the Predicant, still standing on the picnic table. He smiled, head slightly turned with that one eye watching, and it shook Erin to the core. His was the face of the Devil, the smile stretched across his face unnaturally, enjoying her pain.

She felt the fire on her face. Felt as if she were on fire. The heat burned her eyes, and she frantically unzipped her jacket; the zipper was so hot it burned her fingers. Red Head suddenly removed his hands from her shoulders.

"Hold her, brother," said Librarian Bun.

"It's too hot," he said. They were so close it was burning his hands.

Erin ripped her jacket off and threw it to the ground.

"Let me up, you sick fucks," she screamed.

She forgot her hunger. Adrenaline pumped through her, and she was ready to fight. To throw *them* all on the fire.

"Closer," Librarian Bun said, and the men pushed Erin even closer to the flames. Her knees burned now. She couldn't draw back far enough in her chair to get away from it. When she looked over her shoulder, the two men holding her chair drew back their faces as far as they could; the heat was too much for them.

"Closer!" Librarian Bun said.

Again, Erin tried to roll out of the chair. Again, Red Head held her shoulders. She was losing her mind. She leaned back as far as she could and stood in her chair, shrugging off the man's hands. She tore off her sweatshirt and threw it in the snow, where it smoldered. She stood now in front of the youth of Hosanna in a black jogging bra and blue jeans. She was on fire. She started to unbutton her jeans.

"That'll be enough from you, Miss Erin," Librarian Bun said. "Have you no sense of decency?"

"Decency!" Erin yelled. "You're singeing my fucking eyebrows up here. You people are sick." She ran her hands over her sweaty belly.

Librarian Bun scooped up Erin's sweatshirt and threw it at her. "Cover yourself, Ms. Erin."

Erin took the sweatshirt and threw it on the other side in the snow. She glared through the fire at the Predicant, who still grinned at her. Through the heat waves, it looked like the edges of his elongated lips met his ears; it was all teeth.

"And you!" Erin yelled at him. "Why don't you take a fucking picture? It'll last longer."

Then she was off the chair, being carried by the two youth ministers. They took her to her tent, unzipped it, and threw her inside.

"I hope you rot in Hell," Erin said. She balled up on the floor of the tent and punched the hard ground until her knuckles ached.

That evening, Erin was a zombie during prayer circle. She felt like she'd been drugged, like that time she had to have surgery on her hand and the doctor gave her pills to make her relax before she showed up that morning. She could barely keep her eyes open. She was past hunger now; she didn't feel it at all. She felt weak. She hadn't bothered to go to the Dining Tent at lunchtime. It didn't seem to matter anymore.

Librarian Bun gave a long lesson about Lot and Sodom and the ungodly men who lived there. She had verses with more of the same for the boys. Bev's was something about how women shouldn't wear men's garments, and women who dressed like men were an abomination. Oddly, Red Head brought Erin some hot tea halfway through the prayer circle at Librarian Bun's request. Erin sipped the tea, knees to her chest on the fold-up chair. The tea was good. She drank it all.

Then it was time for Erin to read her verse.

"'Let a woman learn quietly with all submissiveness.' First Timothy 2:11."

"Good." Librarian Bun nodded. "What do you think that verse means?"

"That we're supposed to let men just run their mouths and we're to keep quiet," said Erin, looking into the bottom of her Styrofoam cup.

"No, that's not it at all," said Librarian Bun.

"That's what it says," Erin said. "Anyway, can I get more of this tea?"

This time, the Predicant came and took Erin's cup, returning shortly with more hot tea. She raised her eyebrows at him when he returned, holding the cup out to her.

The tea tasted funny this time. Less sweet, with some bitter note that landed on the back of her tongue. She looked behind her. The Predicant sat backward on one of the fold-up chairs, observing everything.

Later, the kids sat in the tent at lights out. Erin had skipped the Dining Tent again. Honestly, she wasn't even hungry; she would starve to death before she gave them the satisfaction of begging for food. But Bev had hid one of those sweet Hawaiian dinner rolls in her pocket. She placed it on Erin's lap. Erinwasn't sure she even chewed it. It was down her throat in one bite, and there it lodged, stuck until someone gave her a sip of water. She hadn't felt hungry till she tasted the bread.

"That's so fucking good," Erin said licking her lips. "I love those stupid rolls. They have them at all those church homecoming dinner things. My God."

"I'm sorry it's not more," Bev said.

"They're just so mean," said Cody. "I don't understand why they're so mean."

"What is today? Sunday?" Erin asked. "So, we got one more full day of this shit tomorrow, then we get to go home."

"What was all that stuff about acting the part, playing the game, like you said last night?" Bev said.

"I didn't know they were going to dangle me over a fire," Erin said. "I mean, all bets were off when they did that. If I could have grabbed ahold of that woman, she'd be dead."

"She looks pretty heavy," Bev said. "You might have needed my help."

"They think we are just doing things to make them mad. Like we *want* to be this way," Cody said.

"What do you mean?" Bev said.

Cody was silent for a moment. When he spoke, it was as if he were choosing his words carefully. "I mean, you didn't *decide* to like girls, did you? You were born like that. Don't you think?"

"When I was five, I knew it," Bev said. "It's never been a mystery."

"But like your parents—well, my parents anyway. It's like they take it personally. Like I chose this just to piss them off or embarrass them or whatever," Cody said.

"If I had a choice to choose it, I still would," Bev said, "but I think I know what you mean."

"My parents. Especially my Dad," Cody said. "He thinks I'm like this because I want to hurt his feelings or something. Like I'm acting out. Like some kid getting hooked on drugs or whatever."

"I'm sorry that happens to you," Erin said. "Parents have a hard time accepting what they don't understand and can't change."

"I always wanted to fix it for them, make them feel better," Cody said.

"How would you do that?" Bev asked.

"I mean, lately I try to go out in the garage with my Dad. He likes to work on these old cars. And I don't know nothing about any of that stuff. But I go out there anyway and pretend like I'm interested. I try to ask him questions about what he's doing, like I want to learn, like maybe he'll teach me. And maybe if he taught me how to work on cars, I'd be more like what he wanted, you know?"

"I know," Bev said.

"Just like...if he had this son who was good at working on cars, like maybe he'd think that was good, like he'd be proud of me, you know?"

"I'm sure he's proud of you," Erin said.

"He's not," Cody said. There was an edge to his voice, like he might cry. "He tells me he's not."

"What about your mother?" Bev asked. "Do you get along with her?"

"I can't fix it for her either."

"Yeah," Bev said, "but she probably doesn't care if you can work on cars."

"No," Cody said. "But she doesn't want a son like me."

Everyone was quiet for a moment. Erin felt the sadness from last night fall over the tent.

Cody continued, "When I was little, I'd try to fix it for her. But I don't know how to now."

"How would you fix it for her?" Kevin asked.

Cody's eyes were far away. "We used to play this game when I was a kid. I'd get on the bed, and she'd be trying to make it. I remember she'd take the sheet and shake it out, and fluff it up in the air, and it would come down over me. I called that sheet the Magic Maker, and when she'd throw it up in the air, I remember looking through it. It was white, and I could see the sun coming in through the window. I'd pretend the sheet was magic and it was going to fix everything."

"How? What would it do?" Erin asked.

"When it came down over me, I'd pretend I could get one wish. And I wished for more than anything that I could make my mama happy, you know? So, I'd pretend that after she fluffed that sheet up and it landed on me, it would make my body different. That when Mama pulled that sheet off —she always jerked it off like we was playing hide and seek—I'd pretend that when she pulled it off, I'd be a little girl."

Erin couldn't breathe.

"See, Mama always wanted a little girl. She told me that a bunch of times."

No one said anything. It was like all the air had been sucked from the tent.

Cody continued, his breath visible in front of his pink lips. "When she was pregnant with me, she told all her friends, her family, church folk, everyone, she told them I was going to be a girl. She told me she'd been disappointed when I was born, and I was a boy. So I thought, if that Magic Maker would just work one day. We'd play that game, and she'd throw the sheet, and when she pulled it back, I'd be what she wanted. And my dad wouldn't expect me to know how to work on cars."

Just then, the gospel music clicked on, the bass so loud, Erin felt it in her chest. The kids all looked at each other. Jack and Kevin eased back into their sleeping bags. Bev studied the floor. No one knew what to say. And anyway, they'd have to yell to be heard over the music.

Erin slid along the tent floor, over to Cody's sleeping bag. He hadn't moved, tears streaming down his cheeks.

"Hey," Erin said into his ear. "I think you're pretty perfect just as you are."

"Yeah?" Cody said.

"Yeah," Erin said. She hugged him, and he wrapped his arms around her neck. Erin felt terrible for all he'd told. But then she thought, why couldn't his mother just hug him like this? Why couldn't she just hug him? It was so obvious that's all he needed.

"Hey," Erin said when they pulled away. "But at least you're not the camp whore, right?"

Cody laughed.

"At least you didn't take your clothes off at assembly." Erin dropped her eyes. "I know what you're going through is way worse, I know that. I just wanted to make you laugh."

"Well, I did laugh," Cody said. "I thought you were going to get butt naked out there."

"I was. I meant to. I was so hot, I felt like I could scream. I was going to take it all off and roll around in the snow in my birthday suit."

Cody laughed again. "That would have been funny."

"For you, maybe," Erin said. She winked at Cody and rubbed her hand on his head like she did her nephew's sometimes.

When she got back to her sleeping bag, she saw Bev crawl over to Cody. They exchanged words, but Erin couldn't hear anything for the gospel music singer wailing about The Old Rugged Cross. Bev hugged Cody, and Erin was happy to see Kevin and Jack chatting with him later, too. Maybe by putting us all together, she thought, maybe these ugly Christians had done some good after all. Cody, Bev...all of them needed people who didn't look down on them. They needed friends. People who would accept them, even if their families didn't.

27 / ERIN ASCENDS

At midnight, Erin struck out for the northern woods toward Lucas. She circled wide outside of the camp, well clear of the campfire light. While the temperature had warmed during the day, it was in the low twenties now, the snow crunching under her boots. There was no chance anyone would hear the sound; gospel music echoed through the mountains under a clearing sky. A few snow flurries caught the wind, but Erin was unsure if they fell from the sky or if they were shaken from the trees. She felt woozy from the lack of sleep and food, but the roll Bev had given her brought her back to life a bit, along with the buzz on her skin when she thought about meeting Lucas. And he'd promised to bring her food. He better have brought food.

She made her way toward the downed tree where she and Lucas smoked the night before, their agreed-upon meeting place. She thought she heard Lucas's footfalls in the woods nearby. She stood still for a moment, listening, but she heard nothing except the music. She sat down on the log, brushing away the snow. It was colder than the night before; her feet were numb. Then she saw the light of a flashlight trained toward the ground, maybe a hundred feet away in the trees. The light looked blue compared to the yellow-tinted light of Lucas's flashlight the night before. Was it Lucas? Or had one of the camp ministers followed her? Erin panicked, sliding on her back over the log to hide behind it. She sat for a moment and tapped her foot in the snow, anxious about sitting still in the cold, anxious for Lucas to show.

Footsteps approached, and the light stopped in front of the log.

She could hear someone breathing. She snuck a peek and saw Lucas holding the flashlight. He wore a red snow jacket and the brown toboggan from the night before. She jumped up from behind the downed tree.

"Lucas!" she whispered.

The poor boy almost jumped out of his skin.

"Jesus Christ, you scared the shit out of me!" he said.

Erin laughed and scrambled over the log. When she got over, she tripped, falling face-first in the snow.

"Serves you right," Lucas laughed.

"Screw you," Erin said, using the hem of his coat to pull herself up. She wrapped her arms around him. "You're a sight for sore eyes."

"My girl," he said.

Then she pulled away from him and looked him up and down.

"What?" he said.

Erin stuck her hands in his jacket pockets. She felt the front of his jean pockets.

"What the fuck, Lucas?"

"What's wrong? Why are you frisking me?"

"Food, you dumbass. You said you were bringing me something to eat! I am walking around, about to pass out. What is wrong with you?"

Lucas smiled.

"That smile better mean you've got a Whopper in your back pocket."

He held out his hand.

"I don't want to hold hands. I want something to eat."

"Come on," he said. "I've got a surprise for you."

They walked quietly for a few minutes, clearing a ridge and beginning to descend on the other side.

"Is it far?" Erin asked. "Oh my God. I don't think I can take another step."

Lucas reached down and lifted her up, one arm under her legs, the other under her back. "Well, then, my lady, I shall have to carry you. But you need to hold the flashlight."

Erin trained the flashlight on the ground in front of them. They were far enough from camp that no one should be able to see the light, especially with the ridge behind them, but it didn't make sense to take chances. She saw another light flickering up ahead.

"What is that?"

"That's our dining place for the evening, my lady."

Up on a rise behind a large oak tree, Erin saw what it was at last. There, nestled between a group of trees, was set up a small two-man tent. There were candles ringing the outside.

"Oh, Lucas!"

"We'll be warm inside, and just you wait and see what I brought you."

Lucas placed her feet gently on the ground and said, "After you."

Erin crawled into the orange tent. Inside, there was a sleeping bag and a battery-powered lantern. The smell of food washed over her. Real food. Cooked food. Like Sunday dinner at grandma's house. She sat cross-legged and waited for Lucas to enter. He zipped the tent closed behind him.

"What is that smell? Oh my God," Erin said.

Lucas crawled excitedly to the back of the tent. He fumbled with a small cooler, producing a bucket of Kentucky Fried Chicken. He placed the bucket between them on the floor.

Erin looked him in the eyes, then ripped off the lid. She grabbed a big thigh and bit into it, closing her eyes. It was like an out-of-body experience. She ripped through the meat, barely chewing what was in her mouth before taking another bite. She ripped off the skin and ate it in one big piece, then tore at the flesh with her fingers, stuffing huge chunks in her mouth. Soon, the thigh was bare, and she was picking at the bones. She let it drop onto the cardboard lid and retrieved a big, juicy chicken leg. She tore into it. She wiped her greasy face with the back of her hand and, with her mouth full, she leaned over and kissed Lucas on both cheeks.

"Mmm," she said. "Holy Jesus, Mary, and Joseph," she said and went back to work on the chicken leg.

"Got biscuits, too," Lucas said, producing a small box.

Erin ripped open the biscuit box, tearing the cardboard, and stuffed a biscuit in her mouth behind the chicken.

"Fuck," she said.

After a few minutes, Erin had polished off two thighs, a leg, and a biscuit and a half. Lucas produced a half gallon of iced tea, and she drank it down like it was the nectar of the gods.

She lay back, still holding the bones of a thigh in her hand, the iced tea jug in the other. "You really know how to treat a girl," she said. Her belly felt taut, and grease streaked her hands and face. She eyed the stack of napkins near the chicken bucket, but it just didn't seem that important.

Lucas beamed. He sat back on his elbows, staring. "I'm not sure I've ever seen anyone eat like that."

"Yeah." Erin burped. "Like, sex is good, but try eating after two days of forced fasting in the snow."

Lucas laughed.

"Oh my God," Erin said. Her head lolled back, and she rested it against the nylon side of the tent. "The tent is a nice touch, too. First time I haven't felt cold since I got out of my sleeping bag this morning. Course," she said, "it got pretty hot by the fire today at Assembly."

"At least they kept a good fire going for you."

"Yeah," Erin said. She thought about telling Lucas about what the ministers had done to her with the fire. But why ruin the moment? She slid down on her side. "Give me a minute," she said. "I promise I'll rally."

"Oh yeah?" Lucas said, his eyes full of mischief.

"Don't get excited," she said. "I meant I'll rally to eat more of that chicken."

He laughed.

"I'm not kidding," she said. "I am going to eat all of it. Just give me a second. I'm gonna eat a bucket of Kentucky Fried Chicken every day when I get home. Original, Crispy, whatever. I'm gonna get so fat you won't recognize me."

Lucas laughed. "Want a cigarette?"

"God, yes," she said.

He shook out two cigarettes and handed her one. He lit them before unzipping the top of the tent flap for the smoke.

Erin inhaled. Her stomach felt enormous. She rubbed it over her coat. Then she was suddenly so hot she pulled off her jacket.

They smoked in silence for a few minutes.

"So, how was it today? More gay Bible verses?"

"Just more of the same," she said. She thought about how humiliated she'd been, pushed up against the fire. How desperate she'd been to get away, desperate enough to take all her clothes off and roll in the snow.

"And I noticed they're playing the gospel music late again?"

"Played it all night last night. None of us got any sleep."

"Holy shit," he said.

"I know," she said.

Erin's eyes wanted to close. She felt the exhaustion in her bones. And here, with the ridge between them and the camp, she could barely hear the gospel music. It was so quiet and peaceful, with just the crackle of the candles outside the tent.

"Lucas?" she said.

"Yeah?"

"Can we sleep and you hold me?"

He snuffed his cigarette out in the snow outside the tent, then did the same with hers. "Anything, sweet Erin."

They took off their shoes and climbed into the sleeping bag. It was made for one person, but it wasn't a problem. Erin pushed back into Lucas's chest, his arms and legs wrapped around her. Her stomach cramped a bit from the introduction of so much food after days of an empty stomach. But soon, peace washed over her, and Erin slept.

When she woke, she panicked; she didn't remember where she was, and then she realized she no longer heard the gospel music from the camp. She opened her eyes and pulled away from Lucas. Outside the tent, the candles had burned out. She checked the time: 4 a.m.

"Oh my God," she said, rousing Lucas. "I gotta go."

Lucas looked around. "It's still dark outside, you're good."

"No, they woke us up so early yesterday. You never know what they're going to do. I've got to get back. And listen—" she held a finger to her lips for a moment. "Hear that? They've turned off the music."

"Oh shit," he said.

They rushed to get their jackets and shoes on and began climbing the ridge.

"Thank you so much for the food. Really, Lucas. It was perfect. The tent. A few hours warm with you. Thank you."

Lucas gripped her hand. "I only wish I could go to the camp in your place today. Let you sleep."

"I almost forgot," he said, reaching into his pocket. "I got you these."

He produced a jumbo pack of peanut M&Ms, her favorite.

"Oh my God," Erin said.

"In case you get hungry today," he said. "This is the last day, right?"

"Yup," Erin said. "I can't wait to see what fuckery they have in store for us to wrap it up."

"Maybe they'll take it easy on you guys."

Erin cut her eyes at him. "That's not how these people think. If the first days were warm-up for day three, I may come back with scars."

"What time will you leave Tuesday?"

"No idea," she said. "They'll probably drag it all out as long as they can. The way an altar hymn has to go on for like a half hour in a Baptist church."

"Well, I'll be ready to come pick you up. Well, as soon as your parents let you get out anyway."

"If they don't let me out, I'm sneaking out. I'll call you quick as I can."

He squeezed her hand again.

When they got to the edge of the woods, they kissed before Erin made her way along the edge of the trees toward the camp.

The night was as quiet as a funeral wake. Erin looked back over her shoulder to see if Lucas was still there, but she didn't see him. Her footfalls felt loud on the crunching snow with the absence of blaring hymns for cover, making her paranoid she'd be discovered. She moved further into the trees, walking with her head down and trying to be as quiet as possible, when she looked up and saw him. The Predicant. He stood at the edge of the camp, looking in her direction.

"Jesus," she whispered. She stepped back into the shadows and stood still for a moment, not knowing what to do. Had he seen her? Although it was cold as hell, he was just in a suit with a white shirt and that stupid red tie. There was no way to get past him, walking along the edge of the woods. She looked into the forest beside her. She could walk back to camp through the woods. Maybe just stay near the edge, using the light of the camp to guide her? She looked back toward camp. The Predicant was walking now. Toward her.

Erin stepped past the first line of trees and began walking toward the camp. With any luck, the bastard hadn't seen her, and in a few minutes, they'd walk right past each other. Maybe he was just out getting some exercise? Down deep, she didn't believe that, but she had to cling to hope.

She walked along for a few minutes. Every time she took a step, it was just so loud. It wasn't just the crunch of the snow; sometimes she'd step on a downed branch, and it would crack under her feet. She peered through the trees toward camp. She couldn't see the Predicant, but she was sure she heard him walking, his feet crunching in the snow like hers. Perhaps she could just stand still and he'd walk right past her? She could sprint down through the trees and make it back to her tent before he came back from wherever he was going.

Erin stood still with her hands stuffed deep in her pockets, cocking her head to the side and listening. Through the trees, she saw him. He crept along slowly, peering into the woods. He was maybe twenty feet away. He would take a step or two, then stop and look into the trees. He'd seen her coming and was trying to figure out where she was hiding now.

Shit. She backed deeper into the woods, edging into the shadows and trying to keep a clear path to return to the edge of the camp. She looked back and realized she could only see the barest trace of light from the torches. If she couldn't see the Predicant, he couldn't see her.

After a while, she decided to walk parallel along the edge of the clearing. The trick was to make sure, after navigating around trees and thickets, that you were still walking in the right direction. Erin tried to keep the light on her left side, so she was sure she was parallel to the field. She'd walked for a few minutes when she realized she no longer saw the light. She felt her heart begin to thump in her chest, and panic rose in her throat. *Stay calm*, she told herself. She decided she would just walk back toward where she'd last seen the light when she saw something on the ground ahead of her.

At first, she thought it was a red tulip poking up out of the snow. But that didn't make sense; flowers didn't bloom in November, and she'd never seen a tulip in the woods. There was a warbled look to it, as if it shimmered somehow, despite there being no sunlight or moonlight to give it this bearing. Erin bent down on one knee. Its light shone from within it somehow; when she looked closer, there was no stem or leaves beneath. It floated inches from the snow. Erin was amazed by it, placing her hand above it. The orb gave off just the slightest hint of heat. When she stood, she saw another red bulb about ten feet away. She walked past the first and bent down again. Where did they come from? She saw there were a half dozen, moving along through the woods, snaking deeper into the trees.

Erin looked back, she thought, in the direction of where the camp might be. Her eyes returned to the red orbs. They swirled on the ground now, alive with motion, their reflections catching on the trees around them. Erin smiled. She knew, somewhere deep inside her, she was witnessing something amazing. She followed the trail of twirling wisps till she reached a point where several were clustered between two thick oaks. There she bent down and tried to touch them, but they wobbled and moved, staying just out of her reach. Then they would dance in again, enticing her to try once more. They were playing with her. She laughed. This was too weird; if she hadn't just eaten a ton of food, she'd have been sure her starved brain was playing tricks on her. The ground rumbled beneath her, and the wisps danced excitedly.

A low growl sounded from within the shadows between the trees. It was so deep it didn't seem real, thrumming over her skin and face like the tickle of a soft breeze. Erin looked between the trees. The wisps moved frantically now, dancing around the tree trunks, lighting the ground.

The growl came again, curling up Erin's spine. A dark snout emerged from the shadows. It was tall. Taller than Erin, taller than the horse she'd ridden that time with her family down in North Georgia. That had been a huge horse, a breed the trainer had called a Belgian. Erin saw the entire head of a wolf come through the shadows. Its torso became visible, at first inky black, but bearing a tint of red throughout.

"You're not real," Erin said, taking a step back.

Am I not? hissed the wolf. The voice echoed in her head, the wolf's face and mouth unmoving.

Erin ran through the woods, wildly pushing through the trees. She ran so hard her hood fell from her head, and she felt the wolf's breath on her neck. This was real. All very real.

After a few minutes of sprinting in and out of the trees, she saw light ahead. The camp! She ran even faster, leaping over a downed log and ducking under a series of low branches.

She cleared the tree line and saw the camp ahead of her. She was almost safe. Was she safe? Would she be safe at the camp? At least she wouldn't be alone.

She saw the Predicant standing by the campfire. She could hear the wolf gaining.

"Hey," she yelled to the Predicant, waving her arms.

The Predicant, who had been facing the tents, turned toward her. When he saw her, he smiled at her, and, as ugly as the smile was, Erin was happy to see it. She ran toward him, screaming.

The Predicant walked toward her, as if to help. He rubbed his bare hands together, the way she'd once seen a used car salesman do when he approached her daddy on a car lot. Did he not see the wolf behind her?

Then Erin was lifted, her feet dangling in the air, and she was carried in the opposite direction. She looked up to see the wolf had her by the hood of her jacket, carrying her away.

"Help me!" she yelled at the Predicant, twisting in the wolf's mouth to look back at the man.

When she saw his face, she almost stopped breathing. The Predicant no longer appeared as a man. He had horns twisting out of the side of his head like those of a goat. His wide-set eyes were black, as if his pupils had drowned out the white. She looked at him, not believing her own eyes. He opened his mouth and snarled, revealing row after row of jagged, pointed teeth.

The Predicant, the camp...all of it grew smaller and smaller as the wolf carried her across the field and into the woods. She looked up at the wolf and saw the vapor of his breath pushing out in front of his face. His nostrils flared, and she immediately knew the sound. She and Lucas had heard the wolf the night before, perched behind the downed tree. The footprints they'd seen belonged to it.

The wolf dodged in and out of the trees, up the ridge, and down past the empty tent site where she had lain in warm safety just a little while earlier. It continued down the mountain, bounding in and out of the trees, the echo of its footfalls shaking the earth. It ran down the mountain and into a valley before scaling another. Up and up, they went, weaving in and out of the trees, Erin swinging like a rag doll in the wolf's teeth. She watched the ground move along quickly beneath them. At times, they traveled dangerously close to vast drop-offs and cliff edges. She felt ice work through her veins, panic rising in her chest.

Erin closed her eyes and tried to will it all away. She began to pray. She prayed the Lord's Prayer over and over, aloud: "Our Father, who art in Heaven, hallowed be thy name. Thy kingdom come..."

Each time she finished the prayer, she opened her eyes. Each time, she found herself still swinging beneath the wolf. Its pace quickened, the terrain growing steeper. Erin felt heat radiating from its body. After a long while, they reached the peak of the mountain, and the wolf slowed, stalking through a ring of ancient trees. Beyond the trees, Erin saw an enormous structure. It had no roof, but the walls were at least forty or fifty feet tall; it appeared to be under construction. In the center of the trees, the wolf dropped her. When she struck the ground, it rang hollow, the sound of some boundless drum. She sat up on her knees. The wolf circled her, its teeth showing. An amber light shone through in the trees in the circle, starting at their bases near the earth and spreading up their massive trunks. Erin's eyes followed the movement of the light. There, in the trees, she saw women and girls held as if behind the thin haze of something resembling ice. In the tree closest to her, she saw a face she recognized. At first, she couldn't remember how she knew the girl. Then she could see the face, in black and white, on a milk carton at school. It was the girl who'd gone missing from last year's Purity Sojourn —Heidi.

PART 4

"There are wrongs which even the grave does not bury."

— HARRIET JACOBS

28 / MINA & THE DISCONNECTED PARTY-LINE

Gabe hadn't looked at Mina the same since the night outside Papa Leo's when they'd discovered Samson's body. The truth was, she wasn't sure how to look at herself either. They'd seen each other a few times since, but neither of them knew how to bring it up. What could she say? *Yeah,* she thought, *I'll just say, so...I can summon these weird supernatural creatures from the shadows, make them into whatever form I want them to take, and then tell them what to do; so do you still want to go out?*

Gabe held something of himself back now. He'd hug her goodbye or hold her hand, but he wasn't pushing forward like he did before, trying to find his way into her heart. Maybe he'd decided it was just too dark a place to go. So that was the way it worked, right? Mina had finally let her guard down with a guy, a very special guy, and he'd found out her secret, and maybe he was just looking for the exit. On Halloween, she'd made up her mind. In the field, when she was above Gabe, kissing his face, she decided she wasn't going to hold back anymore. She was just going to let it happen, whatever was meant to happen. Sure, she was going to go to school in a few years, and she was totally leaving Asheville. But they could be together till then, right? And who knows? They might even go to the same college. It wasn't impossible. But Mina couldn't shake off the way Gabe looked at her after she'd summoned the shadow faces to search for the Red Wolf.

"Your eyes," he'd said, stepping back. "They were gray, covered with some kind of film, when those things came in the trees."

"But they're normal now, right?"

"Yeah, I guess," he'd mumbled. And when he'd walked her home, he hadn't held her hand or tried to kiss her. Was he afraid of her? Was there something he should be afraid of? Did the power she held have a darker side? Mina didn't know, and she didn't have the words to reassure him.

On Monday afternoon, when Gabe drove her home from school, she decided to press for some time for them to hang out. Maybe they could talk. Maybe she'd think of something smart to say about it all, and Gabe would be himself again.

"Can I come hang out at your place?"

"What, like right now?" he asked.

"I mean, if it's okay?"

"I don't think LilyMa or Papa Leo would mind," he said.

"What about you? Do you want me to come over?" she fished.

He didn't take his eyes off the road. "Sure," he said.

It was so cold Gabe turned up the furnace in the basement bedroom. During the day, when Gabe was gone to school, his grandparents turned the heat way down and walked around in big sweaters or coats. Mina couldn't understand why. It wasn't like they didn't have money.

"Do you wanna play chess or something?" Gabe asked, avoiding Mina's eyes.

"Gabe, we need to talk," she said, sitting down on his bed.

"Yeah, okay," he said. He sat down on Papa Leo's old leather recliner opposite her. It creaked when he sat down in it. He looked like an old man when he sat in the recliner; it always made Mina smile.

"You know," Gabe said. "I can't get used to him not coming into my room when I get home."

"Samson?"

"Yeah. I don't think you realize how important a dog can be to your day. Until you lose them."

"I know," Mina said. "I'm sorry."

"What do you want to talk about?" he asked, still avoiding eye contact.

"Look at me, Gabe," she said. "You won't even look at me."

"What?" he said. "I look at you all the time. Used to have to try not to so much, afraid it would freak you out and you'd stop talking to me." He smiled.

"Well, you don't look at me now, at least not in the eyes."

"I'm sorry," he said. "Everything is just so weird right now. Papa Leo is getting worse, and losing Samson, and all that. I just don't know why everything has to be so fucked up."

"You're forgetting one part," she said.

He raised his eyebrows.

"You're forgetting what you saw me do in the woods."

"Oh, yeah," he said, eyes falling to his lap. "That was weird. But I'm getting used to weird things. I mean, an invisible wolf tore into my body when I was high, so..."

"There is that," she said. "Then your girlfriend goes and freaks you out, too."

His eyes met hers. "Girlfriend?"

"That's not the important part here," she said.

They didn't say anything for a while.

"So what was that?" he asked. "What were those things in the trees?"

Mina studied her palms. "I don't know what to call them. But when I was little, I called them the shadow faces."

"What are they?"

"I don't know."

"But you control them? You can just tell them to come, and they do?"

"Yes."

"Like that kid in that Stephen King book?"

"What?"

"*Firestarter*," he said. "It's this Stephen King novel where this kid, a little girl, can make things catch on fire. You know, with her mind."

"Pyrokinesis," she said. "I've read about it."

"Pyro, what? And why would you have read about that?"

"Because of these shadow things. I read all the books in the library at school, plus the ones in the public library, about being able to control things with your mind. I was trying to figure myself out, I guess."

"In that book," he said, "the government tries to catch her so they can study her." He grinned. "We better not tell anyone what you can do. They'll want to take you to a lab to poke and prod."

"They'd probably try to dissect me."

"Let's hope not," he said. He was far away for a moment.

Mina put her hair up in a ponytail, feeling the heat of the furnace on her neck. "I think I first saw them when I was five. They were looking in my window at our old house in the country. Then one time, when I got really mad at my dad, I remember calling them. He was hitting my mom."

"Wow," Gabe said.

"And now they're getting stronger. Like they're more powerful. I can make them do almost anything."

Gabe was quiet for a few minutes. Then he slid forward in the chair, leaning toward Mina.

"Maybe there's a reason," he said.

"I'd rather there be no reason. I'd rather they just left me alone."

"Maybe you have this power so you can fight the Red Wolf."

"I tried," she said.

"What?"

"When you were up in the field. After he bit you. I fought the Red Wolf. Well, the shadows did."

Gabe cupped his face in his hand. "What happened?"

"It was kind of a draw."

"You told me you fell," he said, gesturing to the thin scar on her forehead that ended at her eyebrow.

"It was the wolf."

Gabe stood and paced the room. "Why the hell is he doing this to us? Why did he kill my parents? Why is he after me? I mean, he told Papa Leo I was trying to take his power or some shit. But I never did a damned thing to him."

"That's me now," Mina said.

"What?"

"The Red Wolf told me I wasn't taking his place. That I couldn't take his power," she said. "I don't even know what that means. I just want to go to school, graduate, and get on with my life. I don't want any of this."

"But maybe you're supposed to?" Gabe said. "Like you've been chosen?"

"Out of all the people in the world, some girl from the trailer park? I just want to keep my head down, man. I don't need any of this."

Gabe sat beside her on the bed. "I thought I brought the Red Wolf into your life, and maybe I did. But if you have this power, maybe it was always going to happen, with or without me."

Mina didn't answer. She held his hand. This time, he didn't hold back, unfurling his fingers before lacing them through hers. She looked into his eyes. "I didn't ask for any of this, Gabe. I don't know what's gonna happen now, but you're pulling away from me, and I can't stand it. I finally found someone—"

"Found someone what?" he prodded.

She had to look away.

"What is it, Mina? Now who's holding back?"

She looked back. "I just don't want you looking at me differently. I'm still me. I'm the girl you first met in pre-Algebra. Sat with on the bus. Same girl. Don't treat me differently."

"But what if you got mad at me?" He laughed, then furrowed his brow as if solving a math problem. "The boys that got hurt at the bonfire. That was you, right?"

Her eyes dropped to the floor.

"Mina?"

"Yes," she said.

"Wow," he said. "I mean, they deserved it, every one of them, but still."

"It shouldn't have happened," she said. "I was frightened by the wolf and so angry about what it did to you. They were just there, hurting little girls. I just snapped."

"I get that," Gabe said. "No telling what I might do if I suddenly had that power."

"That can never happen again," she said. "I don't want to ever call them out again."

"Well, maybe you won't have to," he said.

Mina shook her head. "The Red Wolf won't leave us alone now. You saw what he did to Samson. He'll never leave us alone. Ever."

"No," Gabe said. "He won't."

There came a knock at the basement door. Mina stayed on the bed while Gabe walked down the hall. He returned with Lucas.

"Look what the cat dragged in," Gabe said.

Lucas's face was pale. Mina stood.

"I need you to do something for me," Lucas said to Mina, plopping into the leather chair, immediately becoming the old man in the room.

"What is it?" Mina asked. "Are you okay?"

"I need you to call Erin's house and ask for her."

"Okay, why?" Mina asked.

"I sat by the phone all day," he said. "She was supposed to call me. They came back from the Purity Sojourn this morning, at least they were supposed to."

"They didn't come back?" Mina asked.

"They did come back," Lucas said. "But I know some of the other kids who went. One is this dude, Todd. So I called him and asked what time they got back."

"What did he say?" Mina asked.

"He said they got back around ten a.m."

"So Erin is probably just getting settled. She probably has her parents up her ass asking her all about it. Making sure she got sufficiently saved or whatever."

"That's the thing," Lucas said. "Todd said he didn't see Erin on the buses coming back."

"What?" Mina asked.

"He said he didn't see her packing up to get on the bus. He said he heard some gay kid say the ministers came and got Erin's bags before dawn. She was a tentmate with the gays. Todd didn't see her when they all got off the buses at the church parking lot. If her parents sent her to boarding school or something, I swear I'll die."

"Boarding school?"

"They threatened it after they found the condom. Talked about sending her to an all-girls' school. Some Bible-thumper school up in New England somewhere."

"They wouldn't do that, would they?"

Lucas leveled his eyes at her. "You don't know her parents. They're nuts. Please, Mina, just call her."

"Okay. Gabe, where's your phone?"

"Should be under the bed, on the other side."

"It's not the number you know," Lucas said. "Her mom disconnected her party line. You have to call the main house phone." Lucas fished a piece of paper from his jean pocket.

Mina felt nervous when she dialed the number, and she couldn't figure out why. It shouldn't be a big deal. Erin was allowed to get phone calls. But some dark feeling washed over her. When she pressed the buttons on Gabe's phone, her fingers shook.

"Hello, Mrs. Black? Hi, yes, it's Mina. Is Erin home?"

Erin's mom's voice was brittle. "Mina. Have you seen Erin?"

"What? No. She's not there?"

"No, Mina. She's not home. We think maybe she's run off with that boy, Lucas. No one has seen her since last night at the Sojourn."

"No, she's not with Lucas." Mina looked at the boys. Lucas was gripping the arms of the chair, his knuckles white.

"She must be."

"No, I'm sure. We saw Lucas earlier. He was at school today."

"She's with him," Erin's mom said. "I just know it."

"No ma'am. He hasn't seen her. He actually asked me if I'd talked to her," Mina said.

"Oh my God," Erin's mom said. Her voice lost its brittleness. "If you hear from her, please call me right away, okay?"

"Absolutely, Mrs. Black. I will. I promise."

Then Mina heard Erin's mom in the background, like she'd set the phone down rather than hanging it up.

"John! John, honey, Erin isn't with Lucas. Mina just called here."

Mina heard Mr. Black say, "So he says. Of course, he'd say that." Then the phone clicked in her ear.

Mina set the phone down on the receiver.

"They haven't heard from her," she said.

Lucas stood, raising his palms. "I just saw her last night!"

"What? How?" Gabe asked. "I thought they came back from the Sojourn this morning?"

"I snuck up to meet her. I snuck up every night."

"What? Y'all are crazy," Gabe said.

"We just hung out, that's all. I brought her food because they wouldn't let her eat."

"Wouldn't let her eat?" Mina asked. "Why?"

"I don't know," Lucas paced the room. "I was just with her. She was fine. I took a little one-man tent up there so we could hang out for a little while. You know, because it was so goddamned cold. After she ate, we fell asleep, but it was still dark when I took her back. It was like four a.m. Everything was fine. She was fine."

"Do you think she ran away from the camp or something?" Gabe asked.

"She would have come with me if she was gonna do that," Lucas said. His wet eyes scanned the room wildly, as if he could find the explanation in the air around them. His shoulders dropped. "Oh my God," he said.

"What?" Mina asked. She walked over and put a hand on his shoulder.

"Every night I was up there, I would watch her walk all the way back to her tent. Make sure she got back safe."

"Yeah," Mina said, trying to keep her voice calm.

"Only last night," he said, meeting her eyes. "Last night I didn't. I watched her about halfway, and I left. Oh my God."

Mina looked at Gabe.

"I just wanted to get home before my old man got up for work," Lucas said. "Where the hell is she?"

"I'm sure she got back okay," Mina said. "You watched her most of the way. All she had to do was walk back."

"I didn't watch her." He looked back and forth between Gabe and Mina as if he was desperate to make them understand. "I didn't look after her, and now she's gone."

29 / PAPA LEO GOES HUNTING

Lately, Leo remembered the way the widow planted her winter garden on a hill sparsely sprinkled with trees, the way it caught the eastern sun till way past three. He remembered the beets, the greens, the broad beans, the chard. How she'd dig them up and keep them in pots in the colder months, having planted them in October. It was October now, wasn't it? Would the widow be planting her winter garden? Did she need him to come help? Would she have some of those shiny silver quarters for him?

But of course, the widow wasn't doing no planting. She'd been dead a hundred years, it seemed. Still, she came back to him now, and not just in his dreams. Just like Mama sometimes appeared to him. Mama on the roof naked. Mama running through the woods. Mama screaming. All these images of things long past cascaded over him. Daddy coming home from prison, by then an old man. Always casting about with his head down, returning to the bottle. Not living long enough to see his son make something of himself, becoming a policeman, a man of the law. Walking the streets of Asheville on the night beat for years till he got himself promoted. The tests, studying for hours on all the rules and regulations, and later, learning how to match a set of fingerprints, sitting at that old desk in the basement, studying for the detective tests. Well, it wasn't the basement back then, was it? The room that later became Gabe's bedroom in the basement had at one time been part of the one-room house he'd built for him and LilyMa. Laying recycled brick himself with mortar in a wheelbarrow because he didn't have the money to hire help. He'd bartered to get the plumbing and electrical done. All the rest he'd built himself, even laying those first shingles on the roof in the July heat. He'd been so poor he'd had to buy used nails from builders in town, taking hours to tap them out straight so they could be driven.

There were other memories too; they crept in from the dark and rippled over his skin like soft waves lapping a lake's edge. There was the time he'd tried to go talk to Ezra, tried to make peace with him. They were young men then, in their twenties, and Ezra had held his head high, defiant. He'd laughed at Leo's warnings. Somebody said he'd gone to seminary down east, but Leo and Lilyfax had known something everyone else didn't: Ezra was a wolf in sheep's clothing. He'd use the preaching, his new credentials as a reverend, to make the world see him one way, when at night he worked feverishly to conjure the darkness.

Ezra never understood what Leo did. That those dark shadows could be powerful, and while it may make a man more than a man, in the end, it would turn you into something twisted. All these years later, though, it hadn't cut Ezra down, and this perplexed Leo. How long could evil thrive in the world, right under God's eyes? Didn't God see all? Didn't God understand how the darkness worked its way through all Ezra did, how he'd eventually set his eyes on Mulwin Rock, set on rebuilding that evil Temple? Ezra gave himself over to his pride, unable to contain his ambitions, unsatisfied with a church empire that thrived in the daylight. He wanted more. He wanted to become like the Blue Man, who'd terrorized their adolescent years. He wanted power over other men. Something that would make them do whatever he wanted. God could only go so far. But flesh? The flesh is weak. While he hadn't seen it with his own eyes, he knew Ezra's purpose in rebuilding the Temple was to use it just as the Blue Man had. To trap women and girls and use them to control fragile men of power. When Ezra got this control, what did he plan to do with it? That was the mystery of the thing. What would he do when he built the new Temple? Would he lure and woo politicians, the rich and powerful, the way the Blue Man had?

Leo had lived for years, ignoring the growing threat casting its hideous shadow over the mountains. He had his own life, didn't he? A woman he loved, a son, and eventually grandchildren. He had ignored Ezra. Or maybe he'd thought the man would learn, just as he had learned in the days of the wulvers, that what he chased was fool's gold. He would find no peace in it. That's why Ezra couldn't stop. He couldn't help himself. Always pushing for just a little more. A little more power. A little more money. A bigger sanctuary, more tithing congregants, even preaching on the goddamned radio. Ezra didn't have a woman like Lilyfax to hold him close and give him hope. He was still that little orphan boy they'd met all those years ago, seeking something to make him feel superior. He'd never stop, never be satisfied.

Leo was mad at himself when he thought of it. He hadn't felt compelled to act until danger had washed up on his own shore. His son Thom died because he hadn't acted. The twins, Gabe...they too had almost died. And their mother, as crazy as she was, didn't deserve to die like that. Leo had held onto hope. Hope that Ezra would turn someday, decide the price was too high. That he'd come over and sit with Leo and Lilyfax. Maybe drink coffee in the sun. Talk about how things had been when they were teenagers. They'd laugh, and all would be well in the world. When it never happened, and the years just kept piling up, Leo knew deep down why he'd never acted. He never wanted to leave his Lilyfax. He knew that if he'd gone after Ezra, there was a chance he'd be separated from her, either in death or because he'd be behind bars. He smiled when he thought of her. Her long arms and legs, the way they curved around him. The way her dimples had brought him to his knees as a young man, and even now, how they held that same power: the power to heat his old bones, to warm his skin, no matter how cold the night.

That's what had changed. Leo was ready now. No, he didn't want to leave her. Couldn't bear the thought of it. He'd have never survived if she had ever left him. It wasn't that he wanted to be away from her. But how much time did he have left with her now? What would that life be like for her? When he one day forgot his name, who he was. Who she was. Not just for a few minutes of fuzzy-headedness when night fell. But permanently. How would she feel when she came to him, and he knew her not? He wouldn't do it on purpose, the way Peter denied Christ, but it would feel just the same. The sting of it would cut her to the bone. He couldn't bear the thought of hurting her in that way. So, if this was the future, the future he faced, the future he'd bring his beautiful Lilyfax, and if Ezra had his sights set on Gabe and the twins, what choice did he have? Were he a young man, he might have gathered Lilyfax and the grandkids up, and they might have bought a big motorhome and set out for some place out west. They would go so far Ezra wouldn't be able to sniff them out. So far, he wouldn't consider them a threat. There they'd sit and watch the stars under some desert sky like those cowboys in the John Wayne movies.

But Leo was not a young man. He was an old man now, slipping under some dark coming night. If Ezra was coming for them, this was his last chance to do one good thing before he died or wound up in a rocking chair facing a cinderblock wall in a goddamned nursing home. What he feared most was not dying, not going to jail, though it would crush his heart knowing Lilyfax was outside, still in the world without him. No, what he feared most was forgetting what he'd come to the Church of Hosanna to do. That he'd slip under before he did the one task God had left for him. That he'd lose his mind before he fulfilled his destiny. And if he failed, Ezra would come for the twins, for Gabe, and perhaps for Lilyfax herself. He couldn't bear the thought of it. No way in hell could he let that happen.

And so, he had waited in the woods by Hosanna Church for Reverend Ezra to appear. Not only had the man not shown up Saturday, when a bunch of kids were packed on the buses bound for the church's Purity Sojourns, he'd lined up a guest preacher for Sunday. Why was he hiding? And where?

On Monday afternoon, Leo left the house and headed west in his pickup truck toward Mulwin Rock. He kissed Lilyfax on the forehead. Her eyes were suspicious, but she said nothing. He'd already packed his guns carefully under the seat of his truck, where she wouldn't find them, and he was armed to the teeth. He had the over under shotgun, a dozen boxes of shells, two pistols—his .22 revolver and a .45. Enough bullets to kill a hundred men. He had a knife hidden in his boot and a large Bowie knife on his belt, both sharpened to razor edges using a whetstone in his workshop while Lilyfax cooked dinner.

The fog threatened to fall over him that afternoon as he drove. The way it always came at dusk and made him confused. But Leo pushed it away. Not today, he thought, there's no turning back. This was it.

After taking the dirt road as far as he could, he pulled his F-150 off in a cluster of trees to hide it and continued on foot.

It was amazing how much the mountain had changed, and how

much remained the same. Along the trail, he passed several houses covered in tar paper, with tarpaulin awnings spread out in front of them for makeshift front porches. In these little shacks, people cooked food, ate, slept, made love, had babies. These people lived and died on the side of the mountain, the rest of the world not giving a shit one way or the other.

When he snaked along the edge of the mountain, he heard gospel music. There, on a mountain summit nearby, he saw the campsite for the Purity Sojourn, the smoke of a fire, and a few kids milling about in the snow. They were too far away for him to see their faces. He kept on.

After an hour, he was panting. He set the shotgun against a tree and unbuttoned his green army jacket. He had a pistol in each pocket, shells and bullets in a pack he carried over his shoulder. Everything was loaded and ready. He could sense in his bones that Ezra was close.

He saw a cluster of trees ahead, bearing claw marks. Beyond, he saw the ancient macabre trees he remembered. The trees the Blue Man had used to imprison women. Then he saw the Temple structure near the rock face on the north of Mulwin. It was massive. So large it would have swallowed the old Temple Leo, and the others had burnt to the ground back then. Ezra's ambition wouldn't allow him to build something the same size or smaller.

Leo heard someone approaching and ducked behind a tree to listen. One set of footsteps, maybe two. He snuck a peek around the tree and saw a thick bald man coming through the woods, dressed in a heavy coat, snow boots, and black gloves. He held a young girl by the wrist. She had dark skin and wore a thin white gown that clung to her body; she had to be freezing. She might have been a Native girl, maybe Cherokee, but he wasn't sure. She might could have been Hispanic.

The man led the girl down a path opposite the Temple. Leo looked toward the Temple and saw no sign of anyone. Though it wasn't why he was here, he thought of the girl's sad eyes, how cold she must feel in the gown, and made up his mind to follow them.

He crept along the trail, dashing from tree to tree, in case the man decided to turn around.

After a while, they came to a series of tents spread on high ground under a cluster of tall maples and pines. The man went to one tent and unclasped the flaps. He ordered the girl inside. This was where Ezra entertained men while the Temple was being completed, Leo thought. He skulked to the edge of the tent, listening through the canvas.

"Get on that sleeping bag," the man commanded. "You shore are a pretty thing."

Leo heard the man fumbling with his jacket. He waited until he heard the man drop his britches and pull them off. Leo carefully opened the flap, training the shotgun barrel in first. Inside, the man stood in front of the girl, reaching for her with his fat fingers. The girl saw Leo over the bald man's shoulder. He held a finger to his lips and stepped closer, putting the barrel of the shotgun to the back of the man's head.

"Don't you move a goddamned muscle," he said. "Less you want the inside of your head to see daylight."

The man froze, raising his hands.

To the girl, Leo said, "It's okay. It's all going to be okay."

She hesitated, looking back and forth between them.

"I'm not here to hurt you," Leo said.

She rolled off the sleeping bag and stepped around the man, behind Leo.

"What are you doing with a girl so young?" he asked the man. The man moved as if to turn and face him. Leo slammed the barrel down on the man's bald head. "Don't you move, you bastard."

The girl slid to the edge of the tent, holding her knees.

"You speak English?" Leo asked her.

"Yes," the girl said. She had a country accent.

"Put on his jacket, and gloves and all," he told her.

"What am I going to wear?" the man said.

"Doubt you'll be leaving this tent," Leo said.

The man started to whimper.

Leo turned to the girl. "You know the way down the mountain?"

"Yes," she said.

"Okay, put on his snow boots, even if they don't fit. Tie them tight as you can, okay?"

She did as she was told.

"You head down the mountain," he told her. "Run as fast as you can. Don't look back. When you get to the main road, head toward town. Don't stay on the road where anybody can see you. Stay in the trees. Understand?"

"Yes, sir," she said. She laced up the boots, her whole body trembling.

"When you get about 2 miles down," he said, "there'll be a convenience store. You got people you can call?"

"Yes," she said.

"They got a phone. Call your people to come get you. Then wait inside the store for them. All right?"

"Yes," she said.

"Don't talk to nobody, okay?"

"Thank you," she said. She scowled at the bald man and spat on his face. Then she was out of the tent. Leo waited for her footsteps to fade.

He tapped the bald man on the head with the shotgun barrel. Harder this time. The man winced. "Now, I asked you a question," Leo said. "What're you doing with a girl so young? She can't be more than fifteen. You probably got daughters older than her."

"He give her to me," the man said, letting his body collapse to the tent floor. "Said it was God's will."

"Who?"

"Reverend Ezra," the man whispered.

"No man can give you a woman," Leo said. "A woman has to give herself to a man, that's her goddamned choice to make."

"Things are different up here," the man said.

"No hell they ain't," Leo said.

"And anyway," the bald man said, "he ain't just a man."

"He still bleeds, just like you, I'd wager," Leo said. He unclasped the Bowie knife and pulled it free, gripping the handle. "Roll over," he told the man. The naked man did as he was told, his lips trembling. His teeth chattered like a child's. Without saying another word, Leo rammed the knife deep into the man's belly, high, just under his breastbone. The man shuddered, and Leo grabbed the back of his neck to pull him close. "It'll be over in a minute," he whispered.

When had he said those words before? Leo remembered the battlefield in Korea. He'd pulled his pistol on an enemy soldier, but the gun had jammed. He'd pulled out a knife and rammed it deep into the man, holding him by the neck just like this, and said the same words, whispering them into the man's ear even though he knew the soldier hadn't understood them. Maybe they'd eased him anyway? Leo didn't want to ease this man, but he wanted him to give up the ghost quick; he didn't need to linger in this tent. The man didn't make a sound. He lay on his back, blood gurgling in his mouth. Leo tried to still his own breathing as he watched the man die. The man he'd killed in Korea maybe hadn't deserved it, but this man surely did.

30 / FIRST BLOOD
PAPA LEO

Leo made his way toward the Temple, the shotgun pointed in front of him. Somehow, he smelled blood, tasted it. Perhaps it had sprayed in his mouth during the struggle. He thought of spilling Ezra's blood. Hopefully, he'd do it soon. He thought of the girl's bright face, her expression when she'd spit on the bald man. He hoped like hell she made it down the mountain all right. That she'd get home safe. Be able to forget this place someday and go on with her life. How many others like her did Ezra have up on this mountain?

Leo made his way to the center of the trees that circled near the Temple. He remembered their boundless size. He studied their black bark, expecting to see the faces of the girls within them. He couldn't see them, but knew they were there. There was a large tree at the center that drew his eye. There was something familiar about it. Then he remembered. It was the tree that had once held his Lilyfax. He put his fingers on the bark. It gave way, and he saw a girl there. An amber light glowed behind her, a frosty sheen over her body, holding her in place.

She was dressed in a black leather skirt and a bright pink shirt, like young girls wore at the mall, with tall silver heels. Her face was void of expression, her eyes dead-looking, like a fish's when you get it in the boat. It took him a minute to place her. The girl was Erin, one of Gabe's friends. One by one, the trees began to light from within, the faces of all the girls and women visible. Leo shuddered as he spun in a circle, still pointing the shotgun. In another tree, he saw a boy bearing a baby face, narrow through the shoulder. He was dressed in a baseball uniform, a brown leather glove on one hand.

Ezra emerged from behind the tree that held the boy, dressed in a dark red robe, the hood over his head. The train of the robe dragged the snow as he stepped forward. He followed Leo's eyes to the boy in the tree.

"The taste of men changes, twists into perversion. We must meet all their filthy lusts wherever they spring forth."

Leo trained the shotgun on Ezra's chest.

Ezra raised his arms, the robe spreading out beneath them. "It's beautiful, isn't it?"

"It makes me sick. You make me sick."

"Oh, come now," Ezra said, smiling. His face looked old. Older than it had ever looked. A single thick strand of gray hair sprang from the front of his head, disappearing under the hood. "Did you observe that my Temple will be even larger than the Blue Man's?"

"What happened to you?" Leo asked.

"Me?" Ezra spread his hands in front of him. "I've only evolved while you've stayed the same. Look at all I have done. What have you done, Leo? Sat home playing house?"

"You're looking older," Leo said. "This has all caught up with you in the end."

Ezra held his forearm out. "What runs through my veins is the pure energy of the earth itself. Feral, unadulterated, unfettered."

"You'll be found out. All this will come burning down, just like before."

Ezra stopped smiling. "And who will burn it down, Leo? You? You won't even see the sun set."

Leo slid the safety off on the shotgun and clicked the slider to favor the lower barrel.

"It's not too late for you to turn from all this," he said. "You can free the girls and come back down the mountain with me. You'll serve some time, but you can turn to the light."

Ezra laughed and interlaced his fingers. "No bars could ever hold me. We both know that."

"No need," Leo said. He raised the shotgun to his shoulder. Ezra didn't move. Instead, he smiled. As Leo pulled the trigger, he was lifted from his feet, something ramming into his side. He felt an intense pain as he flew through the air, the shotgun careening, the second barrel discharging as it hit the ground. Leo held his side, warm blood spreading over his fingers. He saw a man before him. Something between beast and man. Long black goat horns grew out of its man's skull. He had white-blond hair and skin so pale it matched the snow on the ground. The beast snarled at him, his mouth full of jagged, pointy teeth.

Leo scrambled to his feet, pulling the Bowie knife out with his left hand and the .45 with his right.

"Your friends are as ugly as your heart," he said to Ezra.

Ezra laughed. "Come now, Leo, I've never known you to lack manners. Meet the Predicant. As Christ sits at the right hand of our Father, so does the Predicant sit at mine."

"Two ugly peas in a pod," Leo said, stumbling. The pain made him grind his teeth. He held up the pistol and pointed it at the goat-headed man.

The Predicant took a step toward him. Leo clicked off the safety and pulled back the hammer. The Predicant ducked, dropping to all fours, and loped toward him.

Leo kept the gun trained on the Predicant at first, then remembered his purpose. At the last minute, he swung the barrel toward Ezra and fired, catching him in the shoulder. Ezra cried out as the Predicant's horns tore into Leo's stomach. For a moment, he was impaled, the two of them stuck together like lovebugs on a windshield. Then the Predicant swooped his head and unhooked his horns from under Leo's ribcage. He let Leo drop to the ground on his back.

Everything went hazy. Leo's eyes wanted to close, but he fought against it. He stuck his fingers in the holes of his midsection as if he could stem the flow of blood. His head lolled to one side, and he saw Ezra fall to his knees, holding his shoulder, before red orbs rose on the ground around him. Then Ezra was the Red Wolf, and Leo saw a bright crimson spot at the beast's shoulder. Something like mist rose from the wound, and the wolf groaned so loud the earth shook.

The Predicant stood dumbly by the wolf, hands hanging at his sides. The Red Wolf stumbled for a moment, the crimson mist hovering in the air around him, steadily issuing forth from the shoulder wound.

On the ground, Leo struggled to breathe. He reminded himself he wasn't afraid of dying. He'd come here to die. But he hadn't delivered the kill shot yet. He thought of the .22 in his left pocket, but was too weak to reach for it. He thought of the power he'd wielded when he was young, the wulver he'd been able to conjure from the shadows. He wondered if it would come to him again, but he felt frail. His thoughts turned to God, praying he could finish what he'd come here to do.

The Red Wolf crept toward him. The Predicant remained where he'd stood before, pulling the cloud of red toward his face as if he were trying to breathe it in. When he faced Leo, his cheeks were covered in droplets of dark blood.

Why did you come up this mountain just to die? the wolf growled.

Leo could barely breathe, let alone answer.

Call forth the Shadow Wulver to strike me down where I stand, Old Man Leonard. Call on your God to do it. Is this all you've got?

Leo's vision grew hazy at the edges. He felt blood in his mouth and thought of the way the bald man choked on his own blood before he died.

The Red Wolf turned to the Predicant and saw him pulling the red mist toward his face with his hands, breathing it in. The wolf growled and showed his teeth, stirring the earth. The Predicant fell to his knees in submission.

Throw him over. After three days, retrieve his body and burn it. Burn even the bones to ash.

"Yes, my lord," said the Predicant. He lifted Leo from the ground and walked toward the mountain's rock face.

Leo fished in his pocket for the .22. He pulled it out and chambered a round. When he did so, the Predicant heard the metal click, and he leaned down, biting Leo's hand, rows of teeth sinking into the flesh. For a moment, Leo forgot about his stomach wounds. The flesh of his hand sizzled, the skin burning when the Predicant released it. When they reached the mountain edge, the Predicant lifted Leo overhead and hurled him into space.

Leo fell. He watched the rock face of the mountain race pass in a blur. In that moment, he saw his baby sister, the one he'd called Goldfish. He saw her twirling in the field down by the creek, her gold hair spinning. Like his brothers, Goldfish had preceded him in death, but now she was once again a child of eight or nine. She smiled at him with bright, crooked teeth and put her tiny hand in his. Then she was petting the crystal rabbits in the clearing on that perfect spring day so long ago, the sky so astonishingly blue with white puffy clouds so close Leo could touch them. Lilyfax leaned warmly against him, her soft breath on his shoulder. The breeze lifted the hem of her dress. Leo wrapped his arms around her, and they closed their eyes, turning their faces to the sun. Together, they rose from the earth and floated away.

31 / CONVENIENCE STORE COFFEE

MINA

Mina and the boys found out about the search for Erin when a sheriff's car pulled into the driveway at Papa Leo's at dusk. Mina, Lucas, and Gabe had been sitting on the back porch. They came around the front of the house, drawn by the flashing blue lights. LilyMa was with Sheriff Barnaby.

"No, Sheriff," LilyMa said. "Leo isn't home. He went out this morning, said he was going fishing. Tell you the truth, I'm a little worried. Thought maybe that was why you were here. He gets confused sometimes, driving at night."

"Well, I do want to see him. Get a cup of coffee sometime. But I'm here looking for Lucas Hamlin. His daddy sent me over, said he would be here." The sheriff looked over at the approaching teenagers.

Mina looked at Lucas, who grimaced.

"You must be Leo's grandson," Sheriff Barnaby said to Gabe. "Spitting image of your daddy."

"Yes, sir," Gabe said. He looked from the sheriff to Lucas and back again.

"Your dad was a good man, but I'm sure you know that," said the sheriff. "You, Lucas?"

"Yeah," Lucas said. There was an edge to his voice Mina had never heard before. All the swagger he normally bore was gone.

"We're looking for Erin Black. You seen her?"

"No, sir," Lucas said.

"You haven't seen her at all today?"

"No, sir," Lucas said, looking at his feet. Then, as if he'd made his mind up about something, he blurted out, "I want to help you go look for her."

"Is that right?" the sheriff said, raising his eyebrows. "You know she's missing?"

"No, sir. I mean. Yes," Lucas stammered.

"We called her house earlier," Mina interrupted. "Mrs. Black told us Erin was missing. She said Erin never came back from the church sojourn."

"That's right," Sheriff Barnaby said, keeping his eyes on Lucas.

"I told her not to go," LilyMa said. "After that girl went missing last year. Something strange is going on with that church."

"Yes," the sheriff said. "We haven't given up that search. And there's another woman missing—older lady, not a teenager this time. She was pretty involved over at Hosanna."

LilyMa clucked her tongue. "There will be more," she said.

"How might you know that?" the sheriff asked, turning to her.

LilyMa looked as if she had more to say but held her tongue.

Sheriff Barnaby hesitated, then turned back to Lucas. "When was the last time you saw Erin?"

"Before the sojourn," Lucas said.

Mina and Gabe looked at each other. He wasn't going to tell the sheriff he'd been up on the mountain every night, like they weren't going to find out anyway?

"Some of the folks we questioned from Hosanna, the youth ministers, they seem to think she run off with you because she didn't want to be there. Said her parents made her go."

Lucas said nothing.

Barnaby went on, "We talked to her folks this afternoon. They feel the same way."

"Well, if she run off with me, she'd be right here," Lucas said. "And if she run off by herself, she'd have come here. This is where we hang out."

The sheriff looked at LilyMa, who nodded. "Strange goings-on," she said.

"You don't know the half of it," the sheriff said, shaking his head. "I got teenagers with broken legs, ribs, concussions, all kinds of things, at a big Halloween party a few weeks back. People talking about seeing wolves and panthers all around the county. It's been a crazy fall. Something in the water."

Mina's hands grew cold, and she stuck them in her jean pockets. She felt Gabe's eyes on her.

"You better come with me, son," the sheriff motioned to Lucas.

"I want to help look for her," Lucas said.

"That's nice, son," the sheriff said. "But I'm taking you to the station to get a statement. Your dad can pick you up there after one of my deputies takes your statement. I've got to get out toward Barnardsville, where Erin was last seen. We have men gearing up for the search. Thing is, it's supposed to drop off cold tonight, in the teens, maybe more snow. If she's still up on that mountain, we got to find her."

"She'll freeze to death up there," LilyMa said.

"That's what we're worried about. Her daddy has a bunch of people rounded up to help in the search. And that's all well and good, but I have to keep a handle on this. We don't want anyone to disturb any..." His voice trailed off.

Crime scene. Mina's brain finished the sentence.

"Sheriff," Gabe said. "We want to come help look for her."

"Now we don't need you kids up there. It's not safe. It'll be cold, and the last thing I need is another kid to go missing when we ain't found the first."

"She's my best friend," Mina said.

The sheriff turned his hat in his hand. "I understand how you feel, I really do, but you'll just be in the way. We have to keep organized about this. Best thing you can do is be home, safe and warm, and in case she did run off, she's liable to come here."

"She didn't run off," LilyMa said. "She's been took."

The sheriff furrowed his brow. "You got some strong opinions on this thing."

"I do," LilyMa said. Her eyes were far away. "I'd come help look for her myself, but Leo hasn't come home, and I need to be here when he gets back. I may need to be out looking for him."

"We're going to find her," the sheriff said.

After the sheriff took Lucas, Mina followed Gabe into the house and downstairs to his room. Once they got there, Gabe began rifling through drawers, throwing a pair of long handles, socks, and gloves onto his bed.

"We need flashlights," Mina said.

"Papa Leo has a million in his workshop. Headlamps, too."

"Why didn't Lucas just tell them the truth?" she asked.

"I don't know," Gabe said. "That was stupid."

"They're gonna find out," she said.

Gabe sat down beside her on the bed. He was quiet for a moment, then said, "I can't imagine what Lucas must be feeling. I'd go crazy," he said. "If it were you."

Mina looked at him. "I can't help but think about Heidi, from last year."

"I know," Gabe said. "Two years in a row, a girl goes missing on a church trip. What the hell?"

"That's not what I mean," Mina said. "There was hardly a peep from the sheriff's department when she went missing. Her family doesn't come from money."

"Hadn't thought about that."

"The police kept saying that Heidi must have run off with some man. They never acted like she was worth searching for, not at first."

"That's true."

"But now you got Erin's daddy out there, throwing all his country club money around. Probably helped get Barnaby elected in the first place. Erin said he was big in local politics."

Gabe didn't answer.

"If Erin was a poor girl, a girl from Whispering Pines, there wouldn't be some big search party for her. That's the truth. I mean, if it were me—"

"If it were you," Gabe said, "I'd shake every tree in Western North Carolina."

"Even when you go missing, it matters where you're born, who you are."

"I know," Gabe said. He looked at Mina. "We've got to find her. What do you think happened? Do you think she ran away from the camp?"

"No," Mina said. "Lucas was right about that. If she were gonna run away, she'd have gone with him last night."

Gabe stood up. "Let's get these warm clothes on. Wear my other jacket and gloves. Then we'll get those flashlights."

When they reached the outside door, LilyMa met them, arms crossed.

"It's dangerous out there," she said. "Wind chill down to 10 degrees later tonight, the weatherman is right. It'll be colder up on the mountain."

"I know, LilyMa," Gabe said. "But Erin is missing. She's important to us. We have to go look for her."

LilyMa looked at Mina. "Suppose if I make Gabe stay here, you'll just go out there looking for her by yourself?"

"Yes, ma'am," Mina said.

LilyMa was quiet for a moment. "Gabe, your papaw has been out since early this morning. He never goes off for more than an hour or two these days. I'm worried."

Gabe nodded. "You think we should go look for him instead of Erin?"

LilyMa shook her head slowly. "Papa Leo would want you to look for Erin. I know that about him."

"You're right," Gabe said.

"Now listen to me," LilyMa stood forward and put her hand on Gabe's shoulder. "When you get out there, you've got to stay with that search party. Help them look, but don't go off by yourselves, you hear me?" She looked from Gabe to Mina and back.

"Yes, ma'am," they echoed.

"And you need to understand something," she said, frowning. "Erin didn't run off. I believe what I told the sheriff. She was took. Someone is taking these girls."

Gabe and Mina looked at each other.

"I smell it," LilyMa said, "I believe your papaw did too."

Later, in the car, Mina asked Gabe, "What do you think she meant by Papa Leo knowing about all this?"

"I don't know," Gabe said. "How would he know Erin was going to go missing before anyone else did?"

"I don't know," she said. "How long will it take us to get out there?" she asked.

"About an hour or so," he said. "They were camping up on Hooker's Knob. It's an old, primitive campsite. I went up there when I was a kid. My daddy took us one time."

"There's a name for you. Hooker's Knob."

"I always wondered about that."

"How old were you?" she asked.

"Maybe five or six. Only one thing I remember," Gabe smiled. "It was the first time I learned to wipe my ass with leaves."

"Oh my God," Mina said. "Seriously?"

"Yup," he said. "Daddy made me learn how to bury it after, too."

"There's a life skill for you," she said.

"It's actually pretty important when you're out in the woods and run out of toilet paper."

Mina laughed.

He said, "My mom hated it, though. Not just the shitting in the woods part. All of it."

"She doesn't sound like she was the camping type."

"It was mainly because we had to miss church. She didn't know what to do with herself. She tried to make our own church service on Sunday morning. I'll never forget that."

"Wow."

"I had to sing hymns with her, and then she read verses, and then she got mad because my daddy didn't want to preach."

"She actually wanted him to preach a sermon?"

"She said women couldn't do it, so he had to."

"What did he do?"

"He basically spun some long life lesson. I can't remember a word of it."

"Just the shitting in the woods?"

Gabe laughed. "Yeah, it made quite an impression on me."

"I can see that. I'm picturing little Gabe in the woods with his little shovel," she teased.

"Don't make me regret telling you."

They were a few miles past Barnardsville when Mina asked Gabe to stop at a convenience store. She needed to pee and wanted a cup of hot coffee before they got out in the cold. The gas station was a hole in the wall; she doubted they would have coffee that hadn't been sitting in the pot all day. She found the bathroom out back after getting the key from the clerk, a short man with a black and gray beard wearing a Dukes of Hazzard cap.

Inside, Gabe had a handful of candy bars, Mars and Heath. He'd already poured Mina's coffee and stood with it at the counter. The store sported a dirt floor but was clean otherwise.

"You want anything else?" Gabe asked Mina when she returned.

"Nah, looks like you've got our sugar fix covered."

"Got you a large," Gabe said, nodding toward the coffee. "Didn't know how you take it."

"Hey, man," Mina asked the clerk. "How old is this coffee anyway?"

The man craned his neck, looking at something at the back of the store. "What's that?" he said, never taking his eyes off whatever was so interesting in the back.

"The coffee, man," Mina said. "How old is it? Am I gonna have to spit it out?"

"Made it fresh about an hour ago," the clerk mumbled.

He rang up the items for their order. The spell broke, and he looked at them as he grabbed the cash. "That girl gives me the creeps," he said in a whisper.

"What girl?" Mina asked.

"Can't tell if she's here casing the joint for a robbery or something. Pretty sure she's strung out on something. A lot of them Mexicans are."

Mina followed the man's eyes to the back of the store. Behind one of the rows of food shelves, a girl stuck her head up, just high enough for Mina to see the top of it.

"What's she doing back there?" she asked.

"If I knew that, I wouldn't be so creeped out," the clerk said. "I went back there a while ago to check on her, and she just kept hiding around the aisle like she was afraid of me. She's got on some old work boots bigger than her."

"I'll be right back," Mina said to Gabe.

"We got to get going," he said, but she held up her hand.

At the back of the store, the girl huddled behind a stack of Budweiser cases. She shrank back when Mina approached, her black hair a shock against the whitewashed wall.

"Hey, you okay?" Mina asked.

"I can't talk to nobody," the girl whispered. She wore a thick coat that was so large it reached mid-thigh. She had on a white gown beneath it, and a pair of men's boots that flopped when she took a step back.

"It's okay," Mina said, holding up her hand.

"They got to drive all the way from Bryson City," the girl said. She didn't look Mina in the eyes.

"Who does? Who has to drive all the way from Bryson?"

"My mama and my uncle. They're coming to get me."

Mina leaned against the stacked beer. "Well, that's good. When will they be here?"

"I don't know," the girl said. "I ain't supposed to talk to nobody." She met Mina's eyes before quickly looking away.

"Everything all right back here?" Gabe said, approaching. The girl squatted down as if she were afraid of him. Mina waved Gabe away.

"It's okay. It's just me and you back here," she said. She got on one knee. Gabe's pair of long underwear bunched up under her jeans. She was starting to sweat. "Are you gonna be okay till they get here?" she asked the girl.

"The good man said not to talk to nobody. Just to wait here till they got here. That's what I done. But that cashier, he keeps coming back here."

"I'll tell him to leave you alone," Mina said. "Don't worry."

The girl's breathing quickened, her chest rising beneath the enormous coat.

"Hey," Mina said. "It's okay. You're all right."

"He'll come looking for me," the girl said. Her straight hair fell over her face, shaking in time with her shoulders.

Mina touched her knee, and the girl pulled it back.

"Who is looking for you?" she asked gently.

The girl looked Mina in the eye for the first time. "You believe in monsters?"

"Yes, I do," she said.

"He drug me up on top of that mountain. He put me in a tree. You probably think I'm plumb crazy."

"Who did?"

"Got all kinds of girls held prisoner up there."

"Who?"

"He takes us down for the men to have their way."

Mina felt her skin crawl. This girl wasn't tripping out on some drug. She was terrified to the core.

The girl said, "Took me down, but this old man, he come in and saved me. Set me free."

"Okay," Mina said, "But who put you up there? In the trees?"

"It was the goat headed man and that giant wolf. They done it." The girl's eyes darted in their sockets.

"A wolf put you in the trees? A Red Wolf?"

The girl stared at Mina. "Have you seen him?"

"Yes," Mina said. "I've seen him."

"You better get away from here," the girl said.

"What's your name?" Mina asked.

"I don't think I ought tell that," the girl said.

"It's okay, you don't have to."

"But you better get away from here. He likes the pretty ones."

"Where? Where does he have the girls?"

"It's on top of that mountain. Way up high where it's hard to catch your breath."

"Which mountain? Hooker's Knob?"

The girl didn't answer.

Mina thought of Erin. She wasn't missing—she'd been *took*, the way LilyMa had said.

"How many girls?" she asked.

"Maybe a hundred," the girl said. "They're in all the trees. Near the Temple."

Mina gave the girl a coffee and one of Gabe's candy bars. She let the clerk know the girl's people were on their way, to leave her be. Then she and Gabe got back in the Magic Carpet Ride and headed up Hooker's Knob.

32 / SEARCH PARTY
GABE

The searchers fanned out in a long line over the flat ground where the sojourn campsite had been. They trained their flashlights along in front of them as they shuffled slowly along, looking for any trace of Erin, a few of them calling her name. Gabe and Mina stood by the ashes of the dormant campfire at the center of the campsite, a black circle on the ground, about eight feet in diameter. An ashy half-moon lit the field beyond the campsite intermittently, tucking in and out of the clouds that filled the sky. The wind cut at their faces, the night bitter cold.

"If we could figure out where Erin was meeting Lucas each night," Gabe said. "Then maybe we could track her in the snow. Figure out which way she went." His voice was low, and he leaned his head toward Mina so it could be heard above the wind. Beyond the field, the forest rose in a hush of dark limbs and silver frost. The moon broke free of the clouds briefly, pale and watchful, casting ghostlight through the trees. Gabe thought about the contrast of all the beauty before him against the evil that man brought to this place —a world both terrible and beautiful.

"That girl at the country store," Mina said. "She was there. Where Erin is."

"Where?"

"She said high on a mountain, where it's hard to breathe." A shadow fell over her face. "The Red Wolf has Erin."

Gabe felt his blood run cold. "The Red Wolf?"

Mina looked at the slope of Hooker's Knob, where the peak spread up from the field. "We need to climb to the top."

"What would the Red Wolf want with Erin? I thought it was us he was after?"

"I don't know. The girl said he kidnapped a lot of girls."

"But why?"

"She said they were forced to have sex with men up there."

"Oh my God," he said. "We have to find Erin."

"She said an old man helped her escape."

"An old man?" he asked.

"Papa Leo," Mina said, rubbing her lips with her fingertips. "You think it was him?"

"Maybe he knew about all this," Gabe said, pushing the snow with his boot. "When he confronted the wolf that day, he said something about a Temple. I thought it was a church thing."

Mina tugged at his jacket sleeve. "The girl mentioned a temple. That's where all the other girls are. It's the same place."

"We can't let them hurt Erin," Gabe said. "We have to hurry."

Mina looked back at the sheriff's deputies, still walking in a wide line over the campsite. "Let's go."

They crossed the field toward the tree line. Something grabbed Gabe's eye. "There!" He got down on one knee and traced it with his finger. "It's a paw print."

They followed the paw prints into the woods, where they disappeared.

"This way," Mina said, moving up the slope.

They walked for a while in silence.

"Can you do what you did when we found Samson?"

"You mean using the shadow faces to search?"

"Yes," Gabe said.

"You won't freak out?"

"No."

"Okay."

Mina closed her eyes. Gabe saw the shadows curling in the tops of the trees. They formed terrible shapes, gargoyles, and snakes. They slithered through the branches overhead, and Gabe fought down the sense of panic that welled within his gut.

"I thought I told you two to stay your asses at home." It was Sheriff Barnaby.

"We just couldn't do that," Gabe said. He was afraid the sheriff would see Mina's eyes, milky and cloudy, but Mina turned her back to them. The shadows stilled in the trees, the gargoyles perched on the branches like statues.

"You saw them," Barnaby said.

"Saw what?" Gabe said, his voice on edge.

"The paw prints," Barnaby said. "I followed them here. Reckon you did, too."

Just then, a boom echoed over the mountain. Something like a gunshot. A flare flickered in the distance.

"Shit," Barnaby said.

"What is it?" Gabe asked.

"Told them not to use those unless they found something important."

"Do you think they found her?" Gabe asked.

"They haven't found her," Mina said, her back still turned.

"What's wrong with her?" Barnaby asked, taking a step forward.

Gabe put his arm around Mina. "She's just upset. Give us a minute."

"I got to go see what the flare is for," Barnaby said. "I don't want you out here. I don't have time to babysit."

"No, sir," Gabe said. "You don't need to."

"I need you to get back to the search party. We can't have people wandering off by themselves. There's too much ground to cover, and if you two get lost, we'll have to divide our resources."

"We'll get back with the group," Gabe said. "Just give us a minute."

"Do I have your word?" Barnaby asked.

"Yes, sir, you do," Gabe said.

Then Barnaby was gone. Above them, the shadows came back to life. Mina's fists were balled in front of her. Ugly gargoyles leaped from tree to tree, racing up the slope ahead of them. Mina and Gabe walked along behind them.

"What do you see?" Gabe asked.

"Nothing yet," she said.

Someone in the field had a megaphone. "The search is suspended. Repeat. Search suspended. A body has been found at the base of the mountain."

"A body?" Gabe said.

Then Mina was back, her eyes clear. The shadows dissipated slowly in the trees, like ink spreading in water.

"We're too late," he said.

Tears formed in her eyes. "How could this happen?" she asked.

They caught up with the search party at the edge of the campsite. The men walked solemnly down the trail, their flashlight beams dancing ahead of them. No one spoke. Mina held Gabe's hand, and he felt his body shaking, but not from the cold. He kept thinking about Erin. The way she joked and smiled, the way she put her arms around Lucas and looked at him like he hung the moon. Her laughter when she danced at the Halloween party. The way Erin had brought him and Mina together, with the hand-me-down clothes in his front yard.

It took fifty-five minutes to descend the mountain. When they reached the base, they saw a group of men in a clearing, spotlights from deputy cars lighting the scene. Mina let go of Gabe's hand, and they began to run toward the cars. Together, they weaved in and out of the sheriff deputies and volunteers. When they got close, they tried to see over the paramedics.

"He's got a wound in his side," one said, "but it's the fall that killed him."

Him? Gabe looked at Mina. She met his eyes briefly before Gabe pushed his way to the front.

"Get him out of here," someone said. Sheriff Barnaby. He looked at Gabe and Mina, frowning. "Son—" he started.

Papa Leo was spread out on the ground, his arms out at his sides and his right leg twisted unnaturally. His head was broken open, his mouth distorted. His brown eyes were open. Gabe stared at the body. His breath danced in front of his lips, and he felt his breathing hard and frantic.

Barnaby stepped in front of him. "Son, you don't need to see this."

Papa Leo was wearing his army jacket, and Gabe recognized the brown work boots he always wore.

"I need everybody to back up," Barnaby said. "Coroner is on his way; we need to clear the area."

A large man stepped forward and draped a blanket over Papa Leo's body. It was too small to cover him completely, leaving the lower half of his body exposed, his one leg garishly akimbo.

"Come on, Gabe," Mina's voice broke through his shock. She tugged on his arm until at last he moved.

When they got to the Magic Carpet Ride, Mina sat in the driver's seat. She cranked the car, and after the engine steadied, she turned on the heat. The window fogged from the shock of their warm breath. Gabe's head felt heavy, too heavy for his neck. He stared out the window and tried to make sense of the world outside. Nothing made sense anymore. Someone brought them a bag of sausage biscuits. Mina unwrapped one and handed it to Gabe. He held the biscuit in his hand, staring out the window. The scent of the sausage filled the car, steam from its heat curling around his hand.

"You need to eat something," Mina said.

Gabe said nothing. There were no words within him. There was nothing.

"Gabe," she said. "I'm so sorry."

He looked at Mina. She stared out the window, her face lit by the low dashboard lights. He wanted to cry for Papa Leo, but felt too empty to cry. He wanted to take Mina home, wrap his arms and legs around her, shut the door to his bedroom, and forget that the rest of the world existed for the rest of their lives. Even through the pain, Mina had never looked more beautiful to him, and he felt a rise of terror within him, a fear of losing her like he'd lost his parents that night in the station wagon. The way he'd lost Papa Leo tonight. He thought of going home to check on LilyMa. She didn't yet know that Papa Leo was gone, and he couldn't imagine what the weight of that might do to her.

He hated this. All of this. The dark things that had taken all his joy before were back. He thought of how lost he'd felt when his parents died and how there had been no happiness in the world until Mina had come into his life and he'd found her song on the piano and in the trees and on the breeze alongside the birdsong of spring mornings. It was Mina and the piano, wasn't it? Those were the things that brought him back before. Could they bring him back again?

He heard Mina's stomach rumble. She sipped the cold convenience store coffee and fished out another biscuit. She unwrapped it and took a bite. Gabe felt too sick to eat, dropping his back into the sack.

"The Red Wolf," Gabe said. He couldn't finish his sentence.

"Yes," Mina said. "Your papaw, Leo. He's the one who saved the girl we saw in the convenience store. I'm sure of it."

Gabe looked at her briefly, then back out the window. "He's taken almost everyone I've ever loved."

"And now he has Erin."

"I feel like I'm going to throw up," he said.

"I know," she said.

"He won't stop until he kills us all. Me, you, the twins. LilyMa," he said. "My God, LilyMa. This will crush her."

"I've never seen two people more in love," Mina said, "than your grandparents."

Gabe said nothing.

She said, "At least they had that."

"What?" he said.

"Each other. All those years loving each other. That's a gift."

"Yes," he said. "But now she has to go on without him." He looked at her face. "That feels worse somehow."

"Yeah," she said.

Someone tapped on the window. It was Lucas.

Gabe swung open her door and tilted his seat. Lucas squeezed into the back seat, the ball of his toboggan bouncing.

"Cold as shit out there," he said.

He slid along the back seat, reached up, and put his hand on Gabe's shoulder.

"Heard about your papaw. I'm sorry, man. I really am."

Gabe didn't answer.

"We have to find Erin," Mina said.

"Yes," Lucas said. "I can't believe they haven't found her with all these people."

Mina looked at her watch. It was half past midnight. "How was the police interview?" she asked.

"Say, can I get one of those biscuits? I starve."

Mina handed one back.

"It wasn't too bad," Lucas said, taking a bite and talking through a mouthful. "Had to wait on my dad to get there, on account of me being a minor. Kept asking me the same questions over and over, like they'd trip me up. They think I did something to her."

"He'll kill us all," Gabe whispered. He could see it, the wolf's jaws closing on his flesh. But that he almost welcomed. It would be a relief to have it over. It was thinking of the wolf taking Mina that made him feel sick again. Of the wolf carrying Mina to the top of the mountain, the way it had done to Erin.

"How's that?" Lucas asked.

Gabe didn't answer.

"What's he babbling about?" Lucas asked Mina.

Mina spun in the seat to face him.

"Lucas," she said. "We know who took Erin."

Lucas stopped chewing. "Tell me. I'll kill the son of a bitch cold. You just tell me right now."

"It's...It's not a person."

Lucas swallowed hard. "What the fuck are you talking about?"

"The Red Wolf," Gabe said. "He killed my parents and Papa Leo. He's got Erin up on the peak of Hooker's Knob someplace."

In front of the car, several men passed. The search party was heading back up the trail at the edge of the dirt road where all the police and civilian cars were parked. Snowflakes began to light upon the windshield, fat and fluffy.

"A Red Wolf," Lucas whispered. He leaned back in the seat. "It has Erin?"

"Yes," Gabe said. "We got to find a way to kill it before it kills us all."

"You know about it?" Mina asked Lucas.

"That night at the bonfire," Lucas started. "I saw it. I saw you too. The panther, them monster things. Honestly, I thought it was just because I was so high. Tried to talk myself into believing that."

"I didn't know," Mina said.

"We need guns," Lucas said. "Lots and lots of fucking guns."

"They won't kill it," Mina said.

"And how do you know that?" Gabe said, facing her.

Mina looked out the window at the falling snow. "That night at the bonfire. It was like its body wasn't tangible. Like part of the time, it was just a shadow, like smoke. We—the shadow faces—couldn't get a hold of it to hurt it."

"This is some heavy shit," Lucas said.

"There's more," Mina said. "We met a girl down the mountain. She'd been taken by the wolf too, like we think Erin was."

Lucas slid forward, his hands cupping the back of the front seat. "She saw Erin?"

"No," Mina said. "But she said there were a lot of girls there. They'd all been taken by the wolf. She said they were there for men, like some kind of brothel."

"What?"

"You heard me," Mina said.

"My Erin is up there?"

"We're not sure, but we found paw prints near the campsite. We think the Red Wolf took her."

"Ain't that some shit," Lucas said. He shook his head. "Oh hell no, they ain't doing that to Erin. Ain't no way. They're not making her no prostitute."

"It's not like that," Mina said. "Prostitutes have a *choice*. Those girls have been kidnapped. They're not choosing to be there."

"We got to find her," Lucas said. Tears filled his eyes. His shoulders twitched and Gabe put his hand on Lucas's back.

"We will," Mina said. She turned to Gabe. "Do you want to take the car and go see LilyMa? Lucas and I can keep up the search."

"No," Gabe said.

"You should be with her right now," Mina said.

"I keep thinking about what she said about Papa Leo. She said he'd want us to find Erin, remember?"

"Yes," she said.

"He was like that. He always put other people first. He'd want us to be out looking for Erin. He wouldn't want me moping."

"It's really okay if you need to go," Mina said.

"Let's go find Erin. I'll go to LilyMa in the morning," Gabe said.

"Problem we have now," Mina said, "is all those men ahead of us on the trail. We need to get to the peak of the mountain."

"I know another trail," Lucas said. "A faster way. Found it with my daddy hunting out here one time. I used it to get up to the campsite every night to see Erin."

"Hold on," Gabe said. He turned to Mina. "The Red Wolf. How will we kill it? I mean, assuming we're right and he's got those girls up there. We get up there and do what, exactly?" He reached across and grabbed her hand. "I can't lose you."

"You won't." Mina smiled. "I've got a few things up my sleeve."

"And you're sure guns wouldn't help?" Lucas asked. "My dad has a million. Automatics, too. We could run, get them, and be back here in an hour."

"We don't have time," Mina said. "And they won't help."

Lucas guided them to a trailhead up a steep bank across the road. Snow fell harder now.

"Thought it was too cold to snow," Lucas said. "My uncle always said when it gets this cold, it can't snow."

"Well, it snows in Alaska," Gabe said.

"And Antarctica," Mina said.

"Hell, I never thought about that," Lucas said. "My uncle is full of shit."

"Nah, he's just dumb," Mina said. "Might run in the family."

"All right, wiseass," Lucas said.

They walked along quietly. Gabe felt the cold in his feet and in his bones. He wondered how quickly Papa Leo had gone. Had he lain in the cold shadow of the mountain, his body shivering as he faded? Or had he felt something else—a silence, a softness, the warmth of some bright light finding him at the last?

"There's something else," Mina said. "I kinda forgot about it."

"What's that?" Gabe asked.

"The girl at the store. She said something about a goat-headed man being with the Red Wolf."

"Goat-headed man?" Lucas said. "Fan-fucking-tastic. More monsters?"

"I wonder what she meant."

When they reached the rounded peak of Hooker's Knob, there was nothing there. Just rows of trees and an open rock face that seemed to go on for a mile. Three inches of fresh snow blanketed the mountain on top of the frozen snow beneath.

"Where are they?" Lucas said, spinning.

"It could be hiding them," Gabe said. "The Red Wolf is clever."

Mina looked up into the trees. "The girl down the mountain said he held the prisoners in the trees."

"*In* the trees?" Lucas said. "Maybe she just meant the woods."

"I don't think so," Mina answered.

"There," Gabe said. He pointed to a mountain nearby. While most of the mountain was hidden in shadow, the rock cliff of the neighboring peak was visible in the pale moonlight. He turned to the others. "The girl said they were high on the mountain; did she say it was Hooker's Knob?"

"No," Mina said. "I asked her the name of the mountain, but she never answered me. I thought it would be here because that's where Erin went missing."

"But it could be nearby," Gabe said. "And look at the cliff there. That could be where Papa Leo…"

"Yeah," Lucas said, gesturing around them. "Look at this place. It's pretty round. It would be hard to fall from up here."

"He didn't fall," Gabe said.

Lucas pursed his lips.

"Give me a second," Mina said. She turned to Lucas. "Don't be frightened, okay?"

Lucas looked scared already. "Okay," he said.

Mina closed her eyes. Gabe saw the shadows pull together at the bases of the trees, intertwining there to form a pillar that swirled like a twister.

"Goddamn," Lucas said.

Mina turned her back to them, perhaps so they couldn't see her milky eyes. Gabe shuddered at the thought of them, the way they looked when she controlled the shadows. Mina spun slowly.

"There," she said, her body north toward Mulwin Rock. "Through the trees, I see it."

"See what?" Gabe said.

"I see walls. A building. Looks like a church? They're glowing, the trees around it."

"The Temple," Gabe said.

Her eyes cleared, and her shoulders twitched like she'd caught a chill. "Oh my God."

"What is it?" Gabe asked.

Then a roar swelled up from within the earth. It shook the ground beneath them. Then the Red Wolf howled somewhere off in the distance.

"He's there," Mina said, pointing up at the face of Mulwin Rock.

"On Mulwin?" Gabe asked.

"Yes," Mina said. "He saw me. He sees us."

33 / BLACK CLOUDS
MINA

When they reached the top of Mulwin Rock, Mina's watch read five a.m. The snow now reached mid-calf, well above the top of her boots. Several times as they headed up the mountain, Mina had stopped to scan ahead with the shadow faces. But when Mina looked toward the peak, her visions had become blurry, as if the signal were scrambled somehow. She was sure the Red Wolf had something to do with it; this frightened her, but she didn't let on.

They walked along the trail, and Mina saw a large ring of trees. They passed a group of canvas tents, sagging under the weight of the snow. The face of the moon was obscured periodically by low-slung clouds, some so close Mina felt their weight pressing down on the mountain. "Stay behind me," she told the boys.

"Yes, ma'am," Lucas said.

When they reached the ring of trees, Mina was astonished at how black their bark looked, as if they'd been burnt.

"The Temple isn't finished," said Gabe. "So, if there's no Temple, and the tents are falling down, where are the girls?"

"In the trees," Mina said. An amber glow took form in the branches, and soon they were all visible.

"Holy shit," Lucas said.

There were girls in trees as far as the eye could see. Some were dressed up as if they were going to a fancy ball. Others had no clothes. There was a boy Mina recognized from school, named Cody, dressed in a baseball uniform. Then she saw her—Erin. In a large maple tree near the center. She had on a pink shirt and a short leather skirt the fucking perverts had put on her. She was all leg, her face blank, soulless.

"What's he doing with them?" Lucas said.

"This is sick," Gabe said.

Aren't they beautiful? The ground shook with the words of the Red Wolf.

Mina spun, looking for it. She pulled the shadows from the edges of the trees. Gargoyles formed, clinging to the branches, a thousand dark eyes looking for the wolf. Still, Mina could not find him.

You ought not have come here, growled the wolf. *You've all come here to die.*

"You killed my papaw," Gabe said, anger tightening his words. "Make you feel good to strike down an old man?"

The wolf laughed, its hideous grinding voice ringing throughout the mountain. Mina couldn't find him. Fear began to rise in her throat. Where was he? And why couldn't the shadow faces see him?

Oh, dear Mina, hissed the wolf. *You're like the carpenter who holds a hammer. Everything looks like a nail.*

"Come, show yourself," she yelled.

All you know is brute strength, the biting, the clawing. There's no nuance in your attack. You are already defeated.

"Shut the fuck up," Mina said. "Let's get to the biting and clawing."

His voice drew closer. *Have you forgotten the feeling, the ache of my teeth on your face? I gave you that delicious scar.*

"How's the paw, asshole?"

The wolf growled so loud the trees shook. Mina's teeth chattered. Huddled in the branches, the gargoyles hissed back. Mina focused on each of them. They dropped to the ground and swirled together. Soon, a shadow panther emerged, hissing. It dug its four-inch claws into the nearest tree, as if it would free the girl imprisoned there.

Impressive, said the Red Wolf. *Your power is growing. Too bad you'll be struck down before your peak. We could have done beautiful things together, were you not so stubborn and lowborn.*

"Lowborn? Fuck you," Mina said.

The panther turned from the tree and arched its back, its tail swishing so high it cracked the lowest limbs of the trees.

If I eat you, the Red Wolf said, *all your power will be mine.*

"*If,*" Mina corrected.

The Red Wolf had barely emerged from the darkness when the panther pounced. The two huge bodies slammed into a tree; it leaned caddywompus, its roots emerging from the ground near where Gabe and Lucas stood. The Shadow Panther quickly had the Red Wolf on its back, its claws digging into the wolf's chest. It held the Red Wolf's throat in its jaws, clamping down like a vice. The Red Wolf kicked it off briefly, but after a brief skirmish, it was on top of the wolf again, biting into its back.

"Mina!" Gabe yelled. She was in the eyes of the panther, all her anger and fury ripping through the wolf. "Watch out!"

Mina was lifted in the air, something jabbing into her back. She felt the sting of it, a searing pain down near her kidneys. She was thrown in the air and landed hard on her back. Above her, she saw a tall, thin man with a blond goat's head. His eyes were wide apart, and dark curved horns sprouted from the side of his thin skull. He bore down on her again, and Mina stuck up her feet as he butted at her again and again, his horns piercing her boots, the tips stabbing into her feet.

She cried out as the goat-headed man reached down with his arms—human arms—to lift her and wrap her in a bear hug. Mina conjured the panther, which turned from the wolf and ran to her rescue. The goat-headed man pushed her into a tree, and when he did so, the bark gave way and her arm, from the elbow down, disappeared. The bark closed around it, and it stuck, as if held by concrete. The goat headed man grabbed her leg and pulled her body taut. The next tree opened and received her feet, the bark closing quickly over her boots. Mina looked for the panther. To her horror, it began to dissipate; the shadows curled along the ground, stretching until they were one with those cast by the trees in the moonlight. The goat-headed man took her other arm and pulled it into the tree with the first. She was now spread between the trees, pulled so tight her spine ached, pain searing through the wounds in her back, as if she were being stabbed over and over again.

"Mina!" Gabe ran toward the goat headed man, pushing him from behind. Calmly, the goat man turned and head-butted Gabe in the center of his forehead. Gabe fell back, out cold. For a moment, Mina forgot her own pain and longed to run to Gabe. To cradle his head in her lap, to make sure he was okay.

The Red Wolf paced around the circle, cackling like an old witch.

The panther was a nice touch. Certainly more aesthetically pleasing than those old gargoyles you copied from Asheville's garish architecture. And more you, that's for sure.

The goat-headed man laughed, something between a giggle and a bleat.

The Red Wolf stalked toward Lucas, head high. It towered over him.

"I'll kill you for my Erin," Lucas said. He swung his pocketknife toward the wolf. The blade passed through its body like it was made of air.

Your chivalry is to be commended, young man. But as much as you'd like to rescue her, she's beyond your reach now. He turned to the goat-headed man. *Perhaps he should join her? He's kind of pretty in his own way. A certain kind of patron will like a boy who fights back.* His decision was made. *Put him in the trees,* he barked.

Two figures emerged from the shadows. They wore long flowing brown robes, hoods pulled up over their heads. They looked like monks Mina had seen in a book about the Middle Ages. They grabbed Lucas and dragged him screaming into the woods.

And you? The Red Wolf turned to Gabe on the ground. *I'm going to do now what I should have done long ago. I wiped out your grandfather and your father before him. When this is all over, I'll hunt down those little sniveling siblings of yours. I'll wipe your seed from the face of the earth. There can be no other.*

"You'll do nothing of the kind," a voice said. LilyMa came around a tree opposite where Mina hung. She wore a white overcoat, jeans, and a pair of snow boots. Her hair was pulled up in two clips on either side, and she walked using a staff with a cross shape at the top.

Excellent. The other name on my list. You're making this so much easier. The wolf laughed.

"You old snake," LilyMa said. "Why didn't you choose that form, so you could slither on the ground where you belong, on your belly?"

Old woman, I'll tear out your throat.

"You're just a scared little boy down deep, ain't that right, *Little Priest?*"

Yes, that was what they used to call me, said the wolf. He pulled his body up high, arching his back and poking out his chest. His voice boomed. *Before I learned the power to make the earth shake.*

"You're a coward," LilyMa said. "Still looking for his mother. Is that what all the girls are about? Something you can control, unlike your mother?"

My mother died. I was an orphan.

"We both know that's not true," LilyMa said. "She left you when you were a boy. Left you all alone."

No, said the wolf, taking a step back. Its broad head swayed.

"Remember, little Ezra? The nights in the Elijah Home? Wondering if she would come for you?"

No, whispered the wolf.

"Remember when you were a boy, the last time you saw her at the lake? She held you there. Whispered to you, your head under the warm water, you told us. Then she left for good, ain't that right?"

She died. She had to have died. Why else would she leave?

LilyMa strode toward him, turning the staff around to hold it like a sword. The goat-headed man looked back and forth between the Red Wolf and this wiry woman waving around a staff.

"You're doing all this because you're still mad at her. Admit it."

I hate her, the Red Wolf hissed, showing his teeth.

"Yes," LilyMa said, "finally some truth from your lying mouth. You hated her for leaving you. Making you an orphan with living parents out there somewhere. You didn't have to turn into this hideous thing. But you couldn't let go of it, could you?"

I hate her with all that is in me.

"And the girls in the trees? What're they for? To show your power? You think that's what you're doing?"

Many will be needed, the wolf said. *They give me even more power.*

"You use them to control weak men, just like the Blue Man once did. At least what the Blue Man did was something new, original. You're just a pathetic copycat. Couldn't you think of anything better? You make me sick."

The wolf turned to face her, baring his teeth. He growled, and the earth shook.

"I'm not afraid of you, *Little Priest,*" LilyMa taunted. "You already struck down my husband. Did it make you feel good to kill your oldest friend? Did it make you feel strong to kill an old man with dementia? And doing all this in the name of God? There's nothing of God in you. Christ would never harm girls—harm children. You've put together nothing but a cult. You're worse than the men that do their evil out in the open, in the daylight."

LilyMa's presence helped give Mina strength. In her mind, she called to the shadows that stretched along the ground around the trees. She tried to pull them together, to form shapes as she'd done so many times. At first, they didn't heed her, remaining flat and lifeless on the ground. But finally, a small cloud began to form, floating just above the earth.

The Red Wolf gave a nod to the goat-headed man. It was so subtle, Mina might have missed it, but then the goat-headed man bounded toward LilyMa. She saw him coming and stepped out of the way, but he knocked her staff from her hand. He stepped toward her, holding out his arms as if to subdue her. LilyMa let him approach, get within a few feet, before she moved. With one quick motion, she reached up and pulled out one of her hair clips. Before her hair hit her shoulder, she'd swung the clip at the goat man and sliced open his palms. He stepped back, bleating. Bright red blood dripped onto the snow. He balled his fists, watching the blood lace through his knuckles. He dropped his head and took a step toward her. She reached up and pulled out the other clip. She held them in her hands like a pair of knives, their edges razor sharp.

"Come on," LilyMa said, her long white hair cascading over her shoulders. "This time it'll be your throat."

The goat-headed man stood his ground but didn't approach.

Kill her, you coward, what are you waiting for? hissed the wolf.

Then LilyMa smiled. She started laughing to herself. She kept her arms in front of her but turned to the Red Wolf. "And what is this thing supposed to be? Didn't the Blue Man have a henchman they called Goat?"

The wolf growled, and the goat man turned toward him. The goat man grunted.

Shut up, you fool! howled the wolf.

Then the wolf saw the cloud growing on the ground behind the goat headed man. Mina stretched it taller, perhaps four feet off the ground. Somehow, she could not find the power to make it take shape. She thought of snakes, of dragons, every shape she could conjure, and their horrible faces formed in the pillar.

There now, I see them. The Red Wolf took a few steps toward the goat man. *There on the ground behind you.*

The goat man turned and saw the forming pillar of smoke. He looked back at the Red Wolf, his face confused.

You've always been jealous of my power. Don't think I haven't seen the way you look at me. As if you could eat me yourself. As if you can't stand that I have so much more power than you.

The goat man backed away, shaking his head. He grunted, but could not form words.

Do you conspire, even now, with the girl? You think you'll cut me down like Judas did Jesus? For thirty coins? I see the shadows you conjure even now, against me.

The goat-headed man changed. His horns receded into his skull, and the long goat snout shrank until he was just a man. A thin pale man with long blonde hair. He held his bleeding hands up to the wolf. "I have only ever been loyal to you," the Predicant said, his voice oddly high in pitch.

"This is what evil does," LilyMa said, still holding her hair clips out in front of her. "It breeds jealousy. It takes hold like a cancer in the heart. This man hurts just like your heart hurts, Ezra."

Every heart hurts. Only a few can learn to harness that pain. Turn hurt into strength as I have done. True power. The kind that makes others fear you. It's never been about money or fame. It's always been about fear.

"If he doesn't rise against you," LilyMa said, "Another will. You'll always be looking over your shoulder."

The Red Wolf pounced at the Predicant. It tore into the man's arm and ripped it from its socket. The man backed away, morphing back into the goat. When the Red Wolf pounced again, the goat-headed man lowered his head, but the Red Wolf passed through his horns as if they were not there. The Red Wolf ripped into his midsection, tearing at the flesh and muscle, hot blood spraying the snow-covered ground.

As the wolf battled the goat man, LilyMa stepped over to Mina. She put her hands on the bark holding Mina's feet, and the bark receded, freeing them. She did the same for the opposite tree, freeing Mina's hands. Mina stretched her back, trying to ignore the pain she felt at her kidneys. She closed her eyes and pulled more shadows into the pillar until it stood twenty feet tall, then it morphed into the shadow panther. It crouched low to the ground and crept toward the Red Wolf, who continued to dig into the goat man, pulling at his flesh and stretching his entrails.

The shadow panther leapt on the back of the wolf, biting into the nape of his neck. The Red Wolf yelped and rolled free. It stood to face the Shadow Panther. The two beasts lurched at each other, but when the panther bit down, his teeth snapped together, unable to find a tangible surface. Mina stood between the trees, her eyes milky white, seeing the world through the panther. She tried again to find a place to bite the wolf, but it was futile; each attack failed. The wolf leapt in to push the panther around the forest floor, snow piling up around them. Then Mina saw a place on the wolf, near its shoulder, where the surface was a deeper crimson red than the rest of the wolf. "There," she whispered.

When the two parlayed again, the shadow panther dipped its head and dug its fangs into the dark red spot. The wolf cried out in pain, and as the panther bit down, red mist floated from the wound. The wolf struggled to break free, but the panther held tight like a pit bull with a bone. It pushed its weight over the wolf, pinning it to the ground.

Mina, think of all we can do together, the Red Wolf cried.

"You're finished," she whispered.

It burns, the Red Wolf said, its voice creaking in the trees.

The panther took both paws and placed them on the wound beside its mouth. It ripped the wound open wider, stretching down the belly of the Red Wolf and up to its throat. Red mist rose into the air like fog. It was so thick the others could no longer see the figures on the ground. The panther dug deeper, its head inside the wolf. Through the panther's eyes, Mina saw the beating heart of a man. The shadow panther bit into the heart, ripping until it stopped. The Red Wolf's eyes went dark. The shadow panther pulled free of the wolf and padded toward the trees. Once it was outside the ring, it began to join the shadows that stretched along the forest, disappearing into them.

With her normal vision returned, Mina walked over to the Red Wolf on the ground. Instead of the beast, she found a naked man, curled into a ball, chest ripped open. Reverend Ezra.

Mina put her hand over her mouth. LilyMa, less spry than she'd seemed before, hobbled over, using the staff to help her walk. She looked at the man on the ground. Ezra's face was deeply wrinkled, his hair a dull gray color, almost blue in the moonlight.

"You were given this gift," she said to Mina, never taking her eyes off Ezra, "to defeat the Red Wolf. To bring light where there was none."

"Yes," Mina said, her eyes welling.

"And now that you have done this, you must learn to let the darkness go. Do you understand?"

"Yes," Mina said. "I understand."

LilyMa took Mina by the arm and turned her so they faced each other. "That man on the ground, he surrendered to the darkness. Take a good hard look at him. Look at what he became. That's what *you* will become if you don't let this go. You'll be a gnarled old root in the ground. Tell me you hear me."

"I hear you," Mina said. "But I could never be like him. I would never hurt people like he did. Put people in trees."

"Of course not," LilyMa said. "He was a man with a bitter man's imagination. Or lack thereof. But—" she said, taking Mina's chin in her hand to raise her face, "you can still do evil. You could do more evil than you can possibly imagine. You must let it go and lean to the light, the way sunflowers turn to the sun. Promise me?"

"Yes," Mina said. "I promise. I never wanted any of this to begin with. I never asked for it."

"Neither did Ezra, not at first. Neither did my Leo. One of them learned to let it go." She looked at Ezra's body on the ground. "One did not."

"Papa Leo? You knew about him. That he was gone? And still you came?"

"I felt it the very moment his heart stopped. It brought me to my knees. It was like I was with him when he passed. I believe I was. We were together at the last."

"He had the shadows, too. When he was younger? A dark wolf that walked on its hind legs. I saw it in my dreams," said Mina.

LilyMa hugged Mina close. "A story for another time. Now, let's go get those poor girls and boys down out of the trees. Place your hands on the bark and it will fall away."

34 / A BRIGHTER WORLD
MINA

When the search party began to scale Mulwin Rock, they were greeted by a strange sea of girls and boys walking down the mountain, most wearing few clothes, near froze-to-death on account of the weather. It was a scene a local television station would come to play over and over thanks to an industrious reporter who got wind of the search for Erin and showed up that morning to find the search party had moved on from Hooker's Knob. The reporter had managed to get shaky footage of over a hundred girls and a sprinkling of boys coming down through the trees, their blank faces garish in the low light of the moon, shuffling through the woods like zombies from some horror B-movie.

The sheriffs and other searchers had heard the commotion atop Mulwin Rock and set their sights there. After the girls were settled in police cars and vans, Sheriff Barnaby and his deputies took their eerily similar statements. They'd each been kidnapped by either a monstrous Red Wolf taller than a horse or groups of men who'd turned out to be Elders in the Church of Hosanna. Many of the girls were from poor areas around the county or streets in Asheville known for prostitution. Among the girls were the long-missing Heidi from the church's Purity Sojourn almost exactly a year prior and Erin Black, missing from this year's Sojourn.

Once the kids' statements were taken and they were whisked away to the hospital for treatment, many near hypothermia, Barnaby and his men scaled the mountain and found the good Reverend Ezra dead, his body brutally thrashed open. By what, it was never determined. They also found his right-hand man, the Predicant, also known as Brother Lemuel, dead beside him, his corpse similarly disfigured. They arrested many of the church elders, accomplices in what had gone on at the site of the new Temple they were erecting to serve their nefarious purposes. A number of Elders were captured as they descended the opposite side of the mountain, hoping to avoid detection. The Elders who weren't present were captured over the next few days. None of them could easily feign innocence; the Reverend had instructed each to carve their initials backward in the freshly poured concrete foundation of the Temple on the mountain.

Erin was a different person at first. Mina went to her house every day after school, catching a ride from Gabe. She sat on her bed, legs crossed, staring at her hands, or rubbing the various bruises on her legs and arms. Erin scarcely spoke, and when she did, it was in a whisper so low Mina had to lean in, their heads almost touching, to hear them. She gradually came out of the clouds of darkness, at first reaching out to hold Mina's hand, then by hugging her close to her chest, as if she could help stay the trembling fits that sometimes gripped her. She kept Lucas at a distance, allowing him to come into her room, but not wanting him to be near her.

"Stay over there," she'd whisper when Lucas stepped into her bedroom, allowing the boy only to sit in the desk chair on the opposite side of the room. There he would talk in a low voice, and she would listen, never answering. She'd been worse with her parents, refusing her mom's attempts at affection, her dad's offers to take her for a cup of coffee. She'd only accept the food brought to her door on a tray, as if she was in a hotel accepting room service. Mina was the only person she let near her for many days.

By the time Papa Leo's funeral came around, Erin said she was ready to go out into the world. The funeral was held at a large graveyard at the edge of Asheville, where many of his relatives were buried. Gabe, who had also been mostly silent since that night on Mulwin Rock, was more animated at the funeral, smiling and shaking the hands of strangers like a Baptist preacher. Not the fake smile he'd had after his parents had been killed; a real, open smile Mina recognized from the afternoons they spent together after school. He gave the eulogy at the funeral, LilyMa saying she could do fine without a preacher, despite many offers from clergy in the community.

Gabe talked about Papa Leo's career as a police officer and then as a businessperson after he'd retired. He talked about how Papa Leo's people had found the mountains around Asheville before the Revolutionary War, how they'd landed in Bern, North Carolina, and kept going west until they found the right place to settle—a place that was beautiful but where land was still available. He talked about how poor Papa Leo's family had been when he was a child, how two of his brothers died of diseases that nowadays would be easily treated with penicillin or antibiotics. He never mentioned Papa Leo's final act of bravery at the end, the way he'd scaled Mulwin Rock, freed an imprisoned girl, and died trying to put a stop to all Reverend Ezra had wrought. He didn't mention how Sheriff Barnaby had come to LilyMa in the days after that fateful night to tell her about the slug they found in Reverend Ezra's shoulder, a bullet they traced to Papa Leo's gun, also found at the scene. Sheriff Barnaby attended the funeral; he had arranged for there to be a twenty-one-gun salute.

By Thanksgiving, Erin was mostly back to normal. Gabe was shedding the melancholy of his grandfather's death, and Mina, too, felt almost normal. She thought over and over about the words LilyMa had said to her on the mountain, about how her power could be some tragic path to darkness. About how she should let it go. And she was ready to let it go. She'd never wanted it in the first place, and now that the Red Wolf was gone, why would she ever need it again? The world was a much brighter place now, so she turned her attention back to her grades, planning for the future, still determined to leave Asheville upon graduation and attend college somewhere far away. The natural world around her seemed to heal as well. Mina's parents rarely fought, and she had seen strange moments of tenderness pass between them, which felt at once beautiful and sickening. Chelsea stopped being such a bitch; she began coming into Mina's bedroom when she was home, sitting on the edge of the bed laughing and talking about what went on during her day. In the trailer park, there seemed to descend a blanket of calm over everything. Dana, Twist's young girlfriend, gave birth to a beautiful baby boy with fat cheeks and a cherub's face, clearly favoring his mother's looks. All of this made Mina happy, but none of it tempered her resolve to keep her head down and do what it took to move on from Asheville as soon as possible.

But Mina had also grown resolute about something else: her

relationship with Gabe. The two grew closer after the night on Mulwin Rock. They were together most of the time, whenever they weren't in class, and Mina began to let herself love him in her own way, no longer seeing him as a trap that would get her stuck in the mountains, stuck in Whispering Pines. Instead, she came to think of him as part of her journey toward freedom. She didn't know what the future held, whether they'd wind up at the same college or part ways after graduation, but it didn't matter. He understood there were no guarantees, and so did she. But one night, the night before Thanksgiving, she sat by Gabe as he played her song on the piano, the song he'd composed on Halloween along her back, and she leaned into him, realizing she wanted this closeness. She couldn't get close enough, and she wanted to stop holding him at arm's length, to hold him closer than she'd ever held anyone or anything. Maybe not always, but for as long as possible. They kissed each morning in the car before school, long, warm kisses that Mina mostly initiated.

Once, Gabe had joked about how they could walk around to the Bus Lot instead of the normal path inside. "Let them behold the fireworks of a real makeout session," he'd said.

"I'd rather gag on a spoon." Mina laughed.

It was Gabe's idea for the kids to cook the Thanksgiving meal. He wanted to give LilyMa the chance to put her feet up, to sit back and relax after all she'd been through, after all the years of waiting on everyone else while her food grew cold on her plate. So on Thanksgiving morning, Mina, Gabe, Lucas, and Erin met in LilyMa's kitchen. Gabe produced aprons for everyone to wear, and they set about cooking the grandest meal they could envision. Gabe put the turkey in the oven first, as it would take the longest. Mina worked on a homemade pumpkin pie while he chopped up potatoes. Erin and Lucas were in charge of biscuits and, after rolling out the dough and dusting the cutting board, their faces were soon plastered with white flour, and they were throwing bits of dough at each other.

Erin put a flour-covered hand to Lucas's face. "I kinda like you dirty, old man."

"Careful with that kinda talk, young lady," Lucas said, nuzzling her neck.

"Ew, 'old man?' 'Young lady?'" Mina said. "Jesus Christ."

"He's nearly ten months my senior." Erin beamed. "He's *so* old."

"I try not to use corporal punishment," Lucas laughed. "But I think it might be the only thing that will work on you."

Erin laughed and turned her back to Lucas, poking out her butt. "Better not miss," she cooed.

The biscuits were ugly, and the cake Gabe baked was kind of flat, but the spread wasn't bad. The turkey was juicy and perfect, and he went on and on about how he'd basted it at methodical intervals and kept it in a brine of apples and spices the night before. LilyMa had tears in her eyes as they ate, and Mina put her hand on her shoulder and squeezed. They ate until they were stuffed, then Erin and Mina brought the desserts to the table. They had pumpkin pie, Gabe's flat vanilla cake with frosting, and banana pudding Erin had made the night before.

"You kids have outdone yourselves," LilyMa said. "I only wish dear Leo had got to see this. He'd never have believed it."

"Maybe he's looking down on us," Erin said.

LilyMa cast her eyes to the ceiling. "Oh, I'm sure about that. I'm sure he watches over us every day now."

The kids trained their eyes to the ceiling.

"For one thing," LilyMa said, "the man loved to eat."

Everyone laughed.

"He didn't always know where his next meal was coming from when he was a child," LilyMa said, "so he always went in for a good meal. Wasn't one to turn down dessert neither."

"Remember," Gabe said, "how he'd always say, 'just cut me a piece of that cake about as big as my hand'?"

"Oh yes," LilyMa said. "He'd have loved your cake, Gabe."

Mina laughed, cutting herself a piece. She thought about Papa Leo's childhood, about how he'd been hungry much of the time, the way LilyMa told it. Papa Leo never really talked about it much himself. Though the other kids listened to those stories with a kind of wistful nostalgia in their eyes, she knew exactly what it was like to be hungry. To go to school and try to study on an empty stomach. To live in a trailer with no heat, the water pipes sometimes freezing, her daddy crawling under the trailer with a hairdryer trying to thaw them out. They had no idea, the other three, what it was like to wear clothes from the Salvation Army or to have to wear the clothes your mama had worn in high school. She smiled at the others as she took a bite of her cake. Though ugly, it was delicious, vanilla with just a hint of lemon.

35 / SINISTER RED LIGHTS
MINA

As much as the kids had loved hanging out at LilyMa's and Papa Leo's before, it became a home base for the four of them after Thanksgiving. Every day after school, Mina would ride with Gabe, but instead of him dropping her off at the entrance to Whispering Pines, she'd go with him to LilyMa's. There they'd set up in the living room to study for an hour or two, then have dinner with LilyMa. Sometimes Mina would help her in the kitchen, but mostly she'd just watch the woman work and they'd chat about what was going on at school, what all Mina had learned, her plans for college, what she might study, and so forth. Sometimes they'd get to talking about something, and LilyMa would disappear, returning with a book she thought Mina would like. She gave her books by Flannery O'Connor, Sylvia Plath, and Lucille Clifton. One day, she gave Mina a book of poems by Langston Hughes, a red bow wrapped around it.

"You don't have to give me things," Mina said.

"I know that," LilyMa answered, turning to stir a big pot of beans.

Every day, the house on Elk Mountain smelled like food and, in time, Mina came to think of it as her own home. She sometimes felt guilty when she returned to the trailer at night to sleep, walking through the park by people who lived so differently, just a few miles away from LilyMa's. She'd pass Twist and Dana's trailer and see Dana with the baby on her hip, beaming, Twist scowling in the shadows. The baby had changed Dana, but Twist was the same. *The old fish will always be like this*, Mina thought. Sometimes Mina would bring some food home for Chelsea, some cornbread or maybe a bowl of LilyMa's beans in an orange Tupperware container.

Mina's mama sometimes hugged her when she got home. "Why didn't you come home in time for dinner with *your* family?"

Mina smiled. "I want to see my friends sometimes, too."

From the living room, Daddy said, "One less mouth to feed ain't a bad thing."

Sometimes he'd say, "You get knocked up, you're living over there. You know that, right?"

Mina never answered him. She no longer let his words cut at her the way they used to.

Most days, after Mina and Gabe had done their homework and they were sitting down with LilyMa for supper, Erin and Lucas would show up, his golden 240z winding down the driveway. They'd come inside, their faces red from their long make-out sessions in his car, parked on the dirt road near the junkyard up the mountain. They'd start their homework after dinner; Lucas usually fell asleep, so Erin would do her homework, then his. After she was done and Lucas was in a deep snore, she'd hang out with Gabe and Mina. Sometimes, they'd bundle up in front of the fireplace upstairs with LilyMa. At eight or nine, LilyMa would excuse herself and go to bed, and the kids would stay up till maybe ten, before Gabe drove Mina home. On weekends, they'd stay up later, laughing and making Jiffy Pop on the stove.

On Christmas Eve, the kids had wanted to make dinner as they'd done at Thanksgiving, but LilyMa wouldn't hear of it. Instead, she'd begun baking several days before, slapping the boys' hands away if they tried to sneak a bite. She made a ham and a turkey, mashed potatoes that weren't lumpy like Lucas's, candied yams, a broccoli casserole, homemade biscuits, and gravy. After the meal, they all sat in the living room around the fireplace. LilyMa's Christmas tree was beautiful, strung with colored lights, many red and silver ball ornaments, and an angel on top. The kids had helped her decorate the tree the day after Thanksgiving. Lucas had put the angel on top, after a failed attempt in which he fell off the little step stool and put a pump knot on his head. LilyMa played old Christmas records with songs by Bing Crosby, Frank Sinatra, and other people Mina had never heard of. There was something about the old Christmas songs that felt right to her. Some of the '80s pop stars had made Christmas songs, even one to help starving people in Africa, but they just didn't sound like Christmas. They were like bad knockoffs. She liked the way the old crooners dragged out their notes, the way brass and woodwind instruments curled around their voices.

Later, Gabe played Christmas carols on the piano and the kids sang. Lucas tried to make his voice like the crooners, belting out the notes, often off-key. Mina and Gabe rolled their eyes, but Erin couldn't get enough of it, laughing and staring at Lucas like he was the greatest thing since sliced bread. Afterward, the kids gathered around the tree to exchange presents. LilyMa said they couldn't open the presents from "Santa" until the next day, but they could exchange what they'd gotten for each other.

Erin got Lucas a bottle of Calvin Klein Obsession cologne, which he immediately opened and sprayed everywhere, making Mina's nose burn.

"That cologne makes my toes curl," Erin said, grabbing Lucas's knee.

Lucas got Erin a gold promise ring, and when she saw it, Erin yanked the ring out and threw the box to the floor. She put the ring on her third finger and crowed, "I do, I do" over and over, hugging Lucas's neck.

Gabe handed Mina two boxes. In one was a book titled *Insider's Guide to Colleges, 1987*. She almost cried when she saw it. He knew what she wanted, where she was headed. He wasn't trying to hold her back like everyone else. He wanted to see her do what she wanted. He wanted to go with her—she was sure of that. He'd practically come out and said it several times. But either way, he knew Mina was on her way, and he wanted to help her get there. After she opened the second gift, a brass gargoyle figurine, Mina leaned over and kissed his forehead, letting her lips linger until she felt his warmth radiate within her. Then she handed Gabe two gifts of her own.

The first was a Rush tape. Gabe opened it, smiling. He needed help with his music choices, and LilyMa had said Gabe could add a tape deck to the Magic Carpet ride. Lucas said he'd help Gabe install it and pick out some speakers at the Radio Shack.

Gabe's second gift was a black dreamcatcher Mina had found at the flea market. He had confided in her that he'd kept having nightmares about the Red Wolf after all that had happened.

"I just can't shake it," he'd said.

"It's okay," Mina had said. "That's normal. It's been in your life a long time now."

In front of the other kids, Mina didn't allude to the nightmares, but said, "Dream catchers only catch the bad ones. All the good dreams still come through." They hugged by the Christmas tree, and Erin said, "Get a room, you two!" Then, when she realized LilyMa was in the room, she whispered, "Sorry."

After dinner, the kids went out on the back deck so Lucas and Erin could smoke. Gabe and Mina sipped coffee, and Lucas and Erin had hot chocolate. It was a beautiful, crisp night, the sky so clear you could see all the stars. There was a slight breeze, but the cold felt good on Mina's neck. She leaned back into Gabe, and together they looked up at the moon. Erin and Lucas giggled, first passing a cigarette, then a joint. They shared the joint with Gabe and Mina.

That time between Thanksgiving and Christmas had given her hope. That there could be beautiful days. That there could be happiness and joy. It had been bittersweet to watch Papa Leo lowered into the ground, and what the victims at the Temple had gone through had been horrible. But knowing what Papa Leo had done on the mountain, what they'd all done to free the girls, that brought peace somehow. As if good had won out in the end, and all could be well. You didn't have to live with constant worry, Mina thought. Things could be beautiful. There were warm fires at Christmas, and hot coffee, and LilyMa's hugs, and love. All these things bound the four of them together now, and no matter where they went in life, they would bind them all together forever.

"I love Christmas," Erin said. "I always have, since I was a little girl. It was Santa and Jesus's birthday, and presents and all that. But I never appreciated a Christmas as much as I do this one."

"I didn't like Christmas for a long time after my parents died," Gabe said. "It just wasn't the same. I think we all associate it with the home we grew up in, and the first years, celebrating it here just felt weird, you know? Like it wasn't really Christmas. Not my Christmas anyway. It was somebody else's."

"I never cared about Christmas," Lucas said, "till I got me a sexy elf." He scooped Erin up into his arms, and she squealed.

"Oh," Erin said, her face close to Lucas's. "We need to get me a short elf costume, and you can be Santa."

"Gross," Mina said.

"I'll give you the rosiest cheeks ever," Erin said, rubbing Lucas's nose with her own.

Gabe smiled at Mina. She leaned in and they kissed. It was perfect. Everything was perfect.

"What's that?" Lucas said. He was pointing through the trees to the road that ran to Whispering Pines.

There were blue police car lights kaleidoscoping through the trees. One police car went by, then two, then more. Then came sirens. Maybe ten police cars went by, an ambulance following, its red lights consuming the blue.

"They're going to the park," Mina said. She looked at the others before setting her coffee on the banister. She took off running through the woods, Gabe and the others following. Mina heard their breath as they came. She tried to think of what it could be. A fire? But there was no fire truck. Had her parents gotten in a fight, had her daddy done something to her mama?

They ran through the center of the park, a path lit by Christmas lights that framed the trailers and blazing Christmas trees set in their windows. A few trailers ahead of Mina's, in the back left, there was a trailer with red lights strung around the windows. All the sheriff cars were parked in a ring around it. It was Twist's.

When they got closer, Mina saw Twist bent over a police cruiser, his arms pulled behind him in handcuffs. He wore no shirt or shoes. Just blue jeans, too long for his body, dragging along the frosted grass as he was walked toward the back of a cruiser. A deputy walking behind them carried a big black camcorder.

"I ain't done nothing. It's just resting, surely it's just resting. That's all."

Dana was screaming. "My baby," she said. "My baby."

Mina's stomach twisted, and she had to steady herself against Gabe. As the deputies stuffed Twist into the backseat, he said, "The snake got all in me. All through me."

Mina was shaking when she got to the front door of the trailer. Dana thrashed on the floor, several deputies with their hands on her. She held the baby to her chest, and they tried to pull it from her. Mina sank to her knees.

She threw up. Her eyes were full of tears, the world blurry and streaked with the sinister red Christmas lights that sagged in the trailer windows. The baby was taken from Dana, and she curled up on the ground, shaking. Mina stood after a while, and Gabe tried to put his arms around her. She shrugged him away. She walked to the back of the park, into the trees.

"I'm sorry," he said.

"Don't you dare," Mina said. "Don't you fucking dare!"

Gabe looked at the ground. Lucas and Erin stood nearby, keeping their distance.

"I could have killed him," Mina said. "I *should* have killed him. I had him. I had him!"

"You couldn't have known," Erin said.

"I should have choked him out."

No one said anything.

Mina blinked through the tears. "It's like that thing we talked about in Mrs. Varny's class, you know? If you had the chance. You know, if you had a time machine. If you could go back in time, and you saw Hitler as a little boy, swimming in a lake. And you could just slip out there beside him in that lake, and you could just grab him and hold him under the water. Yeah, you'd be a murderer, but you'd save how many people, how many millions of people?"

"Mina," Gabe said.

"Don't you speak," she said.

Gabe put his hands in his pockets.

"I should have killed him. He was never no good. Not to himself, not to nobody. And he wouldn't have loved that baby. He couldn't have. Even if this didn't happen. How many beatings would that girl have gotten, every time another man spoke to her on the street? Every time she did anything he didn't like?"

"I know," Gabe said.

"He should be dead. He was a sorry piece of shit. Looked in the window on my sister naked. Tried to look in on me. Beat that girl. And I let him live. I had the snake around his neck, Gabe. I could have snapped it like a twig, and that baby would still be breathing. Breastfeeding on his mama."

Gabe dropped to one knee. "I know, Mina. It's not your fault."

"You don't know anything," Mina said. "I'd give anything to have done it. While I was off in the woods focusing on monsters, the biggest monster was right here. Right next door, his fucking Christmas lights strung up."

Gabe hung his head.

LilyMa had told Mina to let go of the shadows. Let go of the darkness, she said. But they weren't the real darkness, were they? *This* was the real darkness. What goes on in the hearts of men. If she'd been home. If she'd been paying attention to what was going on in that trailer. If she'd brought down the shadow faces, crushed that man's bony chest. What would have been wrong with that? Saving a little baby? Shouldn't she have done that? Was that *leaning into the darkness*? Or was it doing what was right, what ought to be done? She was breathing hard, her chest tight, her fists balled. "That baby's dead," she whispered, "because of me."

"No," Gabe said.

Mina called the shadows. Those between the trees, those in the nooks of the trailers. She pulled them together, a dark cloud forming in the woods between her and the others. She made dark faces appear in a twister. The dark faces of demon dogs, stretching and snarling. *Let us go to him,* they whispered to her. *Let us eat him, Mina, oh please, let us eat him.*

Then she was on the ground, sobbing into the leaves. The shadows slid back along the ground, back to their places under the limbs and forming their normal angles beside the trailers. And Mina cried. It rushed over her and into her throat. She howled into the dirt. Gabe lifted her, and she felt Erin's arms around her. Erin kissed her cheeks, and Lucas helped hold her. They walked slowly through the woods, over the back deck, and into LilyMa's house. They laid her down on the couch, and her whole body groaned into the pillows.

Mina wept.

36 / MOMENTS OF LIGHT
MINA

Maybe life was just a series of tragedies, interspersed with moments of joy so high that it too made you want to cry. The joy would come, make the world bright, and you'd get lulled into complacency. Then the dark clouds would return. A baby dying in a trailer on Christmas Eve. Falling in love. A cancer diagnosis. The joy of a perfect book. A terrible car crash that snuffed out your parents. Maybe that's just the way it worked. So in the moments where joy came, Mina thought, we should bask in those, because we know down deep they will be brief, because we know down deep they will pass, as all things must pass.

Mina couldn't feel joy after the baby Dana called Terrence died. She remembered seeing him when he was alive in his mama's arms, his eyes so dark they looked black. Deep, beautiful eyes that took your breath away. People came from all over to see Dana after his death. Old church women who normally wouldn't set foot in a place so poor as the little trailer park on Elk Mountain lined up at Dana's door, steaming casseroles in hand. They cackled like a brood of hens in the little front yard, whispering about the poor blue baby, gossiping about the circumstances.

Mina visited Dana after all the church women left, sitting on the wood-framed couch beside her, listening to all the dreams she'd had for her baby boy. How she knew he was destined for great things, to maybe be a preacher when he grew up, or maybe to work with her uncle, who was a plumber. He'd offered a job to Twist several times, but Twist had explained how he couldn't see that for his life. He'd sent Dana into town to get on food stamps instead. He hadn't worked for over a year, Dana said, other than mowing a few of the small yards in the park using a mower he'd borrowed from Mina's daddy. Mina hugged Dana when the girl broke down and was happy to be there with her, yet guilt gnawed at her. How she'd been so arrogant to think the fear she'd given Twist that night in the park would have changed him somehow, made him afraid to raise a hand to Dana. She knew what she should have done, and no one could ever tell her different.

Mina tried to cling to these moments of light, the moments when she could comfort Dana, or spend time laughing with LilyMa in her kitchen. She clung to Gabe, too. Together they went for hikes up on the Parkway and held hands in his car on the way home, listening to the Rush tape on his new stereo. Sometimes she'd ask him to play her song, the one he named *Mina's Song*. The notes floated over her as she lay on her back on his bed, and the song was perfect. It fit. The B minor key gave it a feeling of melancholy, with brief moments of brightness breaking through the darkness. Just like life. After Gabe would play, sometimes she'd lead him to the bed and wrap her arms and legs around him. Sometimes she'd cry, sometimes she'd burst with so much joy her face would be flushed, and they'd kiss and laugh. There was no in between. Mina felt manic, always rushing from one extreme to the other. But when she thought of LilyMa's words about the darkness and what it had done to Ezra, she began to shrug it away. She'd never use the dark power, she knew, not unless she had no choice. But if she came across another Twist, somewhere down the road, maybe at college, or in whatever city she settled in, she didn't know if she could keep that promise. If she had a chance to suffocate baby Hitler in his bed, she'd do it. She wouldn't hesitate. She wouldn't be haughty like she'd been with Twist. She wouldn't let the devil get away.

One Tuesday, Gabe drove them to school, and they kissed goodbye in the car. As she walked down Clayton's halls, everything was peaceful. She was sure she'd just let it all go. All the darkness. She'd lean into the moments that were beautiful. She'd love Gabe with everything in her for as long as she could. She'd get out of Asheville, permanently unstuck. She'd study in college and thrive under leafy oak trees on some beautiful campus, someplace where her grades and her brains mattered more than how she looked and where she came from. Where no one would think of her as trailer trash, a feral girl to prime with beer and free car rides. She'd maybe go home on Thanksgiving. She'd come home and cook for her mom, give her a break from Daddy beating the wall. She'd kiss Chelsea and tell her all about what it was like to go off to college, and she'd give her the book on colleges Gabe had given her. She'd open her mind to all there was in the world, every possibility. And when she came home, she'd see Gabe. And she'd be single because she didn't have time for stupid college boys. And he'd be single because he was going to wait on Mina forever if that's what it took. They'd eat LilyMa's good cooking, and they'd kiss in the basement bedroom, and he'd play *Mina's Song*, then they'd get under the sheets and turn down the furnace.

Mina was thinking about these things when she passed the Math Hall, and her eyes were drawn to someone behind the last row of lockers. Two people. It was Mr. Bachman and Danni. Mina waited until the hall was empty, but Mr. Bachman didn't back away from Danni to let her go to class. He kissed Danni's neck, his body pressed roughly against her. Then, as if sensing Mina's presence, Bachman pulled away and glared at her.

"What're you doing out here? Get to class!"

Mina said nothing. Did as she was told.

That afternoon, she told Gabe she didn't need a ride, that she'd meet up with him later. She waited patiently in the cold January afternoon, in the teacher's lot. She waited for Mr. Bachman to finish coaching the wrestling team and come out to his car. He walked along, his head high, the cast gone from his arm, now swinging in a blue canvas sling. Mina watched him come. She felt the bile rise in her throat. Her breathing quickened before she focused on it and calmed it. In through her nose, out through her mouth. She focused on the shadows that stretched out in the field between the high school and the woods beyond. She pulled them together. They crawled along the ground toward the school parking lot and swirled together behind a row of white activity buses. Mina conjured the ugliest faces she could, terrible gargoyle faces that drew together and bound until there stood a hideous shadow wolf, standing on two legs, the way the wulver had for Papa Leo.

When Mr. Bachman got to his car, he fished in his pockets for his keys. He yawned and stretched, raising his good arm toward the sky. Then the shadows bore down on him, the heavy footfalls of the wulver striking the ground as it came. Bachman left his keys in the door and turned to see it coming. For a moment, he tilted his head to the side and blinked his eyes as if they deceived him. But when the wulver towered over him, he worked frantically to open the car door. The wulver swiped at him, knocking him away, breaking the key off in the lock.

Kiss me like you did the girl, it said, its voice deep and full of gravel, rattling the car's windows.

Bachman ran.

The wulver grabbed him in its teeth and threw him on the hood, and he lay on his back, drawing up his hands and feet.

I'll eat your guts while you watch, it growled.

"No, please, Jesus, Mary, and Joseph," Bachman said, his jaw spasming, eyes bugging.

Mina stood by the wulver. Bachman looked at her briefly, then back at the wulver.

"Go home to your wife," Mina said. "Don't ever touch Danni again. You got me?"

Bachman didn't answer. The wulver leaned over him and opened its jaws, saliva dripping onto his pink face.

He looked at Mina, studying her.

"You're gonna have to give your word, man," Mina said. "Or I'll let him eat you right here. It's no skin off my back either way."

Bachman kept his eyes on Mina. "Did it give you that scar?"

"No," Mina said. "*I* give the scars."

The wulver dipped its head and chomped Bachman's good arm. Mina could feel its teeth sink in, taste the blood rush over her tongue. He screamed.

"I'll go home. I promise, I won't ever touch her again."

Oh, Mina, let us eat him, the wulver moaned, gargoyle faces working through its shadowy form. It released Bachman's arm. Blood dripped from the wulver's fangs onto Bachman's cheeks, into his open mouth.

"If you ever touch Danni again, I promise I'll let him do it. I'll have him start at your toes and work his way up, so you feel it all. Every inch of it."

"I promise," Bachman said. His pupils dilated, and his entire body shook.

Mina pulled the wulver back, and it ran into the field where it leaped into the earth, rejoining the shadows. She went back to her former hiding place behind the teacher's cars and retrieved her backpack. She crossed the lot, giving Bachman one last glare. He lay, knees to his chest, sobbing.

"Better get that looked at," she said. "You'll bleed out."

Mina stepped into the frosted field and headed down the hill toward home.

THE END

ACKNOWLEDGMENTS

Thank you to my first reader and ever-muse, Casey. Without your gracious candor, I would never have the courage to keep writing.

Thank you to Cassandra Thompson, Alma Garcia, Lisa Morris, and everyone at Quill & Crow Publishing House for believing in this book and for friendships that go beyond business. Thank you to my second readers and writing critique partners: Laura Platas-Scott, Christine Schott, Becky Cartwright, Melissa Cole Essig, and Ewan Marshall. Thank you to early readers Barry Dickson, Meagan Lucas, and Jeff Frisbee for sharing your impressions and helping me strengthen the book. Thanks to the faculty at the Converse MFA program, especially Marlin Barton and Leslie Pietzryk who helped with the earliest drafts of this book. Thank you to the folks who provided blurbs and for all you do to support your fellow writers. Thanks to Bookstagram and the writing communities on Threads and Bluesky. Thanks to my local writing community in Asheville for being such welcoming and supportive folk.

A special thank you to Allison Scott, who generously shared with me her experiences with conversion therapy and bonded with me over fundie trauma. I hope some of your braveness and honesty come through.

Thank you to readers who've supported me by reading and reviewing *Jesus in the Trailer* and *Where Dark Things Grow*. Your kind words about my work have kept me going and I am forever thankful.

Support authors by taking the time to review their books. Please review *Where Dark Things Rise* on Goodreads and Amazon. Ask your local library and indie bookstore to put it on their shelves and get to know the booksellers at your local indie bookstore. Thank you to the many booksellers who've supported my books and for creating community.

ABOUT THE AUTHOR

Andrew K. Clark is a writer from Western North Carolina where his people settled before the Revolutionary War. His debut novel, *Where Dark Things Grow* (2024), was the winner of an IPPY from the Independent Book Publisher's Awards, a Firebird Book Award, and a Literary Global Book Award. His poetry collection, *Jesus in the Trailer*, was shortlisted for the Able Muse Book Award. His work has appeared in *The American Journal of Poetry,* UCLA's *Out of Anonymity, Appalachian Review, Rappahannock Review, The Wrath Bearing Tree,* and many other journals. He received his MFA from Converse College. Connect with him at andrewkclark.com.

Also by Andrew K. Clark
Where Dark Things Grow
Jesus in the Trailer (poetry)

THANK YOU FOR READING

Thank you for reading *Where Dark Things Rise*. We deeply appreciate our readers, and are grateful for everyone who takes the time to leave us a review. If you're interested, please visit our website to find review links. Your reviews help small presses and indie authors thrive, and we appreciate your support.

More from Quill & Crow

Credenza, Wendy Dalrymple

There Ought to Be Shadows, Krissie K. Williams

The Agony of Her, Cassandra L. Thompson

TRIGGER INDEX

Abuse
(*physical, mental, sexual - see below*)
Alcoholism/Drug Use
Animal Death (*dog*)
Bigotry/Bullying
(*misogyny, racism, intolerance*)
Conversion Therapy
Infant Death
(*offscreen/Chapter 35, 36*)
Kidnapping
Religious Abuse/Trauma
Sexual Assault
(*implied, attempted - Chapter 5, 29*)
Stalking/Peeping Tom
Violence
(*fantasy/horror*)

www.ingramcontent.com/pod-product-compliance
Lightning Source LLC
LaVergne TN
LVHW040336100825
818189LV00005B/20